WHITE WOLF WITHIN

Dawn Bramwell

Copyright © 2023 Dawn Bramwell

The right of Dawn Bramwell to be identified as the author has been asserted in accordance with the Copyright, Designs and Patents Act 1988.

All rights reserved.

No part of this publication may be reproduced, stored in a retrieval system, or transmitted, in any form or by any means (electronic, mechanical, photocopying, recording or otherwise), without the prior written permission of the publisher.

Published by Purple Parrot Publishing

Printed in the United Kingdom

First Printing, 2023

ISBN: Print: 978-1-915472-15-1

Ebook: 978-1-915472-16-8

Purple Parrot Publishing

www.purpleparrotpublishing.co.uk

Edited by Viv Ainslie

Follow Dawn at:

www:	https://dawnbramwellauthor.com/
Facebook:	www.facebook.com/dawnbramwellauthor
Instagram:	@dawnbramwellauthor

Dedication

This book is for Belle.

I could say she was my dog, but she was so much more than that. My constant companion during the darkest of days. Her spirit was such she could only have been an angel. I made a promise to her when she died, in honour of that spirit, that I would be my white wolf within. I had no idea of the road this would take me on, but I had absolute faith that she would be with me.

She still is.

Acknowledgements

Thank you, Viv, for the care you have taken in publishing White Wolf Within, but more than that, for the love you have shown to the memory of Belle, or Luna as she is in the book.

This has been quite a journey for both of us, and perhaps here is where the real adventure begins!

Acknowledgements

Thank you, Vix, for the care you have taken in publishing A Little Wolf Within, but more than that, for the love you have shown to the memory of Hellet Pet Luna as she is in the book.

This has been quite a journey for both of us, and perhaps here is where the real adventure begins.

CONTENTS

Chapter One 9
Chapter Two 21
Chapter Three 31
Chapter Four 41
Chapter Five 51
Chapter Six 61
Chapter Seven 71
Chapter Eight 83
Chapter Nine 93
Chapter Ten 103
Chapter Eleven 111
Chapter Twelve 121
Chapter Thirteen 135
Chapter Fourteen 147
Chapter Fifteen 157
Chapter Sixteen 167
Chapter Seventeen 179
Chapter Eighteen 193
Chapter Nineteen 203
Chapter Twenty 211
Chapter Twenty-One 219
Chapter Twenty-Two 229
Chapter Twenty-Three 243
Chapter Twenty-Four 253

Chapter Twenty-Five ... 263
Chapter Twenty-Six ... 275
Chapter Twenty-Seven ... 285
Chapter Twenty-Eight ... 295
Chapter Twenty-Nine ... 305
Chapter Thirty ... 315
Chapter Thirty-One ... 327
Chapter Thirty-Two ... 337
Chapter Thirty-Three ... 343
Chapter Thirty-Four ... 357
Chapter Thirty-Five ... 367
Chapter Thirty-Six ... 377
Chapter Thirty-Seven ... 389
Chapter Thirty-Eight ... 401
Chapter Thirty-Nine ... 411
Chapter Forty ... 421
Chapter Forty-One ... 431
Chapter Forty-Two ... 441
Chapter Forty-Three ... 453
Chapter Forty-Four ... 461
Chapter Forty-Five ... 467
Chapter Forty-Six ... 473
Chapter Forty-Seven ... 479
Chapter Forty-Eight ... 483
Chapter Forty-Nine ... 487
Epilogue ... 495

Chapter One

Suicide had not occurred to me before.

Yet standing on the crowded platform on that cold and wet December day it suddenly seemed the only reasonable action to take.

Perhaps if Gary had been able to break the news to me more gently, given me time to prepare, I may have reacted differently.

But he hadn't.

I was confronted with his betrayal in that classic way, the bedroom discovery.

Exhausted and bleary-eyed from weeks of sleepless nights, I had left the house to attend the funeral parlour to discuss arrangements for my father-in-law, a mere six months after performing the same sad task for my mother-in-law. From there I was supposed to go on to the hairdresser for a cut and to have my highlights retouched. I really had not felt like making the appointment at the time, but Gerald had insisted.

'I want you looking your best Daisy when we have to make our final goodbyes,' he had said in that weakening voice, the light in his warm brown eyes duller than it once was. 'You've run yourself ragged looking after me, and Irene beforehand. When was the last time you spent some time and money on yourself hey? Hmm, exactly,' he had said at the shrug of my shoulders. Then he had picked up my phone and put it in my hands, refusing to settle until I had rung my hairdresser.

Had Gerald known perhaps? Suspected even?

He loved his son but he was realistic enough to know that were it not for me, Irene would have been in a home for people with dementia long since, and he would have ended his days in a hospice rather than in his own bed.

'Not good with the harsh side of life,' Gerald had often commented. 'His mother spoilt him you see.'

Which was why I was the one arranging the funeral and Gary was working from home as his school had an inset day. Only due to my hairdresser coming down with flu, I realised that he was not working at all.

I failed to pay attention to the smart little car parked outside our house. It could quite easily have been a visitor for Violet next door. My elderly neighbour was a lively and popular lady, regularly having bridge meetings and coffee mornings.

I failed to detect the unusual hint of perfume that lingered in the hallway and up the stairs. My nose was full of the overbearing scent of lilies from the funeral parlour, a flower that held painful memories for me. Perhaps it was those memories that also dulled my senses as I numbly climbed the stairs so that I didn't hear the noises, or if I did, they didn't register.

Blind eyes that watched a scene that played out in slow motion.

Was that what Gary's bottom looked like as he made love to me?

White buttocks quivering slightly with the effort of his thrusts. He was working hard, pumping away like a piston, a slapping sound as flesh hit flesh accompanying each movement. Long sleek tanned legs wrapped around Gary's waist. Red nails at the end of elegant fingers dug into his white buttocks. Golly that must be painful I thought as I watched. Gary seemed to like it though. He groaned and increased the urgency of his hips.

Fancy my legs looking that good.

I can't remember painting my nails red though?

'Oh God Cor, I want to fuck you so hard but what about the baby?'

'It's fine, harder Gary, you won't hurt the baby, but I need it harder, you know I do.'

Cor?

Baby?

That's when the room span and my world tilted on its axis, and the fog of utter fatigue lifted so I could see properly, hear properly, observe properly. I was not watching Gary making love to me on our bed. Those were not my long, tanned legs, nor would they ever be.

Nor was that face, flushed and beautiful, framed by silky ash blonde hair that stared at me in shock, mine. And I certainly could not lay claim to those breasts! My eyes slid downwards in reluctant envy, comparing my petite handfuls to those appetisingly full and rounded globes, nipples rosy, dark and erect. Young breasts, not those of a forty-six-year-old woman.

No, that was most definitely not me on the bed. Painfully slowly, embarrassingly so, my mind pieced together the information. My husband was in bed with another woman. Making love to another woman. Or as he was loudly attesting, fucking another woman.

'Oh, Cor I just love fucking you so fucking much,' panting now with the effort.

I wasn't surprised, he was making me even more exhausted just watching.

'Gary stop.'

The legs unravelled from their snake like coil around my husband's hips, the red nails withdrew from the flesh of his buttocks. The silky blond hair swung around her face as her eyes, a Nordic blue, locked onto mine. The fascinating breasts bobbed with movement as she began to pull back from Gary.

'No, no, no, no baby, oh God Cor, hold on.' A long drawn-out moan, more urgent thrusts.

He really could move quite fast when he wanted to. A clenching of those white buttocks, now tight and squeezed together as his whole body began to shudder.

'Oh God Cor, you're the best.'

'Gary!' A hiss, serpent-like, from the no longer writhing length of female flesh beneath him.

'What babe? What's the matter hon, you okay? You went all funny.'

'Sarah had flu.' I spoke as though I had just come in to find him sitting at the kitchen table.

The effect of my words though had Gary catapulting himself off the bed in such a hurry I got an eyeful of his now rapidly shrinking erection and her completely bare nether regions, as sleek as the rest of her. Part of me winced at the thought of how painful having everything waxed off must be. Another part of me registered the fact that, like the hair on my head, the hair on other parts of my body had probably grown a little wild. Gary looked a little wild too as he hopped round the bedroom gathering up his clothes. She continued to regard me coolly as she took her time to dress, aware that my eyes were glued to her perfect body, in the way of a demented masochist.

I must have been demented because I didn't react. Not even when Gary blurted out the full truth. He had been seeing Corinne for some time. Three years to be precise as she calmly told me. But he hadn't wanted to upset his father. No of course not.

Gerald, you knew didn't you!

But he was going to tell me; of course he was.

In the end it had been Corinne who had calmly swatted aside my husband's waffling explanation to tell me that she was three months pregnant, they were getting married as soon as Gary could divorce me, oh and yes, she wanted the house to live in. After all, I didn't have children, so I had no need of such a big place to myself. January would be a good date for me to move out.

So ended my marriage.

It seemed as I waited for the train to arrive, that my life had also ended as well.

I saw Gary's future stretching out before him, not including me.

He was going to be a father and I would not be the mother of his child.

He would live with Corinne in the big Victorian semi, with its enchantingly long back garden, that had been my home for the last ten years. Their son or daughter would grow up there, play there, maybe with brothers or sisters. Christmases with piles of presents under the tree. Birthdays with cakes and candles, balloons and laughter.

There would be so much laughter.

I saw this all playing out in my mind and then I tried to envisage my future.

I couldn't.

There was nothing there.

When I tried to imagine my life from now onwards, I couldn't see a damn thing.

It was like trying to look down the longest, darkest tunnel, desperate to glimpse that light that would tell you there was something at the end of it.

But there wasn't.

There was nothing.

Just darkness.

I felt overwhelming panic. No, too small a word. Terror. Yes, that was what I felt. Sheer undiluted terror that froze the blood in my veins and all but stopped my heart. Around me the noise and chatter, the constant moving of people faded away and no longer existed. In that moment I had ceased to exist too. The next step was really very simple, and once the thought had entered my head there came with it a sense of purpose and also peace.

I told myself it would be quick, and it was even raining heavily now so that would help wash away the blood from the tracks. The train was slowing down but surely at that speed it would not have time to stop completely. I would be mangled beneath and that would be that.

I heard a scream, a few in fact.

The screech of the brakes was awful.

The ground was no longer beneath my feet, but I wasn't crushed beneath the train.

I was flying.

Dead?

No. It was far too noisy for that. I could hear voices buzzing with drama and excitement. In the distance the sound of a siren. A physical presence. I was being held. Someone had me in their arms. Gradually these thoughts penetrated the black dark fog of my mind and the ringing in my ears also began to fade away. My eyes started to focus once more and I could clearly see the mass of faces, as someone carried me carefully away from the edge.

'She's fine, now just feck off and give her some air.'

An Irish accent that I was sure I had heard before. I gave my head a little shake, feeling as though I was drunk or drugged and looked at my rescuer.

'Sean?' I said with puzzlement audible in my voice.

I was rewarded by a wink of his blue eyes and a flash of his smile.

'There you go now, Daisy, you sit there a while and get your breath back. Sure, and that was a nasty tumble you took just now. Blow me down that could have been the end of you, so it could. What a good job I was so near hey?'

He had, I realised now, carried me all the way from the edge of the platform to a wrought iron bench just near the cafe. I also realised just how close I had come to ending my life and the horror of that was another body blow that drained all the blood from my head.

'There you go now, Daisy, let's ease you down on this bench now so I can raise your legs a little. That's right flower, just get the blood back into your head and you'll be right as rain in a jiffy.'

I have never fainted in my life but taking Sean's advice was the only thing to do as everything once more became blurry around me. When it passed and I could sit up again, it was to find a group of official looking people staring at me with a variety of expressions. Easily identifiable were a couple of paramedics, one male, one female and a female police officer. There was also a smartly dressed man who was frowning horribly. Sean was talking to the female paramedic, a youngish woman who was listening carefully to him.

'You may be convinced that your friend is fine sir, but really we do have to check.'

Her male colleague pushed forward briefly exchanging a few words with the police officer before kneeling in front of me.

'Hello Daisy, do you mind if I just check a few things out?'

I shook my head, starting to feel more than a little stupid and more than a little frightened. What had I been thinking off? I didn't want to die. I mean I know I had been feeling down recently, but had I really got that bad?

The paramedic, who told me his name was Steve, checked my blood pressure and my heart rate. Not surprisingly, both were a little on the high side but nothing that was going to have them whisking me off with blue lights flashing. When he had done this, he closed his case and looked me square in the eye. He must have been approaching retirement, a nice enough looking man with a face that inspired immediate trust.

'Tell me Daisy, and no this is not a chat-up line,' he said with a soft smile and a little wink, 'what is a nice young lady like you doing, throwing yourself into the path of a train?'

'Sure, and haven't I been saying all this time, some eejit bumped into her, and she tripped.'

I heard the police officer politely saying to Sean that he must let them deal with things in the proper way. I also heard the words suicide attempt and again I went cold inside.

'Daisy?' Steve was waiting for me.

I got the impression that no matter how impatient Mr. Railway Man was getting, or how many other incidents the police officer may have to attend to that day, that if I needed ten hours to sit there before I could answer, he would willingly wait. He oozed kindness and compassion and that sense of it brought tears to my eyes. I cried so easily these days.

I was filled with shame and yet at the same time, wonderfully relieved. I could tell this lovely man in his green uniform that I was so shattered and weary with life that yes, just for that instant, I had lost all perspective and hope, and stepped forward off the platform into the path of the oncoming train. He could take me to hospital. They could fill me full of drugs. I could hide in a world of medication whilst doctors and psychiatrists assessed my mental state.

After all what else was I going to do with my life?

'I was pushed from behind.' I clamped my mouth shut as soon as the words came out.

Steve, years of experience telling him his intuition was right, continued to look probingly into my eyes. I swallowed a golf ball size lump of awkwardness that had lodged in my throat and tried again.

'It wasn't deliberate, I just got jostled. My fault for standing too close.' The voice was mine, certainly but the thoughts were not. I shook my head. Perhaps I was too emotionally overwrought, not to mention exhausted from looking after Gerald, that I was not capable of thinking straight.

Steve was still waiting patiently, but now the female police officer butted in, gently but even so it was a reminder that there could be a report to file.

'Daisy, I'm PC Wendy Holden, you can call me Wendy if you like.' She was only young, possibly late twenties, cropped dark hair and kind but alert brown eyes. 'Mr. Jones says that he was checking out the CCTV camera and he quite clearly saw you step forward.'

'Jumped!'

Mr Railway Man, or Jones as I now knew him to be, a bland looking man about thirty or so, sounded very annoyed. He went on, with cold contempt in his rather nasally voice. I wondered if he had a cold coming on or if he always sounded like that. Momentarily distracted I had to quickly focus on what he was saying.

'Have you any idea the cost to the railways of suicides on the tracks? Delays. Clearing up the mess. Time off for the drivers who then claim a fortune in compensation for mental suffering.'

He must have seen me wince at that point. Shit. I had not stopped to consider the poor driver. I put myself in their shoes and imagined the horror of someone leaping out in front of them, the desperate attempt to brake, the brutal impact, blood, brain, body parts splattered over the window.

I felt light-headed again and in the dizzying background I could hear Sean, none too politely, telling Mr Jones to 'Feck off behind your desk why don't you'. I closed my eyes, but I knew I could not hide my gaze forever. I had to look up and face the enquiring, if not judgemental eyes of the police officer.

Wendy repeated gently. 'Daisy, it does appear that it was captured on CCTV. That's why we got a call so quickly, along with the ambulance.'

Well, there was no point in lying then. Besides, I hated lying and certainly would not consider doing so to an authority figure such as the police, or paramedics. I cleared my throat, determined to confess my actions and face the consequences whatever they may be.

'I told you. Some idiot pushed me from behind. Bloody sod's made me miss my job interview now.'

Had I somehow banged my head? Where had those words come from? Not only that, where had the feisty spark of anger appeared from? I glanced quickly between the police officer and Steve, who from my reaction seemed to be satisfied that this was the truth.

'Very well then Daisy, in that case you take good care of yourself for the rest of the day now.' Steve patted me on the shoulder and stood up from where he had been crouching all this time. 'Either way you have had a nasty shock. A strong cup of sweet tea and a couple of biscuits is in order at the very least.'

He exchanged a few words with the police officer and along with his female colleague began to make his way back to the ambulance.

'Not so fast,' insisted Mr. Jones. 'The CCTV footage. You can't lie about that,' he crowed rather triumphantly.

Wendy snapped her notebook shut and failed to stifle a sigh. 'Very well sir. If you insist, we can have a look at that.'

'I do insist,'

'Well, I'm coming with Daisy,' said Sean, once more at my side and offering me his arm as I got shakily to my feet.

He gave me a little wink, as if to say he was aware I was puzzling over his presence here. I was, but I was so damn grateful that he had saved me from my moment of dark insanity, that I was happy to let him come along.

Not so Mr Jones. 'Oh really no. We can't have all and sundry in the office, it just wouldn't do.'

What he meant by that, he could not have a homeless tramp with matted hair, a scruffy beard and holes in his shoes, not to mention a rather strong body odour, defiling his domain. At least, I thought, as I clamped down a slightly hysterical giggle, Sean was wearing a lovely smart woollen overcoat. It had belonged to Gerald and was too large for Gary, so I had given it to Sean on one of my weekly trips into town. I always stopped to say hello to the homeless man as he sat hoping for pennies from people who paid money into the car parking machine. Gary told me I was an idiot for doing this, but Gerald had been in approval.

'There but for the Grace of God go you and I, Daisy,' he would say time and again. 'Never stop caring Daisy. It makes you who you are.'

Those wretched tears returned once more to sting at my eyes, and I blinked them away before Mr. Jones could see them. He was arguing hotly with the police officer that Sean should now leave the officials to official's business.

'I rather think as Mr. Murphy has saved Daisy's life, he is entitled to accompany her, that is of course if it's alright with you?' Wendy turned to check with me.

I blinked again and stuttered in reply, 'Yes of course.'

The blue eyes in Sean's grimy face twinkled and I caught a glimmer of a smile from Wendy as she gestured for Mr Jones to lead the way. It was only as we were entering the crowded offices that I suddenly realised I was in deep trouble. I had of course jumped off the platform. No matter what Sean or I might have bizarrely claimed, that is what had happened. CCTV cameras do not lie. These thoughts were echoed by Mr. Jones himself as he clicked his fingers at a girl sitting in front of a desk surrounded by multiple screens.

'You will see Officer, that the cameras do not lie, even if people are inclined to do so.'

I was about to open my mouth then and confess but there was a gentle squeeze on my arm from Sean and the words were trapped in my throat.

'You see, there it is, as clear as day.' Mr. Jones turned the monitor round to show Wendy, his arms folded across his chest and a smug look on his face.

'Yes sir, it is as clear as day. What a good job Mr Murphy you were there.'

'You see. So are there charges to be pressed Officer?'

'Well perhaps if it was possible to track down the person who pushed Daisy here, then maybe, but given how busy the platform was, and seeing how quickly he disappears into the crowd, I very much doubt it. And even if we did get hold of him, or her for that matter, because with that coat and the hood up it could of course be a female, there is some question as whether it was deliberate or not. What do you think Mr Murphy? Run it again,' she finished by addressing the girl on the desk rather than Mr. Jones who had not quite understood.

Mind you, neither had I at this point.

'No, it was an accident, look,' said Sean in his rich Irish accent, you see that woman there bends over to tie her shoe lace, then in doing so she jostles the man next to her, and he bumps into the woman in front of him...'

'Who falls against the person in the hooded coat who, in turn, has no choice other than to collide with Daisy. You have sharp eyes Mr Murphy. We could do with you on the force.

'The poor soul would have been so scared at the thought they could have accidentally killed someone, to be sure they would have scarpered without thinking. See what a blur it all is afterwards.'

'What?' Mr. Jones demanded looking at the police officer and Sean as though they were speaking in riddles.

Wendy swivelled the monitor back towards him. I had been too scared to look initially but now I was compelled to do so. It was at this point that I began to wonder if I really was insane. Perhaps I should have asked Steve to take me with him in the ambulance after all.

I distinctly remember thinking about jumping.

I distinctly remember jumping.

What I was seeing play out before my eyes was telling a different story entirely. The CCTV footage showed events happening exactly as Sean had said. The scene was played back five times before Wendy lost her patience with the baffled Mr. Jones.

'Look sir it's right there before you. Now if you don't mind, I do have other things to attend to, and Daisy here has people to contact about a missed job interview,' she turned to me and offered a sympathetic smile. 'I do hope they reschedule it for you. Here is my number in case they don't believe the excuse and you want me to back you up. And I agree with the paramedic's advice, go and have a good cup of tea and some biscuits.'

'Ooh tea and biscuits, sure and that's a lovely thought,' said Sean rubbing his hands with a hopeful expression on his face.

'Mr Murphy, do you have shelter for tonight? Is there any way I can help you today?' Wendy was now talking to Sean, even while in the background poor Mr. Jones was stabbing angrily at the machine, frantically trying to replay the scene once more.

'Oh, don't you be fretting about me,' Sean replied. 'I'm in the Good Lord's hands so I am, and there's none better to look after me.'

'I'll look after him,' I blurted out, urged by some instinct deep inside.

'Now do I look as though I'm some kind of stray dog needing a home?' Sean tilted his head to one side. I felt a twinge of shame that in some ways that was how he appeared to me.

'Well can I at least buy you that cup of tea and some biscuits?'

'I think that's a grand idea,' said Wendy nodding in approval and then she held out her hand to Sean. 'Well done again sir.'

We trooped out of the offices back towards the main platform areas. WPC Holden went about her business and I stood there feeling a trifle awkward with Sean.

'You don't have to you know,' he said softly.

I stiffened my spine then, thinking what Gerald would say. 'I know I don't, but I want to. Only, I was thinking let's not go to the café here, it's far too noisy and the coffee's probably rubbish anyway. Would you be alright with Lucinda's?'

His grubby face split into a grin. 'I have heard they do a wonderfully wicked hot chocolate with marshmallows and cream on the top.'

'You heard right,' I agreed. We began to make our way out of the crowded station and along the high street to the smart little café that had been a feature of the town for nearly a hundred years.

'And I have also heard they do a wicked plateful of pancakes with bacon and maple syrup?'

'They do indeed,' I said with a smile as I pushed open the door and ushered him into the cosy interior.

It was perhaps not the sort of place you took a homeless man as your guest. But this was not turning out to be an ordinary day. When someone saves your life, they are no ordinary guest. However, I had no idea at that time, just what an extraordinary guest Sean was going to turn out to be.

Chapter Two

I thought that Sean might have been uncomfortable in Lucinda's café, with the crisp white table cloths and waitresses who brought tea and coffee served in lovely china cups, but no. He sat to the manner born in a window seat at a small table for two, pulling out a chair as though he were a regular patron. It had been a favourite place of Irene and Gerald's, so perhaps that is why I liked it.

The café was warm, but on this early December morning, and especially after such a shocking start to the day I needed to keep my coat on. Not so Sean. He shed his outer garment, which was Gerald's quality overcoat I had given him, to reveal the layers beneath. Shabby would be too kind a word. He had on a black jacket, completely out of date, and clearly hanging off a lean frame. This was tied around his waist with a tatty piece of string. Poking out from underneath this was a woollen polo neck sweater which I am guessing was once cream, but now looked a very dirty grey.

His hands, when they reached for the menu, were still encased in his knitted fingerless gloves, an odd pair, one black and the other a jolly red which gave the whole scarecrow ensemble a bravely cheerful look. The finger ends poking out from the gloves, not surprisingly were grimy, nails rimmed in black. Whenever I saw him sitting by the pay machine at the car park, he always had a hat on. Sometimes it would be a woolly one, sometimes a flat cap, and once I had seen him in a trilby. Today it was the turn of an ancient looking tweed cap with ear flaps, the sort I pictured Conan Doyle's Holmes wearing. Combined with Gerald's overcoat, this did at least give him the appearance of a well-dressed man, from a distance that is. Up close and without these superficial trappings, he was clearly what he was.

The manageress Lucinda, who was the great-granddaughter of the original owner, was a shapely, always immaculately groomed woman in her fifties. She spotted him and bustled over, nudging the approaching waitress with her notepad and pencil out of the way.

'There are plenty of tables for two at the rear of the café if you wouldn't mind moving. This is one of my best tables and you are hardly a good advertisement for my establishment, if you don't mind me saying so.'

I had to admire Lucinda's blunt honesty and wished I could be a little bit like her. I was already reaching for my bag and rising from my chair when Sean replied with a warm smile on his face, which considering most of his teeth were black and crooked was not necessarily a good thing.

'And it would be, what with the sun coming in through the window like it now is. And wouldn't you know there is a rainbow to brighten this dark dismal December morning. A gift from God is a rainbow I always say, don't you Lucinda? No matter how deep the shadows, they cannot prevail from the light of a rainbow, 'tis a light that just warms you up inside, isn't that right now?'

I watched mesmerized as Lucinda opened her mouth to speak, shut it again, and then with a little shake of her head as though she had momentarily forgotten what she was supposed to be doing, said in her warmest tone of voice, 'What can I get you both this morning?'

Still stunned, I listened as Sean rattled off a request that sounded like an overload for the arteries in one easy sitting. When it was my turn, it was all I could do to quietly ask if I may have a pot of tea.

'Oh, now and don't be forgetting the biscuits, Daisy. You need the sugar for the shock. What a dreadful thing to happen.'

Underneath her brisk exterior, there was a caring side to Lucinda, one of the reasons her place was so popular, as well as the good food and service.

'What happened? I have to say, dear you do look a bit peaky.'

'And so would you if some eejit had pushed you under a train only half an hour ago,' said Sean in a voice that carried round the café and had most heads turning.

Never mind peaky, I was beginning to blush a healthy rosy red at the sudden attention, but Sean played it for all it was worth. As a result, we were assured of the best service, a plateful of pancakes for him, laden with syrup and bacon, hot chocolate with all the toppings and a large pot of tea and two huge warm scones with pots of jam and cream and pats of butter for me.

I thought there might be an awkward silence between us whilst we waited for our order to arrive. After all, we were virtual strangers. I just knew him to say hello to and to drop a few coins into his cap, or sometimes when the weather was particularly foul, I would take him a coffee or a portion of chips before I would get into my nice warm car and drive back to my nice warm house, feeling that I had done my little bit. But I was rapidly beginning to realise that for all his homeless status, there was nothing awkward about Sean.

He sat there glibly chatting away; offering a highly amusing commentary on the various people who passed by the café window, each oblivious that their every item of clothing, or hair colouring, posture, you name it, was being so carefully scrutinised. Mostly he was kind in what he said, but the odd remark hinted at a rapier wit, lethally sharp and to the point. It was distracting and pleasantly so, but after a couple of minutes, he dropped the cosy monologue.

Ever so casually he said, 'So Daisy my darling girl, do you want to tell me why you look as though your world has just ended?'

The endearment tripped off his tongue as naturally as the air would flow in his lungs and I could take no offence at it. But I was horrified that he was staring at me with such a piercing look in his blue eyes that demanded I answer him. Honestly. Just as I had not been able to do with either the paramedic or the police officer.

I was saved from replying immediately as two things then occurred at once. Our order was brought to the table and my phone rang insistently in my bag. Glad of the disturbance, I rooted out my mobile while Sean thanked the waitress effusively and began to tuck in.

I had completely forgotten to let the school know that I was not going to make the interview. At the other end of the phone was a snooty male voice enquiring as to why I had not shown up. I could understand his attitude. However, as I stuttered my profuse apologies and the reasons why, the frosty attitude remained.

'I can give you the attending police officer's number,' I said falteringly when it became clear that the secretary did not believe a word I said.

'Surely you wouldn't think I would make it up?'

There was a pained sigh and then followed a muffled conversation in the background that clearly was the debate as to whether it was permissible to reschedule the interview. When the secretary came back on the line, it was to request the details I had just offered. They did not believe me. I felt like one of the teenagers I taught when they came into school with bizarre explanations for not having done their homework. I didn't know whether to laugh at it or be insulted. Did I really want to work with these people? Hesitantly, I began to give them WPC Holden's details. Before I could finish, Sean reached across the table, gently, but firmly took the phone out of my hands and spoke.

'Now why on Earth would you be thinking that someone as fine as Daisy would want to work with a bunch of shites like you? Sure, and has she not got better things to do with her time, thank you very much, and goodbye.' He switched the phone off and handed it back to me. 'It's alright, you don't have to thank me. I know you didn't want the job. You were just too polite to say so.'

Horribly aware that my mouth must have been hanging open in a very unflattering manner, I concentrated for a moment on my scone. I would not usually eat such a thing so early in the day, but as I said before, this was not a usual day. Taking satisfaction in seeing the butter melt into the warmth of the fluffy scone, I then loaded it with jam and took a greedy mouthful. It stopped me from having to speak at least. Sean was both determined and patient. He waited until I had devoured the lot, and his plate was halfway to being cleared when he posed the question again.

'So, there's me all this time thinking that this young lady looks like she has everything in the world to be happy about, yet when I look into your eyes, well bless me if I don't see dark despair looking right back at me. So, this gets me to thinking, what in the world has gone wrong in her world, if you see what I mean.'

I lowered my eyes, feeling the heat in my face once more. What must he think of me? I had a beautiful home, a good job, money in the bank, clothes on my back, people who cared about me in their own way. What right did I have to be so utterly despondent? I couldn't form a sensible answer. For the second time that day my surroundings blurred. The fog threatened to engulf me again, but for the touch of Sean's hand on mine, across the table.

I couldn't look at him now because tears were filling my eyes and I couldn't speak because of the lump in my throat. I had the sense that the waitress had come to clear our plates and that Sean had waved her away. When the moment passed, I wiped my eyes with the back of my hand, daring myself to look this kindly homeless man square in the eye and tell him the truth.

'I just feel so lost. I can't really explain it other than that. So utterly, utterly lost.'

He released my hand and let out a soft sigh, leaning back in his seat as he did so. 'Ah Daisy. I would agree. For a minute there you lost yourself, so you did. Just for a minute.' And then he beamed a broad smile, displaying once more those grotty teeth that looked as though it was eons since they had seen a toothbrush and fluoride. 'What a good job I happened to come along, not just to save you from that nasty accident but to cheer you up as well.'

The waitress returned and I gestured to her that she could clear away our table. 'Thank you very much,' I said and then once she had gone, finally found the thought within my mind that begged the question of Sean. 'Exactly how did you happen to be there?'

He shrugged carelessly and began to put on Gerald's old overcoat. 'I fancied a change of scene. I'm not always sat on my arse by the pay machine you know.'

I contemplated this as I paid the bill and then just as we were about to leave the cosy warmth of the café, the heavens suddenly opened. In typical December fashion, a barrage of hail stones as large as golf balls dropped from the sky.

'Well would you look at those beauties,' Sean whistled through his teeth. 'God must be in a bit of a mood at the moment wouldn't you say?' He put his hand on the door to open it and I halted him.

'Wait there's no point going out just yet, we'll get soaked. It'll pass in a minute or so.'

He had put his deerstalker hat back on, the ear flaps firmly tied under his chin making him look slightly comical, or at least it would if the style of hat had been out of choice and not necessity. The look he gave me from underneath the peak was hard to describe but it was his words that came next that penetrated something deep inside of me.

'To be sure it will, Daisy, and there will be plenty more of these showers before nightfall, and the next day and the next. Makes no difference to me if I get soaked now or later. Well, I will bid you goodbye and thank you for the breakfast.'

The bell over the door clanged as a howling draught accompanied a shocking splattering of hail stones into the shop. I pushed the door shut with such force the bell sounded as though it might drop off.

'You can't sleep out in this Sean.'

'There's probably a bed at the hostel if I can get there early enough.'

'There's a spare room at our house.'

We stared at each other then, the teacher and the homeless man.

'I wouldn't want you to be feeling sorry for me now, Daisy.'

Seriously? How could I not? But I guessed there had to be some pride at stake, so I rambled on. 'Don't be daft. You saved my life. Surely that makes us friends. Can I not offer a friend the use of an empty room for a little while?'

He tilted his head and pushed back the peak of his cap a little, scratching the tangle of his beard. 'Friends? Hm. I suppose I could do that. Oh, but look now, the storm has passed. You can take back that offer if you like. I won't be offended.'

I shook my head and moved past him to open the door. 'No. I meant it. No arguing.'

'Oh, I would never be so rude as to argue with a lady like yourself, Daisy, now that would be just bad mannered and one thing my dear, sainted mother taught me, and by Jesus she taught me a lot, was never argue with a lady. Especially a pretty one.'

Ordinarily I would have argued the point that I did not consider myself to be pretty. For once I let the comment go, just taking it as more of Sean's Irish charm that was as natural to him as breathing. We headed back in the direction of the car park where Sean usually sat by the pay phone.

Then he coughed and said, 'Didn't you come in by taxi this morning?'

I stopped dead in the middle of the pavement. 'Yes of course I did. But how did you know that?'

'Well sure and I didn't see you in the car park did I now?'

I was being more than suicidal today; I was being completely dumb as well. 'Taxi of course. Look we need to cross over the road then, there's a taxi rank on Lancaster Road.'

We changed direction and sure enough as we turned the corner to come off the high street, I could see the line of black cabs just ahead of me. Only we didn't get to them just yet. Sean lightly tapped on my arm and nodded his head just to the side of us.

'Would you mind if we just took a tiny detour? There's a friend I want to let know where I will be.'

It was a reasonable enough request. I supposed that there must be a kind of solidarity within the homeless community. At least I hoped that would be the case. Sean led me into Miller Arcade, a Victorian arrangement of shops above which three stories of offices were housed. It had been built in honour of one of the local mill owners of that time and was not the usual place you expected to find any homeless people sitting, even if it was all under cover from the weather.

It was designed in a cross pattern and at the centre was a huge Christmas tree festooned with lights. Usually, it was one of my favourite spots in town and I would enjoy browsing round the clusters of small shops and then take a breather on one of the benches. Now though, the sight of the tree just gave me a hollow feeling inside. What on Earth would Christmas be like this year? More wretched tears made my vision swim and aware of whose company I was in, I quickly back handed them away.

Sean, it seemed did not miss a trick though. 'I know Daisy, you are fair heart sore that you are. Trust me, my friend will give you a lift, you just wait and see.'

His kindness coming from a place of having so little in his life, made me even more blurry eyed and so I didn't quite see at first that he was leading me directly to a shop. I was inside the door before I had chance to see which one it was.

'Michaela my friend, would you have a minute?'

'For you Sean, I have a lifetime,' came back the reply with an accompanying ripple of lovely warm laughter.

I wiped my eyes again and looked around, not seeing anyone at first and wondering what kind of shop this was. It didn't appear to sell anything. And then a pixie came through a curtain which must cover a room at the back. I watched as Sean greeted the dainty lady, who was smaller than I, with a cropped cap of sleek black hair emphasising her delicate features. Eyes as dark as jet and just as shiny stared at me. She greeted me with a dazzling smile. I had to respond in kind, although I am sure I did not dazzle in return.

We appeared to be in a small art studio which I did not remember being in before. It must be new I decided at the same time I was wondering how Sean knew this beautiful lady. She was simply dressed in a black polo neck sweater, black jeans and expensive-looking black leather boots. She was chatting to Sean about a variety of people they seemed to know, and I let their conversation flow over me as I took in more of my surroundings.

There was a round table in the centre, with a large sketch pad and various sheets of paper strewn about, all with different stages of a sketch in black pencil on them. It appeared to be a beautiful drawing of a unicorn with a lady riding it. If this pixie was the artist, then she was very talented. On the walls of the small room were more drawings, all in simple pencil but there was nothing at all simple in the exquisite detail of them.

They looked magical. I was content to peruse the fascinating display of animals, faeries, angels, and mythical creatures that stared back at me. They were all beautiful, but my eyes kept being drawn to one in particular. Or rather I felt that one in particular had its eyes on me.

It was of a wolf standing alone next to a tumbling waterfall with mountains in the background all covered in snow. The more I looked at it, the larger the wolf seemed to be, as though the very picture was changing before my eyes and the animal had moved from its position and was coming towards me.

I shook my head and told myself I was suffering from delayed shock. When I blinked and looked again at the picture the wolf was back under the tree. Only hadn't it been facing left originally? I could have sworn it had. Yet as I looked now, the wolf was facing towards the right, looking away from the waterfall and towards the mountains. I really must get more sleep I decided and then realised that Sean's friend was talking to me.

'So, it is the wolf for you then? A wonderful animal, the wolf. Highly intelligent, loyal, protective, fierce. An animal to be both admired and feared. Yes, yes it would suit you quite well.'

'Sorry?' I looked at her not quite sure what she meant.

'Sean here tells me you need cheering up.'

I looked from her to Sean and back again. Sean was looking at me innocently and yet I had the strangest feeling there was a lot going on under that bland exterior.

'Maybe,' I said cautiously.

Michaela nodded. 'That's what I thought when I saw you. If ever there was a lady in need of cheering up, there she is. And a tattoo is just the thing to do that.'

I gawped. 'A tattoo?'

'Hm, that's what these all are,' Michaela gestured to the drawings around us. 'Designs for tattoos. Of course, I can do whatever you want. There are no limits at all, no limits. But I always say a tattoo picks the owner, not the other way around.'

'I can't get a tattoo,' I squealed.

'And why ever not?' Michaela did not look offended at my outburst, just curious.

I replied stutteringly. 'I'm a teacher. And I'm forty-six. And married.'

Sean raised his eyebrows and I wondered, how? How did he know? My shoulders slumped and yet inside I felt a tiny fire beginning to spark into life. Michaela picked up on it immediately.

'You see, deep down you have this other side of you waiting to get out. It's always been there, Daisy. Sometimes it just needs a little nudge. Expressing it by getting a tattoo can be all the nudge it needs. So, the wolf then.'

Before I could say anything else, Michaela led me through the curtain to the rear of the property. A huge black chair, similar to that a dentist would use only with arm attachments took centre stage and was all I could really focus on.

Seriously, a tattoo?

What was I thinking of?

Then again, hadn't I tried to throw myself under a train a short while ago?

So really, what harm could a small discreet tattoo do?

was in dire need of cheering up, there she is. And a tattoo is just the thing to do that."

"You poof. A tattoo."

Hm, there was meaning there. Shelley is genuinely to the dastardly around he. Does us for tattoos. Of course, I can do whatever you want. There are no limits at all, no limits. But I always say a tattoo picks the owner, not the other way around."

"I can't get a tattoo," I squealed.

"And why ever not?" Michaels did not look offended at my outburst, just curious.

I replied stoutly uppy, "I'm a teacher. And I'm forty-six." And that stuff.

Sean raised his eyebrows and I wondered how. How did he know? My shoulders slumped and yet inside I felt a tiny fire beginning to spark into life. Stomach picked up on it immediately.

"You see, deep down you have this other side of you waiting to get out. It's always been there, Daisy. Sometimes it just needs a little nudge. Expressing it by getting a tattoo can be all the nudge it needs. Say the will then."

Before I could say anything else, Michaels led me through the cut barn to the rear of the property. A huge black chair, similar to that a dentist would use only with an attachments foot centre stage, and was all I could really focus on.

Seriously, a tattoo.

What was I thinking of?

Then again, hadn't I tried to throw myself under a train a short while ago?

So really, what harm could a small discreet tattoo do?

Chapter Three

Having made this impulsive decision, the one next was where to have the tattoo?

'Are you a show it off to the world kind of person, or let's keep it private so only you and a few others may know it's there, kind of person?' Michaela was saying, her voice as beautiful as the rest of her with a soft accent, hinting at Welsh ancestry. The answer must have been clear in my face as she nodded. 'Hm thought so. On the back then maybe, between the shoulder blades?'

'Yes, yes, that should be fine,' I agreed hastily, thinking of a delicate tiny image somewhere above my bra strap.

Michaela then went on to explain what the procedure entailed, and I listened carefully. There was a form for me to sign and a list of after-care instructions that she waved airily away.

'You don't need to worry at all Daisy, that's just paperwork – that's all it is. Now then, Sean are you going to make us all a brew whilst I get Daisy ready?'

I was still full from my pot of tea and scones but Sean busied himself with the kettle and mugs which were kept on the side. He obviously knew his way around here.

'Now Daisy,' Michaela focused her attention on me and as I perched on the edge of the huge black chair, I was transfixed by the darkness of her eyes. 'Do you trust me?'

Somehow it was impossible not to. I answered in all good faith. 'Yes. I do trust you.'

Her beautifully dainty face beamed with happiness and the room was lit up with her smile. 'I love it when people do. That's when I do my best work you see, Daisy. Leave me to give you the tattoo you deserve. I promise you won't regret it. The right tattoo can be life-changing, can't it Sean?'

Sean was now perched on a stool in the corner of the room sipping at a mug. 'Life changing indeed Michaela and Daisy is sore in need of a life change right now.'

Michaela then showed me how to place myself on the chair in order for her to do her work.

'We'll just step back out through here now for you to undress,' she said, nodding to Sean who got off the stool straight away.

I hadn't thought of that and felt myself blushing.

'Daisy, it's just skin to me, and skin is my canvas.'

When she put it like that, I felt reassured and once they had gone back into the front of the shop and the curtain was in place, I took off my top and after a moment's hesitation my bra as well. Then I laid myself on the chair which Michaela had put into a reclining position, covering myself as best I could with the towel she had provided.

'I'm ready,' I called out and back in they came.

What happened next was far more cathartic than any number of professional therapy sessions. For a start, there was something hypnotically lulling about the soft buzzing of the machine. I had always expected a tattoo to be painful; strangely this wasn't. Michaela had asked Sean to fiddle with the music centre and there was a background noise of seemingly all my favourite tracks.

'I like this one,' I kept saying and would begin to hum along. 'Funny how we have the same tastes,' I commented after about a dozen songs had played, all of which I loved, even if they were from way back in my teenage years.

'Isn't it just,' agreed Michaela, sitting almost statue like at my side, only her hands seeming to move so deftly and softly.

And then from Sean, the gentle and casual questions that teased out various chapters of my life story.

'It's such a pretty name, Daisy. Are they your mother's favourite flowers now?'

I gave a little snort which was most unlike me. 'No. I would say roses are definitely my mother's favourite flower, no matter that they have sharp nasty thorns which can cut right into you.'

'Hm, it is true. Roses do have a shocking way of doing that,' Sean agreed. 'I prefer a wildflower myself, don't you Michaela? No one ever pricked themselves making a Daisy chain, that I know of anyway.'

I found myself laughing and then blurted out without meaning to, 'My elder sister is called Rose. She's glamourous and vibrant and takes after our mother, Marigold, whereas I do not.'

'Is that a fact? Now forgive my ignorance but do Marigolds' have thorns or not?'

'Not,' I replied. 'But they are greedy for sunlight and can overshadow other flowers around them.'

'Are they indeed? I'm not so sure I like the sound of Marigolds then,' he said solemnly.

There was a pause and even though I have never been one to feel uncomfortable with silences, I suddenly felt the need to fill it by explaining about Rose and Marigold.

'I think it's their Hungarian blood. I mean it's very diluted. I think it was Marigold's great grandmother who came over from Hungary. By all accounts she was a trapeze artist in a travelling circus. She met her husband here and never went back.'

Sean was quick to pick up on two points. 'You share the same blood though, Daisy do you not?'

'Well yes of course I do. It's just that with them you can see their heritage. They are both dark and fiery-tempered, and that hint of gypsy blood still flares up from time to time. Tempestuous is a good way to describe them. I am nothing like them.'

Practical. Boring. The unspoken words in my mind.

'Hm,' Sean seemed to ponder this and then asked. 'So why do you not call your mother, Mum, or Ma, why do you call her Marigold?'

I turned my head to look at him, careful not to alter the position of my body in any way. 'We were both told not to call her Mum once we started high school. She said it made her feel too old. She's not the most maternal of women.'

'Hm,' was Sean's only comment on this. He then distracted me with an anecdote about his own mother. Whether this was done to take my mind off Marigold, or simply because he wanted to share some of his life with me, I don't know. But his mother, Eileen Murphy sounded a real gem.

'You must miss her,' I said, thinking she was still in Ireland by the way he talked. 'Isn't there anyway you could go back home to her?'

'One day my darling, Daisy I'll be chatting to Ma again, but the Good Lord isn't ready for the both of us just yet. I shall have to bide my time.'

'She's dead? I am sorry Sean.'

'And what have you got to be sorry for, Daisy? She was nearly ninety and, if I say so myself, she went in a grand old fashion, that she did. You remember me telling you about it, Michaela?'

Without moving an inch, Michaela grinned and replied that she had not forgotten. 'If I get chance to book my flight out of here, that's what I would do for sure.'

Curiosity overtook me. 'How exactly did she die, if you don't mind me asking?'

'She walked herself to death.'

'I beg your pardon?'

'Well you see, she had always been a keen hill walker, loved the outdoors with a passion did Ma. When they told her, she was dying and would need to go into a hospital, she shook her head. 'Sean, my son,' she said to me, 'my mother gave birth to me in the fields where she was working and I have never spent an entire day inside in all my life, and I don't intend to start now. Outside is where I was born, and outside is where I will die, with the sun and the rain on my face and the smell of heather and thyme and the Good Lord's fresh air in my lungs, not the stink of disinfectant and old folk's piss."

I had to laugh, and Sean grinned with me. 'Aye she had a way with the words did Ma. Any how she took to walking as many hills as she could, the higher and steeper the better, with good old James and Bob for company.'

'James and Bob?'

'A bottle of Jameson whiskey and Bob the collie dog.'

He was painting such a picture in my mind I was entranced, seeing this defiant old lady hiking up hillsides with a dog at her side and a bottle of bottle of whiskey in her rucksack.

'What happened?'

'Exactly what she intended. She got to the top of the mountain one day, she drank her whiskey and she fell asleep. Bob came back down to the village and that was when the priest knew it was time. He fetched his own hiking boots and followed Bob back up the hill. He got there in time to give her the last rites and sit with her whilst she took her last breath. The priest took Bob back with him and wouldn't you know it, but the dog went to sleep in his basket that night and never woke up in the morning.'

I now had tears running down my face and I let them fall unashamedly. 'Sean, that's beautiful,' I snuffled and thanked him as he passed me a tissue. It was only after I had composed myself that I thought to ask him where he had been at the time.

'The Good Lord was keeping me busy with other things,' he said with a wink. 'Isn't that right Michaela?'

'Indeed it was. But that was how your mother wanted it Sean. She was never one for a fuss was dear Eileen. And she didn't need you by her side to know that you loved the very bones of her and she you.'

Sean nodded quietly.

'Oh hell, give me another tissue; you're turning me to mush.'

'No Daisy, you already are a bag of mush, I am merely letting you see it.' He went quiet then and I think he realised I needed a little time of reflective thought myself. I relaxed into the chair, and with the gentle buzzing of the machine and the music, it was enough to send me off to sleep.

'That was a good little nap now Daisy, wasn't it?' I heard Sean's voice some time later. I hoped I'd not dribbled as I snoozed. 'Shall I be making you a cup of tea now?'

Groggily I nodded and Michaela paused a little in her work so that I could move a fraction and have my drink. Sean then returned once more asking me about my life and enquired about my father.

'Dad? We get on fine I suppose. He was always busy working when Rose and I were growing up but to be honest, I think that was more to do with escaping from Marigold's moods than anything else.'

'Are they still married then?'

'God no. Dad waited until Rose was sixteen and I was fourteen and then left.'

'Did he have somebody else?'

By now I had lost all sense that Sean could be prying and after what he had told me about his mother it seemed natural to just let it flow.

'He didn't. Marigold did. She was just never satisfied with what he could do. She criticised him if he wasn't earning enough money for a new kitchen or bathroom, or fancy holiday, but then she yelled at him if he worked late to make the money. She blamed the fact that she took lovers on what she deemed his inadequacies. I suppose one day he just had enough.'

Horrible memories that I had worked so hard at suppressing came rushing back. Ours had not been a happy family home. Discord and dissatisfaction were two permanent residents. I had felt abandoned when Dad had left but looking back, I could see so clearly how Marigold had manipulated my feelings and thoughts to her own advantage. I was so desperate to have peace and harmony that I would do anything to placate her vicious temper, even if it meant siding with her against my dad.

I felt a little worm of regret twisting deep in my belly. As I reviewed the condemnations my mother had poured upon Dad in the past, could I really blame him for just walking out of the door one day and not wanting to come back?

'She was an absolute cow,' I said suddenly, as if a light bulb had been lit up in my head illuminating what I could not see before. 'And so was I. I shut the door on him too.'

'You were fourteen, Daisy. A child.'

'I'm an adult now though aren't I'?

'Then there's chance for you to change things if you want to,' said Sean evenly. 'Do they both still live locally?'

'Oh yes. As soon as I was sixteen, Marigold did go off travelling for a while with a string of men, one after the other, leaving me in Rose's capable hands.'

Sean raised his eyebrows. 'Daisy, do I detect a bucket load of sarcasm in that sweet voice of yours?'

I ignored him and continued. 'But when Dad remarried some years later, she decided that she wanted to be back on his doorstep to meddle in his happiness.'

For the first time, it struck me that I could see this was exactly what she had done. Odd how today, after a lifetime of blurred vision, I was seeing things differently.

'I think it was getting harder for her to keep hold of her men as she got older. She's currently single and living on a canal boat her latest lover left her when he died.'

The words had left my mouth and I realised they held a sting of bitterness that took its root from somewhere else and the blame could not be laid at Marigold's door. That dreadful vision of emptiness I had felt at the train station came hurtling back towards me. My breathing grew quick and shallow.

'Is it hurting?' Michaela was quick to ask. 'You're doing grand, Daisy, you're sitting so well. Isn't she Sean, never flinching or moving a muscle.'

'It's not the tattoo that's hurting,' I choked out. 'It's Gary and Gerald.'

'Now Gerald would be your lovely father-in-law for whom I have to thank for my overcoat.'

I nodded. 'He was a lovely man, Sean. You would have liked him.'

'Ah. When did he die, Daisy?'

'Two weeks ago.'

'Grief can take a soul in many different directions. Some of them really not good.' Sean fixed me with his arctic clear blue eyes. I had the horrible feeling that for all he had said at the station, he knew I had actually jumped. I saw no judgement in his stare, just a wonderful kindness that again, coming from his position in life, was truly humbling. Gerald would have really liked him.

I began to talk about my father-in-law. 'He was a quiet man, thoughtful. I think he had always wanted a daughter and when Gary and I got married he made such a fuss of me. It made a change from my own Dad.' I paused here and wondered if Dad's hurtful disinterest in my wedding had been because of Marigold's behaviour. She had certainly made it feel like a movie premiere, only you would have thought that she was the star of the show and not the bride.

I went back to Gerald. 'He never interfered in our lives, but he was always just there. He was a retired woodwork teacher and he used to spend hours in his workshop at the bottom of his garden. I used to love joining him there at the weekends, sitting amongst the shavings having a cup of tea and some of Irene's cakes. She was a great baker until she got ill.'

Sean had got off his stool to refill his mug of tea and asked me if I wanted another one. I looked outside at the sky. It had never really got light today but now the darkness was drawing in and I wondered how long I had been in this chair. For a small tattoo I seemed to have spent rather a long time here.

'Is there much more to do Michaela?' I asked tentatively, not wanting to offend her.

'No, my lovely. Maybe ten minutes or so. And yes, Sean I will have a coffee thank you very much.'

'In that case I'll have one too, thanks Sean.'

'Go on then,' he prompted me. 'What happened with Irene?'

'Dementia. It started slowly at first when she was still relatively young. But then, as it got progressively worse, Gerald asked if we would move in with them to help. They had been together since they were at school, and it was just too dreadful to contemplate putting her in a home. She was happier anyway in her own surroundings, but she did get to needing a lot of help.'

'Not many daughters-in-law would have agreed,' Sean commented.

'She wasn't like many mother-in laws. I adored her. I adored them both.'

'And when did the poor lady pass over then?'

'Six months before Gerald. We had barely buried her when he got his diagnosis.' I screwed my eyes tight as I remembered the scene in the hospital waiting room. Gary had been unable to get out of a meeting at work and I had promised to go with his father instead. Gerald had sat there quietly as the doctor gently explained.

"There is cancer of the prostate, but as well as that we have found that cancer has spread to the bones. It's stage four I'm afraid."

"Well at least I know what I am going to die of," Gerald had said quite calmly.

Afterwards I had grabbed the doctor for a private word to double check that there was nothing they could do.

He had shaken his head sadly. *"I hate seeing cases like this,"* he had admitted to me. *"We could so easily have treated his prostate cancer if he had come to us sooner. As it is, no there is nothing now to be done. I understand he has just lost his wife?"*

I had nodded and the understanding dawned the same time as I saw the thought reflected in the doctor's eyes.

"It is very often the case. When a couple have been married for so long, the knowledge that one of them is dying makes them want to cover up their own health problems. He probably doesn't want to be here without her."

'He made the best of the six months,' I told Sean and Michaela. 'He contacted all his old friends and at weekends or in the school holidays when I wasn't working, we went for days out. He loved stately homes and gardens. Castles too.'

It was good to remember the happy times even though it brought more of the wretched tears. Sean was ready once more with the tissues.

'Ah Daisy it sounds like you did him proud. And your husband, did he go on all of these treks with you?'

My smiled vanished, 'No. Gardens and castles are not really Gary's thing.'

"No off you two go together," Gary had said so often. "You know I'll only get fidgety and bored and this is Dad's special time, I would hate to spoil it. You two have a smashing day and I will sort out tea for when you get back."

I realised now that although yes, there was always a lovely meal upon our return, our days ticking off items from Gerald's bucket list had given him plenty of time to spend with her. Just then Michaela switched off her machine and announced with a satisfied sigh that she was finished.

'As good a work of art as I have ever done, even if I do say so myself,' she declared with a smile.

Sean had been able to see the tattoo progressing and he nodded in agreement. 'I think you will be pleased, Daisy.'

Clutching the towel to my chest, I clambered awkwardly off the chair. My body had become rooted into position and it was only then that I could look at the clock on the wall. I saw that four hours had passed. Four hours!

'Well, what do you think?' Michaela asked as she turned me towards the mirrors. She had a couple of them that she could angle together so it was possible to see over my shoulder.

What did I think?

'It's…'

For a minute I literally could not speak as I stared and stared.

My silence could have been taken for disapproval, but Michaela and Sean were grinning in such a way they knew that my only reaction could be of delight, even if that was a little delayed in being expressed.

'It's…' I tried again and had to close to my mouth as I struggled to find the right words. For one thing it was huge! I had expected a tiny discreet drawing but no. My back was now a complete work of art. There was a wolf living and breathing between my shoulder blades, or at least so it seemed.

It was stunningly, beautifully alive with every delicate, feathered touch of ink.

It was wild, savage, gentle, soulful.

It was all these things.

'Well?' It would appear, that my silence had been drawn out a little too long.

'She's beautiful,' I whispered in awe.

I couldn't take my eyes off it as I struggled to comprehend that this was now a part of me. This wonderful wolf was going to live on my back forever. I experienced a thrill of unexpected excitement running through me. Suddenly the despair of the morning seemed a long time ago. I looked at the eyes of the wolf in the mirror and from somewhere, a tiny spark of hope trickled into my veins.

'She's magical,' I said in a louder voice turning now to Sean and Michaela, still holding the towel to my chest, reluctant to cover the wolf up.

The tattoo artist and the homeless man exchanged a smile and then high fived each other.

'She certainly is, Daisy, we would agree with you on that one,' said Sean with a beaming smile.

Chapter Four

Michaela and Sean went through to the front room so that I could dress. I realised that most of the day had slipped away. The clock on the wall was nearing three. It seemed an age since the morning when the task of getting dressed had almost been too much.

When life had not felt worth living.

My back was tingling.

My whole body was tingling.

It was a reminder that I was alive.

A wave of optimism flooded into me, warming hitherto frozen veins. I felt giddy and I nearly forgot to ask Michaela how much I owed her for her glorious artwork. My hand was on the door of the shop to finally go and get a taxi home with Sean when I remembered this.

'Oh, my goodness what must you think of me?' I clapped my hand to my mouth in horror. 'How much do I owe you?'

Michaela laughed. 'You owe me nothing, Daisy.'

'I must pay you! It took four hours. It's huge. It must be a lot.'

Hastily I stepped back into the warmth of the studio, my hands already fumbling inside my bag for my purse.

She stepped towards me and placed her hands over mine. 'There is no charge, Daisy.'

I gawped at her. 'I can't just not pay you!'

Her shining eyes stared, darkly intense.

'And why not? Did you ask for the tattoo?' She shook her head. 'It was offered as a gift. You cannot pay for a gift, Daisy.'

Even so.

She could see I was about to argue and said over her shoulder to Sean, 'Tell her, Sean, it is a gift and a gift cannot be bought, only given with love and hopefully received with love.'

Behind me, his soft Irish tones agreed. 'That is how it is. Given with love and received with love, that is the true essence of a gift and as such no monies should ever change hands. You do love it, Daisy, don't you?'

'I do! Absolutely. She's the most beautiful thing I have ever seen. I can't believe she is part of me.'

I received then a brilliant smile from Michaela. I had clearly made her happy with my answer.

'She is a part of you now, Daisy and you are just as beautiful as she is, and that's the God's honest truth of it. Now off you go and no more frowning. You should be smiling Daisy.'

On impulse I leant forward and kissed her on the cheek. 'Thank you so much. You don't know what you've done for me today.'

She laughed a musically merry sound. 'Oh, Daisy I think you may find that I do.'

Slightly puzzled by her last words I left the studio with Sean, and we resumed our steps towards the taxi rank. My stomach growled and I realised we had completely missed lunch.

'Crikey I'm starving,' I said as we left the undercover shelter of the arcade back into the heavy rain, dashing to cross the road. 'We didn't have any lunch.'

Sean shrugged and I cursed myself again for my stupidity. As if he could expect to have three solid meals a day. I shooed him into the taxi and gave the driver my address. The taxi began to follow the route out of town, past the university and the sprawling buildings of student accommodation.

I wondered if Sean had ever attended university and with that thought was the realisation that I knew nothing about him. A moment of panic hit me, and I cast a sneaky side long look at him. What the hell was I doing? He could be a murderer for all I knew. As if in tune with my thoughts, the taxi then passed by the prison, an imposing-looking building on the corner of a major junction.

'I wonder if the food in there has improved?' Sean said breezily, making the driver cast a sudden look in his mirror. 'Shocking it was. I wouldn't have fed it to my pigs no, indeed I would not have done. *"Sean,"* they would have squealed back at me, *"what God awful shite is this you're giving us?"* If pigs could speak, which of course we all know they cannot. So, there you go, they couldn't have really said it. But they would if they could. Oh yes, I am sure about that. They would if they could.'

His expression when he turned and looked at me was bland as if he had been talking about a hotel, or guest house and I struggled to make any fluent response.

All I could manage was a high pitched, 'Oh really?'

He grinned at me wickedly and I didn't know if he was teasing or not. Then I reminded myself once more that this was the person who had saved my life and miraculously caught me when I had jumped off the platform. As I remembered this, my head now a little clearer than it had been this morning, I suddenly had another blinding thought whizz into my mind.

I had jumped.

There had been no one immediately behind me, despite what I may have said back at the station, regardless of what the CCTV footage had shown.

'Sean...' I began tentatively. 'You know this morning.'

'Ah yes, when that eejit pushed you and made you tumble off the platform.'

'Yes, but he didn't. There was no 'eejit' Sean, only that of myself.'

'Daisy you saw it as clear as day on the CCTV. There was a muddle of folk all bumping into each other, just like dominoes toppling so they were. And you were the last one in the line. Just lucky I was right there with you when you toppled.'

I opened my mouth to argue, but he gave me such a look that I shut it again.

'What?' He said with a rather mocking tone to his voice now. 'You are going to suggest, Daisy that somehow I, a homeless scrap of humanity, could somehow have tampered with the CCTV tapes? And wouldn't that make me greater than the late Paul Daniels himself, God rest his soul with all his magician's tricks? And in front of the police officer and that arse Jones as well? Sure, and Daisy don't you think my lovely that if I had those sorts of skills up my sleeves I would be sitting by the pay phone in the car park every day?'

When he put it like that, I could see his point. 'Sorry,' I mumbled.

Maybe there had been a jostling of some sort behind me as I took my leap which made it appear as though I had been accidentally pushed. That, I rationalised could be the only explanation as I know I had jumped.

'Forget it now, Daisy,' said Sean softly. 'Tis over. Look forward, not back.'

I nodded, my eyes fixed outside the rain smeared window, not on him. 'Good advice.' It was just the sort of thing Gerald would say and I turned back to him with a smile. 'You're right, Sean.'

'I know,' he replied with quiet assurance. 'Is it far to your house Daisy?'

His tone told me that in his mind the subject was now well and truly closed.

'No, not much further now.'

Ours was a northern mill town, built on the back of the industrial revolution and as such had block upon block of solidly built terraced houses, some of their streets still retaining the original cobbles. Spreading out from this mass, where the workers used to live, grew the larger houses that belonged to the factory managers, office workers and the like. Tree lined avenues began to appear in these more affluent areas, and garden fronted semis with deep bay windows and grand front doors sat well back from the roads. As we turned the corner into Park Road, so named because it ran parallel to one of the parks the town was lucky to have, I repeated my address to the driver.

'It's just past this bend here, on the right. That's it; the one with the red door. Thank you.'

'I do love houses with red doors,' said Sean as he opened the taxi door and, quick as a flash, he came round to my side to help me out. 'Always so cheerful and welcoming I think, a house with a red door. And it looks like we have a welcoming party. Look.'

I was busy paying the driver, so I had not noticed there was a familiar car parked on the pavement in front of the house.

'Keep the change,' I said, in a fluster all of a sudden.

'Daisy, Daisy, Mummy says we can decorate biscuits, we've got coloured beads and icing and all sorts of things!'

Abigail came flying towards me, her auburn pigtails bouncing either side of her freckled face, her mouth wide in a beaming smile. Her hugs were something akin to a rugby tackle and I had learnt to brace myself but today she caught me unawares and Sean had to steady the pair of us.

'Easy now tiger, we don't want you falling over now do we?'

Abigail looked at Sean and with the wonderful unquestioning approach of a seven-year-old, she simply giggled at him as she extricated herself from my hug.

'I'm not a tiger, silly.'

Sean cocked his head at her. 'No maybe I was wrong. You're possibly more of a giraffe. All tall and long legged.'

Mirroring his actions, she cocked her head back at him. 'I think I prefer tiger.'

'Tiger it is then. So, we're going to decorate biscuits, are we? I cannot remember the last time I did that. I can't wait.'

'Are you going to help us then? Are you a friend of Daisy's?'

'Yes, Daisy, who is this?' Abigail's mother caught up with the hurricane that was her daughter, holding a bag of baking ingredients.

'Samantha this is Sean. Sean this is Samantha.'

Sean smiled warmly at the tall attractive woman with a smart crop of auburn hair. In turn, Samantha's brown eyes furrowed into a frown as she recognised Gerald's overcoat.

Sean spoke first. 'Lovely to meet you, Samantha. And you would be perhaps a colleague of Daisy's, or, let me guess, you two were at school now. I can see that would be the case.'

He held out the hand that wore the red fingerless glove for her to shake. Her whole body had stiffened but it was hard to say whether it was because of his comment, or that she had seen the grubby and betraying state of his fingernails.

'Wrong on both counts,' she replied, declining the offer of his hand and refusing to explain either. She turned her gaze to me. 'Daisy, where have you been all afternoon? I was hoping you could pick Abigail up from school, but your mobile kept going to voicemail. Gary said you would be home. Anyway, never mind, the thing is, something has come up and I have to be somewhere. Abigail needs these biscuits doing for school tomorrow. I knew you wouldn't mind.'

'Come on then,' Abigail reached for Sean's red gloved hand and was tugging on it with all the enthusiasm her mother lacked. 'Biscuits to bake and decorate.'

'Who exactly is this, Daisy?'

My usual response would have been a ramblingly long and nervous explanation. I always felt inferior in Samantha's presence. But today had been far from usual and my response was bluntly different.

'I told you, this is Sean. Come on Abigail, it's too cold to stand around out here and your mother has things to do.'

I caught a glint of amusement in Sean's eyes that was a distinct contrast to the scowl in Samantha's.

'I'll pick her up at nine, she's got spare night clothes here, hasn't she? Good, so if you wouldn't mind bathing her for me as well.'

'Not a problem,' I said, used to this routine which was one I enjoyed.

'I take it your 'friend' will have gone by then?' She hissed this under her breath.

Sean, standing at the front door with Abigail, which was a good ten feet down the driveway, must have ears like a bat, I thought, as he cheerfully replied.

'Oh no. I'm staying the night so I am. But don't worry about young Abigail here and bath time, I will be well out of the way. You've no need to worry on that account. I only spent time in prison for bank robbery, I'm not one of those, you know, funny people.'

For a split second, I saw Samantha contemplating changing her mind. Then her phone pinged and the message she read was clearly prompting her to hurry up.

'I have to go. Daisy we will speak later.' She turned sharply on her heels giving Sean another wary look and then shot a backward comment to me. 'Does Gary know about this?'

'Not yet.'

But he soon will I thought and decided not to ponder too deeply what my feelings were on that subject. There was tea for three to make and biscuits to decorate. Reprisals could wait.

'Hurry up Daisy.'

Abigail was hopping around on the front step, and if I didn't get a move on the bag of ingredients she was swinging around was going to spill everywhere.

I opened the front door and Abigail darted through, at home here as she was in her own house. She took off her coat and scarf and placed them on the old wooden settle under the stairs. Her blue and grey school uniform that I knew would have been pristine that morning now looked in total disarray, ink, paint and various other stains splattered here and there. Her white socks were crumpled around her ankles, and there was mud on the shoes that she had taken off.

'Come on Sean, this is where we put our coats,' she said tugging her new friend towards the settle.

I shut the door, glad of her chatter. It masked the silence that would otherwise have been far too loud. In my mind, I was calling out to Gerald and waiting for his welcoming reply.

'This is a lovely house, Daisy,' Sean said as he began to unbutton his coat. 'Feels like a proper home.'

Those bloody tears threatened to return.

'Thanks Sean. It is. I mean it has been.'

Gerald and Irene's Victorian house where we had lived together as a family for the last ten years, was embedded with memories and for the most part they were the happy sort. There was plenty of space, with four large double bedrooms and two separate sitting rooms as well as a huge kitchen that had room for an enormous dining table.

When Gary and I had moved back in as a married couple, Gerald had insisted that he paid for alterations to have an ensuite added to the second largest bedroom as well as a full refurbishment for the room itself.

"You've been used to your own place," he had kept saying. "And you moving back here means my beloved Irene won't need to go into a home. Least I can do, now stop arguing, Daisy and go and pick some pretty bedding and curtains for the windows."

My reverie was cut short by Abigail's exclamation.

'Oh, that's so funny, Sean. You're wearing Grandad's coat.' She was helping him undo the buttons as if he could not quite manage to do so himself.

'Gerald was your Grandad, was he?' He asked her gently, happy it seemed to let her help.

'Not exactly,' she answered, her bright face crinkling as she thought. 'Daisy, I can never remember exactly.'

I met Sean's eyes above hers.

'Abigail called Gerald Grandad, and he was like one to her, wasn't he sweetheart? He loved you.' I gave an affectionate tug on her plaits. 'But technically, he was her great uncle in law. I think. I was never too sure myself to be honest.'

Sean looked as though he was working this out as Abigail led him through to the kitchen.

'So, you two are related then? Not just a friend of family type of thing?'

'Daisy's my sister silly,' Abigail pushed her sleeves up at the sink and turned to him. 'Come on, we have to wash our hands first and yours look sooooooo dirty. How did you get them like that?'

She sounded rather envious of Sean's blackened nails. He laughed good-naturedly.

'Ah well that would be a long story now.'

'I like long stories.'

'I will tell you one later,' he said to her solemnly. 'So, if you are Daisy's sister, then Samantha is…'

'My stepmother,' I provided.

I had never seen anything remotely amusing, that ten years after walking out on me and Rose, my dad, a successful GP with his own practice, had married one of his junior doctors. So junior that in fact I was three months older than her. To rub salt into what was a very sore wound, they had married the same year that Gary and I had, infuriating Marigold.

Happy families indeed.

All these years later when my heart was so desperately ripped into little pieces, I suddenly saw that there was a funny side to it. Maybe it was the wicked light in Sean's eyes that illuminated the whole situation into something different.

'Do you call her Mummy, Mum, or is it Mother?' He asked looking up from scrubbing his nails, the water in the sink now a gloriously muddy black.

I laughed. A half held back snort that somehow rolled into a great monster of a belly laugh. I quickly clapped my hand over my mouth, not wanting to upset Abigail. My little sister though just rolled her eyes in a spectacularly grown-up fashion and then swiped at Sean with a tea towel, tutting.

'Don't be silly Sean. How can Daisy call her Mummy? She is older than her.'

'You are actually older than her?' Sean took the towel and began to dry his hands.

I had to contort my face into a scowl against all its better instincts to grin widely back at him.

'It's not so unusual,' I said.

He shrugged. 'Well anyway, I think you are very lucky to have been blessed with such a wonderful little sister.'

He handed the towel back to Abigail who hung it neatly on the rail to dry. I watched her do this as I had done so a hundred times before and never actually noticed. I was filled with a rush of love and affection for the little girl. If anyone had asked me if I loved my youngest sister, I would have answered that of course I did. But in truth I suppose there was always something of my heart holding back, part of me had been frozen long before Gary's betrayal.

'Okay then, let's crack on. We've got biscuits to bake and decorate.'

'Can we make them all sparkly Daisy, really, really sparkly?'

'Of course we can. The sparklier the better.'

'Sean, have you ever made sparkly biscuits?' Abigail looked at him with curiosity aglow in her eyes as she sat at the table.

'Indeed, I have,' he replied rolling up the sleeves of his tatty sweater.

'I'm going to make one like an angel,' said Abigail rooting through the bag Samantha had provided. 'Look. Mummy bought me an angel shaped cutter. Do you like angels Sean?'

'I do,' he answered. 'I like angels, fairies, wood sprites and all sorts of things.'

He turned to look at me then with a smile that despite his rotten teeth, grimy face, and ungroomed hair and beard, was disturbingly beautiful. I felt something tugging at my heart that shot down to my core, a sensation I vaguely remembered as desire.

Somewhat shaken, I turned away and put the kettle on.

Chapter Five

We made two batches of biscuits, or rather Abigail and Sean did whilst I took a quiet back seat at the kitchen table. They chattered away as though they had known each other for years but I think this was also a natural skill that Sean possessed. It should have felt unbearably odd to have this scruffy stranger looking so at home in my kitchen. But it didn't.

Then again, everything was different.

I would not normally be sitting down at this time of the early evening having a cup of tea. I would be seeing to Gerald's needs, preparing a meal for Gary, before marking work for the next day, sorting the washing and ironing, all the usual daily tasks. I was more than redundant in not having Gerald to care for. I was bereft. I did not like to dwell on having no husband to cook for. I did after all have my little sister to feed, not to mention Sean. In keeping with the unusual day, I suggested the chip shop.

'On a Tuesday, Daisy? Really!' Abigail was gazing at me as though I had suggested Father Christmas was going to turn up early.

I shrugged. 'Why not Abigail. It feels like that kind of a day.'

She nodded enthusiastically and then said through slightly pursed lips, 'Perhaps we can tell Mummy we had shepherd's pie though.'

Samantha was a health freak. The notion of a chippy tea mid-week would have sent her into an apoplectic fit.

Feeling rebellious, I said to Abigail. 'Yes well, steak pud and chips is what I fancy eating and as this is my house, that's what's on the menu. Unless of course you would prefer fish or a pie.'

Abigail shook her head. 'Pudding please.'

Sean nodded in agreement and added that if it was not too much to ask, please could he also have mushy peas. I hesitated for a second as to whether I should leave Abigail alone with him. Samantha would freak if she knew. Once more he had that habit of reading my mind and spoke for me.

'We can all go together if you like?'

Instantly my hesitation vanished. I could not explain how or why but I knew with certainty that Sean would care for Abigail as I would myself.

'If I go now there shouldn't be too much of a queue. And then Abigail, my darling little girl, we can have one of your biscuits for afters?'

There was an extremely good chippy just at the end of the road. It was now completely dark with the street lamps lit and the odd car passing by with headlights on and windscreen wipers swishing to and fro. I pulled the hood of my coat up and dug my hands deep into my pockets. The air was much colder, and I wondered absently if this rain would turn to hail once more. It was almost too cold to snow but if it froze tonight the roads would be treacherous tomorrow.

I would have to remind Gary to get up a little earlier if that was the case in order to defrost his car, as he set off for work before I did. And then I remembered that just as I no longer had Gerald to care for, I no longer had a husband to fret over. Well technically I did. He just wasn't living with me anymore. It would be young, glamourous Corinne who would have to remind him.

Young, glamourous, pregnant Corinne.

I must have been looking a little lost by the time I was waiting in the queue at the chippy because Nellie who owned it had to ask me twice what my order was.

'Sorry Nellie. Miles away. Steak pud and chips three times and a portion of mushy peas please.'

'Nowhere nice either love by the look on your face.'

She bustled about behind the counter whilst her young male assistant got busy serving someone else.

'I heard from your Rose that Gary has moved out? Lousy timing for you, what with losing Gerald so recently and so soon after Irene. Then again, when is a good time hey? My git of a husband walked out on me when I was pregnant with the twins. Mind you, I wouldn't have met my Malcom if he hadn't. Best thing since sliced bread my Malc, so you never know love. Silver linings and all that.'

'Thanks, Nellie.'

Right now, I would be lucky if I had a brass lining never mind a silver one.

'You take care of yourself now love,' she said as she passed over the parcel of well wrapped food in a brown paper bag. I handed over my money or tried to and she shook her head. 'Don't be daft girl. You look done in. Have this one on me. And try and get some sleep.'

I opened my mouth to argue but she shook her head firmly at me.

'I know what you did for Gerald, and Irene before him. And I remember how bloody hard it was nursing my folk with cancer. Leaves you like a wet dish cloth when it's all over. Go on with you and like I said, try and get some sleep.'

I shoved my purse back in my bag, nearly blinded by more tears.

'Thanks Nellie,' I said again with a sniffle and made my way back out into the dark.

Her kindness at the end of such a weird day was almost too much and I was choking back a sob as I began the short walk home. Distracted, I didn't pay any attention to the soft sound of two push bikes coming up behind me until they were right alongside, hemming me in.

Two dark-clad figures, hoods up with indiscernible features loomed in close. I had always considered where I lived to be a safe place but now, I was under threat and totally ill-equipped to deal with it. I cried out helplessly as the one on the left swiped my bag of food from my hand whilst the one on the right yanked hard at the strap of my shoulder bag, almost pulling me over as he did so. Anger overcame my fear. I didn't stop to think as I began a tug of war with him. I might consider losing my chippy tea but not my bag with everything in it!

Then out came the flash of a knife, glinting dangerously in the flickering light of a street lamp.

'Give it up you stupid bitch!'

Already there was a trickle of blood on my right hand. I had taken my gloves off in the shop and not put them back on. I yelped and this made the youth with my food laugh, but only seemed to irritate my attacker further.

'Fucking let go!' He yelled into my face.

The knife moved again so fast my breath caught in my throat. He was going to slash me I thought, terror now replacing anger.

He didn't get the chance though.

It was his turn to scream and shout and there was genuine terror in his voice. 'Jesus fucking Christ, get it off me!'

The movement was so sudden, so silent it was impossible to say where it came from. One minute my attacker was wielding a knife in my face, the next he was knocked off his bike, sprawled on the floor and a huge white beast was pinning him to the ground.

'It's a fucking wolf!' his accomplice shrieked as he dropped my bag of food on the floor.

'I know it's a fucking wolf,' came back the high-pitched reply followed with another entreaty for me to do something. 'It's going to rip my fucking throat out!'

'Please Miss, we're dead sorry, we shouldn't have tried to mug you, it was for a dare, don't let it eat my brother!'

I managed to tear my eyes away from the wolf on the floor with the body beneath him, to the hooded figure wobbling now on his bike the other side of me. I thought I recognised his voice, but I was too stunned by the appearance of the animal to contemplate putting a face to it.

'Miss, please!' His brother pleaded with me from the floor. He was as still as a stone apart from the fact that his breathing was rapid and there was now a certain wheeziness creeping into it.

'He's got asthma miss. He's only doing this as a dare cos the lads in his class think he's a wuss for having to have an inhaler! Please miss call your wolf off!'

Two things clicked in my rather slow brain then.

Firstly, this was Jed Williams lying prone on the floor. I had taught him last year so this would be his brother Ted, who, at thirteen, was two years younger.

Secondly, my wolf?

As I thought this, the creature turned its huge head and looked at me. At the same time, I felt the whole of my back prickle and burn.

'Oh. My. God,' I whispered in disbelief.

'Miss please,' Jed was starting to wheeze now.

I blinked just in case I was seeing things. When I found I was still staring into the eyes of the creature that was tattooed on my back, I considered that I had maybe stepped into some kind of parallel universe, or that I was dreaming.

But then Jed's wheezing broke through that.

'Shit, you need your inhaler.'

I suddenly grasped the severity of the situation and without thinking took a step towards Jed and the wolf. The instant I did so, it moved away from him and went to sit watchfully over by Ted who scuttled as far away as he could without deserting his brother. I helped Jed to a seated position, and he scrambled in his pockets for his inhaler. The knife clattered to the floor beside him. I saw now it was a kitchen one, similar to those I had at home.

'I think I should take that don't you?'

I reached for it once I saw his breathing was getting under control, but he shook his head and his younger brother spoke for him.

'Please miss don't. It's one of Mum's best. She'll skin us alive if she knows we had nicked it to do this.'

Mrs Williams was a decent mother, and her boys were not really bad. Perhaps just too easily led and in Jed's case, vulnerable to bullying peer pressure.

'Promise me you won't ever do anything so stupid again.'

I looked at the pair of them and helped Jed to stand up. As soon as he was on his feet, so was the wolf, right by my side.

We both stared warily at it.

It was huge, wild looking.

Totally out of place on Park Road.

It had its gaze fixed on Jed and he gulped. 'I promise Miss. I was just trying to be one of the gang.'

'Well make me another promise Jed. Find different friends; those lads are no friends of yours.'

He hung his head and looked ashamed; his face clear to see now with his hood pushed down.

'I know miss, but they pushed me into doing it. They were picking on our Ted and when I tried to stop them, they said that they would stop bullying him if I did this for them. To prove I was hard like they are. Ted was telling the truth when he said they think I'm soft cos I've got asthma.'

'It's true Miss.'

Ted nodded, still keeping a distance from me and the wolf. I didn't blame him.

'Look, go home now the pair of you. I think I know who you are talking about Jed. They need stopping.'

'But Miss if you say anything, they'll know I snitched.'

'I promise I will be discreet,' I assured them, but right now I had more pressing things on my mind.

Like a wolf.

The animal was waiting silently at my side and remained like a statue until the boys had pedalled off. The scent of steak pudding and chips reminded me that our tea was probably cold by now and Sean and Abigail would be wondering where I had got to.

Sean!

I had almost forgotten about him.

I looked at the wolf and thought about the homeless man who was baking biscuits in my kitchen and decided that this was turning out to be the weirdest day ever.

'Right,' I said to no one in particular and certainly not to the wolf because now that the boys had disappeared, I was trying my best to pretend that it was a figment of my imagination brought on by too much stress and not enough sleep. 'Home for a chippy tea.'

My steps were brisk, and I refused to look sideways to engage eye contact with the animal that was loping along next to me. I ignored it until I was about ten feet away from my house and then in exasperation turned to it.

'Look shoo! I don't know who you belong to. You've obviously got out from somewhere.'

It crossed my mind for one second that perhaps I could look to see if it had a collar and identity tag but no. There was nothing domestic about this creature. Still, I tried once more and waved a hand at it repeating my command to go.

The wolf then smiled at me. Yes, it really smiled. I saw lots of terrifyingly sharp looking white teeth and a pink tongue, but in no way was it snarling and threatening as it had done to Jed. Then, to my further disbelief it pushed past me and in one graceful bound, cleared the garden gate and went to sit on the front step.

I had no choice but to follow and was rummaging in my bag for my keys when the door was opened by Sean. Illuminated behind him in the hallway was Abigail who understandably squealed when she saw the huge white animal sitting in front of her.

'Daisy, it's a wolf!'

Her wide eyes grew rounder as Sean stepped back and it walked calmly into my house.

I shrugged my shoulders at Sean who didn't seem in the least bit surprised to see it.

'Ah great, you've got the chips. We were wondering where you had got to?'

Not, where in the bloody hell has this beast come from Daisy? Or what the feck are we going to do with it now? No. Just ah, great you've got the chips!

'There was a little incident,' I said as I stepped into the hallway to watch the wolf nudge open the door to the kitchen.

To Abigail's utter delight, it then sprang up onto one of the chairs and sat at the table as though waiting to be fed. My little sister could not contain her excitement.

'It's like The Tiger who Came to Tea Daisy, only you've brought a wolf back with you, a real wolf! Are you going to keep it?'

I passed the bag of food to Sean.

'I give up,' I muttered quietly. 'I have gone utterly mad. That's the only possible explanation.'

'Ah but mad can be a good thing,' said Sean airily. 'Shall I pop these in the oven to re heat a little, it's still hot from the baking.'

'Good idea,' I replied, as I went to drop my coat onto the settle into the hallway.

Perhaps by the time I had done that and returned to the kitchen, my brainstorm would have cleared, because surely that must be what had happened, and the apparition of the wolf would be gone.

No. It was sitting there next to Abigail who was feeding it one of the iced biscuits by hand.

'I'm not altogether sure you should be doing that,' I said faintly, wondering how on Earth I would explain to Samantha if she turned up to find her daughter eaten by a wolf.

'She likes them,' said Abigail. 'She's had three already.'

'She?'

'Oh yes,' declared my little sister confidently. 'Of course she's a she. She's so beautiful, she has to be a she.'

I swear then the wolf actually turned its head to her and batted its eyelashes.

'What are you going to call her?' Abigail was now nuzzling up to her like she would a teddy bear. Remembering how fierce the wolf had been with Jed, I was feeling more than a little anxious.

'What do you mean what am I going to call her? She's not mine!' I protested.

And then Sean looked at me as he began to serve up the belated supper onto plates. Out of nowhere, as suddenly as the wolf itself had appeared, came the answer in my head.

'Luna. I'm going to call her Luna.'

'For the moon,' Sean nodded as if he approved. 'Good choice.'

'You're going to keep her Daisy! Wait till I tell my friends you've got a wolf!'

I opened my mouth to protest and once again I thought of what had happened at the station that morning. I tried to speak the words that I knew I should be uttering but different ones came out of my mouth instead.

'Yes of course I am going to keep her.'

Really Daisy?

'Daisy, your food will go cold again,' Sean gently chided me as I sat at the table blankly staring at the wolf.

Luna.

I ate my supper and at Sean's prompting, as though there was nothing out of the ordinary at having a wolf at the table with us, I told him about Jed and his brother. Sean agreed that something must be done, but not necessarily through the school.

'What are you suggesting?'

'Well, if you know where these other lads hang out, maybe I could have a little word with them. Warn them off, like.'

'Sean, I can't ask you to do that!'

'Mummy says we should always tell the teacher if someone is bullying us,' piped up Abigail as she finished her meal, having shared half of it with the wolf.

'And Mummy is quite right,' I agreed with her, whilst trying to give Sean a pointed look at the same time. 'Now, I really think I ought to go and run a bath for you. Your Mummy did say she wanted you bathed and ready for bed when she picks you up.'

'But I wanted Sean to tell me a story and to play with Luna.'

'Bath first,' said Sean firmly and to my amazement Abigail nodded, her pigtails swinging by her ears.

I settled my little sister in the bath with lots of bubbles and told her not to stay in too long and then at last I could speak to Sean alone. I had asked him to light the wood burner in the back sitting room which looked out onto the garden. We never drew the curtains in there as we were not overlooked and Gary had had lights installed outside so that even in winter, the garden was beautiful to look at. Sean was sitting in one of the chairs by the fire and he stood up as I entered the room.

'I spotted a bottle of whisky in the cabinet,' he said and held out a glass. 'I thought you could do with one.'

He wasn't wrong. I took it off him, noticing he had made himself a cup of tea.

'Do you want one?'

'Tea's grand for me. Another time maybe.'

Stretched out in front of the log burner was the elephant in the room. Or rather the wolf.

'Sean,' I began tentatively.

'Ah, I know what you're going to say, I shouldn't have done the washing up but honestly it was no bother. Sure and wouldn't my mother have tanned my arse if I had left you with dirty plates?'

'No, that wasn't what I was going to say at all! Sean, the wolf!' I hissed, not wanting to risk Abigail overhearing.

'And what a fine specimen she is.' He gave me one of those oblique looks.

I persisted. 'Sean, you know what I mean. That... animal... that wolf is exactly like the tattoo that Michaela did on my back.'

'Do you know, Daisy, now you come to mention it, yes there is a slight resemblance.'

'Slight resemblance? Sean, she's identical!'

Michaela had taken some artistic licence with my tattoo in that wolves, as far as I knew, were not actually pure snow white and they did not have silver eyes which glowed with the luminosity of the moon. But the drawing on the wall in her studio had and so did the tattoo on my back. Right then, the wolf raised its head and looked at me with those amazing unearthly eyes.

'She's not real, is she?' I whispered to him. 'I am going mad, aren't I?'

The wolf, Luna, as I had called her, rose and came to settle beside me, her great head resting on my lap. It was impossible not to touch that thick, soft fur and stroke her.

'Does she feel real?'

'Yes but…'

Sean shrugged his shoulders. 'You know, I never really like that word, 'but'. It's always so negative.'

I opened my mouth and he grinned across from me as I realised that I was about to say it again.

'Sometimes, Daisy you just have to believe in things. Whether they make sense or not. It is all a matter of faith. You do have faith don't you, Daisy? You do believe in miracles?'

At eight o'clock this morning as I had headed into town, utterly depressed and convinced my life was not worth living, I would have said 'no'.

Twelve hours later, with a wolf laying with its head in my lap, I could only answer, 'Yes Sean. I do have faith and I do believe in miracles.'

He nodded his head in approval. 'Well, that's all right then.'

Chapter Six

I woke the following morning aware of two things.

Firstly, there was a gentle knocking on my door and secondly, there was a heavy, warm and very furry presence occupying the bed with me. When I had finally got to bed, after waiting an extra thirty minutes for Samantha to pick Abigail up, and then sorting out some fresh bedding for Sean in Gerald's old room, and getting him towels etc so he could have a bath, I had tried to persuade the wolf that she was going to sleep in the nice warm, cosy kitchen.

Oh really?

It turned out that as well as being able to leap over gates, the wolf could also open doors. No surprises there. I had just settled myself deeply under my duvet, desperately tired but with my mind whizzing, when I heard my bedroom door click. Raising my head, expecting to see Sean in need of something I had forgotten to provide, my gaze was met instead by those two silvery orbs of knowing and other worldly understanding.

I was about to get up and shoo her back downstairs when I had to watch in disbelief as the wolf turned her head and nudged the door firmly back shut before covering the distance from there to my bed in one giant leap. She padded about a bit as though testing out the comfort my bed was going to provide, before flopping down on the pillow next to me.

'Are you quite happy now?' I asked, not believing I was actually talking to her. In reply I heard a deep and what seemed to be a contented sigh.

"Sod it", I thought, letting myself flop back onto my pillow, switching the light off once more. I would worry about her, and Sean, and Gary, and

Corinne tomorrow. Dark thoughts came again of how much my life was going to change and how empty it was going to be. More wretched tears – of the lonely silent type – slid down my face as I stared up at the ceiling. I felt the bed move and then there was a cold nose, nudging into my neck. Without thinking or questioning it, I turned into the warmth of the wolf and within seconds I must have been asleep.

Groggily I heard the knocking on the door again and looking at my clock I realised that for the first time in years, I had slept through. My alarm was about to go off in five minutes time, but before it could, I heard Sean's voice calling from the other side of the door.

'Are you decent? I've brought you a cup of tea?'

Was I decent? I was in Winnie the Pooh fleecy pyjamas that Gary had bought me for Christmas last year, a sure sign I realise now that he no longer viewed me in any passionate sense, and besides, Sean was sixty if he was a day, so really was I bothered? No.

'Yeah, come in Sean,' I yawned thinking how nice to have someone bring me a cup of tea.

Only the person who entered bearing a breakfast tray, was not Sean.

Or at least he was not the Sean I had brought home with me.

'I thought after all the excitement yesterday you might like a spot of breakfast in bed before you get up. I've made you a boiled egg, soldiers and toast and marmalade. You can't beat a boiled egg and soldiers, so my dear old Ma used to say. And if toast and marmalade is good enough for Paddington then its good enough for my dear friend Daisy, I said to myself.'

I really couldn't speak. I was too stunned to say anything.

'Shall I put it here for you Daisy or would you like it on your lap?' He gestured to the bedside table, and I shook my head and reached out my hands to take the tray from him. 'Are you alright now, Daisy only you are looking at me as though you are seeing a ghost or something?'

I realised I was perhaps being rude in my appraisal of him and blushed as I mumbled my thanks for the breakfast.

'This looks lovely, Sean it really does. I can't remember when I last had breakfast in bed.'

Despite last night's filling supper from the chippy, I was ravenous and tucked in greedily. Sean looked happy to see my enjoyment of the food and then perched himself on the end of the bed to drink a mug of tea.

'I've made a list of jobs I can be doing whilst you're at work,' he said cheerfully.

'You don't have to do that,' I protested.

'I do.'

He began to regale me with a comprehensive schedule of what he could be doing whilst I was teaching. I had to admit all the things he mentioned did need doing. This was a big old house and the last few years with both Irene and Gerald's illnesses things had been left to slide. Not to mention the fact that Gary had been pursuing the furthering of his career to head of science department, as well as pursing the glamourous Corinne. Perhaps having Sean was a solution to all the jobs that desperately needed attention.

'You know what Sean,' I said, as I finished my toast, 'that sounds like a really good idea. I was planning on getting some of it done when the school closes for Christmas but that is a couple of weeks off yet.'

He looked pleased and he reached to take the tray off me. 'Good. I shall leave you to get dressed. It's frosty out so I will go and warm up your car for you before you set off.'

'Am I living in some kind of fairy tale?' I asked the wolf. 'I mean, did I accidentally walk through a wardrobe yesterday, or fall down a rabbit hole?'

No, came back a voice in my head.

You tried to throw yourself under a train.

Maybe I wondered just then, I had actually done it, and maybe this was some kind of heaven? Well breakfast in bed and my car being defrosted before work wasn't such a bad version of heaven, not to mention having a magnificent white wolf as a sleeping companion.

But I was pretty sure that you didn't get mobile phones in heaven and mine was ringing insistently now. My first thought when I saw Gary's name flashing was that something was wrong with him. You cannot just wipe out eighteen years of caring. Especially when as far as you are concerned there is nothing wrong with your marriage. As soon as I heard his voice, I knew that this was not the case.

'Daisy what the bloody hell are you doing? I had Samantha on the phone late last night and I tried to ring you three times. You didn't answer.'

'Oh, did you? Sorry. I was asleep. I must not have heard it.'

I had slept right through the calls which was astonishing considering how light a sleeper I had become over years of being watchful for Irene and then Gerald.

'Is something wrong?' I dared to venture in as innocent a voice as I could.

'Something wrong?' He all but exploded down the phone. 'Samantha tells me you've lodged some old homeless tramp in Dad's room and got a bloody great dog or something.'

'Hm.'

'Hm? What kind of answer is that? Daisy have you or not?'

His voice thundered down the phone and I had to hold it some distance from my ear. I felt that old familiar twist in my stomach. I really hated conflict of any kind. Marigold had been such a master at creating chaos in my childhood home that I avoided arguments at all costs.

'Daisy will you bloody answer me? Have you got a stinking tramp in Dad's bedroom?'

I was shaking a little from the anger in his voice, knowing my answer would enrage him further. The wolf came over to my side and swiped a massive paw at the phone, knocking it out of my hand. It fell to the floor with Gary's voice still echoing into the room. Then she sat on it, and I could hear Gary no more.

You're not a normal wolf Luna, are you?' I spoke to her as I would a human being. My back prickled and almost glowed with a lovely warmth where my tattoo was.

I then spoke to myself. "Of course, she's not a normal wolf, you bloody idiot, Daisy. She's the figment of your imagination; she's the creation of an incredibly talented tattoo artist and even though you have had a good night's sleep, you are still having some kind of post traumatic hallucination."

Either way, as I contemplated how she sat on my phone and absolutely refused to budge to let me get it back, there were compensations for being temporarily insane. At least I could excuse myself from having to talk to Gary. Even if when I did get to speak to him, he may well decide to have me committed.

Shrugging all of this off for now, I had a quick shower and dressed for work. Black trousers with low heeled boots provided me with my base uniform. I had, in the early days of my teaching career, opted for heels to give me a little more height but that went in place of comfort a long time ago. I varied my tops with an assortment of blouses and jumpers or cardigans, nothing too fussy but hopefully not too dreary either.

Looking in my mirror I knew I had scored on the first point and failed miserably on the second. When had my wardrobe gone all black and navy? It really did nothing for my brown and greying hair and grey eyes. Not like bloody blonde Corinne who went for bold scarlet dresses or ice cool blue suits teemed with spiky killer heels. Would she still be as glamourous as her body swelled with pregnancy? Would she care? Would she hate the changes to her body?

Luna nudged me away from the mirror and I took the hint.

'Yes. I know. I am just bringing myself down.'

Definitely in need of certifying I thought, as I talked once more to the wild animal that had appeared in my life as though someone had waved a magic wand. But as far as I knew I did not have any fairy godmothers around. That being the case, I had to be going insane.

Downstairs I could hear the washing machine going in the utility room. I was ashamed to say that I hoped Sean had not put his filthy clothes in with my pristine white work shirts.

'That's a grand washing machine you've got, Daisy,' he said coming out of the utility room and into the kitchen. 'There's a programme for every type and colour clothing possible. It even has a pre-wash setting for filthy old tramps' clothes just like mine.'

He grinned and again I felt discomforted at the change in him over night.

'Your car is all defrosted and I have made up your lunch for you. Tuna and mayo sandwich, an apple and an orange and, of course, one of the biscuits we kept back from last night.' He winked. 'Couldn't let Samantha take them all now, could we?'

Once again, I was nonplussed. 'Er, thanks Sean. Are you sure you will be okay here by yourself? I'll write my mobile number by the telephone in the hallway. If you need anything just ring.'

And then I stopped in my tracks.

Luna.

I had a wolf in my house. What the hell was I supposed to do with her?

'Don't worry about Luna,' said Sean as he followed my gaze to the wolf who had settled herself by the warm cosy range. 'I'll take care of her.'

I held my hands out in a sort of 'what the heck' kind of gesture. 'I've never had a dog, Sean, never mind a wolf, I mean is she really a wolf? Not just some kind of weird hybrid, overgrown dog?'

Luna then moved herself into a sitting position, leant her head back and gave a long, high pitched howl the like of which you hear on a horror film with werewolves.

'Okay, she's an actual wolf,' I said shakily.

Sean grinned. 'And I am guessing she'll eat the same kind of stuff as a dog, so if you leave me some money I can nip to the supermarket and get her some food.'

'Yes of course, how stupid of me.'

'Not stupid, you have a lot on your mind.'

'But how will you get there?'

'I spotted a bicycle in the garage, if you don't mind me using that?'

The bike in question was Gary's pride and joy which cost over a thousand pounds. He would hate, absolutely hate the thought of a 'stinking old homeless tramp' using it to get food for a 'bloody dog'.

'Of course, you can Sean. The lock number is 1928. And here's fifty pounds. If there is anything else you need for yourself, please get it. There's a rucksack in the garage too you can use to carry things.'

Satisfied with these arrangements I left for work, convinced that by the time I returned I would be coming home to an empty house and the last twenty-four hours would prove to be an illusion. I had gone into teaching because I loved literature and the steady nature of the job appealed to me even though Marigold and Rose both declared it a boring profession

Maybe it lacked the excitement of Marigold's life full of travel and different men, or the glamour that Rose created within her world with her own beauty salon, but it had been where I had met and fallen in love with Gary. Years later, he moved to the private boys' school for the better salary. The job he had persuaded me to apply for had been at a private girls' school. I had argued that I was happy where I was. My ambitions trailed behind his.

Besides, I was so damn busy caring for his parents.

It hadn't crossed my mind at the time that he was nudging me in this direction, so I would not need to claim as much support from him when he divorced me. The irony was that as he had met me at work, so he had met Corinne. My mind was full of this all day. I was not in the mood to deal with a bunch of kids who were merely counting down the days to the Christmas holidays and really could not give a shit about Shakespeare.

I hated this empty feeling of desolation that had led me down such a dangerous track yesterday. Immediately the image of the wolf came into my mind and I felt my back prickle and tingle with life. It was as though she was right there with me in the room. I felt a surge of energy and suddenly I could face the thirty teenagers. Into my mind came the dilemma of how I was going to solve the problem of Jed and Ted Williams being picked on by that gang.

I shouted at the class to be quiet in a way I had never done before, surprising myself, never mind them. Then I organised them into two groups to debate how Henry V should approach the oncoming battle with the French. Should he stand and fight, or try and negotiate?

It was a rowdy, boisterous hour but at the end of it I had thirty engaged pupils. I had also realised that Jed and Sean were unfortunately right. It appeared that negotiation only showed weakness. The enemy would only see this as an opportunity for further exploitation.

'I was saying this to Jed the other day Miss.' Chris, one of the boys, seemed keen to talk to me as the others filed out of class to go to their next one. 'He's been having bother with Larkson's lot. They think he's a soft touch cos he has asthma, and he can't read properly.'

I stiffened suddenly. 'You know Jed?'

The two boys were at opposite spectrums of the school. Chris was in all the higher sets, and Jed with his dyslexia, in most of the lower sets, hence his rubbing shoulders with Baz Larkson and his motley crew.

'He lives down my road. His mum cuts my mum's hair and I heard her talking about how worried she was that Larkson was going to get Jed into trouble. I tried to have a word with him, but he's scared. So, I reckon we have to stand up to them. What do you think Joe?'

This was to one of his friends who was also hovering.

Joe, a tall, stocky boy who was in the rugby team nodded. 'Deffo.'

I opened my mouth to protest that perhaps they had better not, but they merely grinned at me and went to their next lesson. At the end of the day, I bumped into Chris again on my way to my car.

'It's alright Miss,' he said with a cheery grin, 'I've had a word with the lads and some of us are going round to Larkson's to sort him out. Bloody good bloke that Henry the whatever he was. Can't beat a good scrap can you Miss?'

Oh heck. I tried to protest again but he had dashed off in order to catch the school bus.

I knew vaguely where the Larkson's lived. They were only a few blocks away from my house in Park Road and Manor Drive where Chris and Jed both lived. Victoria Avenue was arguably posher in that all the houses there, built in the same era, were detached not semis. Most owners were professionals of some sort, and that included the Larksons.

They were not a family to mess with. For one thing, Timothy Larkson was one of our school governors, which went a long way to explaining why his revolting son Barry got away with so much. He was also a solicitor and Barry could often be heard using the refrain, 'My dad'll sue you for doing that.'

I did not go straight home. Instead, I passed Park Road and went on to Victoria Avenue just in time to see a tangle of boys really going at each other. There were no cars parked in the wide gravelled drive, but I didn't expect there to be. Both parents worked and would not be home yet.

'Boys, stop it now!'

Horribly aware that even at fifteen, most of them topped me by a good few inches, I jumped out of my car and raced towards the rugby like scrum of bodies. As satisfying as it was to see Chris and his friends giving Barry and his cronies a convincing thrashing, I had to stop it.

'Lad's, really now, enough!'

Wading into the middle of it was perhaps not the best idea but what else could I do? I came up close and personal with Barry who glared meanly at me.

'Fuck off Miss why don't you! I'll see my dad gets you sacked, you dried up old bitch. Not surprising your old man left you for a younger tart and got her up the duff. I heard my mum talking about it.'

There was a momentary pause and both sides backed away, a glorious mish mash of bruised lips, reddened jaws and the odd beginnings of a black eye. Barry took his moment to gloat and to take this as an overall victory, despite that fact that his lot seemed to be the more battered and bruised.

'Ha, it's true isn't it! You going to cry now are you, Miss? Go on fuck off the lot of you. Get off my property before my dad sues you all, and as for you Jed,' he focused his bullying eyes on the boy who had stood his ground as best he could with the others. 'You just wait till I get you alone.'

I was shaking and to my horror I was on the verge of tears. What a shambles! How could I have let this happen? All I had succeeded in doing was to give the detestable Barry even more power.

Then I felt my back begin to burn. Not prickle and tingle, really burn. Something fierce lit within me. 'Now you listen to me, you nasty little piece of work, you are going to leave Jed and his family alone from now on otherwise you will have me to deal with.'

He laughed. 'Yeah right, you don't scare me. Nobody scares me.'

She came then.

In an echo of last night, only this time she was not coming for Jed, but for Barry. She must have known the difference though. Last night she had merely pinned Jed to the floor, silently snarling at him, warning him relatively gently. With Barry I could only guess that she sensed the deep animosity in him and was reacting to it. Her body language was such it looked like she would rip his throat out. There was utter silence apart from Barry's whimpers and in the background a hissed remark from Jed.

'I told you she had a bloody great wolf.'

Then Chris suddenly started laughing. 'Not so brave now are you Baz, you've pissed yourself!'

As Luna finally came to my side Barry scrambled to his feet, red faced and looking even angrier.

'You wait till my dad hears about this. He'll have that fucking dog shot.'

'It's not a dog, you turd; it's a wolf.' Jed went up to him and gave him a shove on his shoulder. 'Now go and change your pants before your mummy gets home.'

Even Barry's group sniggered at that and although I knew I had opened up a whole can of trouble for myself, at least I thought he would no longer be a problem for Jed.

'Is this really your wolf?'

Chris and the others were now making a fuss of Luna. And there was I thinking that I would get home tonight and the hallucination would all be over.

I gave in. 'Yes Chris, she really is my wolf. Her name is Luna and I had better get her home for her tea.'

With that, the wolf trotted to my car and stood by the passenger door.

'Awesome Miss,' called out Chris, a thought that was echoed by Joe, Jed and the others.

As I drove the short distance back home, I looked at the wolf sitting regally on the passenger's side.

'Are you going to make a habit of this, Luna?'

If this was going to be the case I would either be making a lot of new friends, or enemies. I wasn't sure which. As I turned down Park Road, I saw Gary's car. I groaned and Luna decided to howl in unison.

Chapter Seven

'Jesus bloody Christ Daisy! Samantha wasn't joking. You have got a bloody great wolf!'

Gary had got out of his car as soon as he saw me pulling up. He was standing with his hands on his hips, looking understandably taken aback. The last conversation I'd had with my husband was the day I had found him in bed with Corinne. He had then hastily packed a bag and we had not got any further in discussing things. Now, here we were on the front path with a huge white wolf standing between us. The expression on Gary's face was so comical I let out a ridiculous girly kind of giggle.

'What? It's a joke? Is that it, Daisy? I tell you Corinne is having a baby and you get yourself a wolf to have a laugh at me or something?'

My mood swiftly changed, and I slammed my car door shut. 'No Gary. I don't think you getting another woman pregnant is anything to laugh at. What do you want? I have had a very tiring day and you were the one to leave if I remember correctly?'

The pain of his betrayal thumped into my gut like a sledgehammer. This was my husband. The man I had fallen in love with twenty years ago. He had not changed much from the young enthusiastic teacher I had met. Tall, of average build with a thick mop of brown hair that now, like mine, was going grey, and intelligent hazel eyes behind tortoiseshell glasses.

Still attractive.

This hurt.

'Well obviously I thought you needed some time to take in what I had to tell you, but this is still my house, Daisy and I have a right to know what the hell you are doing in it? I mean, a fucking wolf for Christ's sake? Where the hell did you get it?'

I shrugged. 'I didn't get her. I mean, she just sort of followed me home last night.'

His expression cleared a little. 'Oh. You mean it's a stray. Well, obviously we need to ring the RSCPA straight away. I am surprised you haven't done that already.'

I opened and shut my mouth like a goldfish as the thought filtered through my befuddled brain. Why had I not done that already? Surely that would have been the right thing to do. I was so used to automatically following Gary's suggestions that I agreed.

'I suppose you are right.' I looked at the wolf by my side. 'I can't possibly keep a wolf. It's ridiculous.'

But just like last night, Luna then leapt over the garden gate and went to sit at the front door.

Oh hell!

I then remembered Sean who had temporarily flown out of my head. I was so full of cotton wool between my ears it was ludicrous. Right on cue, my new lodger and presumably the other reason for Gary calling round, opened the door.

'Ah there you are, Daisy. I've got a lovely meat and potato pie in the oven with some red cabbage. One of Ma's best recipes.'

He stepped back to let Luna lope past him, clearly not concerned that she had escaped from the house.

'And you must be Gary. I am sure Daisy won't mind if you stay for tea. Now if you will excuse me, I will go and get some more clothes on. I got grubby scrubbing out the utility room Daisy, so I was just in the shower when I heard your car drawing up.'

'Daisy what the fuck is going on?' Gary's voice hissed behind me as we both trekked up the garden path. 'Samantha said you had an old homeless tramp staying last night, now I turn up and you have some Steve McQueen look alike baking a fucking meat and potato pie in my kitchen! Is this a wind up?'

'He is the homeless old tramp,' I whispered back as quietly as I could, hoping Sean wouldn't hear.

Judging from the wicked grin on his face as he held out his hand to shake Gary's, I think he did.

'Pleased to meet you, Gary. I'm Sean Murphy. Your lovely wife has the heart of an angel, so she does. Didn't she bring me in out of the cold yesterday, hail stones and all, to offer me a bed in the warmth and the dry here? I mean how many women do you know would do that?'

Gary was in essence a gentleman, and he automatically took the hand that Sean was offering. He seemed unable to speak though, just silently stared at the man who was looking so at ease in his hallway.

I couldn't really blame him.

Sean's appearance this morning when he had brought me breakfast had surprised me. Standing in front of me wearing just a pair of Gerald's trousers, surprise was not the thought that instantly came into my mind as I looked at him.

Let me clarify.

The Sean I knew from sitting by the pay machine in the car park had been a bedraggled wreck of a man. Filthy hair and beard, which I thought to be brown, overshadowed a lined and craggy face with a mouth full of shockingly bad teeth. The only bright spark about him had been his amazing blue eyes which Gary quite rightly said, made you think of Steve McQueen from those old films.

Washed and cut, presumably with my kitchen scissors, his hair was a blond so light it was silver in places. With no beard you could see he had a sharp jawline and cheekbones that could have blunted a chisel. There were deep lines on his face, but the intensity of his blue eyes was such that it was hard to put an age on him. When he grinned, he displayed a gleaming white set of teeth. How was that possible?

Then again how was it possible that I had a wolf in my kitchen right now?

Best not ask too many questions, Daisy.

You might not like the answers.

Suffice it to say, my shabby homeless old man was anything but and his lean torso was sculpted in a way that every muscle was defined with not an inch of fat on him. He winked at me and then turned to go upstairs. I watched him move lightly in his bare feet. His actions were more like those of a professional dancer than a man in his late fifties or sixties, which is what I had originally thought.

'Seriously Daisy?' Gary took my arm and almost pulled me into the kitchen shutting the door behind us. 'Christ Daisy! Call the RSPCA now, I had nearly forgotten about that bloody thing.'

'I don't think she likes you grabbing at me,' I said quietly as Luna had moved in a flash to nudge Gary's hand from my arm.

Now looking thoroughly unsettled, and who could blame him, Gary moved edgily around the wolf to pull out one of the kitchen chairs.

'Sit down Daisy, we need to talk before he comes back down.'

'What about?' I asked innocently as I went to switch the kettle on. 'Tea or coffee?'

'Neither,' he snapped back at me. 'Exactly how long is he going to be staying here? And who the fuck is he anyway? He could be a bloody murderer for all you know. Or a con artist. He's probably already done an inventory of the entire house. Wouldn't surprise me if you came home tomorrow to find it completely emptied!'

He went white at this thought and for a second, just a second, I could share his horror as I envisaged such a scenario. Then I thought about Sean. I thought about what had happened in the last thirty-six hours. Whilst it had all been decidedly strange there was no way I felt that Sean meant to do me harm.

I said so to Gary who looked at me rather oddly.

'Are you, you know?'

'What?'

I sat down opposite him hugging my cup of tea in my hands to take the chill off them.

Gary's face took on an interesting expression. 'Are you and him having sex?'

I choked on the mouthful of tea at the same time that Sean, now wearing one of Gerald's bright golfing jumpers, walked into the room. He moved so quietly neither of us had heard him come down the stairs which considering they creaked in this old house was saying something.

'Shall I be dishing up the pie now, Daisy?' He asked casually.

The way he moved around the kitchen he looked as though he had lived here for years. A fact that was not lost on Gary.

'Make yourself at home why don't you?' He muttered under his breath as Sean began to lift plates out of the cupboards as well as cutlery from the drawer.

I was still clearing my throat and trying to calm my blushes. What was Gary thinking asking that ridiculous question? As usually is the case when you least want to think about something, there it is, right slap bang in the forefront of your mind.

Sex with Sean.

Good God, Daisy seriously?

Sex with the person you had brought home out of charity for shelter yesterday. Utterly bloody ridiculous.

Sex with the silver blond, twinkling blue-eyed man, with the ruggedly lined face and balletic way of moving?

I realised they were both waiting for me to speak. 'Sorry, what was that?'

'How hungry are you, Daisy?' Sean was holding a knife over the pie, a definite look of mischief in his eyes. He had heard Gary's comment. No doubt about it.

'Very,' I answered and at the crinkling of the lines around his eyes I blushed even hotter. 'The pie looks lovely, Sean. Doesn't it, Gary?'

'Never mind the fucking pie!' My husband, soon to be ex, was looking at Sean as though he would like to throttle him. 'What exactly are you doing here? My wife is in a vulnerable state right now. I am really not sure she is capable of making any sensible decisions, let alone inviting a total stranger to take up residence in my late father's room!'

'You'll not be wanting the pie then?' Sean nodded his head amicably. 'No bother. I'm sure Luna will love it. There you go my beauty.'

He set a plate down on the floor for the wolf who seemed quite happy with what was on the menu before settling himself down next to Gary with his own meal.

I began to eat, my eyes darting between the two men. Sean was enjoying his first mouthful, nodding to himself as though applauding his efforts and Gary was looking as though he had stepped into some kind of twilight zone. Maybe he had? I considered the huge wolf who was now resting her heavy head on my lap and gazing at my plate with soulful eyes.

Gary managed to spit out another word. 'Well?'

'Well what?' Sean replied. 'Is Daisy vulnerable?'

He laid down his knife and fork and looked at me. There was such a depth of knowing in his eyes I trembled inside. Vulnerable enough to try and kill herself? I knew what he was thinking. At least I thought I did.

'Yes. I would say that right now Daisy is very vulnerable.' Then his expression changed with lightning speed to one of pure mischief. 'But you don't have to worry Gary. I am here to look after her so you can stop fretting. After all. You have another woman and a little one on the way.'

'My private life is none of your damn business!' Gary hissed, shooting me a furious look 'But my house and who lives in it, is! My father is barely cold in his grave. In fact, my father would be turning in his grave right now if he knew what was going on.'

Sean continued to eat his pie and cabbage as he considered this. 'I think you may be wrong there.'

I spoke for the first time. 'I agree. Your dad was the kindest man I knew. He would be happy with my decision.'

As I said this, I felt a warm glow inside me, and any last remaining doubts disappeared. It was as though Gerald was right there with us. For a second, I swear I felt a gentle touch on my shoulder, but it was so fleeting it was hard to be sure. I blinked as right in the corner of my eye I got a brilliant flash of white light. I turned my head quickly but there was nothing there.

Sean gave me a gentle smile. 'Have you had enough to eat, Daisy?'

'Thank you, yes Sean. The pie was lovely.'

Gary shook his head with an expression of disbelief on his face. 'You've gone completely mad, Daisy. That can be the only explanation. I'll ring our doctor and see if I can get an emergency call out appointment.'

'Now why would you want to do that?' Sean asked as he filled the large Belfast sink with hot soapy water having declared the dishwasher to be a thing of the devil. 'Daisy is as sane as the rest of us.'

'I disagree,' Gary said mulishly and reached into his pocket for his phone. 'I am calling the doctor now. Daisy, you need help.'

'And haven't I just said that I am now here to help?' Sean said lightly as he began to wash up.

'And haven't I told you to mind your own fucking business! Oh no, not you, sorry I didn't mean you,' Gary spluttered hastily as someone answered his call. 'I need a doctor to come out and see my wife immediately. She's gone mad. No, no, I mean she is clearly mentally very unstable. What? No. She hasn't tried to kill herself.'

I lowered my eyes at that point not wanting to meet either his gaze or that of Sean's.

'Can I bring her into the surgery now? Well not really. I need someone to come out here, you see she's got this homeless person in our house and frankly, I don't trust him an inch. I can hardly leave the house with him here.'

Gary had obviously run out of good manners at this point, but Sean didn't seem to mind that he was being talked about in such a way.

'No. It isn't a kind thing to do with Christmas coming up! It's fucking irresponsible, sorry, sorry, I didn't mean to swear. And she's got a bloody wolf as well. Yes, I did say a wolf. Hello, hello, are you still there?' He held the phone away and looked at it. 'I don't believe it, she cut me off!'

'It's probably just the weather,' said Sean. 'Look, it's coming on to rain now cats and dogs, so it is.'

'We never have a problem with reception here,' snapped Gary and began redialling only this time the engaged tone was clear to hear. He swore and tossed the phone onto the table. Then immediately he snatched it back up again. 'I'm ringing your father. He can come round and talk some sense into you.'

However, before he had chance to do that the front doorbell rang.

Sean moved as though to go and answer it, but Gary blocked him.

'I don't think so mate. Not your house, remember.'

'Stop it,' I hissed at Sean the moment Gary stepped out of the room. 'You're winding him up!'

'No. He's doing a grand job of that all by himself.'

I considered this but I did have to give Gary some credit. Most men would find it difficult to swallow that their wife had suddenly installed an old homeless man into their house. I had to refine this. Most men would find it difficult to swallow that their wife had suddenly installed an extremely charismatic and attractive man into their house.

Not to mention a huge and hairy wolf.

The other side of me was arguing the case that he had slipped between the sheets with a woman nearly twenty years his junior, so tit for tat. Not of course that I was even remotely considering slipping between the sheets with Sean because that would be so wrong! I was saved from having to pursue this line of thought by Gary returning into the kitchen with a female police officer.

Sean was quicker off the mark than I.

'PC. Wendy Holden. Grand it is to see you again. Would you be liking a cup of tea now?'

It was easy to recognise the police officer from yesterday, but Wendy Holden understandably was doing a double-take as she compared Sean's appearance to the tramp she had met at the station.

'Mr Murphy?'

'As I live and breathe. Do you take milk and sugar?'

'I beg your pardon? Oh, erm, well really I shouldn't, I'm on duty.'

'Isn't all work washed down better with a cup of tea? Oh, you've met Luna I see, she seems to like you. Now, what brings you to our door at this time of an evening, Wendy?'

'Our door?' Gary snorted incredulously. 'Unbelievable. Daisy, once we have sorted out whatever it is this police officer needs, oh in fact yes that would work. Officer, Sean here really does need some other form of alternative accommodation. My wife is clearly not in her right mind, and I am sure there are hostels for the likes of him.'

Wendy though was temporarily not listening. She was being feted by Luna who had moved from her place by the range to go and rub herself against the police officer in a pathetically adoring manner.

'Aren't you just beautiful,' cooed Wendy, crouching down to stroke the wolf who to my amazement rolled over onto her back and exposed a soft furry belly for the police officer's touch. 'What a softy.'

'Yes, isn't she,' said Sean sliding a mug of tea across the table to Wendy with a couple of biscuits for good measure on a side plate.

'Yes, well wolf or not, that's another thing you can help me with officer. We need the RSPCA. Oh, is that why you are here?' Gary looked a little brighter. 'Has someone reported the beast missing?'

Wendy shook her head. 'No, actually sir but the dog is the reason I am here.'

'It's not a dog it's a wolf!' Exclaimed Gary.

She opened her notebook. 'Hm,' she muttered. 'It does say wolf here.'

'What exactly is the problem, Wendy?' Sean, lolling against the counter was by far the most at ease in the room. You could be forgiven for thinking it was his house.

'There has been a complaint that your wolf attacked a young boy, Barry Larkson of 7 Victoria Avenue.'

'Jesus! Can we not get the RSPCA now? I mean, surely it needs putting down or something.'

'Gary!' I glared at my husband across the table.

'If it's a dangerous animal that's what you do isn't it?'

We all turned to look at Luna who had rolled back onto her belly and was regarding us all with her fathomless silver eyes. She had curled up into a ball and made herself look so much smaller. She heaved a big sigh and then with one paw, covered her eyes as though she couldn't bear to look at us.

'See, you've upset her!' I hissed at Gary.

'Which proves how mad you are!' He hissed back.

Sean seemed happy to ignore the marital hissing ping pong match and addressed Wendy. 'I think you mean the bit of bother that happened earlier.' He gave a shrug of his shoulders as though it was nothing to worry about. 'It was a group of lads from Daisy's school, Wendy. Weren't they all having a good blow out if you know what I mean. Lad's stuff. Pack order so to speak,' he added with a wicked grin. 'Our Daisy here only got herself in the middle of it, so she did, what with being their teacher and all. Not surprising the little dog went to help his mistress. I had opened the door to let her in the garden and she shot off like a rocket.'

'Little dog? It's a fucking wolf!' Gary tutted and shook his head again whilst Wendy chewed on the end of her pencil and considered her notes.

'That's not quite what it says here,' she said, and then got distracted again as Luna shuffled up to her, resting her head on her lap, her ears soft and flat and not a trace of a wild animal about her. She was transforming herself into a teddy bear whilst we watched.

'I am sure Mr. Larkson wouldn't make up something like that,' said Gary stuffily. 'He's a respected solicitor and does a lot for charity. He's on the board of governors at Daisy's school.'

'He's a fucking crook,' said Sean as though he was discussing the weather. 'More tea, Wendy, you've drunk that as though you've been in the desert all day long.'

'Feels like it, Mr Murphy and yes thanks.' She pushed her mug across the table towards him. 'What do you mean, he's a crook?'

'Oh, you know, this and that. And call me Sean, please.'

Wendy smiled at him. 'This and that being what exactly, Sean?'

'Well let me see now,' Sean paused as he refilled her mug, and I could see Gary fuming with impatience. 'There's the tax dodging of course, though mostly it's the money laundering. Got friends with some very colourful business interests has Mr. Larkson. And there's the brothels, although to be fair to Mr. Larkson, that might be purely a personal thing if you know what I mean.'

Wendy was now in alert police officer mode and although one hand was still stroking Luna's head, she was giving Sean her full attention.

'How exactly do you know all this?'

'He doesn't!' Gary exploded, clearly at the end of his tether. 'He's making it all up so you will lose interest in having that wild animal put down.'

Was he? From what little I knew of Sean, I wouldn't put it past him. But he just shrugged and answered Wendy's question.

'You see and hear a lot when you are invisible. I can't give you any details. All I would say though Wendy, is that if you fancy earning yourself a promotion, I would do a little digging.'

'Indeed. Well,' she said snapping her notebook shut. 'I shall bear that in mind. As for this evening's fracas at the Larkson's, there is absolutely nothing about this animal that suggests to me that she should be destroyed. I've got a dog myself, well my parents have, and she is always protective of me. It's their job after all. And the boy has no signs of dog injuries at all. It looks as though he was using that story as a decoy to get himself out of trouble with his father for fighting.'

'So, I shall bid you all good evening. Thank you, Sean for the tea, and Daisy it is good to see you looking a little better than yesterday.' She nodded at me and winked. 'And what a transformation hey, didn't see that coming did we?'

It was clear she meant the peeling back of layers of dirt and grime to find a diamond beneath in my new house guest.

'What do you mean, better than yesterday? What happened yesterday?' Spluttered Gary standing up once more. 'And what about the RSPCA? Not to mention him!' He pointed first at Luna and then at Sean.

Wendy regarded my husband calmly. 'Are you quite alright sir? You look as though you might be having problems with your blood pressure. You need to watch that at your age. From what I can see sir, your wife has made a jolly good decision and it is utterly refreshing to see someone prepared to give another human being a second chance at life.'

She turned back to me, leaving Gary looking as though he did indeed have high blood pressure.

'I will tell my colleagues at the station that you are giving Mr Murphy, Sean, the use of your spare room for a while. It will really cheer them up. We get so much negative stuff to deal with, especially at this time of year. It will give them all a real touch of Christmas spirit.' She replaced her hat and offered a final comment to Gary. 'Seriously sir, I would give the doctors a call. You don't look too good.'

I led her back through to the hallway, Luna trotting quietly beside her to give her one final gentle sniff and then shutting the front door went back into the kitchen before Sean and Gary killed each other.

Chapter Eight

'Which room do you want to tackle first?'

'Neither.' I looked at Sean as I dithered on the landing between the four bedrooms. In my hands was a roll of black bin liners that I was reluctant to fill.

'We don't have to do this yet you know, Daisy. You've got a lot on your mind at the moment.'

'You're telling me,' I grunted in a half-heartedly mocking way. 'Two weeks ago, I was caring for Gerald and consoling myself with the thought that at least I had a happy marriage and a good job, with the prospects of an even better one lined up for me with that interview. And now…'

Sean smiled at me, a soft look in his cobalt blue eyes.

'And now you have me and Luna, and the chance to start a whole new life. It was time you left teaching anyway, Daisy. There is far more in store for you than can been found in a dingy old school.'

The most bizarre week of my life had ended with me being suspended thanks to Mr Larkson's input as governor. The head teacher had been reluctant to do so, but Mr Larkson's money was funding the new gym. English teachers were easy to replace; wealthy sponsors were not.

Thursday and Friday evening, I had been visited by Gary, both my parents and my sister Rose. My husband was clearly regretting his swift decision to move out giving me the chance to move Sean in. Yet, at the same time, he was obviously under pressure from Corinne demanding that he stayed with her.

We had ended up exchanging more bitter words in the kitchen. I had finished by screeching at him to go back to his high maintenance husband stealing bitch, fuelled by self-righteous anger. To my astonishment Gary had been quiet in his reply.

'She's not high maintenance. And she's not a bitch. And do you know what, Daisy, she didn't have to steal me. You gave me away.'

My stunned retort had been a splutter, a gasp of incredulous disbelief. The cheek of it! I was mustering a blistering retort when he continued with another stab to my heart.

'You need to take a long hard look in the mirror, Daisy. And I am not talking about your looks either.' He then left saying that he had asked Dad round to come and talk to me.

Staggered at how he had the audacity to turn things around and blame me for the end of our marriage, I had looked at Sean who had been sitting quietly in the corner. I had asked him to stay feeling the need to have a witness to whatever Gary would say. The look he gave me was long and thoughtful, and left me feeling a little uncomfortable.

When I raised the subject to Dad who turned up later, I got no support from him. I suppose this was stupid of me to expect it in the first place. Hadn't he done the same as Gary in marrying a woman much younger than him? He just gave me a sad look and tentatively mentioned the menopause. Even more cautiously, he suggested that I was more like Marigold than I perhaps realised. I quickly showed him the door.

Like my mother indeed!

I was the total opposite of Marigold.

She arrived in due course with my sister Rose. They both made a shocking play for Sean who batted away their flirtations with an easy grace and good humour. Then they stirred things up further by insinuating that perhaps I had been 'grooming' Sean to take Gary's place all along.

They were also shown the door.

So much for family support in my time of need.

Thank goodness for Sean and Luna.

The animal seemed to have a telepathic way of reading my thoughts and emotions. Luna was at my side with a silent warning curl of her upper lip should anyone raise their voice at me. Suggestions that Gary was right, and I could not possibly keep her were immediately dropped.

I didn't care if they all thought I was having some kind of break down. I was. Sean knew this and wanted to help make some sense out of my shattered life and move on. Hence the notion that clearing out Irene and Gerald's rooms would be a good thing to do. Only now, the thought of emptying the two bedrooms of their personal belongings was proving an impossible task to face.

As I dithered, I felt Luna's cold nose nudge into my side. Placing my hand on the warmth of her neck I was instantly calmed. I still was not ready to face whatever magic had been wrought, or even how insane I might be, all I knew was that the wolf at my side gave me strength when my own courage was lacking.

'Irene's' I said decisively, my hand still on Luna. 'We moved Gerald into his room in the last two years of Irene's illness,' I explained to Sean. 'She was so unsettled at night and when she forgot who he was, she would wake up screaming if he was in bed beside her. It broke Gerald's heart not to share a bed with her but as he said at least they were under the same roof.'

'They were Daisy, and it was a grand job you did keeping them united to the very end. Irene's it is then.' He opened the door which had been shut these last six months and then paused. 'Unless of course you would rather be alone to do this?'

I shook my head vigorously. 'Oh no Sean, please, I would value your company.' We made a start on one of the most painful jobs a person is faced with in life. 'It could have been so much worse,' I kept saying to Sean each time I felt the tears washing down my face. 'She was seventy-two after all, some people die so much younger.'

'They do Daisy. But death is death and grief is grief. There is no age or time limit on it.'

He was gentle, respectful and compassionate with a quiet stillness about him as we worked that made me think he could have been a priest. Distracted by this thought, I pictured him in clerical clothes, and it would be easy to imagine him in a pulpit commanding a flock with his warmth and charisma. Thinking how Marigold and Rose had all but thrown themselves at him, I could also imagine how women in a congregation would be utter putty in his hands.

'What?' he cocked his head at me as I stopped in my task of folding up some sweaters.

I blushed. 'Nothing.' And then because it was impossible to keep anything from him, I added, 'I was just wondering what you used to do, Sean?'

He was taking Irene's dresses off the hangers in her wardrobe and folding them with so much more care than the average man would.

'What do you think I used to do?' There was a gentle teasing in his eyes that prompted me to blurt out exactly what I had been thinking. 'Ah, a priest now? Hm. Well that would have made my dear old Ma happy indeed.'

'You have never been connected to the Church at all?' Somehow this thought would not leave me.

'Well now, are we not all connected to the Church in one way or another if you believe in God?'

He was being deliberately vague, and I let it drop. After the first hour or so we got into a steady pattern of work, deciding which clothes and belongings were suitable for charity shops and which were frankly only fit for the bin. The more methodical we became the easier the job, and some of the knots in my stomach and the tightness in my chest eased a little. Even so it took the whole of the morning and we had filled twenty bags of clothes, shoes, books and ornaments.

'I think we've done really well there,' I said with satisfaction looking at the pile of bags.

Then the sight of the empty wardrobes hit me like a hammer, and I was instantly wishy washy all over again.

'Fresh air I think,' said Sean. 'Look, it's a grand day now. Why don't we go and take Luna for a walk and clear the lungs? We can start on Gerald's room this afternoon.'

'Brilliant idea.' I leapt at the chance to abandon this sad task. 'I feel guilty, as it is that you have been walking Luna yourself all this time. Are you absolutely sure she doesn't need a lead or micro chipping at all?'

'I'd like to see the vet who could manage to do that,' he said with a grin as we both made our way downstairs. 'As to a lead, I think you will find she will just follow you like a little lamb.'

I paused as I reached for my coat which was lying on the settle in the hallway. 'Sean. She's a wolf. She's a wolf just like the…'

'I know I know. Just like the tattoo on your back of all the mad crazy coincidences.' He stopped me by gently placing a finger on my lips. 'Stop questioning things, Daisy. Just trust and believe.'

I couldn't move.

He had never touched me before.

Or at least not like this and I was shocked by the sensations rippling through me, not to mention the effect of having his blue eyes so close to mine. It was enough to banish any thoughts of how on earth I had ended up with a wolf in my life.

'You see,' he said with a flashing smile. 'Life can be so much simpler, Daisy if you just accept things for what they are. Now then, fresh air and exercise. Always good for the soul.'

I agreed with him on the first count. Exercise had never been high on my list of priorities but ten minutes later when we reached the park, I found myself being urged to run with Luna.

'Go on, she wants you to run with her,' said Sean as though he was an authority on wolves.

He probably was for all I knew.

'I can't run,' I protested as I looked at the huge animal that was alternating between tugging at my coat with her teeth and nudging me up the bottom with her nose. 'Oh, surely not?'

She threw her head back and howled and to my amazement something unfurled from deep inside me and rose all the way up to my throat. It was, I realised, laughter, and with it, an emotion I had thought was long forgotten.

Joy.

'Come on then, Luna.'

In the winter sunshine I ran and played, and tumbled and rolled on the leaf covered grass as though I was a child. I got muddy. I got grass stained. I got red faced and breathless, sweating under the padding of my thick coat. I moved my body more in half an hour than I had done in a month.

'Sean that was so good!' I gasped when I could run no more. Luna still looked as though she had miles left in her, but I was done for. 'I must have looked a complete idiot,' I suddenly realised as I saw the state of my clothes.

'No Daisy,' he said reaching forwards to gently take a twig from the tangle of my hair. 'You could never look an idiot. A beautiful wood nymph, yes maybe that, but never an idiot.'

I was glad my cheeks were already red from exertion as my blushes were hidden. It must be the unexpected amount of oxygen that had flooded into my lungs that was making me feel light-headed.

'Mummy look, a wolf!'

A child's shriek brought me back down to earth. I focused my dreamy gaze on a group of women with a clutch of preschool age children and babies in prams. Not surprisingly they were regarding the very muddy Luna with more than a little horror on their faces.

'Shouldn't that... dog be on a lead?'

The oldest looking lady in the group frowned at me.

'Oh, don't worry,' I called back blithely. 'She's quite tame.'

'Even so,' said the lady, 'it says quite clearly that dogs should be on a lead in this area. We are near the duck pond you know.'

I had not realised we had strayed close to the children's play area and the duck pond.

'She is very well behaved,' I insisted, just as Luna decided to abandon all pretence of domesticity and hurtle towards the pond at break-neck speed.

There then followed ten minutes of quacking, flapping, and shrieking.

The ducks made almost as much noise as the women and children.

Sean was holding his sides as he rocked in silent laughter whilst I attempted to show that I had some measure of control over a now wet, and very wild looking animal. Luna had decided that jumping in and out of the duck pond, shaking herself over everyone and snapping at the feathers of the ducks was far too much fun to consider stopping. It was only when the suggestion was made that the police should be called that things changed.

Sean stopped laughing and went to talk to some of the children.

'Ah look now, have you ever seen anything funnier than a big silly dog playing tig with the ducks. And look she wants to play tig with you now. Shall you let her?'

I watched in amazement as Luna changed before my eyes from a mad duck hungry beast to a playful bundle of fur. She was worthy of an Oscar in how she could switch roles in the blink of an eye. At the same time Sean doled out his Irish charm to the ladies and soon they were laughing coyly with him.

'Unbelievable,' I muttered under my breath, then louder, 'when you have quite finished playing Luna, perhaps we can get going?'

I didn't know whether to be surprised or not when the wolf stopped mid chase and trotted straight back to me as meekly as the lamb Sean had called her earlier. There was nothing meek about the glint in her eyes though. They positively sparkled with something that I could only call magic. But just as I did not want to question the effect Sean was having on me, neither was I ready to think about what exactly Luna was.

'I think we had better be going,' I repeated as Sean said a cheery goodbye to the women.

'What a lovely well-behaved dog,' I heard one of them saying and I laughed in disbelief.

'Now that was a grand little interlude.'

Sean offered to hose down Luna when we got back to the house. I wondered if she would object but she stood there happily enough.

'It was.' I was glowing and not just from the fresh air. 'Soup and sandwiches alright for lunch?'

'Perfect.'

After we had eaten, we began the task of Gerald's room. I had asked Gary if he had wanted to do this, after all Gerald was his father. There was no doubt in my mind that my husband had loved Gerald, but theirs had been a rather reserved relationship. Maybe that was just how it was with fathers and sons. Yet even so, I did expect him to want to go through Gerald's belongings.

It only ended up in another row over Sean's presence and Gary told me that under no circumstances was I to give anything personal of Gerald's to him. He didn't mind the clothes, but I was to box up every item of his father's personal items to give to him.

'You can have his clothes Sean, but really they don't fit you all that well,' I said as we began to take things out of the wardrobe. Gerald had been a little bit shorter than Sean and a lot bulkier, until the cancer had stripped the flesh from his bones.

'They suit me grand, so they do,' said Sean with a smile as he held up one sweater after another.

'Yes, but really Sean we ought to go shopping for some clothes of your own.'

'I am fine as I am, if you don't mind seeing me in Gerald's things that is.'

I shook my head.

'You look so different in them anyway Sean. But we ought to think about how we can help you get back on your feet properly. Not that I don't like having you here with me,' I said hastily, 'but I am not sure what Gary's plans are for the house, what with the divorce and everything.'

'Don't you worry about that, Daisy my girl. One step at a time and it will all come clear, you'll see. For now, let's just focus on this and take the time to remember Gerald.'

'Yes. You're right, Sean,' I said as the impact of what I was doing hit me once more. I let Sean make a start with the clothes, and I began to go through the bedside drawers and dressing table.

There were the usual items, toiletries, brush, comb, a dish for loose change. Then a few photographs in silver frames of Gerald's own parents and a brother who had been killed in the war. There was a picture of him and Irene on their wedding day and placing it carefully into a carboard box for Gary brought tears to my eyes.

'He loved her just as much on the day she died as on the day he married her.'

I sank to my knees, weeping silently, my shoulders shaking with the effort of trying to contain it. Gentle arms came around me, and the familiar scent of Gerald's after shave, only of course it was Sean. He knelt down on the floor with me and eased me into a caring hold.

'Let it out, Daisy, you need to.'

It took a while. The control I had exerted for too long was reluctant to break. Gradually though between hiccupping sobs, I released some of my emotions.

'She died just before their fiftieth wedding anniversary,' I sniffled. 'They never got to celebrate it and even though she had kept forgetting who we all were by then, those last few days it was as though she had come back to us, to Gerald. She knew what date it was, she could remember their wedding and knew it was nearly their golden anniversary. But she died and they couldn't even have that moment to cherish.' The unfairness of it had me pummelling at Sean's chest but he just held me closer and rocked me liked a child.

'He was so brave at her funeral,' I cried remembering the dignity which Gerald had displayed, 'and so brave afterwards with his own illness. He never complained once Sean and he must have been in so much pain. He never grumbled, was always kind. I miss him. I miss him so much. I never thought I would. Isn't that stupid.'

I was angry with myself, angry with my loss.

'Why do we not realise until it's too late? Why don't we tell them more that we love them, that they're going to leave a bloody big hole in our lives that no one will ever fill! And it hurts Sean; it really, fucking hurts!'

He held me so close then and softly whispered Gaelic words of comfort as I grieved not just for Gerald but for Irene and all the suffering that they had borne together because of her illness. When some of that pain had passed, I was then tipped into another pit of painful emotions.

'I used to think Gary and I were going to be like them. Stay together forever. I meant to you know. When I said my vows in the church, I really meant them. But he doesn't love me anymore, he loves Corinne and they're going to have a baby and I am never going to be a mother.'

The deepest, cruellest grief of all ripped through me. There were no words to express my pain.

Yet Sean found them. Whatever he was whispering in his Gaelic, like the softest rain drops falling upon granite, eventually found a way to soften the pain. He whispered to me. He held me close and comforted me. Luna had joined us and curled her huge furry body as close to me as she possibly could.

I was sheltered, protected.

Loved beyond measure.

When the pain finally eased, this was the feeling that was foremost in my mind.

Loved beyond measure.

Dazed, and a little confused, I raised my face to Sean's. He was so close I could see every line in his face that told me he was older than me, but the light in his blue eyes was so dazzling he seemed so much younger. The love I saw there was deeper than any emotion I had ever seen in Gary's eyes.

I kissed him.

Chapter Nine

I did not just plant a little peck on his cheek.

I reached my hands up behind his neck so I could scoop his mouth down to mine. That first touch was electric and sent a jolt through every muscle in my body. Warm firm lips obeyed my command to open. A tongue met and parried with mine. I wriggled around until I was nestled on his lap and deepened the kiss. An overwhelming hunger and desire overtook the place of grief and pain.

I felt alive.

More than alive.

Sensations overwhelmed me as I took in the taste of him, my fingers tangling in his thick hair, hot wet desire flooding into me. A dam bursting the banks as I let go of repressed emotions. The torrent that was surging through me was unstoppable and I kissed Sean as though my life depended on it.

Maybe it did.

Sensuously, tenderly, he gave what I was asking of him. Light hands cradled my hips, the softest pressure moulding me to him so I could feel how much his body was responding. I groaned against his mouth, moving so in my kneeling position I was straddling him more. I hadn't felt this turned on since… My mind stopped at that point because it was so long ago and that thought included Gary and he was the last person I wanted in my head right now.

Here and now was all that mattered.

The two of us on the floor in Gerald's bedroom.

Good God almighty what was I doing?

I gasped and broke away. 'Sean.'

I stumbled backwards and clambered inelegantly to my feet finding that my legs were like jelly as I did so. He rose in one fluid movement that made me look like a baby elephant beside him and gently placed his hands on my shoulder.

'Daisy,' his voice was as gentle as his touch. 'You are a lovely, beautiful woman. And that was a lovely beautiful kiss. I thank you for the gift of it.'

'But,' I felt as gauche as a teenager on their first date. 'Sean I shouldn't have. I mean...'

I gestured with my other hand to Gerald's belongings in piles around us. How on Earth could I have started snogging the face off my newly acquired lodger, let alone taking things further on the floor of my recently departed and beloved father-in-law's bedroom? My cheeks already flushed with passion burnt even hotter. Shamefully, I could imagine Gerald watching me and that felt awful.

'Daisy, it was a kiss. It was a need. It was emotions running wild within you. You are human, Daisy, not a machine.'

'Yes but... Gerald.'

'Don't you think Gerald ever felt like that in his life Daisy? From what I know of him he was a man of honest emotions. So are you. Well a woman that is. But your emotions are locked away in here,' he tapped a finger lightly on my chest, 'and you've put a mighty fine padlock on them, so you have.'

I thought of Gary's betrayal and how the whole of my life seemed to be a complete waste. Then I thought that it was the notion of having sex with someone in Gerald's bedroom that had stopped me, not thoughts of my husband. I grew even more confused, and it must have shown on my face.

'It was just a kiss, Daisy,' Sean reiterated.

'You're right,' I said, determined to get a grip. I brushed my hair back from my face and nodded at him. 'I am an emotional wreck. I wouldn't otherwise... I mean I wouldn't like you to think I make a habit of behaving like that.'

His grin was pure seductive mischief. 'You mean like a woman with fiery passion in her veins?'

I had a moment to acknowledge the sharp stab of lust that hit me in the belly. Then as quick as a flash he was back to the job in hand.

'Now, shall we carry on up here or perhaps take a break?'

Disturbed by the way I was feeling I nodded decisively. 'Let's carry on.'

'Alright. But how about I go and make us a cup of tea and fetch some biscuits whilst we do it?'

As he went downstairs, I nipped into the bathroom to use the toilet. I went to the sink to wash my hands and got a shock when I saw my reflection in the mirror. I had grown used to seeing a tired middle-aged woman with greying brown hair and sad grey eyes, skin the dull pasty colour of dough.

Kissing Sean had taken years off me.

'Crikey!'

I blinked and opened my eyes to check that I was not imagining what I was seeing. Sparkling eyes, glowing cheeks and lips that looked soft and pouty, curling upwards into a slight smile, rather than drooping down in a sad arc. I wiped the mirror with my sleeve.

She was still there.

The woman with a smile in her eyes.

'You look like someone I used to know,' I said to my reflection 'You look like the girl I used to be. Minus the grey hairs of course.'

And then I snorted.

'Daisy get a grip woman. You are a forty-six-year-old woman whose marriage has screeched to a halt and you've just let yourself get totally carried away snogging your lodger for Christ's sake!'

I splashed cold water onto my heated cheeks. It was one thing to insanely accept a magical wolf into my life, and quite another to be so bloody stupid as the last ten minutes had just proved.

Insanity I could excuse, stupidity no.

Thankfully, Sean was casual about the whole thing, as though it had never happened. He came whistling back into Gerald's bedroom five minutes later with a tray of tea and biscuits. In true Sean fashion, he began a conversation about my neighbour Violet Woodrush.

'She's invited me round to make up a foursome in bridge,' he said blithely as we began bagging up the clothes.

'You play bridge?' I said and then flushed as I realised how patronising I sounded.

'I do.' He looked smug as though he enjoyed confounding me with his list of never-ending talents.

'I am sure she will be glad of your company,' I commented. 'Gerald used to play. I never quite got the hang of it. Now, I think we have finally finished. How many bags have we got in total?'

'Around thirty I reckon, with all of Irene's things.'

I looked at the pile of black bin liners we had filled. The charity shop was going to benefit hugely. Yet there still pervaded in me a sense of loss. I was bundling up and giving away two people's lives.

'You will always have your memories,' Sean said softly as though he was reading my mind. He was very good at that. 'These are just clothes and what would Irene and Gerald be saying to you now?'

'*Crack on girl and get rid*, that's what Gerald would say.'

'Well then. We have an hour before the shop closes. If we do crack on, I reckon we can get it done.'

I raised my eyebrows. It was no small task but then I was to find that with Sean the most difficult of things seemed ridiculously easy. In no time at all he had hauled half a dozen bags down the stairs, opened my car, put down the back seats and filled it up. Leaving Luna in the kitchen, I set off with Sean. I thought we were pushing our luck to get the various loads to the charity shop and back before it closed. It was Saturday tea-time and the roads were busy with Christmas shoppers.

I had not allowed for the Sean factor.

That is to say that within minutes of meeting him, the lady in charge of the shop had agreed to stay open for longer. She then went the extra mile and in between us ferrying back and forth with bin liners, she rooted out a selection of clothes that she thought would suit Sean.

'Such a lovely story,' she said more than once with a smile as she watched Sean dart in and out of the changing room to try on the outfits.

'Indeed it is, Cynthia,' he charmed her in his best Irish accent as he exchanged the clothes of Gerald's he was wearing for a well cut pair of jeans and a cream cricket sweater with a bold red shirt underneath. 'What do you think?'

Cynthia, a petite blonde lady about my mother's age exchanged a look with me and replied, 'Well if I brought home a lodger as dashing as you, I think my husband would have something to say about it.' It was said with a laugh in her voice and a wink at me.

Her choice of words made me blush as I was hit once more by a surge of completely inappropriate lust. Sean was even more attractive in clothes that fit him. I mumbled some meaningless reply and thanked her effusively for her extra time in staying open for us.

Cynthia spread open her hands. 'We are a charity shop my dears. The clue should be in the title.'

Nevertheless, I was sure if I had just turned up by myself, I would not have been so fortunate. We left with her calling out to Sean that if he ever wanted something to do with his time until he got back on his feet, she would be happy to have him help her in the shop.

'I'll bet she would,' I muttered a touch grumpily under my breath.

'What was that?'

'Nothing,' I said to Sean who was looking thoroughly pleased with himself and why not.

The clothes that Cynthia had picked out for him were so much more his style than Gerald's had been. It was rather discomforting to see yet another dimension to this mysterious new companion in my life. Shooting him a sidelong glance as I drove the short distance back home, it was hard to fit him with the homeless man I had offered shelter to a few short days ago. Every cell in my body wriggled with embarrassment at the thought that I would never have considered being attracted to him then.

So why was I now?

My head started to spin as I considered the change in him. Or had I only seen what I expected to see when I looked at him before? It was all rather mad but, as with Luna, I was happy for now to go along with the madness. I would take the mad wild wolf and sexy lodger for now and worry about my sanity at some point in the future.

But first there was Christmas to overcome.

At home with my parents, it had always been something of a battleground with them continually scoring points over each other until they finally parted. It was not surprising then that I fell in love with Irene and Gerald's idea of a traditional Christmas. Gerald was an absolute star at Christmas, full of jovial spirit which extended to Marigold and Rose who often appeared either with a man on their arms or without. He also had the ability to play host to Dad and Samantha at the same time without anyone launching a barrage of Brussels sprouts. The more the merrier as far as Gerald was concerned.

What on Earth was I going to do without him this year?

What on Earth was I going to do without Gary this year?

Where on Earth would I be spending Christmas next year?

These thoughts were spinning morosely around my head early the following morning. I got out of bed and dressed as it was still dark. Sean's bedroom door was shut, and I wondered if he was still asleep. Then I wondered what he looked like sleeping. My thoughts began to veer off in a wild direction and I crossed the landing to the top of the stairs just as his door opened.

'Morning beautiful,' he said with his voice husky and ridiculously sexy from sleep.

My reply resembled something a frog would utter. I was trying not to stare at his lean torso which was bare. His jogging trousers were hanging dangerously low on his hips, also lean without an inch of spare flesh to spoil the line of his stomach muscles.

'Are you not cold?' I stammered, aware that heat was rising in my cheeks. 'It's freezing outside today, there's frost in the garden, it looks beautiful.'

Stop gabbling, Daisy and stop staring.

But I couldn't. My hand was frozen onto the pommel of the banister and my legs would not move. He yawned and stretched, which only made more of a show of his physique. His grin was slumberous and seductive when he looked back at me.

'I only put these joggers on to be decent going to the loo, didn't want to scare you wandering around naked, but you've got the heating on awful high, Daisy. I'm not used to being warm at night.'

'No, right, course you aren't.'

My tongue was glued to the roof of my mouth at the thought of him naked under the duvet.

'Would you like a cup of tea?' I squeaked.

'That would be just grand. I'll throw some clothes on and come and join you in the kitchen.'

Downstairs, I let Luna into the garden and slipping my feet into a pair of clogs by the back door I went to join her. The garden was coated with white and shimmering under the light of the moon which was still out. Huge and glowing, it caught my gaze and held it. Standing under its light it was easy to believe in magic. Luna turned her head and her silvery eyes shined intensely at me.

She was magic.

She had to be.

Back in the kitchen I put the kettle on and started cooking some bacon. I had not been eating properly this last couple of months and my appetite for food appeared to have returned.

Sean walked into the kitchen with a handful of mail. 'You're popular this morning.' He placed the pile of envelopes on the table. 'Ooh thank you, darling, a bacon butty just grand.'

The endearment I knew was as natural as breathing to him but when he leant forward to peck me on the cheek, I felt a quivering inside. An appetite of another kind was coming back to me it seemed. I munched on my breakfast, feeding Luna tiny bits as I did so and surveyed the pile of mail. At least it was a distraction from my lustful thoughts.

'Boring, junk, or personal?'

'I'm sorry?' I raised my eyes to Sean. He was wearing a blue sweater today which made his eyes seem even brighter. His hair was slightly damp and I caught a hint of the shower gel he had used.

'The mail. Which order do you open it in? Boring, junk, or personal first?'

'Oh yes I see what you mean. Junk first,' I replied, tossing aside the annoying pile of leaflets 'Then boring.'

I chattered on, trying not to feel the intensity of Sean's blue eyes from across the table. This included my car insurance renewal and a letter about bin collections over Christmas.

'What's next,' asked Sean indicating the other white envelopes.

There were rather a lot but then it was December.

'Christmas cards by the look of them?'

'Oh hell.' I looked at the name on the first one. It was addressed to Gerald. 'Should I open it?'

'Of course. Someone knew him but doesn't know he has died.'

It was a sad task and there were two more like it. Gerald had so many friends he had met over the years, it had been hard to know who to contact when he died. I perused the cards with a leaden feeling of sadness growing. My mood dropped further when I sifted through the next handful.

'Gary hasn't managed to tell all of our friends yet the happy news then?'

As I looked at the cards addressed to both of us, it was another blow to realise that all my friends, were jointly his. When had I become such a nonentity that I had no friends to call my own? With the benefit of hindsight, I could see that I had made the classic female mistake. I had been so wrapped up in my love for Gary, and the stability of his family that I hadn't needed anyone else in my life. I had been a fool to let my friends drift away and it hit me now how alone I really was.

'This time next year you'll have lots of new cards, Daisy, from lots of other lovely people.'

Sean's quiet comment was sweet, but I doubted the truth of it. I managed a weak smile reminding myself that he would have no cards at all.

'Two more personal letters. Oh great, thanks Gary. It's from his solicitor drawing up the initial terms of the divorce.'

I scanned the letter, not wanting to look too deeply.

'He wants the house, so he is going to use some of Gerald's money to buy me out.'

'I suppose that's reasonable.'

'Hm. But he wants me out by the end of January. Apparently, he needs to get the house redecorated and Corinne settled in here well before the baby is born which is sometime in June. So New Year beckons, Sean, no husband, no job, no home. Great.'

Then it hit me who I was talking to.

'Shit. I am sorry you must think I am such a spoilt cow. I mean, I will have some money after all and I can get another job, it's just…'

He brushed aside my waffling. 'You have every right to feel on the glum side. Now the last letter, that looks more interesting. It's got a Scottish postmark.'

I frowned. 'I don't know anyone in Scotland.' I looked at the envelope, surprised it had been delivered at all. The name and address were barely legible. The envelope had got thoroughly wet and the ink had smudged terribly.

'Well?' Asked Sean as I read the letter twice and puzzled over it.

'It says *Dear Ms Bolton, thank you so much for replying to my advert, I would be delighted to invite you to stay with us for a couple of days in order that we can both assess the suitability of each other. Sincerely Catriona Munro*. It's not for me at all. It's come to the wrong address.'

'How funny,' said Sean with a light of mischief in his eyes. 'Where was it sent from?'

'Wolf Lodge, Kinlaggan, Grampians, Scotland.' As I read it Luna rose silently from her place in front of the aga and placed her head on my lap. I looked at her and then looked at the letter in my hand.

'Sean what's going on?'

He shrugged his shoulders and looked at me blankly. 'How should I know? Haven't I told you before Daisy, I am just a poor old soul from the streets, how can I know anything? Let's just leave it there for now shall we and get going.'

'Going? It's Sunday, Sean, where are we going?'

'Christmas shopping.'

I stared at him blankly. 'I'm not really in the mood, Sean.'

'Which, my darling Daisy, is precisely why we are going. We are going to do Christmas.'

'We are?'

'Christmas is a time of magic and miracles Daisy and you do believe in both don't you?'

Pinned down by Luna's silver eyes and his blues ones, somehow, I had to.

Chapter Ten

After we had taken Luna for a quick run in the park, he chivvied me into getting ready to go shopping. The fresh air had put some colour in my cheeks, so I didn't look quite as peaky as I had done. On impulse, I changed my black sweater for a pink one that I had not worn in ages. The colour was far kinder to me, and I wondered when I had stopped making the effort with how I looked. I was reaching for an abandoned lip gloss when my eyes questioned my reflection in the mirror.

Why was I doing this?

Who was I doing this for?

'Are you alright up there?' Sean's voice carried lightly up the stairs.

My eyes taunted me with the answer to my question and angrily I tossed the lip gloss back onto the dressing table.

'Coming,' I said as brightly as I could and went back downstairs to meet him in the hall.

'Now that's a pretty colour. It suits you so well and it's perfect for these.'

He was ready and waiting, wearing a silver-grey sweater from the charity shop paired with black jeans. Around his neck was a bright red scarf and of course he was wearing Gerald's overcoat. The effect was all rather dashing. He looked like the type of man that a woman would wear lip gloss for.

A very stupid woman.

'Why the frown?' Sean asked as he reached into his jeans pocket and brought out a small package. 'Here, these are for you,' he said, not waiting for an answer to his question but handing me the bundle.

Curious, I took it from him. 'What is it?'

'Sure, and if you open it you'll see,' he teased.

Within the folds of the tissue paper were a pendant and matching earrings. Polished rose-pink stones set in silver.

'They're beautiful,' I said admiring the handiwork but also wondering at the how and the why of them.

'I didn't steal them if that's what you're thinking,' said Sean with a wry smile that made me suddenly ashamed. 'Violet gave them to me.'

'Violet?' I wondered why on earth my neighbour would have done this.

'I did some gardening work for her, and she wanted to pay me. I said that I didn't want payment. So then she said she must give me a present and I said to her that I didn't want a present but if she wanted to give you a present for being so kind to me then that would be alright. Her great-niece makes them from all sorts of different stones. She let me choose.'

I was touched. 'They are beautiful stones Sean.'

He took the pendant from where it was cradled in my hand. 'Rose quartz,' he said softly looking into my eyes. 'They bring love to a person. Here, let me put it on for you.'

I was too shaken by the proximity of him and the look in his eyes to protest as he came to stand behind me, moving my hair away from my neck so he could fasten the silver chain. It was the lightest of touches from his fingers, but the contact of his skin on mine was enough to make me tremble.

'I can put the earrings in myself,' I said, aware that my voice was not sounding quite like my own.

'That's grand you look now, Daisy, just grand. Now, shopping.'

We took the bus into town to avoid parking. Getting on to it, the touch of his hand on the small of my back was barely even there, but through the thickness of my winter coat I was aware of it. I wondered as he slid onto the seat next to me if he was feeling the same effect. It was so hard to tell. One minute he could be flippant and light-hearted like the brightest of butterflies, and the next it felt like he was probing my soul with the solemn compassion of a priest.

Except that he made me feel nothing like a priest would.

As the bus arrived in town, he took my gloved hand in his. 'The market first Daisy, what do you say?'

I looked at my hand in his and I thought it was almost as though I was on a date. And what woman would not want to be seen out with him? Silver blond hair, the brightest of blue eyes, enough lines on his face to make him rugged looking and not too pretty, and with a smile that bewitched. I shook away my feelings of reserve. Why not just enjoy the moment? Have a little fun. Feel like a teenager again.

The town had a huge open-air market and I had forgotten that this weekend it was staging a Victorian extravaganza. The stall holders were dressed up in costumes, there was a brass band playing carols, and instead of the usual burgers and pies, hog roasts and chestnuts were the fayre on offer. It was noisy, lively, colourful and just what I needed.

It was fun.

It seemed that Sean knew pretty much every one of the stall holders. Soon it was impossible to hold hands as we were becoming laden with bags full of things for presents. It crossed my mind a couple of hours later, as we paused for a warm sandwich of roasted pork and apple sauce, that I had completed all my Christmas shopping and not yet set foot in one of the main chain stores.

'Commercial crap,' Sean said in reply to my comment on this. He waved his hand around the buzzing market. 'Every person here Daisy, is working hard to put food on their tables, to pay their bills, to keep the kids in school shoes. Every purchase you made today makes their lives a little bit easier. You go into the big fancy stores with the glitzy lights and the gifts all wrapped in that bloody plastic that's killing the planet, and where does your money go then, Daisy? To some overpaid fat corporate lard arse who doesn't give a shit about people or the planet, or Christmas and its true meaning.'

He was utterly compelling when he was serious. Again, I had the sense there was so much more to Sean than what you saw on the surface. I looked at the collection of presents I had acquired, quite a few of them handmade and simply packaged in brown paper bags and I understood what he meant.

'I'd never thought of it like that before, Sean.'

Quick as lightning he was the jovial teaser. 'Now there you go again, loading yourself with that wretched guilt, Daisy, I can see it in your eyes. Stop it now will you. You're giving yourself a frown on that pretty face of yours.'

He leant in towards me and brushed a finger across my brow. He had taken his gloves off to eat his sandwich and I felt the warmth of his hand. Then I felt the gentle heat of his lips as they ever so briefly brushed against mine. I responded as if I had known him all my life, sitting on a bench at the side of the market, with the hustle and bustle of Christmas shoppers and carols singers the background to our kiss.

'Daisy are you snogging Sean?'

It was a loud and delighted shriek that broke up the moment. I opened my eyes to see my little sister hurtling towards me.

'Abigail!' I exclaimed just before she plonked herself between us and looked at Sean with a comical expression on her face.

'You were snogging Daisy.'

''Twas not a snog,' he answered with mock indignation. 'It was a Christmas Kiss. It's the law.'

'The law?' queried Abigail as I searched the crowd looking for Dad or Samantha.

'The Law.' Sean insisted. 'Where there is mistletoe, there must be kisses.'

I had not noticed the mistletoe just above my head, tied onto a wrought iron lamp post.

'Abigail you shouldn't run off like that,' Samantha, looking stunning in a forest green belted coat that set off her auburn hair, appeared with Dad right behind her.

'Daisy and Sean were Christmas kissing,' Abigail explained.

'Were they really?' Samantha looked at me first and then Sean. She did a double-take. She had not seen him since that first night. The look she then gave me was difficult to interpret.

'Daisy, what are you doing here?' Dad, as handsome as ever with his thick shock of white hair and dapper style of dressing, had already seen the transformation in my lodger.

Abigail explained again, 'They were Christmas Kissing Daddy, it's the law.'

'Snogging under the mistletoe,' Samantha drawled with amusement and maybe envy in her voice.

'Not snogging, Mummy, kissing, isn't that right, Sean.' Thankfully, she filled what could have been an awkward moment. 'I'm going to be an angel in our school nativity.'

Sean gave her the most beautiful of smiles. 'And perfectly fitting I would say, Abigail.'

I don't think Samantha liked the way her daughter was beaming up at him. 'I see you have been busy helping Daisy spend her money?'

'We have been busy preparing for Christmas. It's going to be such a special one this year for Daisy.'

'Really?' Samantha now looked amused.

'It's going to be grand,' said Sean and then turned back to Abigail. 'You're going to come aren't you, and see what Father Christmas leaves under the tree for you? And play with Luna in the snow.'

'Yes, please Sean! Mummy, can we go to Daisy and Sean's for Christmas?'

'I think you mean Daisy and Gary's,' Dad corrected her with a sharp look at Sean.

Samantha crowed unpleasantly, 'Not for much longer, he wants her out by the end of January.'

'Which is precisely why we are going to have one heck of a shindig, isn't that right, Daisy?'

Thankfully, Samantha said tartly that it was out of the question.

'We always go to my family in the Cotswolds. It's utterly charming there.'

'Mummy your phone is ringing.'

Samantha took her call and Sean continued to chat to Abigail whilst Dad and I looked at each other uncomfortably.

'I don't bloody believe it!'

'What's wrong, darling?' Dad asked his young wife.

'Bloody Alistair is coming home for Christmas. Mummy's over the moon.'

'That's alright, isn't it?'

'No. It bloody isn't. You know I can't stand Felicity and as for their awful kids; Christ, ten minutes in their company and I want to throttle them. Bloody Alistair.' She stuffed her phone back into her expensive leather bag. 'Very well then Daisy, we will come to you for lunch.'

'Yippee!' Abigail jumped up and down and hugged first me and then Sean.

'Are you sure?' Dad looked at her.

'You can't cook a bloody turkey and I certainly am not going to do all that hard work.'

'That's sorted then,' said Sean with a broad smile on his face. 'You can eat with us, and Abigail can play with Luna in the snow.'

'Don't be stupid,' snapped Samantha. 'It never snows on Christmas Day!'

I looked at Sean and he winked.

Somehow, I thought, it might just snow on this one, if only to piss

Samantha off.

After finishing our shopping, Sean suggested we get off the bus a stop earlier at the garden centre that sold Christmas trees. With his usual charm, he talked the owner into delivering the enormous tree after the place had shut so that we could decorate it that evening.

The smell of fresh pine in the room lifted my spirits which had dipped again from coming home to the empty house; although there was a bittersweet sadness in the mix. I was so used to doing this job with Gerald, my adorable, gentle, father-in-law. His missing presence stung. As I hung each bauble on the soft feathery branches, I had to wipe away a tear.

Sean got the wood burner going and some lovely Celtic music playing softly. Seeing my tears, he poured me a large glass of sherry and tempted me with a mince pie. At this rate, I would not need any tea. Never mind, it all worked to combat the sadness and I was beginning to feel a little merry when the doorbell rang.

Marigold never casually dropped in without wanting something, so the presence of my mother at seven o'clock on a Sunday evening was cause for concern. In she flounced, wearing a swirling black skirt, shiny patent boots and a cerise top in soft cashmere that hugged her full figure. Her thick wavy hair, carefully dyed to hide the grey bounced softly on her shoulders. Gold earrings and a matching necklace were bright against her tanned skin, and her lips and nails matched the colour of her top. She had the looks of her Hungarian Romany ancestry and she used them to full advantage.

'I didn't think you would be celebrating Christmas this year,' she said accepting a glass of sherry from Sean and eyeing the tree with surprise. 'Not after Gary dumping you. It's good that you are though.'

I paused, a strand of silver tinsel in hand. 'Oh?'

'Mm, why don't you let Daisy get on with that and come and join me over here,' she patted the space on the sofa beside her and gave Sean a flirtatious look.

'It's not right for a person to decorate a tree alone,' Sean easily rebuffed the request. 'It's a job to be shared with love and friendship, isn't that right, Daisy?' His hand touched mine briefly, lingered for a minute and the sadness over Gerald disappeared.

'As I was saying,' Marigold's husky voice broke into my head which was probably a good thing.

I turned to look at her and noted the sharp glint in her eyes as she glanced from Sean to me.

'Cheryl has gone and let me down. Her daughter has had a car accident or something and she has to stay in England this year to help look after the grandchild, so she doesn't want to go to Tenerife after all.'

'Poor woman,' said Sean. 'I will pray for a speedy recovery for her.'

Marigold looked at him. 'Didn't have you down for the religious type?'

'I believe,' he said with that winsome smile of his. 'In all sorts of things. You'll be wanting to come and join us then on Christmas Day.'

'If you're sure it won't put you to too much trouble,' she smiled seductively at Sean.

'Oh no. No trouble at all. We've invited Violet from next door as well, so you can keep her company.'

I shot him a look. Had we?

'Did I not say,' he went on glibly, as he rooted in the box of decorations for the angel to go on the top. 'I saw her in the garden when we got back from shopping. She was going to her nephews', but his mother-in-law is also ill, so this year they are going there to look after her. And I knew you wouldn't want her to be on her own.'

'No of course not,' I replied quickly and meant it. I liked my neighbour and certainly, she would be a buffer for Marigold's usual sniping at how I did everything.

'Hm so there'll be four of us then,' she said finishing her sherry.

'Don't worry, there'll be plenty of turkey,' said Sean, not mentioning that he had already invited Dad, Samantha and Abigail. Then he escorted her to the door in such a way that she didn't even realise she was being asked to leave without being offered a refill.

'So, we're cooking for Dad, Samantha, Abigail, Violet and now Marigold?' I queried as he came back into the room. 'Are there any more people you think we should invite?' I couldn't prevent the tiny sting of tartness from sharpening my voice. 'Like my soon to be ex and his pregnant girlfriend?'

He just shrugged. 'It's Christmas, Daisy,' and then handed me the angel and went to hold the step ladders so they didn't wobble as I climbed up.

As I held the angel in my hand, I could hear Gerald's voice as clear as if he were in the room with me.

'It's Christmas Daisy. It's a time for forgiveness and love.'

I nearly dropped the angel.

'Are you alright, Daisy?'

'Yes, yes, I'm fine Sean. There, all done.'

'That's perfect, Daisy, just perfect.'

'Thank you,' I said quietly and turned in towards him.

Maybe it was the magic of the tree.

Maybe it was the sherry.

Maybe it was sheer loneliness.

But he was there, and he was smiling at me. I took the step to move closer and knew that this time I had to have more than a kiss from him, mistletoe or not.

Chapter Eleven

I have never seduced anyone in my life.

Now was not the time to start. I wouldn't even know how to begin. All I knew was that kissing Sean was what I absolutely had to do right here, right now. With the smell of pine from the tree and logs burning in the stove and the harshness of the world shut out, now was the perfect time to lose myself in a fantasy world.

After all, there was a magical white wolf sprawled out in front of the fire, and she came from goodness knows where, so why not fall under the spell of this man who had saved me from myself. Why not take that magic a little further?

He didn't hesitate to open his arms to me and there was a gentleness in his touch as his hands cradled my face. His lips met mine with the perfect match of someone who has been a lover for a lifetime. Which of course he was not. He had never been my lover. I barely even knew him. Yet that touch of his mouth on mine was like coming home.

The first few kisses were soft and slow, but not tentative, there was nothing questioning about it. It was so completely right. Lazy, unhurried, with all the time in the world. You could be forgiven for thinking this intimated that there was no passion there; that the spark was not ignited between us. Nothing could be further from the truth.

As soon as we touched, I came alive.

I walked out of my frozen tomb and began to feel again.

All over.

Inside and out.

It was as though Sean was breathing oxygen into my body and bringing life into cells that had been shrivelling up and dying. Just as my back prickled and burnt when I felt Luna's energy spilling over, so I felt every inch of my skin glowing with a warmth I had never experienced before. Such a meltingly fluid feeling that trod softly through my blood and my bones, and I was in no rush to hurry past this. Why should I? Who would not want to linger in this heady place of sensations?

But without thought, without effort, we had soon tumbled to the floor, Sean gently halting my fall as my knees gave way beneath me and I found myself on the carpet. The lower branches of the tree brushed at my head and the needles lightly teased my skin as the pink sweater I was wearing was removed along with my bra.

Unfair not to return the favour, so Sean's sweater was tossed aside. My fingers were as eager as his to touch, to feel, to explore. Between touches, there were kisses and these were much deeper now; more searching, more giving. Not a word between us and there didn't need to be as next came the fumbling jumble of unzipping jeans, wriggling them past hips and losing the underwear; again tossed carelessly aside.

Not a moment to be lost, to be wasted as soon as we were both naked. I had forgotten the thrill of feeling skin against skin, the contrast of hard muscle against soft flesh. The agony of need. The pulsing desire that bursts through a dam of lonely deprivation to bring forth life into an otherwise arid desert.

I had been shrivelled up, dying of thirst, not even aware of it.

Until he lay upon me, eyes flashing blue fire as he nudged his hard tip between my legs.

I gasped at the contact, nearly lost myself there and then.

Anticipation, a touch of fear, excitement, blinding need.

'Please,' I whispered as he seemed to be waiting for permission.

His mouth slowly curved into a knowing smile.

Eyes wide open I was lost in his gaze as I felt every inch of him fill me. He held me close, poised and immobile for a few long sensuous moments. Enough time to get used to the feel of him inside, the fullness, the pressure the sense of being made whole once more.

A moment of wonder on my part.

How?

How was this possible?

How could I be laid here, on the living room carpet, beneath a Christmas tree, with a white wolf next to the fire, and this man, this virtual stranger, lying on top of me, his body now deeply embedded in mine?

How?

Because I thought dreamily, there was magic in his eyes.

And I so wanted to believe in magic.

I needed to believe in it.

I needed to believe in something.

I let myself believe in him and it was the most intense feeling I have ever had in my life. As if nothing before this moment had ever really mattered. I had not been living before but now I was. Tears were forming in my eyes but not from any sadness.

I was overwhelmed.

His smile as he bent to kiss them away was so full of impossible love that I felt my own heart bursting. Then he began to move inside me, and my feelings grew far more physical. Yet with each deep stroke, each kiss and caress, I felt myself being lifted higher and higher to a place I had never been before. Someone had spiked the sherry I thought. It wasn't possible to feel this good.

But it was and with every move he made it got better and better.

We had long past the slow and lazy now, but still with the faster pace of passion he cradled me within a world of tenderness that had me softly whimpering in wordless ecstasy. There was no beginning of me and no ending of him, totally entwined with each other, hardly an inch of air between us. I was melting into him as much as he was heating up ready to melt into me.

My body writhed beneath his with long-forgotten movements. My hips lifted to meet his, to match his rhythm. My legs found their way to coil around his waist, opening myself further to his entry. My fingers began to snake into his hair, pulling his mouth back to mine. My lips bruised against his, tongue exploring, seeking, demanding.

Demanding?

I had never felt so demanding of sex before in my life.

Yet here I was, grasping and greedy.

Panting and breathless.

Moaning and biting hard to suppress the words I suddenly wanted to use but never had with Gary.

I heard his low throaty laughter, and looked up to see him poised above me.

At that moment his eyes had gone so dark they were almost purple. Rich, velvety, full of secrets and dark desire. I swallowed a lump in my throat, nearly choking on the urgency of my lust, the need he had stirred within me.

He created that need.

And then released it.

Slow lazy strokes grew faster and harder, fuelling the fire inside me until I felt I was scorching through to my bones. Then a tormenting control that pulled back and slowed, altering the pace, the tempo so that I was nearly there but not quite allowed to fly.

Not yet.

I began to grow dizzy with the desire he was making me feel. My breath grew ever shallower, even as his never altered, never grew ragged and harsh. He was passion controlled and I was a puddle of limp lust on the carpet.

Finally, he paused. He held his weight lightly above mine. My insides were throbbing, burning for that wet, hot release. I could feel the tip of him nudging, pushing even further until it felt as though he was going to lose himself completely within me.

I no longer felt like Daisy.

I was a part of him.

A slow curving smile made his mouth look even more beautiful; teeth white in the darkness of the room. I wondered that not one bead of sweat dampened his forehead, yet I was slick with moisture, both over my body and within. A molten mass of damp, warm femininity, pliant beneath his hard cool masculinity.

My body was beginning to shudder.

His smile grew.

The length of him inside me grew.

How?

How was it possible that he could fill me more?

How could I surrender even more to him?

But he did, and I did, and finally he spoke.

'Now, Daisy, now.'

With the words, firm hands on my hips and three long hard thrusts that lifted me off the floor, I was helpless to do anything else. My body belonged to his now, we were one and the same. When I came, so did he; it could be no other way.

Shockingly intense.

Almost painful.

Soaring in the arms of an angel to a heavenly place I had never dreamt I could visit. Totally and utterly enveloped in love and fiery hot passion. Brought back down to earth with soft feather-light kisses, tender caresses and magical words spoken in Irish that brought tears to my eyes without even knowing what they meant.

Then he rolled us both over so that I could lie on top of him, pillowing my head drowsily on his chest. I listened for the beat of his heart, surely it must be thumping madly as was mine? But even though I could feel the steady rise and fall of his chest, I couldn't hear anything.

'You must be incredibly fit,' I murmured sleepily, which was possibly not the most romantic of comments to make at a time like this.

'I'll take that as a compliment Daisy. You're trying to tell me I've worn you out?'

With the inevitable rush of embarrassment, I prised myself slightly up and away from him, too conscious now of his nakedness and mine. Which was ridiculous as I could still feel him inside me.

'I mean I can't hear your heart beating but mine is going ten to the dozen.' I dared to look him in the eyes now, my vision unclouded by passion.

'I am naturally blessed with a good constitution,' he grinned and then gently toyed with the damp strands of hair that were tousled about my face. 'Which is fortunate Daisy, cos it matches my appetites.'

His easy nature quickly dispelled my embarrassment. Moulded against his lean body I felt as though I had come home. It was so natural. So utterly right. So deliciously sensual. I felt my body becoming sinewy and elegant like a cat. It was a nice way to feel.

'What appetites Sean?' I all but purred at him and he laughed low in his throat; a wicked sound.

'Appetites for everything Daisy. For food, for drink, for life, for love. For you.'

I felt him then stir to life within me, shocking me that he could ignite with passion so quickly after such intense lovemaking. Yet he was, and so was I. This time I could not be silent. My contented purring grew into a rumbling growl of need that again had him laughing.

'Go on Daisy, find the wildness within you. It's been there all along just hiding below the surface.'

He lifted up his hips at the same time he stroked his fingers down the length of my back. I had the feeling he was outlining my tattoo and each spot he touched came instantly to life, burning and prickling with heat.

I felt something inside me burst into life, something breaking free.

Luna sprang up from her place by the fire and trotted quickly to the old-fashioned French windows that opened into the garden. With ease, she swiped her paws at the handle and let herself out into the cold dark December night.

'Is she alright?' I hated to tear my eyes away from his, but Luna was a part of me, as much as he was now.

'She needs to be a little wild,' he said softly. 'As do you.'

He coaxed me gently, hands now moving to push my shoulders up and away from him, encouraging me to rise up. The Daisy that I had become had long since forgotten the heady days of passion and lust. They were lost way back when… I couldn't think about that not here, not now. Besides, with Sean moving beneath me it was impossible to think for more than a fragment of second.

I lost my worrying modesty that my breasts were no longer those of a young girl or woman, I didn't care that I had soft folds of flesh around my belly, and that there were lines around my eyes and grey in my hair.

I was here in this moment, and this moment was a man who was looking at me with desire and love in his eyes. This moment was a sensation of being filled to the brim with this man and needing to take those feelings further. This moment was my awakening from a long and very dark, lonely sleep. This moment was life itself.

I took it, reached for it, grasped hold of it with everything I had within me.

I went a little wild.

I was glad that my neighbour Violet was slightly deaf and that she had the habit of having the TV in her lounge on very loud at times. I was glad that Luna was in the garden howling her head off. I was glad that I could find my voice and release those cries. All the time he urged me on, whispering in the Gaelic I had no hope of understanding. The language of our bodies was clear enough. He wanted me and his own husky moans mingled with mine. The second climax when it came was sudden, explosive, shattering in its force; a moment of life and death intertwined. I felt so good I had to be dying. Being alive could not feel this good.

'Oh but it can, Daisy darling,' groaned Sean beneath me and I wondered as I collapsed against him if I had uttered those thoughts out loud.

I didn't think so. Then again, who knew what I had said, uttered in that obliteration of passion. And who cared? Not me. I was tempted to simply stay where I was, moving required too much effort even though the night air, let in the room by Luna, was quickly chilling me. It didn't seem to concern Sean, but he noticed that I was suddenly shivering.

'Come on,' he said. 'We don't want you getting ill.' Carefully he eased me over to the side and finally withdraw from me.

I felt horrendously bereft and had to bite my lips to stop myself from calling out his name. Ridiculous. Instead, I opened my mouth to call for Luna, but I had no need to. She was back in the room, looking bright-eyed and fresh with the scent of the garden. She came up to me where I huddled hardly able to move, under the Christmas tree.

Snuggling up against her fur in my naked state was primeval. She folded herself into me and nuzzled up to my neck, licking and ever so gently nibbling at me. At that moment I didn't feel like a woman, I felt more like a wolf, the same as her and with that feeling came a glorious sense of contentment. This is who I am, I thought, heady with the after-effects of passion and goodness knows what other magic was in the air.

Or maybe the half bottle of sherry from earlier.

Telling myself this was the case, I gently eased Luna away from me and I reached up to take the hand that Sean was holding out.

'Come on my darling, Daisy, I think we need to get you into bed before you fall asleep down here. As much as I am used to sleeping on a hard surface, trust me, you won't thank me in the morning if I let you do it.'

Here was another bridge to cross.

'Sleeping with someone can be more intimate than sex you know,' he said softly.

'I know.'

I had not thought of Gary at all since I had kissed Sean, and yet now at this point suddenly he was there in my head. My husband with whom I had slept for eighteen years. But he had left me alone in a cold empty bed and I couldn't face that desolation anymore.

'Are you sure?'

Sean gave me chance to change my mind as I tugged at his hand and opened my bedroom door. I wasn't sure about anything really, other than for now the rest of my life had just been paused and all that existed was this man and this wolf beside me.

I took them both to bed with me.

Although Luna had, in a short space of time, settled on the spare pillow beside my head as being her spot, she allowed Sean's head to rest there instead, and curled up at my feet. I was beyond drowsy now and as soon as Sean reached out an arm to cradle me in towards his chest, I was asleep.

I don't think I moved for the next eight hours or so and it was still dark with the December morning when I finally stirred from the deepest sleep I had had in years. As soon as I did move, I became aware that there was another person in my bed and that it was not Gary.

In the raw cold chill of morning, I should perhaps have felt uncomfortable with this. Regrets should have gnawed away at me. Guilt should have pierced me in the heart. All these 'shoulds' melted in an instant as Sean moved with me and then within moments was once again inside me.

This time was once again silent. Touch was everything. Touch and taste, and smell. Eyes closed for the most part, lost in that early morning cocoon of darkness. Wrapped up in a blanket of bliss that felt too wonderful to be real.

It was real though and there was no imagining the intensity of the feelings as once more Sean took me to the edge of a shattering climax and rode along with me. When I finally could breathe steadily, again I couldn't stop myself slipping back into a drowsy state. How on Earth was I possibly going to manage to get out of bed this morning?

'You have a lie in.'

Sean had quietly got out of bed and dressed before I realised I had nodded off again. He leant down towards me and kissed me gently on the lips.

'Daisy you look so beautiful, so you do. And wouldn't I be happy to stay there all day with you.'

That seemed like a jolly good idea. Wantonly I tossed the duvet aside and beckoned him sleepily.

'Why don't you?'

I hardly recognised my voice. Sultry, inviting. Sexy. Where had the exhausted teacher gone? He had turned me into a siren overnight. I rather liked it.

So did he judging by the look in his eyes, but he shook his head and gently covered me back up.

'I promised Violet I would clear out her gutters today before the snow comes.'

I was tempted to sit up at this, but I couldn't. My bones had dissolved into the bed somehow.

'Snow?'

'Sure. We're going to have a white Christmas. I said so to Abigail yesterday, didn't I?'

'Yes, but you saying it won't necessarily make it happen, Sean.'

'Hm, we'll see. Anyway, that's what I'm about today. I'll take Luna with me. She can play in her garden. You stay right there and sleep. It will do you good.'

'No, really I should get up.'

Old habits die hard and even though on this Monday morning I had no job to go to, no elderly relatives to look after, no husband to think about, I still felt like I should be doing something. Sean though did not seem to view it this way.

'No. You stay right there and sleep. You need to heal Daisy.'

'I don't need to heal Sean, there's nothing wrong with me. I'm not ill.'

He placed a hand then on my chest, right over my heart. I felt it pumping madly under his touch and a sudden surge of intense heat.

'Oh, but you do, Daisy. Your heart needs to heal, it's fair broken so it is. You've lost all the love inside you darling girl. It's been wrung out of you like a used-up dishcloth.'

He toyed with the rose quartz pendant he had given me yesterday which still hung around my neck. 'But with a little love given back it will mend so it will.' Then he kissed me ever so gently on my brow. 'Now do as I say and sleep.'

The protest died on my lips as my eyes closed. Faintly, I heard the door opening and closing. Then I was asleep once more.

Chapter Twelve

When I next opened my eyes, it was going on for lunchtime. Yawning and stretching out my body under the duvet I waited for the rush of guilt to swamp me. I had slept with another man. I had slept with Sean. No guilt. That surprised me.

I was calm and clear-headed for the first time in a very long while. I even hummed to myself as I showered. I was not on the scrap heap. This old body of mine, with its saggy bits and untoned flesh, had been well and truly loved. It was singing with joy at feeling like this and when I saw myself in the bathroom mirror, there was a smiling face looking back at me.

'Sean Murphy, you are better than any face cream I've ever bought,' I said to my reflection, admiring the new sparkle in my eyes and glow in my cheeks. I touched the rose-pink pendant around my neck and smiled even more. It would bring me love he had said.

Was I in love with Sean?

Could I possibly have fallen in love with someone so quickly?

Maybe.

The practical side of me argued that I was emotionally vulnerable right now and therefore an easy target. I knew that anyone with an ounce of sense in their head would advise caution here. Then again, anyone with an ounce of sense in their head would not have given a room to a homeless stranger and a mysterious wolf either. So that was that argument lost.

And really did it matter?

I had been gloomy for so long I was more than happy not to question

Sean or Luna's presence. Life was simply so much nicer with them here so that was all that mattered for now. There was no sign of Sean or Luna downstairs, but he had mentioned clearing out Violet's gutters before the snow came. We still had ten days to go before Christmas and after the early chilly start to the month, the weather had become milder again.

Would we really get snow?

I started thinking about the invitations so casually issued yesterday. I would be cooking for Dad, Samantha, Abigail, Marigold and Violet. I no longer cared. That was the wonder of Sean's lovemaking. Not only had he unravelled every knotted muscle in my body, made my skin glow and eyes sparkle, he had magically detuned the programming of a lifetime in my brain.

I must be good.

I must be practical.

Daisy Practical Barton.

The Daisy who could have had practical as her middle name, would never have let herself go with such wild abandon with a man she had just met. The Daisy who was, truth be told, more than a little sore this morning seemed to have acquired a different way of thinking.

'Bollocks' I said to myself as I loaded an extra sugar in my mug of tea and reached for the biscuit tin. I was ravenous. Not surprising really as our marathon love making session had taken place on a few mince pies and half a bottle of sherry. We had skipped tea altogether and having slept in, I had also missed breakfast.

I picked up my mug and plate of biscuits and my eye caught sight of the mail that I had placed on the shelf yesterday. On a whim, I picked up the letter that had been wrongly delivered and put it in my pocket. Then I went through to the sitting room where the tree now proudly stood. It was lovely, and the scent of pine had its usual brightening effect. Our discarded clothing that we had so merrily strewn around was nowhere to be seen. No doubt Sean had already loaded it into the washing machine along with any other laundry.

'Really', I thought with a twisted little smirk on my face, what was I missing without Gary? My husband could hardly tell the difference between the washing machine and the dishwasher, and God forbid if he ever had to iron his own shirts. I wondered if Corinne was doing that for him now – I doubted it. She would make a much better job of training Gary than I had ever managed to do.

I pushed thoughts of them aside, not wanting to spoil my mood. Sitting in a chair by the tree I opened the letter and perused it as I drank my mug of tea. The person to whom the letter should have gone must have applied for some sort of job, although it was hard to ascertain if an interview had already taken place. It mentioned arranging a visit in January, so maybe they had just discussed details over the phone, or by email? Either way, Catriona Munro deserved to know that the lady she had written to had not received her letter. I keyed in the number to my phone.

'Yes!' After a long time ringing a male voice growled into my ear.

'Oh, sorry to bother you, is Catriona Munro available.'

'No.'

I opened my mouth to ask when she would be available, when I realised that I had been cut off.

'How rude.' I muttered.

I was about to toss my phone aside. Then an odd thing happened. I felt Luna on my back, burning and prickling with heat. I felt a compelling urgency to redial the number.

It was the same voice that answered; male, Scottish, gravelly and annoyed. 'You again!' he snapped.

'How astute!' I snapped back, most unlike myself. 'Now, you ignorant arse, I have information for Catriona Munro so tell me when she will be available to speak to.'

There was a pause and then the voice queried in a slightly quieter but no less aggressive tone. 'Did you just call me an ignorant arse?'

'I did. Or would you prefer arrogant prick?' I clapped my hand over my mouth appalled at myself. Seriously Daisy, where had that come from? I never spoke to people like that! Astonishingly though, it seemed to have the desired effect.

I heard a choked gasp and then muffled as though speaking away from the phone, 'Mother, there's a madwoman who wants you.'

Madwoman? He could talk. The next moment I heard another Scottish voice, only this time it was like listening to a soft mountain stream bubbling, as opposed to a lump hammer cracking against rock.

'Please forgive my son, he's not himself at the moment. To whom would I be speaking?'

'Hello, you don't know me, my name is Daisy Barton. I'm afraid I accidentally opened a letter that you had written to a Ms Bolton who also lives in a Park Avenue, but it came to me instead. The rain must have made the ink on the envelope run.'

'Oh, yes I see, do go on.'

'Well, it's just that you see. The person who should have got the letter hasn't done.'

'Of course. Och, well it matters not anyway, I'm afraid.'

I was curious. 'Oh, why is that?'

'As a matter of fact, I had another telephone call about five minutes before you rang. It was from the recipient of your letter. She had phoned me to say she had changed her mind after all.'

This sentence was finished with such a sigh that I was drawn in further to ask more. 'What had she changed her mind about?'

'The job. I had advertised it a while ago and had a few replies but for one reason and another they weren't suitable, or our position wasn't right for them. Diane, the lady, seemed like the answer to my prayers. She sent a lovely letter with her CV and on the back of that I gave her a lengthy interview over the phone. The letter you received was to confirm a meeting face to face.'

'I see. And she no longer wants the job?'

'It would seem that way.' She sounded disheartened. Then as though someone had flicked a switch inside her, her tone altered completely. 'I don't suppose you are looking for a new job?'

My tattoo tingled, burnt, itched. The words came out of my mouth, 'As a matter of fact I am.'

'Really?' I could picture her sitting up straighter, as her tone sharpened. 'What did you used to do?'

'I'm an English teacher.'

'And you no longer wish to do this?'

'I got sacked. Well, suspended but it's the same thing really.' I couldn't lie to her.

'Sounds intriguing.'

I explained what had happened and heard her laughter down the phone.

'Would you like the job then?'

'Oh well, I mean, what exactly is it?'

'Silly me, I haven't said. Hard to put a description on it really. Sort of manger come housekeeper. We run a hotel and a number of self-catering chalets in the Highlands. Have you ever been to Scotland?'

'No, I am afraid I haven't. The Lake District is as far north as I have been.'

'I am sure I can forgive you that wee error of judgment. Shall we arrange a date then in January for you to come and visit?'

My mind was whirring. This was going too fast. 'But I have absolutely no experience at all of running a hotel or holiday lodges,' I protested.

'From your voice, you don't sound over young, if you will pardon me for saying so.'

'I'm forty-six.'

'Married? If you are and your husband wants a change of career, I am sure we could find something for him to do.'

I didn't immediately answer, and an awkward laugh filled the pause. 'Oh dear, now I sound utterly desperate, don't I? Truth to tell I am.' A weariness I recognised overshadowed the brightness in her voice. It was the weariness of someone who has been carrying a burden for too long.

Gently I said, 'No it's just that it's all a bit raw. I have been married for eighteen years and my husband is divorcing me to marry his younger woman.' As if Catriona was a life-long friend I found myself telling her about Gerald dying six months after Irene and then Gary making his announcement.

'You poor dear, how utterly wretched for you. But it does answer one question.'

'It does?'

'Of course. If you have managed your own home for eighteen years as well as being a teacher, and cared for your ailing mother-in-law on top of all that, before your poor father-in-law took ill, you more than have enough experience to do this job.'

'Really?'

'My dear I think it will be an absolute walk in the park after what you have coped with. And by the sounds of things, you could do with a fresh start? What do you say?'

At that moment I heard the back door shutting in the kitchen and a cheery hello from Sean. Seconds later, Luna bounded into the room and dropped her heavy head on my lap.

'Oh heck, how can I?'

'How can you what?'

I stroked Luna's head and looked into her fathomless silver eyes. As exciting as this opportunity sounded, I could not possibly do anything that meant parting with her.

I explained. 'I've sort of got a dog. No, that isn't strictly true. I've got a wolf.'

'My dear then in that case you must be destined for the job. Bring her with you of course. How fabulous to have a real wolf at Wolf Lodge. Now, diaries, lets agree on a date.'

I was hesitating again as Sean came into the room. His jeans and sweater were on the grubby side but that was to be expected from a morning clearing gutters. His sleeves were pushed up to his elbows, his hands resting light on his hips. The thought of what those hands had done to me was momentarily distracting and threw me right off course from my conversation.

'Sorry,' I said to Catriona, as my pause had lengthened. I waved the letter at Sean to indicate who I was talking to. Then I mouthed to him that she had offered me the job and shrugged looking to him for guidance.

In typical Sean fashion he took the phone from me. I then had to listen to a lengthy one-sided conversation with Sean at his Irish best. Didn't he have cousins three times removed on his Ma's side, God rest her soul, who had stayed at the very lodge where Catriona lived, and sure hadn't they told him how beautiful and wild it was up there, almost as magnificent as God's own country from which he hailed.

'So that's grand then isn't it?' said Sean with that angelic smile of his, that had the power to rob a person of the ability to speak and think sensibly. He handed me back my phone with a nod of satisfaction. 'New year in the highlands. Will you do the highland fling with me, Daisy darling?'

He pulled me up from the chair and whirled me round singing, 'Oh you take the high road and I'll take the low road, and I'll be in Scotland before ye, but me and my true love will never meet again, on yon bonnie, bonnie banks of Loch Lomond.'

I had never heard him sing before and his voice stunned me with its haunting quality, tears springing to my eyes.

'I know, it's a heart-wrenching tune so it is. And it is not about taking a different turn on the map you know. The high road is the spirit road, did you know that Daisy?'

I shook my head, still feeling more than a little overwhelmed that in the space of half an hour I had been talked into a job interview in the new year for the position of a housekeeper at a hotel in the middle of the highlands.

'No I didn't.'

He pulled me close and tenderly brushed away a lock of hair from my forehead. 'Yes, Daisy darling, some of us walk the spirit road, so we do.'

Then he kissed me deeply and thoroughly and thoughts of new jobs, hotels in Scotland and lunch for that matter went right out of my head. Sean, for all his talk of spirit roads, was demonstrably earthy in his appetites. Now that we had crossed that line of becoming lovers, he seemed keen to demonstrate how attractive he found me, and I was certainly not going to stop him.

I couldn't remember the last time Gary had made love to me. But I do recall with sadness that in the last few years the passion had been replaced with a familiarity bordering on complacency and that complacency had withered gradually into nothing at all. With the strain of Irene being so ill at times and living in the same home, it was understandable that passion could be lost amongst the stress.

But touch itself.

Human contact.

A kiss that went beyond a peck on the cheek.

A hug that was more than a brief encounter as two busy timetables and lives collided?

Surely there should have been more than that?

For Gary there clearly had been – in the form of Corinne.

The sting of rejection and betrayal leaves a deep and nasty wound.

Salve for this was to be found in Sean's arms.

I was aching and a little sore in places from last night but my hunger for more matched his own. It was like being given a massive shot of a youth drug. What woman my age wouldn't want to experience the intoxicating high that sudden infatuation can bring?

In broad daylight and feeling all the more decadent for it, clothes were tossed aside and once more we tumbled to the floor in front of the Christmas tree. Luna heaved a massive sigh and took herself out of the room.

'Daisy you're beautiful so you are,' said Sean as he reached for handfuls of my flesh, the curves of my hips, my bottom and my breasts.

He squeezed, kneaded, nibbled, bit, kissed and caressed every inch, but not delicately as though I was a gourmet platter. Oh no. He feasted upon me as though he was a starving man who had been offered a huge plateful of honest down to earth hotpot. I was being devoured with a greed that was in itself a huge turn-on. The need he was so freely displaying was something I had to return.

It was playful, honest, rough and tumble sex.

It was absolutely glorious, and I had no mind for the carpet burns as the pace began to spiral out of our control and Sean started to slam his hips into mine. As hard as he was thrusting, I could see he was holding back some of his force.

'All of it Sean, I want all of it.' My greed for him was overwhelming at that moment. A tornado could have ripped off the roof of the house and I would not have moved for it.

'All of it?' His eyes darkening as they did with passion, teased me.

I was still shy with him in some ways and could not yet bring myself to utter the raw coarse words that were pounding in my head. I silently begged him, pleaded with him to fuck me. Fuck me hard and fast and furious and don't ever, ever stop fucking me. My eyes were communicating my thoughts and my cheeks burnt with embarrassment. I never thought like this. I never felt like this. I certainly never would speak like this.

But he knew.

Wickedly he let me know.

His lips soft against my ears, he murmured the words I had withheld. 'Daisy darling, so it's fucking you want is it my girl, hard and fast and furious? Never-ending fucking like this?'

His lean well sculpted body began to demonstrate exactly how he could do this. I groaned an indecipherable reply, too dazed in my lust to wonder that he could read me so easily.

'I'll take that as a yes then,' he said in between hard, deep kisses.

My groans were more like whimpers now. Shameless, weak willed, desperate whimpers.

'My pleasure to oblige,' was his answer to my moans.

Oblige me he did.

Twice in fact.

I lost myself in a loud out of control orgasm, only to catch my breath and feel Sean still hammering away inside me. He had stamina; however old he was. I worried for a second about his heart, but his breathing seemed so easy compared to mine. Then I could no longer think, just surrender to the blinding sensations he was creating within me.

'Earth to Daisy,' he teased me a little while later.

I could not move. If I died right there, right at that moment on the carpet with pine needles in my hair, I would die happy.

Then the doorbell rang.

'Shit!' Now I felt like a teenager again, caught out having a sneaky fumble.

Sean, not surprisingly, found this highly amusing and with his lazy grace pulled on his jeans and his sweater and went to the door. 'I'll go and see who it, is shall I?

'Bloody hell Sean give, me a moment.'

He was still laughing as I scrambled into my jeans which had been peeled off in haste and were, of course, inside out. There wasn't time to put my bra on again as I heard Sean opening the front door. I stuffed it under one of the cushions and pulled my sweater over my head, frantically trying to smooth my tangled hair with my hands, just in time for Rose to walk into the room.

'You'll never guess what's bloody happened.'

'What?' I asked as casually as I could.

'Shall I be making a pot of tea?' asked Sean from behind Rose. Then he chortled and ruined any chance I had of trying to maintain my dignity by adding, 'Daisy darling you've gone and put your sweater on back to front so you have, but you know, a reverse v neck might soon be all the rage.'

My stunningly beautiful sister shot her dark eyes from me, to Sean and back again.

'I'll leave you sisters to it while I brew up,' he said and conveniently disappeared.

'What the fuck is going on, Daisy?'

'Well Rose, rather a lot of that since you mention it. Fucking I mean. And he is really jolly good at it Do you want biscuits with your tea or are you dieting again?' I don't know who was more surprised by my reply, her or me. I never, ever used that word. I never fucked. I had sex, I made love. I did not fuck.

Times, it appeared, were changing.

I brushed past her and went to join Sean in the kitchen leaving her to trail open-mouthed behind me.

It appeared that Rose was also after an invitation for Christmas Day.

'But I thought you were going to Spain with Pablo?' I liked Rose's current boyfriend. He was hard-working and seemed able to keep the wild Rose from rambling off. Pablo owned a small but very popular bistro in town. He was also not married which was a definite plus.

'We were. I was. He still is.' Rose answered my questions, but her eyes were following Sean as he bustled about heating up some soup and making sandwiches.

'So why aren't you?' I tucked into my lunch with an appetite that made Sean smile.

Rose frowned at me. 'His wretched grandmother's dying.'

'Oh, that's terrible.'

'Too right. The old hag can't stand me, she's doing it on purpose.'

'Rose, nobody dies on purpose to annoy someone else.'

'She won't actually be dying,' Rose said scathingly. 'It's just to get Pablo to change his mind.'

'About what?' Sometimes Rose's thought processes were hard to follow.

'Proposing to me of course. I know he's building up to it.'

'And his grandmother dying has what to do with this exactly?' I glanced across at Sean whilst Rose examined one of her nails. He returned my gaze with that bland look that told me he found it amusing.

'She won't actually be dying,' said Rose huffily, 'she just wants Pablo to promise her that he won't marry me. She wants him to marry a prissy little Catholic virgin from his home village.'

'And you think it's a good idea to let him go back home to his dying, or maybe not dying, Grandmother by himself?' I said slowly, earning a snort from Sean that betrayed his humour at last.

Rose gave us both a sharp look. 'I don't need to prove I am good enough for him. When have I ever chased after any man?'

Frequently, I felt like saying, and all of them married. It struck me as bizarre that when a decent one came along, she was prepared to gamble with him. Then I reminded myself, who was I to dish out relationship advice? I let her waffle on until she delved into her handbag for the keys to her Mercedes.

'Right, well I can't sit here all afternoon. Some of us have got a business to run.'

'I thought Mondays were your day off?'

She gave me a scathing look. 'Daisy, if you have your own business, you never really get a day off. But then you do get your rewards,' she added dangling her car keys. 'Not like you with your little part-time school job. And even that's gone now, hasn't it? Marigold told me you had got the sack.'

'Ah well, when one door closes there's a far better one waiting to be opened,' said Sean.

Rose stood up from the table and shot him a look. 'Oh? Has she got something in mind already?'

Behind her I shook my head. I didn't want anyone to know about the job offer.

Sean shrugged. 'There's bound to be something special for Daisy. A woman with her talents, personality and looks, sure she'll not be twiddling her thumbs for long.'

Rose turned and looked at me thoughtfully. Talented, with a good personality and looks. That was not how she viewed me, and it showed on her face.

'If you get really stuck, I'm sure you could do some reception work for me at the salon, and there's always plenty of cleaning to do.'

'I'll bear that in mind,' I said as I ushered her to the front door. 'Do say hello to Pablo for me and tell him I hope his grandmother gets better soon.'

'She's not bloody ill,' tutted Rose as she trotted off down the front path. 'Oh, and don't forget, Daisy I hate sprouts so don't bother cooking any of them on Christmas Day.'

'Right, no sprouts,' I muttered and shut the door behind her. 'So that's eight for Christmas Day now including us,' I said as I went back into the kitchen. 'Honestly, Sean it's like somebody is conspiring to gather all my family members around me, just when I really don't want them!'

'Ah but Daisy my darling girl, sometimes it's not a matter of wanting, it's a matter of needing.'

'What, you think I need to have all the people who seem to put me down and use me, and who never really have any time for me when I need help, sat round my table whilst I cook for them? And let's not forget that it's not going to be my table for much longer anyway cos bloody Gary wants me out of the house so that Corinne can get cracking on decorating the nursery!'

Whoosh went the geyser of hurt as it blew up from deep inside. Sean just looked at me calmly.

'And maybe Daisy, you need to really see that for yourself and then you can move on properly.'

I was still rattled. 'And I suppose it would be a good idea if Gary and his bloody pregnant girlfriend turned up too, would it?' I ticked things off on my fingers. 'I mean so far we've had one car accident, an inconvenient brother visiting the family home, and a dying, or maybe not dying grandmother all conspiring to ruin my family's plans so they then feel it's perfectly alright to ruin mine. All I need now is for some catastrophe to fall on Gary and Corinne and I'll end up having to feed them as well!'

Sean grinned. 'We wouldn't want that would we? Now, why don't you go and take Luna out for a walk. You're making her agitated with your fretting.'

He was right.

He was always right.

I bundled myself up in my coat, hat and gloves and set off with Luna. I don't know how many miles we walked that December afternoon. We fell into a brisk pace, her trotting easily, me working up a sweat beneath my coat. The rain began to fall. The sky began to darken. Sean was waiting for me when at last I returned to the house on Park Road, the front door opening as soon as I set foot on the front path.

'There you are now. You see, I told you that would do you good. You can't beat fresh air and the company of a wolf to lift your spirits. Now, I've run a bath for you and there's a glass of wine poured by the side of it. You go and have a good soak and I'll clean up Luna.'

A bath at four o'clock on a Monday with a glass of wine?

Life, I concluded really wasn't all that bad.

'You are an angel,' I said to Sean as I started up the stairs.

'I don't know about that,' he replied with a grin far too sinful to be angelic. 'An angel would not be having in mind what I want to do with you in the bath. I can have a touch of the devil in me at times you know.'

A while later I had to agree with him.

I also had to acknowledge the little devil emerging witin me that had to answer his call when I was with him.

Water went everywhere as Sean as squeezed in with me, turning me around until I was straddled on his lap. He then massaged every inch of me with soapy bubbles, his fingers sliding over my flesh and deep inside me, one hand caressing my bottom at the same time. Another of those wicked laughs as his longer sensitive fingers explored me in a way Gary had never done.

'It's alright you know, you can enjoy your body and how it feels.'

I wasn't so sure anyone could be allowed to feel this good. And how had I ended up here anyway? Soaking wet in a bathtub, a man so ruggedly beautiful lying beneath me, sculpted muscles that made my fingers itch to touch, and an erection throbbing and waiting once more to pleasure me. Only this time it was his hands that so were so skilfully working their magic and making me twist and turn and rub against him in sensuous joy. And his knowing eyes that directed my hands to stroke and caress him.

Oddly more intimate this.

To have his fingers inside me, wherever they could go, and for me to cup him within my grasp and explore the thick, long, heavy length of him. Strangely more intimate considering he had already been inside me. Yet it was and as the bath water emptied around us and I could no longer contain my movements, I felt more exposed than ever beneath that bright and mysterious gaze. When my climax had me quivering, he prolonged it, gently coaxing more rippling shudders of pleasure with careful teasing strokes, so that I rode out another way of ecstasy as he spilt into my hands and a slow lazy smile flickered across his face.

I was all but ready to collapse into bed and fall asleep. But no. Sean had other ideas. Scooping me up and out of the bath, showing no signs of sleepiness at all, he then proceeded to wrap me in a towel. Once dry he repeated his massaging of my body, top to toe and every crevice he could expose and explore. This time with a body oil until I was sleek and silky as a seal.

'I need to sleep,' I murmured, now lying naked on the bed, yet as my eyes were closing, my body was responding once more to his touch.

'Soon Daisy, darling. Soon.'

If I thought I had become more intimate with him in the bath, there was more to follow. His mouth went the way of his hands and he moved me gently around so that I was in a position to do the same with him. All I could focus on was the taste and smell of him as he filled my mouth, yet never too much that I felt he was choking me. Full to the back of my throat and then no more.

Deep, satisfying a hunger I never knew existed within me.

Deep went his tongue.

Deep went the feelings of desire and overwhelming passion.

Out of my head flew the thought that he could be an angel because feeling this good could only be sinful. His laughter filled the room and then once more, I cried out in pleasure.

Chapter Thirteen

'Oh, don't you look festive in that colour! It suits you my dear, so much better than those dark clothes you usually wear, and so suitable. Red Riding Hood with her wolf! Merry Christmas, Daisy. I know I am early, but I thought I could give you a hand with the sprouts.'

'You look lovely too, Violet and Merry Christmas to you too.' I stepped back to let my elderly neighbour into the hallway. She was wearing a plum-coloured velvet dress with a string of pearls around her neck.

Sean came through to greet her and taking both of her hands in his, gently guided her to the centre of the hall where he had hung an extravagant bunch of mistletoe.

'May I be allowed a Christmas kiss from a beautiful lady?'

Violet's blue eyes twinkled behind her silver framed glasses. 'You may indeed.'

Looking resplendent in a pristine white shirt and a brightly patterned waistcoat he placed a respectful kiss on her cheek. Violet blushed and went a trifle teary eyed.

'Goodness, it's been a long time since I had a kiss from a gentleman. Not since my darling Roger, oh and that is so long ago.' She sniffed. 'Dear me, how ridiculous to be maudlin at such a time.'

'Not ridiculous at all,' Sean soothed. 'Far more ridiculous to not feel the need to shed a tear for a lost loved one. Now, never mind helping Daisy with the sprouts, how about a small sherry? Or perhaps a large one?' He soon had her comfortably settled at the pine table in the kitchen.

'Are you quite sure I can't do anything to help?'

To gird myself up for the arrival of my family I had already started on the gin and tonic. I was serenely mellow as I answered her, 'Honestly I'm fine. It's all prepped, just a couple more things to chop.'

'And the turkey?'

'Done.' I took a large mouthful of gin, pleased with having already accomplished this task.

'I tell you how you can help Daisy though, Violet,' said Sean as he deftly removed the sharp knife I was holding. 'Why don't you just sit down with Violet and let me do the rest,' he smiled. 'I know you are wearing a red dress but it would be an awful shame if it got blood-spattered and gin and tonic and sharp knives are maybe not such a good idea.' He steered me into a chair next to Violet and then continued. 'Daisy has a decision to make, perhaps you can persuade her she is doing the right thing?'

'Oh, what's that?'

I told Violet about the opportunity to go and work at the hotel in Scotland.

'You mustn't let your family being here stop you,' Violet agreed with Sean about this.

I thought about this. 'I would miss Abigail.'

'But you look after her a lot in the school holidays don't you, and what is to stop her from spending time with you in Scotland then?'

'I'd miss you,' I said truthfully. Her quiet presence next door, always happy to chat over the garden fence, always there to share a cup of tea and a biscuit. Yes, I would miss Violet.

'Silly! I'll come and stay. See, you haven't got any excuses. Do it Daisy.'

Sean then refilled our already empty glasses. He had also managed in the time we had been talking to turn the table into a thing of beauty with place settings for everyone, glasses polished till they shone, fancy napkins, crackers and candles.

'Ooh you are good at this Sean,' said Violet appreciatively. 'But forgive me for saying and I know I have had a little sherry or two, but haven't you set too many places?'

Before he could reply the doorbell went. I slugged back a mouthful of gin and stood up. 'Let battle commence,' consoling myself that at least I would get to see Abigail.

I did not expect to see my soon to be ex-husband on the doorstep, accompanied by Corinne. I was so sure I was seeing things and blamed it on the gin, that I shut the door immediately, only to slowly open it again hoping that my eyes had deceived me.

'Don't play silly buggers, Daisy, it's fucking freezing out here and it's started to snow.' Gary growled at me and stated the obvious as large feathery snowflakes appeared out of nowhere.

'What are you doing here?' I was still slow to react.

'Our boiler's packed in,' snapped Gary. 'We've no heating, no hot water and no gas to cook with. And Corinne's not very well.'

I turned to look at my nemesis. She was wearing a cashmere wrap in an icy blue colour over a dress in a darker shade. Her face was immaculately made up and I could see no signs of illness whatsoever.

'Er we're freezing here, Daisy,' Gary snapped. 'And it is my house remember.'

Silently Luna had appeared at my side. Her presence bolstered my courage.

'You'd better come in then.' With my hand on Luna's neck, I stepped back into the hallway. 'But would you not have preferred to go to your parents?' I asked Corinne.

Pregnant or not she towered over me and so could look down her nose as she replied, 'They're in the Maldives for the winter and they've got house sitters looking after their home.'

'Course they have,' I nodded thinking of all the reasons leading to me being inundated with surprise guests. But her next comment got my hackles up, never mind Luna's.

'Besides, this is going to be my home soon, baby can experience her first Christmas here even before she is born.' She opened her wrap to reveal her tiny bump and cradled her hands around it. She looked me square in the eyes and I could see a challenge there that despite Luna's presence, was wounding. But not as much as her words.

'She?' I managed to get out. 'You know it's a girl.'

'We had the scan last week. Gary was so excited to see her moving, weren't you?'

'You went to the scan?' I was beginning to sound stupid. I was staring in dismay at my husband, the man part of me still loved, when Sean came to my rescue.

'Ah so it's you two, well would you have believed it, oh and look Daisy it's starting to snow just like I said it would to Abigail. Come on in now the both of you. There's a place set and everything's nearly ready. Just got to wait for the others to arrive.'

I looked sharply at Sean, but he deftly avoided my glance. How had he known to lay two extra places? How could he have predicted the snow? But then I was distracted by his handling of Corinne.

'You come through right away and take the weight off your feet now. Sure, and don't you look all pasty-faced and washed out. Pregnancy can do that to you, and Lord would you look at the boots you're wearing, if those are not a recipe for swollen ankles, I don't know what are? My Ma, God rest her soul, she suffered terribly with swollen ankles so she did when she was carrying me. Ah God love her, the tales I could tell you about childbirth that she told me. Enough to put you off sex for life, but I think that was her intention with me. Not that I would be pregnant of course. Just the fear of getting a girl that way, do you see.' He ushered Corinne into the kitchen.

Gary meanwhile was loitering in the hall looking at me. 'You look different,' he said stiffly.

'I had my hair cut,' I answered, so glad now that I had finally made a trip to my hairdressers after that fateful morning when she had cancelled my appointment. It had been months since I had been and Sandra beamed with approval when I told her I wanted a restyle.

"You've such a dainty face, Daisy," she had said, *lifting my hair up in different ways before she had started cutting. "And your neck and jawline are really good you know."*

My eyes had met hers in the mirror. "For a woman my age, you mean?"

"You're as young as you feel," she had replied. *Then added with a sly wink. "Or as young as the man you feel. I copped an eyeful of your lodger cutting Mrs Windrush's front hedge the other day."*

I had opened my mouth to protest but then we had ended up laughing together. I was glad now, that with my new pixie cut, red dress and makeup, I was looking as good as I could do. Comparisons with Corinne were never going to be easy.

The next couple of hours passed in a chaotic, and rather bizarre manner. Rose had arrived on the heels of Gary and Corinne. My sister, clearly not missing the lovely Pablo one little bit had dressed herself up to the nines in a figure-hugging black lace dress; voluptuous bosom amply on show. I was used to her overt flirting with Gary, something which on reflection he never attempted to stop or play down. I noticed now though, that in Corinne's presence, he reacted very differently to Rose.

'Looks like Corinne has him on a tighter leash than I ever did,' I whispered to Violet as I refilled our glasses, well onto the wine now.

My mother had arrived in a cloud of perfume and an outfit so colourful it was almost painful to the eyes. Her makeup and costume jewellery were fairly jaw-dropping too. Finally, Dad, Samantha and Abigail were seated around the table. It was easy to lose the awkwardness of Dad and Marigold in the same room together, along with the much younger Samantha, with my little sister's bouncing enthusiasm.

'It's snowing! Sean, you said it would snow today and it has!'

And then it began.

Christmas without Gerald and Irene.

Christmas with my lodger and lover. Christmas with my husband and his girlfriend. Christmas with my mother and sister both flirting madly with Sean. Christmas with my dad, my glamourous, clever stepmum and my cute, adorable little sister. Christmas with my kindly neighbour.

Oh yes, and Christmas with a wolf.

Abigail insisted that another chair be squeezed in next to her so that Luna could join in as well just like she had that very first night, in an echo of 'The Tiger Who Came to Tea'.

'Well, isn't this just grand,' said Sean brightly as he deftly began serving up the best Christmas lunch I had ever eaten. 'All here to celebrate Christmas, ah the miracle of Christmas, a toast everyone, to the miracle that is Christmas!'

'No such thing as miracles, and Christmas certainly isn't one,' said Samantha crisply, 'But I must admit this is a good glass of wine and the food looks excellent, so I will raise my glass to that instead.'

I looked across at Sean and he caught my eyes to smile, but only after I saw the cold stare he had given my stepmum, unusual for him. Then I was side-tracked by Marigold's comment.

'Corinne, have you given any thought to how you're going to redecorate the house?'

Thanks, Marigold, for your show of loyalty. Appreciate that.

Corinne smugly replied that the main room to do would be the nursery, naturally it would be pink and then, 'Would you like to see the photos of the scan?'

The only salve to my hurt at this point was that neither Marigold nor

Rose was in the least bit maternal. They were more interested in interior design schemes. Samantha gave the photo a passing glance and continued eating her meal. At least I was saved from gushing baby worship. Dad though displayed as much sensitivity as a rhino as he spoke to Gary.

'So how does it feel to be a father at last then?'

I glugged on my wine, to numb the pain of this blow.

Gary pointedly looked away from me as he replied, 'Oh I can't wait. It's going to be the best thing that's happened to me.'

I felt the nudge of Sean's leg against mine under the table. Luna silently got down from her chair next to Abigail and came to press her nose into my hand. With the touch of my lover and my wolf, I rode the wave of hurt that my unfeeling family had sent my way.

Violet was also on my side. 'In my day it would be considered rude to show such a personal photo at a meal and without the host's permission, but then what do I know?'

Corinne snatched back the photo and muttered something under her breath that was clearly not complimentary towards my neighbour.

The next moment she squealed. 'Ouch! That wretched wolf has just bit my bum!'

I blinked. Luna was no longer by my side, but equally, she was nowhere near Corinne either.

'Don't be silly,' said Abigail as though Corinne was utterly deranged. 'She's been sitting with me the whole time. How could she have done?'

I looked at Luna and then quickly at Sean who gave one of his wicked smiles. 'Abigail's right, Corinne. You are a silly thing now. Why would Luna want to take a bite of your arse, it's all skin and bone? In fact, would you like me to get you a cushion to sit on? Maybe it's the piles that's making you uncomfortable.'

'I don't have piles!' Corinne snapped back at him and glared at Abigail who to my delight gave her the cheekiest of grins.

'It's the stretch marks you need to worry about,' snipped in Samantha from her end of the table. 'Carrying Abigail totally ruined my stomach. Honestly, the pains women go through to have a child!'

'You're still the most beautiful woman here,' said Dad gallantly to his wife. The pair of them failed to see the downturn of Abigail's mouth at her mother's comments.

Marigold snorted into her wine glass. 'I never had a single stretch mark and I still have a fabulous figure. I am always being complimented on it.'

'Abigail, what did you get for Christmas?' Sean cut across this unseasonal conversation and smiled at my sister who was silently chomping on her sprouts, too well-mannered to leave them.

She chirped up at this and began to regale us with a description of everything she had been given.

'That all sounds rather lovely,' said Violet kindly listening to Abigail, whilst the other adults mostly tuned out and started a conversation about holidays for the year ahead. I zoned out on them and listened to my sister instead.

'Did you get everything you wished for?' I asked her and told her that she did not need to eat all her sprouts, she could still have the pudding.

Abigail looked at me a little wistfully. 'Not exactly,' she said with a glance over to her parents.

'That sounds absolutely fabulous,' Corinne was saying to Samantha, who was now looking extremely animated. 'I'd love to do something like that obviously once the baby is born.'

'Yes, but it's not the sort of thing you can do with a baby or child in tow. That's why Abigail's going to stay with Daisy when we go.'

My ears pricked up at this and my head swivelled round. 'Go where and when?'

'On safari in Kenya. Some friends of mine are going, and they have asked if we want to join them. It's going to be fabulous isn't it darling.' She reached across the table and squeezed Dad's hand.

Marigold gave a raucous laugh. 'Daniel on safari, don't be ridiculous. The most adventurous he ever was with me and the girls was a week in Snowdonia. He complained that it was too cold and windy.'

'I hardly think it will be cold and windy in Kenya,' replied Samantha snootily. 'And maybe it was the company that was cold and windy when he was with you.'

Violet and I both thought this rather apt but managed to hide our appreciation by coughing at the same time.

'I must admit Dad, I never thought you would be one for snakes,' said Rose clearly not liking the implied dig that it could have been her company as well that had made Dad so unhappy. 'Then again…' She gave one of her dark and deadly looks at Samantha over the rim of her wine glass.

'As a matter of fact, I have always wanted to go on a safari,' said Dad in an over loud voice, as though he was trying to persuade himself that this was indeed the case.

'I'd love to see giraffes,' whispered Abigail at the end of the table.

'And one day my sweet little Abigail, you shall,' Sean smiled at her benevolently.

'Really I do wish you wouldn't say things like that to her,' Samantha complained. 'You shouldn't fill children's heads with things they may or may not do.'

'But surely children should be allowed to dream?' Violet put in.

Samantha shook her head. 'We don't believe in that sort of thing, do we darling,' she reached for Dad's hand and clasped it tightly. 'Fairy tales and nonsense only lead to being let down in life. We want our daughter to grow up with a practical head on her.'

'Sounds a bloody boring way to bring up a child if you ask me,' said Marigold blithely ignoring the fact that her version of child rearing had been rather free range with as little input from her as possible.

'Nobody was asking you, Marigold,' said Dad stiffly.

'Well,' butted in Sean before things could escalate, 'if you have all had enough turkey, who would like Christmas pudding and brandy butter? Abigail, my angel, perhaps you could be my little helper?'

She jumped up from her seat and I could see from the smile on her face that she was happy to play waitress for Sean. I sent him a look of gratitude, appalled at Samantha's cold-hearted approach to being a mother. If only she realised how lucky she was. When the plates for the main course were cleared and the pudding displayed in the centre of the table so that it could be set on fire, Sean made a pointed remark.

'Well, regardless of other's opinions, I know magic to be real, and I believe in the power of wishes, so Abigail, you may have the honour of the Christmas wish as you blow out the flames. Here, let me hold back your lovely hair so that it doesn't singe. Are you ready? No, don't say it out loud; it won't come true if you do.'

To cover Samantha's rude snort at this, I clapped my hands loudly as did Violet. So did Marigold and Rose but I think that was more to annoy Dad's wife than anything else. As we tucked into the richly moist pudding, there were a few moments of blessed silence.

Then Sean, with that impish note in his voice, said to Abigail, 'So, if we cannot get you to see a giraffe next year, how about a reindeer?'

Her face lit up with pleasure. 'Like Father Christmas'?'

'I told you, he isn't real,' Samantha sounded cross. 'he's just a made-up character, just as unlikely as the nativity story itself, donkeys, guiding stars and a baby in a manger and all that rot.'

I saw Sean's face in profile as he looked across the table at her. I had never actually seen him look angry and it surprised me.

'You should be careful you know. Treading so carelessly over other people's beliefs. The nativity is a story of a miracle.'

I had never heard him speak so coldly either.

Samantha slashed back with a sharp retort. 'I told you before, I don't believe in miracles or a God of any kind for that matter, or angels, fairies and unicorns and I certainly don't want my daughter growing up believing in any of that nonsense, so I will thank you to keep your ludicrous opinions to yourself!'

There was a moment of utter silence and I swear the temperature in the room dipped by a few degrees and not just emotionally either.

I felt chilled to the bone.

Then with a quick laugh, Sean turned to Abigail. 'Well, as it so happens little one, if it's reindeers you would like to see, you will get the chance in April.'

We all looked at him.

'Really?' asked Abigail wide-eyed.

'How exactly?' asked Dad.

Sean gave one of those fabulously nonchalant shrugs. 'Sure, and if you two are beggaring off on Safari and leaving Abigail behind to stay with Daisy, then she will be in Scotland so she will, and I know for a fact there are reindeer in Scotland.'

Now they all turned to look at me.

Suddenly, the tattoo on my back did that thing of feeling as though it was becoming alive, as though there was a wolf inside of me waiting, yearning to be set free. So instead of blustering and dodging the bullet, I took it square on.

'Yes,' I said and then delayed the moment further by finishing off my pudding.

'Daisy what does he mean you will be in Scotland. I thought you were going to come and clean for me at my salon?' Rose looked put out at the thought I wouldn't be her skivvy.

'Actually, I had been going to suggest that Daisy just do a swap with Corinne for her flat, so we don't have the bother of selling it,' Gary sounded a little peeved. 'How can you do that if you are in Scotland? Or are you just going on a holiday there?'

Marigold's turn. 'Of course she is. Daisy wouldn't leave her home town. She's never been one for adventures; takes after her Dad of course for that. I've never been so boring.'

'I don't consider going on safari at all boring,' sniped back Dad. 'And if Daisy feels like a holiday in Scotland, then that will work very nicely for Abigail to go with her.'

I put my spoon carefully back down into my bowl.

'Actually, I'm going to live there. I am going up for New Year with Sean to discuss arrangements for my new job.'

When I told them what it was going to be, they all looked at me as though I was mad, apart from Abigail that is who wriggled with delight.

'Will there be a wood there? Like in Narnia'

'I am pretty sure there will be a wood of some sort,' I said looking at Sean who grinned.

'A very big wood. Big enough for wolves, witches, faeries, goblins and trolls of the very worst kind.'

'Of the very worst kind,' echoed Abigail in a whisper, her eyes round with fascination at his words.

'The very worst.'

Amidst more of Samantha's tutting, Dad and Marigold for once united, voiced their doubts.

'Seriously Daisy,' Dad went first. 'I think you need to go and see your doctor. I agree with Gary. You really are not coping well. First you, well I mean with Sean here, you were lucky. He could have been a mad murderer for all you knew, and now this ridiculous idea.'

'Exactly.' Marigold nodded, 'You're just running away from life, Daisy and no good ever came of that.'

This from someone who had spent her entire adulthood doing precisely that.

A final dig from Rose was added to the mix. 'Not to mention you have no business experience whatsoever. I give it two months Daisy and then you'll be back. But don't worry. I will always find work for you as I said, cleaning in my salon.'

I turned to Sean and in his eyes was a satisfied knowing look as if he had arranged this all along. It was enough to make my head spin. I pushed back my chair and stood up.

'Frankly, what any of you think doesn't matter. Right now, I am going to build a snowman with Abigail. If anyone wants to join me, great, if not there is plenty of cheese, biscuits and mince pies to go at. You all know where everything is, and hey, Corinne as it's soon going to be your house, you can always start on the washing up. Come on Abby.'

'Her name is Abigail,' said Samantha.

'I like Abby,' said my little sister gleefully taking my hand and I did get some pleasure from shooting a look of triumph over my shoulder to my stepmum.

I turned to Sean and in his eyes was a satisfied knowing look as if he had arranged this all along. It was enough to make my head spin. I pushed back my chair and stood up.

"Really, what any of you think doesn't matter. Right now, I am going to build a snowman with Abigail. If anyone wants to join me, great, if not, there is plenty of cheese biscuits and mince pie to go at. You all know where everything is and hey, I ensure as it's soon going to be your house, you can always start on the washing up. Come on, Abby."

"Her name is Abigail," said Samantha.

"I like Abby," said my little sister gleefully raising my hand and I did not some pleasure from shooting a look of triumph over my shoulder to my stepmum.

Chapter Fourteen

Sean had left the table to don coat, scarf and gloves, and so had the valiant Violet.

'Are you sure you won't get too cold?' I asked her as she made to join us.

'My dear girl, this may be the last chance I get to build a snowman. Do you think I am going to pass it up? Don't worry, I've got enough good food and wine inside me to keep me warm.'

I lent Violet a pair of spare boots with some woolly socks to go with them and then we were ready. I had always loved the garden with this house. We lived on a busy road but once you stepped into the garden you could believe you were anywhere. It was long and narrow with a winding path that wove past flower beds, with evenly placed trees that gave it a delightfully hidden and secretive feel. Right at the very end was a summer house, a favourite spot to sit with a good book.

With the fresh fall of snow, it was a winter wonderland. Who could not find the child within on a Christmas Day like this to want to make the most of it? Well clearly my family, but we forgot them as soon as we started to make the first snowman. Naturally with Sean around we didn't just make a snowman. Violet suggested we make a wife and child for him which we did. Meanwhile Sean enchanted Abigail by creating a garden scene of magical snow creatures. There were three of us, four if you counted Luna who proved to be particularly adept at rolling the snow into balls with her nose.

'Look, look,' said my sister a while later as Violet and I were putting the last touches to the snow child, in other words one smaller ball on top of a larger one. 'Come and see what Sean has done.'

She took hold of Violet with one soggy gloved hand and me with the other. 'See, there's a reindeer, and that's a goblin, and that's a troll but Sean says it's okay, it's not one of the very worst sort, and that's a wolf just like Luna, isn't she amazing!'

'Wow!' They were more than amazing. They were so real as to be lifelike.

'You are incredibly talented.' Violet was as stunned as I was. 'You put our snow family to shame.'

'I do not,' he was quick to reply. 'There is nothing more magical than the good old-fashioned snowman, and you and Daisy have made a lovely family there. Mother, Father, and Daughter snow people. Just like you and your Mummy and Daddy,' he added to Abigail.

Abigail looked at the trio of snow figures and it seemed that some of the glow inside her dimmed. She was clearly considering something as a frown wrinkled her rosy cheeked face. Her next actions shocked me. She went to the smallest figure, the child and carefully took off the top ball representing the head. She placed it on the floor and then began kicking at the body of it.

'What are you doing dear?' Violet asked in the gentlest of voices. I was too surprised to speak. I looked at Sean and he had that unreadable, all-knowing look in his eyes.

'They don't really want the child,' she said matter of factly. 'She wasn't supposed to come along.'

'Whatever do you mean, Abigail?' Violet crouched down beside her, at her age no easy task.

'I heard them arguing. Mummy was shouting at Daddy that they had agreed no children and he should have let her get rid of the child.'

'Abigail when was this?' I helped Violet to her feet and took her place next to my sister.

She gave a little shrug. 'Oh, I don't know. When I was smaller. They went on that long holiday soon after. Remember, Daisy I came to stay with you in the summertime.'

I did remember. It was the first of many a holiday that Abigail had been with us. Dad had taken Samantha away on a cruise. He had said at the time that Samantha had needed a break and I had thought it so selfish.

'That's why I have to be so good,' explained Abigail. 'In case Mummy decides to get rid of me.'

I scooped her up into my arms. 'Abby darling that is never going to happen. I promise you. Your Mummy does love you. Sometimes grown-ups are stupid. Really, really stupid in what they say.' I hugged her close to me and looked at Sean over the top of her bobble hatted head.

'How about I go and make us some magic hot chocolate and we have it in the summer house?' Sean's idea of magic hot chocolate meant marshmallows, cream and a chocolate flake in Abigail's and for us adults a hefty dose of whisky. He also brought out mince pies and brandy butter.

'You know, a lady could get used to this sort of treatment,' sighed Violet wistfully as we snuggled together in the summer house, Abigail tucked up between us.

'This is yummy.' My little sister looked content to sit there sipping her hot chocolate.

I felt a pang of sorrow on her behalf. Part of me wanted to go and throttle Samantha. 'Are they all behaving themselves inside?' I asked instead.

Sean grinned. 'There's nothing like a common cause to bind people together.'

'What do you mean?'

'He means,' said Violet with an acerbic edge to her voice, 'that they are probably all discussing you and your idea of moving to Scotland, which Abigail and I think is utterly brilliant, don't we darling?'

Abigail nodded 'I can't wait to come and stay with you Daisy and see the reindeer. Are you going to come too, Violet?'

My neighbour patted Abigail's hand. 'I may well do little one, if that's okay with Daisy.'

I pointed out that I was not guaranteed the job yet, nor was I exactly sure what it would entail. 'I can't make promises just yet, Abigail, other than of course wherever I happen to be, you will be able to stay with me when Mummy and Daddy go on safari.'

She nodded and swung her head around. 'Are you coming too Sean?'

Across the top of my sister's head, my eyes met his. Stupidly, in all the talk and ideas about moving to Scotland, I had not allowed any space in my mind to consider where Sean might fit in all of this.

'I most certainly will come and see the reindeer with you,' he said to Abigail solemnly.

'Cross your heart and hope to die?'

'Cross my heart and hope to die,' he assured her, completing the necessary actions.

Violet then coughed in a not-so-subtle way.

'But I may not be helping Daisy with her work.'

'What do you mean?' I asked him, feeling my stomach plummet at the thought of him not being around, which considering the length of time I had known him was absurd.

'Forgive me my dear,' said Violet quietly. 'I fear I may have inadvertently put a spoke in the wheels of your romance.'

Sean shook his head. 'Not at all Violet.' He looked at me in that mesmerising way of his that I knew that whatever he was about to say I would completely understand and agree with. 'You see the thing is Daisy, I need to be helping people. Just like you helped me by bringing me off the streets. It's good to pay it back, or forward if you like. Anyhow, Violet's nephew is involved in a project building a shelter for homeless people in Manchester and I feel I need to be involved in it.'

Of course, he did. How could he not? And how could I be so selfish as to consider stopping him? After all, this thing between us, it wasn't love.

Was it?

I swallowed the lump of uncertainty with a large last mouthful of my hot chocolate and gave him what I hoped was a breezily reassuring smile.

'Of course, you must.'

He leant over and kissed me gently on my cheek.

'Sean, do you love, Daisy?' Asked Abigail chirpily.

'I do, Abigail.' He said this looking squarely into my eyes. I felt such an inner glow of warmth and joy that must have been visibly lit up from within. 'And love you know is like a diamond. It has many different faces. It sparkles like a star, and it can never be dimmed.'

I thought of Gary. 'Are you sure about that?'

'Pure love, he means,' said Violet sniffing suspiciously and dabbing at her eyes. 'Pure, unselfish love. No, that can never be dimmed, not even with the passing of years. Deary me Sean, you're turning me into a very silly sentimental old lady.'

I considered her long marriage and knew that whatever I had had with Gary had not been remotely equal. How could it? Within a couple of weeks of discovering his infidelity, I had hopped into bed with Sean. Violet had spent the last ten years resolutely alone, and cheerful with it.

'Come on, Violet,' I said to her, 'let's go and brave the others, you must be getting frozen out here, even with the hot drinks and mince pies.'

'I don't have to go in, yet do I?' Abigail pleaded, tucking her small hand into Sean's. 'Sean promised me that we could watch the snow figures dance.'

Violet and I exchanged a glance and then I nodded at her. 'As long as you aren't cold.'

We walked back up the length of the garden carrying the tray with the empty mugs and plates.

'I do hope you aren't cross with me, Daisy. I didn't ask Sean to get involved with Timothy's project, he offered.'

'Honestly Violet, I really don't have any claims on him.' I said this with a wistful realisation that it was true.

'Do you love him?'

'I really don't know. It's all sort of strange, Violet.' I paused with her in the magical snowy wonderland of my garden complete with sculpted figures. 'He just sort of came into my life and changed it so wonderfully. I was... well I really wasn't coping truth be told. It was like I was lost in this very dark scary place and since he came home with me, everything seems brighter.' I laughed. 'It's like he's some sort of fairy godmother. It wouldn't surprise me at all if somehow he did make those snow figures come alive for Abigail.'

Violet laughed. 'Now that really would be magic.'

'I tell you what would be magic,' I replied as we continued up the path and towards the kitchen door, 'if my family have cleared away the table and washed up.'

They hadn't. That would have been a miracle too far. Not in the least perturbed by this, Violet and I set to. Coming from the other room there was the hum of a lively conversation. But at least it appeared to be punctuated with bouts of laughter.

Violet commented on this. 'They all seem happy in there,' she said with a flick of the tea towel and a nod of her head. 'Doesn't it irk you that your family have so readily accepted that Gary wants you to move out of your own home, even if you do have plans otherwise?'

'Again Violet, I have Sean to thank for this. Without him, I really would be stuck in a slump, and I certainly would not have considered the job in Scotland without his prompting.' I looked at her. 'That was such a lucky coincidence the letter coming here by mistake.'

'Hmm,' was Violet's thoughtful reply but when I pressed her, she could only shake her head and mutter that she was not a great believer in coincidences.

'What do you mean?'

Her gaze went out of the window down to the garden where Sean and Abigail were still playing in the snow.

'I mean that sometimes Daisy, people come along in your life that you were absolutely just meant to meet at that moment. Even if they don't stay for long, they sweep you into sudden changes. Like you said before, a bit like a fairy godmother.'

I laughed. 'Except that in real life things like that just don't happen.' Even as I was saying this, I could feel the tattoo of Luna tingling on my back in response, taunting my words. 'Come on, I suppose we had better go and join the others. See if they want coffee or something?'

'Let me do that,' offered Violet, at home in my kitchen as I was in hers. 'Least I can do.'

I went through to the sitting room where the tree twinkled and shone in all its festive glory. My family looked remarkably cosy together and it hit me briefly that this time next year I would not be standing there asking anyone if they wanted coffee. Corinne would be doing the honours, or maybe she would get Gary to do that as she nursed her daughter?

I waited for the bucket of cold water to drown me in sadness, but it didn't come. It felt as though I was watching from afar. Looking past them all towards the French windows that overlooked the garden, I wondered again if this was more of Sean's effect on me.

Or simply large quantities of gin and wine?

Either way, detachment was better than emotional pain.

A few minutes later, Violet and I had joined them with coffee and mints being passed around. Once more back in the spotlight, it was Rose who decided to get out the wooden spoon and start to stir.

'Daisy dearest, is lover boy going to hot foot it to Scotland with you?' This was said with a sly glance over to Gary who choked on his coffee. 'What? You didn't realise Daisy and Sean were at it?'

'I suppose that was your way of getting your own back, was it?' Corinne stunned me by leaping in with her retort. 'You do realise, you won't get Gary back by making him jealous.'

To be fair, my husband did look a little uncomfortable with all this.

Especially when Marigold threw in her bit. 'Well sauce for the goose and all that. And to give Daisy some credit for once, I certainly wouldn't kick Sean out of bed.'

To which Dad muttered something along the lines of Marigold never kicking anyone out of bed, more like her dragging any odd sod into it. Knowing how this was all going to deteriorate and rapidly, I hastily stepped in.

'No, as a matter of fact he is not. He will be coming to Scotland with me for the New Year but after that he has his own plans.'

'You mean he's got bored of you already,' sniped Rose. 'Well, if he wants some other company whilst Pablo is away?'

'Don't be ridiculous!' Violet clanked her cup against her saucer angrily. 'Why on Earth would he be tiring of Daisy?' At this she gave Gary a wonderfully arch look. 'But if you must know, not that it is anyone else's business, Sean is going to help my nephew on a project in the new year.' She began to explain about the homeless shelter when Abigail burst into the room.

'They danced, they danced, they really did!'

'What do you mean, Abigail?' Dad asked her, at the same time Samantha told her to stop jumping around because she was scattering snowflakes all over her.

I went to take Abigail's coat from her shoulders as she continued to hop about in excitement.

'The snow figures. He made them dance!'

'How wonderful!' Violet clapped her hands in delight.

Samantha tutted. 'Abigail what have I told you about telling lies?'

'I'm not lying!' Abigail looked close to tears. 'He made them dance! He can do magic.'

Just then the magician himself entered the room.

'Now see what you have done?' Samantha scowled at him.

Sean shrugged carelessly. 'I've made a little girl happy, so I have.'

Abigail turned away from her mother to look at me. 'You believe me don't you, Daisy?'

Did I believe that Sean could make snow figures dance? I thought of all the odd things that had happened since that day at the station. Yes. Anything was possible with him.

'Yes. I do Abigail.'

'Your sister is as mad as a box of frogs,' said Marigold with a little laugh, but then at least she did say gently to Abigail, 'But if you think they danced, then that is all that matters.'

'Why don't we go and see if Luna wants feeding?' Violet got up and took hold of Abigail's hand.

I could hear my sister muttering intently to Violet that she was not telling lies. The snow figures had danced. The focus then in the room was on Sean and it was Gary who began to question him.

'When exactly are you going to start work on this building site?'

Sean was delightfully vague, deflecting the interrogation that came from not just Gary but Dad as well. It seemed that both men wanted to get a clear picture of how soon this vagrant person would be out of my life. When Violet came back into the room with Abigail and Luna, she clarified matters in a way that astonished us all.

'The actual building work won't start until much later on,' she explained. 'They have only just managed to get the funding cleared.'

A bubble of happiness grew inside me. Maybe Sean would be around a little longer?

Gary fairly snarled at Sean 'I presume you can get work on another building site as a labourer until then and stop scrounging off my wife. Ex-wife' he added following a sharp nudge from Corinne.

'Why ever would he want to do that?' Violet asked Gary in amazement. 'I know Sean is not afraid of hard work, but why would he want to waste his talents?'

At which there was a shared scoffing from Dad and Gary and a muttered comment from Rose that I seemed happy to enjoy his talents. Sean sat there smiling blandly and again it was Violet who clearly losing patience with my family, blurted out the truth.

'Sean has very kindly volunteered to draw up the plans for Timothy's project for free.'

Dad and Gary looked at each other.

'Draw up the plans?' Dad queried as we all turned then to look at Sean.

'Well hasn't he said?' Violet looked at him. 'Sean really. Why be so modest?' Then she addressed the room with a smile on her face. 'Sean is the architect.'

I think if it had been in her to add 'Duh!' at the end of that sentence she would.

'You're an architect?' Gary spluttered and inwardly I was laughing. 'I don't believe it. Who have you worked for?'

Sean replied with a grin. 'Well, you could say I have worked for the greatest architect there has ever been.' And after that, he refused to discuss it.

she would.

"You're an architect, Gary splintered and inwards. I was laughing. I don't believe it. Who have you worked for?"

Sean replied with a grin. "Well, you could say, 'I have worked for the greatest architect there has ever been.'" And after that, he refused to discuss it.

Chapter Fifteen

Soon after Sean's announcement, Gary declared that he and Corinne were leaving. I had expected them to have gone long since, but I was forgetting Gary's love of whisky. I was cross when I saw that he and Dad had nearly finished the bottle of malt that had been a leaving gift from the school.

'Don't forget, Daisy we want everything completed as soon as possible,' he said, swaying slightly as he stood up.

'There is so much to do before baby comes,' said Corinne. She sent a disparaging look around the cosy room that I loved and would never have changed for the world.

I felt the heat of my tattoo prickle on my back. 'If it's all so shabby for you, why on Earth do you want to live here?'

Gary scowled at me, 'My bloody house isn't it.'

I had forgotten how bullish alcohol could make him, especially whisky. For once I bit back. 'Only if I sign the bloody papers.'

'You see,' Gary said to all assembled, 'this is why I left her. Argumentative is putting it mildly. You always have to have your own way, don't you?'

I stared at him open mouthed. The unfairness of the retort left me speechless.

'She was like that as a child,' said Marigold, 'always me, me, me. So needy.'

I looked at my mother in astonishment, then from her to my dad. But as he had shared half the whisky on top of a large amount of wine at the meal, he was in no state to comment on anything.

'We really must be off as well now, hey Samantha, time to get Abigail to bed.'

'I suppose so.' She elegantly uncoiled herself from her chair and rooted in her bag for her car keys. 'Don't forget what I said about Easter, Daisy, you have to have Abigail.'

Then Dad dropped a clanger as he was prone to do when drunk and suddenly the reason for Gary wanting to hurry with the signing of papers, became so much clearer.

'Let me know if you have any problems with the planning application,' he said to Gary, clapping him on the shoulder. 'I have friends in that department if you know what I mean.'

'Planning application?' I looked in confusion from him to my husband. And then to Corinne who was now shooting a look angrily at Dad.

'It's nothing to do with you,' she snapped, tugging at Gary's sleeve. 'Come on, we need to go.'

Gary, blurry with drink nodded in agreement with her. But he couldn't keep his mouth shut. 'That's right Daisy, nothing to do with you. If you have your way, nothing would ever change, Dad was like that too. I told him of my plans and he pooh-poohed the idea. Shows how much he knew. Silly old sod. Sat on a fortune all these years and he never knew it.'

'Gary come on.' Corinne tugged some more and managed to hustle him towards the door.

'What the hell do you mean, Gary?' I was angry at his dismissal of Gerald who I had adored and suspicious now that I was being played for a fool in more ways than the obvious.

Just to meddle, because that was what she loved to do, Rose chose to join in. 'Yes. Come on you two, what's the secret? You know you can tell me, Gary, you know how I can keep a secret.' Rose had also had plenty to drink and there was a sly undertone to her comment that had both mine and Corinne's heads swivelling towards her.

Then it was Marigold's turn to shine. 'You're selling the plot, aren't you?'

'What plot?'

'You snake in the grass!' Violet exploded. 'How could you? Gerald would be turning in his grave.'

'Well, Gerald isn't here. We are, and I am going to have the best for my baby, so that's that. I don't know why you are so bothered anyway,' Corinne said to my elderly neighbour. 'Chances are you'll be in a home soon, or dead,' she added in a none too quiet undertone.

I looked at Violet who was quivering with what appeared to be more rage than indignity. 'They want to build on the land at the back of these houses,' she explained.

'What a dreadful shame,' I said, thinking of the patch of land that had always been used for allotments. 'But what has that got to do with Gary and this house?'

'It's the access required,' said Marigold knowingly. 'I saw the letter one day when I had called round and you were upstairs with Gerald.'

'You opened my mail?' I stared at her in disbelief.

'Not yours silly, it was addressed to Gary, but I recognised the stamp on the envelope.'

'You've no right to do that!' Corinne snapped at her, but Marigold never gave a damn what she did or what anyone thought of her.

She merely shrugged and replied, 'Always good to know what's going on around you.'

'And what exactly is?' I was on the verge of exploding myself by now.

Dad finished the explanation. 'Simple Daisy. This house is at the end of the road. It has the largest back garden. The builders need more space to create their access road. Without it, planning permission will be denied.'

Now it all made sense. To add to the betrayal of his infidelity, Gary was also trying to con me out of what was no doubt a large sum of money by getting me to sign the house over to him before he sold the necessary bit of garden to the property developers.

It was all too much.

'Just go!' I ordered them, quickly adding to Violet that she was welcome to stay.

Abigail hugged me and then turned to Sean. 'Thank you for making the snow figures dance, Sean. I love you.'

'I love you too my sweet little Abigail,' he replied much to her mother's snort of disgust.

Rose was the last of them to go. She was dithering in the hallway, having taken her shoes off somewhere and was now struggling to find them.

'I won't be long,' she called to Marigold who had the local taxi service on speed dial and was currently standing in our driveway calling a cab.

Finally, my sister located her shoes and managed to get them on the right feet. 'Very entertaining day, Daisy,' she said leaning towards me to press a glossy kiss on my cheek. Sean deftly moved to avoid the same gesture which would no doubt have turned into a smacker on the lips. 'Naughty,' she tapped him with a long-nailed hand on his arm. 'You should share. Sister's always share everything, don't they Daisy?'

'What?' I was tired now and just wanted some peace.

But Rose was about to show her thorns. 'Sisters should share. And I don't see why Sean should be any different to the rest, even if he does seem a little reluctant.' She laughed and spoiled the effect with a hiccup.

'Different to the rest how, Rose?' I had to ask but I think by then I knew.

'Your boyfriends at school of course. And Gary! Oops, have I let it slip, silly me. Corinne wasn't the first you know. Not by a long way. She's just the one who managed to snare him with a baby.'

'Goodnight Rose,' Sean actually pushed her through the doorway and shut it behind her. We both heard a loud exclamation as she clearly fell into the snow.

Then he looked at me. 'Well Daisy, that was a success don't you think?'

'A success?'

'Indeed. Now you cannot possibly have any doubts about leaving your family behind.'

Had that been his plan, I wondered? I opened my mouth to ask but the words never came out as Sean trapped my lips beneath his and began kissing the hurt away. Which I have to say he was remarkably good at. Later, with the moonlight filtering through the gap in the bedroom curtains, I asked him another question.

'What happened, Sean?' I was lying with my head cradled onto his chest, sleepy and slumberous after our lovemaking but with my head spinning round to wonder. Who indeed was my lover?

'What happened when?'

I paused not quite sure how to phrase the next bit. As ever he saved me the trouble.

'Ah. How did an architect end up on the streets?'

I pushed myself up on my elbow so I could look him in the face. I felt suddenly ashamed of my probing. Whatever had happened could not have been pleasant. I mean who chooses to live rough? No one.

'I'm sorry. It's no business of mine. I was just being curious. Nosy.' I sighed heavily. 'It's the effect of having spent a day with my family. They bring out the worst in me.'

He snorted then. 'They would do that to anybody. But it's a fair enough question, Daisy my darling girl and I am surprised you have not asked me before.'

I considered this. 'It wasn't that it didn't cross my mind, or that I didn't care. I suppose it just didn't matter in the respect that, to me, you are Sean who saved me from... getting killed by the train.'

I shifted slightly and felt the warmth of his naked body next to mine and a shivering echo of the pleasure he had just given me rippled through me.

I added, 'You are the Sean who is now my lover and who has cooked the best Christmas dinner ever. Not to mention making a garden full of snow creatures for my little sister!'

'Exactly. That's who I am.' He shrugged and pulled me up on top of him. 'Does anything else really matter?'

I could feel him stirring to life once more beneath me and in an instant any questions melted from my mind as easily as the snow figures would melt when the sun came up.

'No,' I whispered as I bent my head for his kisses. Nothing mattered at all other than this moment.

I kissed him back passionately. He answered with a throaty chuckle and a firm grip on my hips, moving me slightly so that I could allow him entry once more. Even then, with the sensation of him filling me, I still could doubt that this was what I was feeling.

'What?' he murmured as we began to move so perfectly in time with each other. The first time this night had been quick, hard and fast, an outlet for my anger with Gary and the family, but now without sharing a word, speaking in that invisible language that lovers have, he knew that I needed to savour each moment of this.

'I can't believe I can feel so good,' I whispered.

A tear surprised me by making its way silently down my cheek. It rolled off and landed on his. Being with him like this brought joy to my soul. I hadn't recognised how depleted in this emotion my heart had been. In the beginning, I had been overwhelmed by a lust that had hit me sideways. But in such a short space of time, Sean had managed to craft those feelings into something else entirely.

He rolled me over in a swift sure movement, as graceful in bed as he was out of it, remaining deep inside me. When he had me on my back, he cradled himself over me on his elbows so he could support his weight and look me deep in the eyes.

'Believe it, Daisy. You do feel so good.' He slowly withdrew from me nearly all the way before thoroughly driving back deep inside. 'You feel good here,' he said just as he could penetrate me no further and had me gasping in delighted shock. He closed his mouth over mine, lightly teasing at first then again deeper, seeking further pleasure with his tongue. 'You feel good here,' he repeated just as I thought I was going to faint from being kissed so madly.

My response now was to groan. As he continued to move his hips, he bent to lavish attention on my breasts. I was soon quivering beneath him and clutching my fingers through his hair as his mouth moved from one breast to another.

'Oh yes Daisy, you feel good here, can you not believe it my darling girl?' He raised his head to look at me and in the dim light I could just about make out the sparkle in his eyes.

'I think so,' I managed to respond and earned myself a rumble of laughter from him. Another thing I loved about him. We laughed as we made love. It was fun. Then I froze slightly, and he sensed it.

'Tell me,' he said, ever so gently.

I shook my head, my hair now mussed and messy. 'It's nothing.' My voice was breathy and impatient at the sudden stillness of his body entwined with mine.

I saw the devilment then in his eyes. 'Tell me,' he insisted now and slowly began to withdraw.

'No!' I squealed in the most undignified of ways. 'I mean, no Sean it was nothing, don't stop, please, don't stop what you were doing.'

He was ever the imp though and whereas my body was a wriggling mass on the brink of exploding with passion, my mind damn near numb with it, Sean seemed able to control himself perfectly.

'No more sex, Daisy, until you tell me,' he said with a laugh in his voice.

And that was the thing.

This was sex.

But I had fallen in love with him.

Hadn't I just said it to myself. The fact that we could laugh together in bed was another thing I loved about him.

'Ah,' he said reading the confusion in my face. Slowly now, gently he moved back within me and lay so close to me it was as though we were one body, his chest pressed against mine. My heart was pounding as it always did when we were in bed together, yet he remained so still and calm.

I couldn't stop the breathy little gasps turning into soft sobs as he began to move once more, this time he held me to him, rocking me gently as I cried. And when those cries became whimpers of passion growing to joy and finally breaking over the edge into ecstasy, I clung to him as tightly as a drowning woman to a rope thrown from the shore.

When the last tiny tremors left my body and his, and stillness fell upon us, I hardly dared to breathe. If I breathed, I would have to move and if I moved, I would have to acknowledge that I was now clear from the passion that had so brilliantly blinded me. And if that was the case then I would have to now hear what 'Ah,' meant. Which I suddenly decided I now was not really in a hurry to listen to at all.

'You see the thing is, Daisy,' he began as he carefully, pulled out of me and rolled to his side, still cradling me in his arms as he did so.

'You're married aren't you.'

He would be I thought. I still had no clue as to his age, sometimes I thought he was younger than me, maybe late thirties, early forties, and sometimes older, fifties, or sixties even, there was such wisdom in his eyes, his face was both lined and boyish at the same time.

'I am not!' he punched me lightly on my arm. 'And what kind of a man do you think I am, Daisy darling? Wouldn't my dear old Ma come down from her saintly perch and knock me round the head if I were, so she would.'

I had to laugh. From what he had told me of his beloved mother I could picture this. 'I don't know anything about you, Sean,' I said in a quiet voice.

'What do you need to know, Daisy, other than I am here with you, right now and that I love you and will always love you?' He had turned slightly so that he could look me in the eyes. I saw a truth so pure reflected in his gaze; eyes the brilliant blue of the sky on a perfect summer's day.

Dazzling.

The lump of ice that had been frozen around my heart melted a little. I dared to voice my reply, the thought that had flown through my mind a little earlier.

'I love you too, Sean.' I did not think it possible that those words would fall from my lips so soon after the cutting death of Gary's double betrayal.

'I know you do, Daisy darling,' he moved closer and dropped the lightest of kisses on my brow, a sweeping touch of a feather no more than that but it burnt through to my soul with its intensity. It tingled through every cell in my body, and I would not have been surprised if anyone had told me that I was glowing with light.

I felt as though I was.

But such moments cannot last forever, and I knew that as it passed there was the truth of reality to deal with now. Fear no longer twisted inside me though. I was calm and I could serenely say to him.

'But we don't have a future together do we, is that what you are trying to tell me?'

A long and resounding sigh. 'Not in the way you would see it, Daisy.' He cupped my face in one hand 'I am a wandering spirit. A traveller. I cannot stay in the same place for a long time.'

'Cannot?' I queried boldly now, 'or don't want too?'

'Cannot,' he replied gently with a wistful smile on his face. 'We all have our roads to travel, Daisy. Some are more defined than others, that is all. My road is to wander and to watch.'

'Watch?' Curious now.

He nodded. 'Yes Daisy. I am a Watcher. I see life, I see people. I like to flit in and out of it, but I cannot stay in the same place for too long. I am simply not made that way. And sure, would it not be fucking boring if we were all made the same?' A gentle poke accompanied the warmth of his smile.

It was impossible not to smile back at him. Equally, I could feel no sting of hurt at what he was saying. How could I? He had never said anything to give me the impression he was looking for a relationship, if indeed that was where my thoughts had been heading.

'You're right. It would be boring.' My husband's face was suddenly before me, and I felt a stab of disloyalty at the connotation this produced. Then I giggled. His face, and that of the others when Violet had told them all so imperiously that Sean was an architect.

Which of course brought me full circle.

This time I tried to skirt around the subject with a little more tact. 'Do you enjoy doing what you do, I mean when you did it? Being an architect.'

'Oh yes, it's a grand job so it is.' He grinned wickedly at me. 'You can make a lot of money doing it if you are so inclined.'

'Which you are not?'

He shrugged. 'Money is good. But it does not provide all the answers in life, Daisy.'

I realised that I was never going to be able to pin him down to anything more specific. I may as well try and catch hold of a moonbeam, or a rainbow! And then I smiled to myself. He was just as bright, and magical as both of those things, not that I would tell him of course. No need to pander to his ego.

On a practical note, I asked instead, 'Will you keep in touch with me, Sean when I move to Scotland? If I move to Scotland that is. For all we know I might get to this place and meet with Catriona Munro and hate everything about it. Or she might hate me for that matter!'

'As if anyone could possibly hate you Daisy. And yes of course I will keep in touch with you. But please don't ask me to write letters or anything,' he said with a mocking smile. 'A letter writer I am not.'

'But you will at least have a phone won't you by then. I mean if you are working for someone, they are going to need to get hold of you, and maybe an email address?'

He visibly cringed. 'I might concede to a phone, but only for you Daisy. Only for you. Now hush my darling girl and get some sleep. It's been a long and busy day.'

It certainly had.

Christmas Day with a difference I thought as I nestled deeper beneath the duvet, content to lie next to Sean, enjoying his warmth, his friendship, his love, however light and casual it might be, for as long as I could. As I drifted off to sleep, I had fleeting images of the past year slip before my eyes, but they no longer held quite as much pain.

Chapter Sixteen

'Daisy we are going to Scotland, not the North Pole,' Sean's voice was full of amusement as I clattered my way down the stairs with two well stuffed holdalls behind me.

I had given him an old rucksack of Gerald's which he insisted was enough for his belongings. He had more than he used to but even so, his was a light load to carry. I reached the bottom step with a grunt of relief.

'And I suppose you would know the difference, wouldn't you? Between Scotland and the North Pole.'

I looked at him archly. Since the revelation on Christmas Day that he was a qualified architect, followed by announcing on Boxing Day that he was doing a stint at the children's ward at the local hospital as a magician, I would not put it past him to have explored the North Pole at all.

'Oh yes,' he said solemnly. 'They don't hunt Haggis for sport in the North Pole like they do in Scotland.'

I wished I had something at hand to throw at him. He was such a tease at times. But he made me laugh and each time he did I felt a little tear in what had been my heart, mending.

'I am pretty sure that Haggis is not an animal.'

'Sure it is, of the tartan furry variety.'

'Sean,' I said to him, 'fuck off,' and then I planted a smacking kiss on his lips, feeling the quivering of his laughter turn into something a little different. When I let him go there was a deep twinkling in his blue eyes and a hint of satisfaction in his voice.

''Tis grand to see you like this, so it is. I much prefer defiant Daisy.'

'Defiant?'

'Sure. And are you not?'

I considered this.

Since the revelations of Christmas Day, my attitude towards Gary and the rest of my family had certainly changed. I had told Rose to sod off the day after Boxing Day, when she rang up to say her receptionist had let her down at the salon and could I go in and help. Marigold had turned up on my doorstep wanting a room for the night when the gas heaters in her canal boat packed up on her. I suggested she go and cosy up with Gary and Corinne.

When Samantha asked me to look after Abigail so she could go shopping in the sales I said yes with a smile on my face. I delighted my little sister by taking her to the cinema to see a film I knew my stepmum disapproved of. I filled her up on popcorn, ice cream and fizzy drinks so she was as high as a kite upon her mother's return.

Dad was the only one who was not shown the new face of Daisy the Defiant, but perhaps that was because he showed me a new face himself. Clutching a bottle of Laphroaig, he sheepishly asked if he could have a little chat with me. This was the day after Boxing Day. I had received a vitriolic text from Samantha as Abigail had bounced off the walls with giddiness following our trip to the cinema.

However, it turned out that my little sister, in her sugar fuelled explosion had rocked Dad with the sort of brutal truths that only a child can give. We had shared a glass of the whisky in the back sitting room as I took the decorations down from the tree in preparation for my trip to Scotland, and he had told me what Abigail had said.

It would appear that I had quite a champion in Abigail. She had told her parents in no uncertain terms that she thought I was the nicest member of the family and the rest of them were all simply quite horrid. She had added that she also thought Gary was a stinking nasty twit for hurting me and making me sell my home and that Corinne was also a stinking nasty stick insect and that if Dad and Samantha were on their side then they must be stinking and nasty too!

Quite a few more holes in my heart mended there and then when I heard this. Bless my little sister. It was new territory also for Dad as he shamefacedly offered an apology for how he had treated me. There was a huge amount of ground to cover, years of hurt and indifference that had scarred me as a teenager and young woman, but sharing the whisky was a start.

And wouldn't you know it, but Sean had burst in at that point, having just done a volunteer shift at the charity shop where we had taken Gerald's things, with a silver Scottish quaich. He had insisted we pour some of the whisky into it and we all sipped from the same cup.

'There,' he had said with that twinkle in his eye. 'And things begin to mend, so they do.'

For the first time in my life, Dad had told me he was proud of me. Again, it had been something Abigail had said. She had shouted at Dad and Samantha that she couldn't wait to stay with me in my new home in Scotland and that she thought I was really brave, having a proper adventure going to live somewhere new, not just a silly stupid safari.

So here I was now, ready to leave. 'Right, let's go.' I smiled as I caught sight of myself in the mirror.

Red Riding Hood and her wolf indeed.

'It suits you, so it does,' said Sean with an admiring look at me in my new red coat.

'Well, you bought it for me.' Or rather he had traded some hours at the shop with Cynthia who had a crush on him. I loved the bright red duffle coat with its wooden toggles and deep cosy pockets.

'Red suits you,' he said. You should always wear red, Daisy.'

'I am learning you know,' and I pouted my lips at him which were coated in a bright red I would never have dared wear previously.

All togged up we got in my car and began the drive further north. It was the day before New Year's Eve and there was a fair bit of traffic on the roads heading up the M6 towards the Lake District. But the motorway got quieter once we had passed the turnoff for Windermere and then there was even less traffic after Penrith.

Now I was driving through countryside I had not visited before, and enjoyed that lovely sense of discovery when seeing new vistas for the first time. We stopped for a quick hot chocolate at Gretna and then Sean offered to drive so that I could take in more of the scenery. Miles and miles of rolling hills and then the plains of Stirling where the castle stood proudly above the landscape and the Wallace Monument was clearly visible.

Further north still until we crossed the fault line that took us into the highland region. Heavy snow was falling, and we were driving through a winter wonderland. I found myself singing a song I remembered from years ago.

'It is a big country,' agreed Sean joining in and we finished the refrain together which ended with the words, stay alive. 'Oh yes, Daisy, stay alive my darling girl for there is much to live for.' He took my hand then across the gear stick and gave it a squeeze.

I was instantly cast back to the day when he had saved me from the train. We had never talked about that since, but looking at him, he knew the truth no matter what had been said at the time.

'Stay alive, Daisy darling,' he said again and raised my hand to his lips to kiss.

Then, in true Sean fashion, he changed the subject entirely and had me laughing as I listened to his rambling tale. A few hours later, we approached the mountain resort of Kinlaggan. Sean asked if I wanted to stop and have a coffee and refresh myself before reaching our destination. But the afternoon light was already fading fast, pink and gold shimmering on the snowy white caps of the mountains.

'No let's get there. I'd hate to be arriving in the dark and from the instructions Catriona has given me it can be a little difficult to find, even allowing for sat nav.'

'Don't worry,' he said, 'I never get lost. I have an inbuilt tracking system.'

I laughed. 'I am sure you do. Even so, I would like to get my first glimpse of it in the daylight if I can.'

'That I understand,' he said, and we turned off the main road, ignoring the way into Kinlaggan itself.

I let myself enjoy the stunning scenery and tried to quell the sudden bout of nerves. What if this place was horrible? What if I didn't like Catriona or she didn't like me? And for the thousandth time, what the heck was I doing here anyway?

'Oh no you don't,' said Sean into my silence.

'Don't what.'

'You have that look on your face. Daisy the Doubter. No doubts Daisy. Believe in yourself.'

I smiled at him and then as we turned a final corner, let out an exclamation. 'Oh wow!'

We had arrived at Wolf Lodge.

Or maybe Narnia.

We had been driving for some time through a densely forested landscape, mountain peaks visible in the distance through the trees, and here and there was the silvery light of a river, winding its way from mountain to sea. Hidden in the middle of this forest, with majestic Caledonian pine trees, natural and wild, was a turreted grey stone building that belonged in a children's fairy story.

'I think it was the French influence at the time,' Sean said in reply to my comment. 'There were strong links between the two countries and once the landowners no longer needed to build fortified castles to withstand attacks from neighbouring clans, they could indulge their whimsical side.'

'It's really pretty,' I said getting out of the car and catching my breath at the chill of the air.

Stupidly, although everywhere was covered with snow, I had not expected quite the difference in temperature. I reached for my red coat. Sean didn't seem bothered by the cold, used to life on the streets. He didn't seem to be cramped from all the driving either, getting out of the car looking as fresh as the flower I am named after, whilst I had to stretch a little and ease the numbness from my bottom.

'Well then, shall we see if there is anyone at home? It looks pretty quiet.'

There was a gravelled area in front of the lodge, with a sign that indicated parking for hotel guests, and another pointing to a path that led towards the rear of the property which said 'Chalets.' The gentle evening light cast a rosy golden hue over the rooftops and caught silvery glints of crystals in the snow that hung heavily upon the dark green boughs of the surrounding trees. The air was intoxicating with its crispness and the scent of fresh pine.

'Yes, come on. Should I leave Luna in the car at first?'

Sean gave a nonchalant shrug. 'Didn't your host say she loved dogs, and wolves, and sure, we are at Wolf Lodge after all. Luna knows how to behave anyway.'

'True,' I considered this as Sean opened the car and out she jumped. I had to rush to catch up with her as she bounded up the set of stone steps that led into the Lodge.

'Jesus bloody Christ woman, why don't you watch where the fuck you're going!'

This exclamation came from the brick wall that I collided into in my haste.

'I am so sorry.'

My years of being polite were too deeply ingrained to not react at the way in which I been spoken to. I stepped back to let the towering hulk of a man with his dark angry face and glaring eyes push past me. As he did so I caught a strong whiff of whisky. A bit early I thought to be drunk, and rather alarming as he strode past Sean to get behind the wheels of a black Porsche.

'Do you think we should tell someone that a guest has just driven off in that state.'

'If indeed he is a guest?' Sean had an amused expression on his face.

'Oh, you don't think that was the person I spoke to on the phone?' I recollected the deep Scottish growl I had encountered on my initial enquiry. 'Surely he can't be involved in the running of this place? Not with manners like that!'

'No doubt we shall soon find out. Standing out here however, won't get us anywhere. Shall we?' Sean nodded his head inwards.

At his prompting I gathered my wits and followed Luna inside, hoping whoever I met next would be a little more friendly. They were. I found I was looking into the green eyes of a pretty dark-haired girl who I guessed to be about fifteen or sixteen years old.

In a delightful contrast to the previous greeting, I was met with, 'Oh look at you, Red Riding Hood and her wolf, oh you beautiful creature, just look at you.' She showed no fear at all with Luna, instead she crouched towards her and hugged the huge animal as though she were a teddy bear.

I watched as Luna coiled her body into that of the girls and a moment of silent bonding seemed to take place between the pair of them. The girl lithely got to her feet and with a smile as graceful as her movements guided me into the rather grand hallway, with Sean following behind.

'Granny, she's here, and the wolf is too. It worked! It really worked.'

I was trying to take in my surroundings, getting an impression of stone flagged flooring, wooden panelling, mounted stags' heads, gilt-framed oil paintings, as well as a pair of crossed Claymores over the reception desk, all of which you might expect in a highland lodge hotel. At the same time, a tiny fragment of my brain took notice of the girl's choice of words.

'What do you mean, 'it worked'' I asked her, realising that we had not introduced each other.

She gave me a typical teenager's shrug and rolled her eyes 'The spell of course, to bring you here.'

'Away with that nonsense, child. What have I told you about trying to scare our guests?'

Coming down the wide, green and blue tartan carpeted staircase, was a woman, dainty in stature who bore a striking resemblance to the girl. Her silver hair was cut short and feathery and there were lines and wrinkles aplenty on her face. I thought they added to her beauty. She wore a cheerful berry coloured sweater and grey woollen trousers with flat-heeled boots. I liked her style. I also liked the warmth of the smile that was beaming in our direction.

'Welcome to Wolf Lodge, you must be Daisy, and Sean, and this of course is Luna.' Her direct gaze encompassed us all, but it was to Luna that she went first. 'Aren't you a beauty,' she murmured. Having fussed over Luna, she turned back to me. 'I am Catriona Munro.' She held out her hand, nails painted a colour that matched her lipstick and sweater.

I liked her instinctively. Sean and Catriona took to each other straight away. I expected nothing less and as I had seen with Abigail, the young girl also appeared to naturally feel at ease with him.

'Come on,' she said, gamely trying to pick up one of my heavy bags, 'I'll show you to your rooms. Granny's put you both in the red tower. It's got the best view over the river.'

'That sounds lovely,' I said picking up my other bag.

'Has my granddaughter introduced herself?' Catriona raised beautifully groomed eyebrows.

'Oops, forgot Granny, sorry.' We were partway up the main staircase which split in two. One side continued left, the other right. She stopped on the mid-way landing, 'I'm Lily.'

'Pleased to meet you, Lily.'

I was glad that Sean could cover my silence. I felt a piercing pain in my heart on hearing her name.

'Are you alright?' She asked me. 'You look like you've seen a ghost.'

Maybe I had.

A ghost of my hopes and dreams. I felt the warmth of Luna at my side, and I shook off the chill. It was a name, I told myself. Just a name. 'I'm fine, probably just a little hungry.'

'Don't worry about that. No one goes hungry at Wolf Lodge.' She chattered on as she led us up the left staircase to the second-floor landing and then opened a door. She took us through, not to a bedroom, but to another a smaller staircase.

'It's worth the climb I promise,' she said, and I had to admire how she manhandled my bag up this narrower set of stairs. At the top there were two doors. 'Here you are. The rooms share a bathroom but you can lock the doors on each side of that if you want to.'

She turned to face us with a mischievous grin as her flashing green eyes flicked between Sean and myself. It was impossible not to be charmed by her and I couldn't help comparing her to so many of the hard-faced girls I had taught back at the high school.

'You see, just over the tree-tops there's the river.' Lily placed my bag on the floor and as naturally as if she had known him for years, took hold of Sean's hand and steered him towards the window.

'That is some view,' he said nodding his head in approval, 'and let me tell you young Lily, I have seen many a beautiful view in my time. I have seen views so beautiful they make the soul want to weep with joy and that to be sure is one of them. Is it not, Daisy?'

I had been enjoying the view of the room itself, squarely proportioned with a huge four-poster bed in the centre, cosy furnishings with various shades of red, orange, and cream. A wardrobe that could well have led to Narnia and through the doorway to the bathroom, I could see a large roll topped bath, immaculately glossy tiles and a stack of fluffy white towels. I turned to look out of the window and gasped.

A mass of thick dark forest, snow-capped mountains, a silvery river and an endless sky.

'It looks enchanting,' I said and felt a warm tingle where my tattoo of Luna lived and breathed. 'I just want to follow the river and see where it leads.'

'To Wolf Falls, and it is enchanted,' said Lily seriously. 'That's why it's so good that you are here.'

'Really?' I turned to her all goggle-eyed. I loved a good fairy story!

She opened her mouth to speak but remained quiet as her grandmother came into the room.

'Lily, what have I told you about such nonsense, you'll be scaring away our guests before they've even had something to eat. Hush and away with you child.'

'I forgot to bring these up earlier,' said Catriona, explaining her presence.

In her hands were two carefully presented packages of toiletries. 'They are made locally, all from natural products and with as little damage to the environment as possible. The bottles are glass, and we refill them after each guest has gone. I hope you like them.'

'They look lovely,' I thanked her and commented that she shouldn't have felt the need to come all the way up the many stairs just for that.

'Och 'tis what keeps me fit,' she brushed aside my concerns. 'Now take your time refreshing yourselves after your journey and come down whenever you are ready. Then we can have something to eat and get to know each other a little better.'

I waited until they had both gone and then did what I had been itching to do. I flung myself back on the bed and bounced.

'Sean, this has got to be the comfiest bed I have ever been on.'

He joined me with a bouncing flop as did Luna who declared her satisfaction with the new accommodation by letting out a long and happy sounding sigh.

'You'll be sleeping soundly here, Daisy,' said Sean and for a second, I wondered if he would be taking up the use of the room next door. He laughed at my puzzled expression. 'Don't worry, Daisy darling, I will be right here beside you, if that's what you want?'

Odd how quickly I had grown use to his presence in my life. The thought of him not being with me was like imagining the sun never coming out from behind the clouds. I knew that he would be leaving at some stage to work in Manchester for Violet's nephew. I knew that some relationships could last over distance. I ignored for now the little voice that told me Sean was a one of life's butterfly's and I should not try to hold onto him. I pulled him towards me for a passionate kiss that had we not been expected downstairs for tea I would have taken further.

'Of course, it's what I want,' I said as I reluctantly let him go. 'I know what we have is not permanent, Sean, but I also know I do love you.'

'As I you,' he returned with a soft and gentle kiss. 'But love, Daisy comes in many forms and should never be defined by rules.' He was echoing my thoughts as though he had read them clearly from my mind. Perhaps he had. Then he added something that had me shaking my head with mock laughter.

'Besides, Daisy, you have so much more love to give and receive in turn. And with this new beginning here, who knows what may happen?'

'No Sean, seriously I am not looking for love, not in that sense.' I snuggled into his arms, as safe as a boat in any harbour when I told him, 'You have gone a long way to making me feel whole again, but I don't think my heart will ever truly mend. Some wounds are just too deep.' I thought of Gary's betrayal. Then I thought of my other hurt, the pain I carried in that deepest place of me.

'Hmm, we'll see,' said Sean with a kiss on the top of my head. 'Now, shall we go and see if the food on offer here is as tempting as the bed?'

Lily was waiting for us at the bottom of the main staircase in the entrance hall. 'I hope you are hungry,' she said with a smile on her face.

She led us through a large room which was laid out with a dozen tables and was clearly where the guests would eat, into a smaller room which I suppose the term parlour would fit, or perhaps snug. It had a dark wooden table and carved chairs to seat six people, an open fire which was lit. Upon the table were platters of food that had my mouth watering.

'Do come in,' Catriona was standing by a sideboard upon which stood bottles of wine and a couple of glass decanters. 'Everything is home made, we have the most wonderful cook, there's game pie, a stilton and broccoli quiche if you prefer vegetarian, sandwiches as you can see, smoked salmon, the obligatory turkey at this time of year of course, roast beef and horseradish, cheese, egg. Well, you can see for yourselves.'

'It looks amazing,' I said as my mouth watered, and my stomach gave an embarrassing growl. 'You've gone to a lot of trouble.'

'Well, not really to be fair,' said Catriona as she ushered us both into a seat and then asked us if we wanted wine, whisky, or water. Then when our glasses were filled, she explained. 'Mary and Alex, our cooks have done all the hard work. And you will have seen as you came through the dining room that they will be busy tonight with our guests, but I thought it would be cosier and less formal if we all got to know each other in here, if that's alright with you?'

'More than alright,' I assured her.

'Where's Dad?' Lily asked Catriona as she took the chair next to mine. 'He promised to be here.'

For the first time, I saw a darkening in the expression on Catriona's face. Mind you, if the dark bear-like man who had sped off drunkenly in his car was her son, I could understand it.

'Will you excuse me a moment?' Catriona invited us to begin helping ourselves then she left the room for a couple of minutes. When she returned there was a strained look on her face, but she took her place at the table and began to talk with the natural ease of a hostess.

Later, when I was completely full of delicious food, the door into the room opened once more.

'As requested, I am here.'

'Dad!' Lily hissed across the table, and I caught a flash of angry disappointment on her young face.

The door was behind me but even without turning my head I knew from his voice that her father was the man we had met earlier.

'Greetings,' he said with a faint slur to his voice 'Welcome to Wolf Lodge.'

'How could you Dad, you promised!' Lily's cheerful disposition dissolved to display a vulnerable core and my heart felt for her. She pushed her chair back and fled the room.

I looked properly at the man who was her father. He was taller than Sean, much heavier built, and currently swaying where he stood. His dark hair was unruly and in need of a good cut. He was unshaven, but his growth was not quite a full beard just not groomed properly. His eyes, forest green, were puffy and red-rimmed. They seemed to have trouble focusing on me but when they did, a twisted smile appeared on his mouth.

'You must be the woman who has come along with her wolf to break the curse and clear my name.'

'Please excuse my son, and take no notice of what he is saying,' Catriona's voice was like ice. 'Robbie if you have nothing better to say than perhaps you should return to your room.'

He snorted and reached for the whisky decanter. 'For God's sake you make me sound like a child.'

'Well stop acting like one then!' The words erupted from my mouth unbidden.

His hand paused for a second as he poured yet another drink. His stare was darkly intense.

'And just who the fuck do you think you are to speak to me like that?' His eyes burnt hot, his voice was arctic.

I reeled not just from the alcoholic fumes that wafted from him, but from the burning I felt on my back where Luna lived in ink form. As though the wolf on my skin was also reacting to him.

It seemed she was.

Luna rose from where she lay at my side and went to lay her great head on his lap as he sat, or rather almost fell into one of the chairs. We watched in silence as he went completely motionless. It was as though he had stopped breathing. Then he raised the glass to his lips and downed it in one, his other hand coming to rest on Luna's head. When the glass was back on the table he looked once more at me.

This time he spoke calmly. 'Well then, assuming you are who I think you are, are you going to tell me your name?'

I hadn't used my maiden name in over eighteen years. Now it escaped my lips. 'Daisy Flowers.'

In my mother's family it had been a tradition for girls to be named after flowers or herbs, and my father's name was Daniel Flowers. I had forgotten how it could make people smile. It had that effect now on the surly drunken man sitting opposite me. The grim line that was his mouth lifted at the corners. His smile was slightly crooked, and the flash of white teeth made me think of Luna somehow.

Wolfish.

'Daisy Flowers. And are you as hardy as our wild mountain thyme and heather lassie? Have you got what it takes to brave the highlands? Or will you blow away on the wind?' His voice had softened; still gravelly but with a musical lilt at odds with the sharp glint in his eyes.

I felt that prickling on my back and I stiffened my spine. 'I have no intention of blowing anywhere thank you very much.'

Out of the corner of my eye, I caught the look on Sean's face, grinning from ear to ear as though he was very pleased with himself.

Chapter Seventeen

It had been a long day.

My mind was buzzing but as soon as Sean slipped into bed beside me there was no need for thinking. I had grown used to the feel of his naked body next to mine. Rarely now did I wear nightclothes to bed. Whatever kind of day it had been, whatever mood I was in, with Sean it always ended the same way. Our bodies entwined and me utterly helpless as he skilfully brought me to orgasm.

He had unleashed another side of me that was scary at times.

Where had all this fiery passion come from?

And how would I cope without it when he left me?

I couldn't think about this as he began to make love to me, the curtains of the tower room open so that the moonlight spilt onto the bed. Sometimes he was playful with me. Sometimes he urged me to take the lead. Sometimes it was quick, hard and furious as he seemed to know just when I needed to let out something deep within me.

Tonight, I felt as though he was conducting a symphony of pleasure, using my body as an instrument to bring forth sounds and sighs of blissful ecstasy. With his mouth and hands, he coaxed and teased responses from me, caressing, kissing, and biting gently on every inch of my skin until I felt he had not left a single spot untouched.

I burnt feverishly with desire, sweat coating my limbs even though the night air was cool. His legs tangled with mine, over and over we rolled together, endless kissing and caressing, touching and searching mouths. The hard hot heat of him pressing against me, teasing, probing, taunting the throbbing slick folds of my flesh but never going further than that.

Rubbing against me, gliding back and forth, dipping in for a tantalising touch and then pulling away and flipping me over onto my stomach, leaving me howling in need, begging for him to fill me. He laughed as I knew he would, always the laughter. Never cruel, full of love, and something else.

Devilment?

Oh yes, there was more than a hint of devilment in Sean's lovemaking.

And magic.

Definitely magic, as he began to cover my tattoo with kisses, reverently now so the burning fire he had stoked gentled slightly and soothed my senses until I was drowsy and dizzy with sensual pleasure.

Once more rolled over and then with those stunning eyes glittering as he looked at me, he drove in deep, hands on my hips to fill me completely. A moment of stillness, just my breathing to break the silence of the room. Only mine, I could never hear his, he always remained so in control. And in control he was now, holding me as close as it was possible to hold another person, pinning me down as much with his eyes as he was with his body.

Not moving.

Just holding me.

Staring at me.

And with the stillness and the feel of him so very deep, I then began to feel it build. He never took his eyes from my face, but his lips curved in that smile that utterly bewitched me and I knew that he was aware of what I was feeling.

I desperately wanted to move.

To writhe beneath him and let my body somehow release the tension he was creating within me, simply by being inside of me.

But I couldn't.

He wouldn't let me.

He held me still, poised above me, and smiled as I began to quiver and tremble, tiny whimpers becoming a ripple of cries that rose into screams as wave after wave of pleasure crashed over me. Only when I was half-drowned in my passion did I feel his own body shudder and a sigh slip from his lips.

A masterpiece of lovemaking.

I told him so. 'You're like a musical maestro, coaxing the most beautiful of notes from the plainest of instruments.'

'You are not a plain instrument. You are beautiful, Daisy. I see that and perhaps one day you will too. Shh,' he placed a finger on my lips knowing I was going to protest. Then he placed his hand across the centre of my chest. 'You have a beautiful heart. I know you are going to tell me it is broken and wounded. But wounds heal Daisy. The scars may linger, but the wounds eventually heal. And your heart is healing nicely I would say.' Then he had kissed me deeply and I had fallen into a long a dreamless sleep.

Next morning, I was eager to throw back the covers, get dressed and start the new day. Sean as usual had woken before me, showered and dressed. He handed me a cup of tea from the tray in the room and I drank it in between getting myself ready.

I picked out a bright emerald green sweater that Sean had bought me for Christmas. There had been a huge sack of presents under the tree for me from him. All bought from a charity shop, or gifts he had accepted in return for favours he had done for other people. The colour looked vibrant against my winter pale skin that I had lightly dusted with blusher. I took the trouble to outline my grey eyes with a soft pencil and applied a coat of mascara as well as a touch of peachy lip gloss.

I still looked my age, or rather I now looked my age once more, instead of perhaps ten years older. The rest of my outfit was made up of a new pair of jeans and a pair of low-heeled chunky biker style boots that Sean had also bought, again assuring me they cost hardly anything.

'Ah it's grand you look, Daisy Flowers just grand.'

The second time in twelve hours my maiden name had been used. It felt good.

We went downstairs to find our host waiting for us in the hallway. Her smile was bright, but I thought perhaps a little forced. Was she having doubts about me already? Had I offended her last night in the way I had spoken to her son?

'I hope you slept well?'

We assured her we had, and she led the way through the main dining room, the smaller snug where we had eaten last night, to the kitchen. The original fireplace was still there and in the centre was a long oak table with two benches either side. Other than this it looked to be kitted out how I would imagine any professional kitchen should look.

A tall thin young man with dark hair was busy overseeing the cooking of all that was required for a full highland breakfast. He had his back to us as we came in and carried on silently with his work. There was a woman in catering clothes also bustling around putting the finishing touches to the plates as they were assembled. She wore her greying hair in a thick plait down her back. She was round in both figure and face but bonny with it, a welcoming smile in her blue eyes.

'Good morning to you. I am guessing as Catriona has brought you in here for your breakfast you will be staying on with us then, joining the family so to speak. I am Mary and this is my son Alex.' I was enveloped into a bosomy hug. She added quietly into my ears. 'Don't mind Alex, he doesn't talk much. He isn't being rude, he is autistic.'

'It's lovely to meet you. This is my friend, Sean.'

Mary dimpled and smiled as Sean took hold of both of her hands and kissed them in greeting. Then he spoke across the kitchen to the white-coated back of Alex.

'And a good morning to you, Alex. I hope it finds you well.'

The young man paused for a second and turned from his task at the grill. He smiled at Sean.

'Well I never,' said Mary sounding surprised. 'You must have a rare gift.'

'He has many,' I said dryly.

Catriona then explained how the breakfasts were co-ordinated and served to the guests and that there was also a cold selection available in the dining room itself.

'We can ask Alex to cook something for us now,' she said, or we can go and help ourselves to the cold buffet and bring it through to eat in here so we can chat a bit more about everything. If you do stay, this is where the family eats.'

'What about Luna?' I asked anxiously as my wolf had let herself out of my room to follow me here.

Mary exclaimed on seeing her which brought Alex's attention away from his cooking once more. Laying down his skillet he approached Luna who went all soft and teddy bear like.

'Beautiful,' said Alex. 'Bacon?' He asked this of me.

'Yes, yes, she can have bacon.'

We watched as he went to fetch a rasher of bacon and cut it up methodically into neat pieces. He placed it into a metal bowl, next to a similar bowl with water in it.

'Hotel inspectors?' I said faintly.

'Don't worry,' Sean declared confidently. 'Luna will know not to be here if they ever arrive.'

'She's that clever?' Mary asked in some awe.

Sean nodded. 'She's that clever.'

'Well Alex seems to like her, and he is in charge of the kitchen so that's fine with me,' said Catriona making the final decision.

Then, considering how busy Alex was, we opted for the cold breakfast. Sean loaded up his plate in a manner that made me wonder how earth he never put weight on. He saw my hand dithering over a pastry, and he winked at me.

'Go on, Daisy, you know you want to. And you need to put a touch more flesh on your bones.'

'You're a bad influence,' I said with a grin as I reached for one but acknowledged that he was right. I had got too thin whilst looking after Irene and Gerald.

'That's what I like to see,' said Catriona back in the kitchen as she sat next to me at the table. 'Can't abide fussy eaters. Ah there you are, Lily, I was wondering where you had got to?'

The young girl looked slightly subdued. 'Sorry Granny. My phone rang. It was Mum.'

'Ah, well never mind my dear, help yourself to breakfast and then perhaps you can tell Daisy and Sean all about Wolf Lodge and what we do here.'

I looked across at Sean, but he returned my gaze blankly. I knew that he would not have missed the inference that things were not good between Lily and her mother, wherever she was. It crossed my mind to wonder what sort of a woman could possibly cope with Robbie Munro?

Then Sean tilted his head at me and winked which made me wonder not for the first time if he wasn't some sort of mind reader. Disconcerted by this, I addressed Lily who was now sitting at the table with a plateful of croissants and jam and an adoring looking Luna at her side.

'Yes Lily, I am eager to hear all about it, the Lodge and the chalets.

'There are six chalets in total. They're named after animals. Pine Martin, Osprey, Wild Cat, Stag, Ptarmigan, Red Squirrel. Is she allowed some?'

She asked me as Luna was silently requesting a jam covered mouthful of croissant.

Having learnt that trying to stop Luna from getting what she wanted was completely futile I nodded.

'She's so gentle,' said Lily, clearly entranced by my wolf and Luna in turn was gazing adoringly at her.

'The chalets are all self-catering,' Catriona continued. 'But we do offer the guests the chance to come and have meals here if they wish. We get many a party booking the lodges for birthdays and such, although we don't particularly encourage stag or hen groups.'

I could see the sense of this having listened to Rose regale me with the wild antics of the hen parties she went on. But it did strike me that this would be a wonderful setting for a wedding, and I blurted this out before I could stop myself.

'I keep saying that!' Lily turned to Catriona. 'Granny, see, Daisy thinks it's a good idea.'

'It was just a random thought,' I said hastily. 'I have no experience of these things at all, so perhaps you shouldn't listen to me.' I didn't want to cause any trouble between them.

'I can understand it on a general level,' said Catriona slowly. 'It's just the overall management.'

'By which she means, Dad,' said Lily. 'You saw how he was last night. It's tricky enough keeping the hotel guests happy with him around, can you imagine the effect he could have on a wedding if he crashed into it like he did last night. Knowing him he'd probably try and shag the bride!'

'Lily!' Catriona admonished her granddaughter who got up from the table and turning her back to us, cleared away her plate.

'Why don't you show us these Chalets then, Lily? They sound grand and Luna could do with a run outside.' Sean's easy manner smoothed over the outburst in an instant.

'I'd like that. Granny shall we go?'

I was still rather horrified at what Lily had said about her father. Seriously?

Catriona seemed happy to gloss over it. 'No time like the present, although the girls might be in a couple of the chalets getting them ready for tomorrow as it's changeover day. You'll need your coat my dear, it might be wonderfully sunny but don't be fooled.'

It was still extremely cold with the ground crisply white from another layer of snow. We togged ourselves up with coats and gloves and followed Catriona and Lily outside.

'I'll meet you there, Granny,' said Lily. Then she stopped in her tracks and asked, 'Daisy can Luna come with me?'

It looked as though Luna already knew the way as she was ahead of Lily and waiting for her. I knew better now than to wonder how she did it. She was magic my wolf and that was a fact.

'Of course you can. She'll be fine with you.'

'That's a joy to see.' The words were breathed out on a sigh from Catriona. 'Life has been a little tricky for Lily with one thing and another. This place is where she is happiest, and even so, well, you met Robbie last night. My son is not the easiest of people.'

That, I thought, was putting it mildly. Ten minutes in his company was enough for me.

Sean though saw things in a different light. 'Isn't the road we travel so much harder for some than others. But as long as we just keep walking and helping each other along, that's the main thing. Isn't Daisy? We just keep walking and helping others.'

It was one of those moments when his words pierced something deep in my soul and I found I was suddenly ashamed of how I had viewed Robbie Munro on first meeting. What did I know about what lay beneath that hostile exterior?

'What a beautiful way of putting things you have, Sean. Tell me are you a poet?' Catriona asked.

'Ah well,' he laughed. 'Now if you want to meet a poet, you should meet my cousin Fergus. He could make an angel weep with his words so he could.'

'Maybe you could bring him here some time,' said Catriona.

'Maybe I will,' replied Sean with that easy manner of his.

'Anyway,' she said brisk now, 'we just follow this path along here, and you will soon see the chalets.'

At the back of Wolf Lodge there were formal gardens with box hedges clipped neatly into shape and what I imagined to be well thought out beds, although now everything was covered in snow. There was some creative topiary and an archway covered in what was currently a bare climbing rose, leading through the centre of the gardens. At the far end was a round pond with a water feature in the middle.

It would certainly make a beautiful setting for a wedding I thought, but for now we were going away from the formality of the eighteenth century. Catriona led us along a path through a winter-bare wood. Snow hung heavy on the empty branches of the silver birch and our footsteps made a gently crunching sound. A bright-eyed robin appeared and seemed to guide us, flitting from one tree to the next.

'Here we are,' said Catriona a couple of minutes later. 'Our chalets.'

'How lovely!'

The path opened into a clearing, and I could see a cluster of timber chalets. We were on slightly hilly ground now and some of them were higher than others. They had been thoughtfully positioned as they faced away from each other, the surrounding trees offering privacy. There was a parking space beside each unit as well as a picnic bench and brick-built barbeque and I could imagine sitting out here in the spring and summer months. I could also imagine the whole area being booked for wedding guests, or multiple groups for any special occasion.

'Pine Marten, Osprey and Stag all have balconies that overlook the river,' Catriona pointed out and I could see the glistening strands of moving water. 'Red Squirrel, Ptarmigan and Wild Cat are those you see a little higher up. They look down the glen towards the mountains. The road you see there comes from the main driveway but as we have just done, they can follow this path to the Lodge. It looks like Shona and Moira are here as I thought. Ah and here is Lily with Luna.'

'We gave Shona and Moira a real fright,' she exploded with laughter. 'You should have heard their shrieks; in fact, I am surprised you didn't.'

Catriona gently scolded her granddaughter. 'Well so would you if a wolf suddenly appeared.'

Lily looked at me and grinned impishly. 'Daisy come on in, let me show you around. The girls have finished this one now.'

Shona and Moira lived locally and took care of the chalets on changeover days. Shona was the younger of the two women, about thirty and pretty with reddish-blonde hair and a curvy figure. I was told she also worked in the Lodge on reception and wherever help was required. She was the first one we met on the steps of the chalet.

'Fair scared me to death you did missie with yon great bloody wolf!' She addressed Lily before stopping to take in our appearance. 'Och sorry

Miss Catriona, I wasna aware you were coming up this morning. Madam here thought it amusing to sneak up on us with that great beast.'

Out of the corner of my eye I saw Lily pull a face and I was about to say something apologetically feeling responsible as Luna's owner. But then a second voice was accompanied by another presence.

'Don't make such a fuss Shona! It's just a big hairy dog that's all, and yes aren't you beautiful my lovely.' The older of the two women, Moira was nearer my age, as lean and wiry as Shona was soft and curvy, with short iron-grey hair, and a no nonsense look in her blue eyes.

Catriona made the introductions and I had to yet again hide my smiles as both ladies blushed when Sean greeted them with a cheery grin. Really, was there no female immune to his charms?

'Daisy is going to take over running the Lodge and the chalets,' Catriona said as though it was a forgone conclusion. Yet hadn't I already made that announcement myself last night to Robbie Munro?

'Oh well that's marvellous news isn't it, Shona?' Moira greeted this with a firm shake of my hand.

Shona was less welcoming. 'I told you, you need a local woman who wouldn't run scared from the tittle tattle like the last two did. What's to say Miss Daisy here won't pack her bags and make a run for it when she hears what happened?'

There was a challenge in her green eyes, and I was disturbed by her words. More so when I looked at Catriona who had gone rather pale. What was I missing?

Before I could ask, Lily showed another side to her sunny nature. 'You're just being a bitch, Shona. How can you even mention that?' She looked darkly furious.

'Are you going to let her talk to me like that?' Shona glared at Catriona who was still looking uneasy and lacking the previous confidence she had shown.

Moira stepped in and nudged Shona. 'Come on, we need to crack on. Lily why don't you go on ahead and show Daisy the bedrooms?'

A look passed between the girl and the other woman who was giving me what I guessed was meant to be a reassuring smile. I was more unsettled to see that when Lily turned to me there was a sheen of tears in her eyes, but she followed Moira's suggestion.

'Come on Daisy, Moira's right. You will love the bedrooms, they're so cosy.'

As she led me towards the wooden stairs, I heard Moira say quietly to Catriona, 'Where on Earth did you find this one, I thought you had all but given up?'

Lily had obviously heard the remark and called carelessly over her shoulder. 'That was me Moira, I did the spell you told me about, you know the one with the wolf? It worked!'

'I'll be off now then, Catriona,' Moira's voice said breezily. 'Lovely to meet you Daisy, let me know if I can help you with anything. Byeee!'

'Lily, what have I said about listening to Moira and her magic?' Catriona's voice called up the stairs a touch of anger and something else I couldn't identity. Fear maybe?

'Daisy doesn't mind, do you?' was Lily's reply as she opened one of the bedroom doors and ushered me in. 'I mean you do believe in magic, don't you? You must with a wolf like Luna.' She sat on the double bed, oblivious to the fact that it had just been newly made and patted it so that Luna jumped up beside her.

I wasn't sure what to think of the comments about the spell and magic. Lily had mentioned it twice now and it seemed that there was a local witch on the scene as well. But with a wolf who had appeared out of nowhere and was the echo of my tattoo, how could I not believe in magic to some degree?

'Yes of course I do.'

Lily said solemnly. 'Not everyone does. Granny certainly doesn't, and neither does my Mum for that matter. Mind you, all she cares about is fashion and money so that's not surprising really. But Moira does. It was Moira who helped me do the spell to bring you here.'

'Lily hadn't we better concentrate on finishing our tour?' Catriona stuck her head through the door. The look on her face told me what she thought of magic and spells. Whatever they may be!

Lily for the most part appeared to be a sunny natured child and readily sprang up from the bed. We continued with our tour around the chalets, and then down to the river. It was shallow at the point where the chalets were clustered together, and large flattish rocks had been carefully placed to form stepping stones to the other side. Here was another small natural clearing.

'We let guests also pitch tents here if they wish in the summer, only those who have already reserved a chalet, which might sound a little daft, but it gives the option of extra guests, or a bit of a sense of adventure for children and young ones.'

Lily and Luna went straight across, followed by Sean who nimbly hopped, skipped and jumped over the stones to the other side. I followed a little more carefully.

'Are you not coming?' I asked Catriona as she stayed put where she was.

'I'll let Lily guide you from here. There is a lovely path that leads along the riverbank and towards the waterfall. I have things to attend to back at the Lodge. You are in safe hands with Lily. Just to the bridge mind, and then turn back,' she added to her granddaughter. 'It is not really a day to go too far.'

I looked up at the crystal blue sky. 'Really?'

Catriona nodded solemnly. 'Oh yes. There is more snow coming later.'

It seemed impossible but Lily assured me that this was what I could expect from good Scottish weather. To which Sean added it had a lot in common with good Irish weather. I muttered something inanely about English weather being pretty unpredictable, but this only earned me a look of puzzlement from Lily and Sean, so I shrugged my shoulders and followed on.

Catriona was right this was a lovely path. As we walked further away from the chalets the river grew narrower and faster, and the ground began to change from gently undulating to steeper and rockier. Sean and Lily kept having to stop for me to catch my breath.

'I'm sorry,' I said at one point. 'I hadn't realised how unfit I was.'

'It's not much further to the bridge where we turn round,' said Lily, 'but you can sit on that boulder and rest if you like.'

I shook my head, making a promise to myself that if I moved up here, I would have a good daily walk with Luna. I had got into the habit of taking her to the park each day but there was a huge difference between that easy amble for me and this type of activity.

'I am fine honestly, and you can stop grinning,' I poked a finger at Sean who was laughing at me. 'Don't you ever get tired?' I already knew the answer to that. He hardly needed any sleep and always had tons of energy. It really was most annoying. 'Stop it,' I playfully slapped away the hand that he held out to help me along. 'I'm not that decrepit.'

'We can go back now if you prefer,' said Lily as though anxious that she was doing the right thing.

I looked around me. The scenery was breath-taking. Following the river along its' twists and curves had taken us deeper into a forest of huge Caledonian trees. Towering majestically above them were the snow tipped peaks of mountains. It was wild and untamed. It was also oddly familiar although I knew for a certainty that I had never been here before.

'No come on, show me this bridge Lily and then we will go back and join your grandmother.'

'You are going to stay, aren't you? We need you here, Daisy. You have to stay.' There was an intent look in her green eyes, almost as dark as the pine trees.

I felt compelled to ask her, 'Lily what spell did you cast and why?'

'Granny doesn't really want me to tell you. Promise you won't tell her I told you, and promise me that you'll stay and help, no matter what.'

I wasn't a huge fan of making promises about which I knew nothing, but I was drawn to Lily despite myself. It was as though she had spotted a chink in my well-crafted armour and with arrow like accuracy, pierced it, threatening the defences of years.

'I promise, Lily. To both. I won't tell Catriona, and I will stay and take the job here.'

Really Daisy?

'Alright then, I will tell you. Moira and I cast a spell to bring a woman with a warm heart with a white wolf to Wolf Lodge to break the curse. And here you are.'

My footsteps faltered at this. 'I agree that Luna is a white wolf certainly,' I said tentatively, 'But I hate to say it Lily, my heart has been pretty frozen of late.'

Ahead of me I heard Sean's chuckle.

'And what exactly are we meant to do, Luna and I that is?'

'You're going to break the curse.'

'And what curse would that be, Lily?' I asked as though this was an everyday occurrence.

'That the Lairds of Wolf Lodge all go mad and kill themselves. Grandfather did, and my great grandad, and next it will be Dad. You do see don't you, Daisy? That's why you have to stay.' She now took my hands in hers and implored me with eyes made even more beautiful by the swell of tears.

Once more I had no control of the words that came out of my mouth. 'Of course I will stay, Lily.'

Really Daisy?

You are going to stay and break a curse involving that mad, wild brute of a man. I was desperate to see Sean's face, but he seemed to be deliberately keeping his back to me.

'It's just round this bend and then you get to see the way up to the waterfall,' Lily announced.

I could see the bridge that crossed back over the river and the start of the trail that led away from the thick forest and up the mountain. Luna was poised at the bridge looking at me. Then I realised why this seemed so familiar.

I was looking at the setting of the picture that Michaela had drawn in her tattoo studio. Ahead of me I could see the mountains, the forest, the river and most importantly of all, the waterfall where I had first set my eyes on the sketched version of Luna, who then was imprinted on my back in ink, who was now grinning at me from her place where she stood on the bridge.

I looked at Sean who returned my stare blankly, as though there was nothing at all unusual in this.

Once more I had no control of the words that came out of my mouth.

'Of course I will stay,' she said.

Really, Daisy.

You are going to rest and break a curse involving that mad, wild pursuit of a man. I was desperate to see Sean's face, but he seemed to be deliberately keeping his back to me.

'Yes, just round that bend and then you go on to see the way up to the waterfall,' Lily announced.

I could see the bridge that crossed back over the river and the start of the trail that led away from the thick forest and up the mountain. I now was puzzled the bridge looking at me. Then I grasped why this seemed so familiar.

I was looking at the setting of the picture that Michaela had drawn in her upstairs studio. Ahead of me I could see the mountains, the forest, the river and most importantly of all, the waterfall where I had first set my eyes on the sketched version of Fiona, who then was imprinted on my back in ink, who was now gurning at me from her place where she stood on the bridge.

I looked at Sean who returned my stare blankly, as though there was nothing at all unusual in this.

Chapter Eighteen

I was too stunned to frame any questions to Sean, or to Lily for that matter, about the notion of a curse. It was in something of a daze that I made the walk back, vaguely aware of Sean and Lily chatting away as if they had known each other for years. Back at the lodge, Catriona asked me to join her in the office for freshly brewed coffee and home-baked pastries. Sean was included in the invitation, but he gracefully declined.

'You don't need me to help you out with this Daisy,' he said with a gentle nudge when I looked at him for support. It was all very well promising a teenager that I was going to stay and help break some peculiar family curse, the details of which Lily had yet to tell me, quite another thing to agree a contract to run a business I knew nothing about!

But he merrily gave me a little push into the office and offered Catriona a dazzling smile. 'Would you excuse me; I have some phone calls to make about a project I am due to start work on.' This was another reminder that I was going to have to wean myself off him, at least for a little while.

Catriona got straight to the point, 'Well Daisy, will you be staying?' The same question as her granddaughter but I hoped for different reasons.

'I would love to stay,' I answered, the words belying the doubts my mind was screaming at me.

I could see her relax a little at this and she waved aside the fact that I had no experience at all.

'As I said over the telephone, Daisy, most of it is housekeeping on a grand scale and organisational skills. I will be able to work closely with you until you get the hang of things. We have ten letting bedrooms here in the

Lodge itself and as you have seen, each chalet can sleep up to eight people if they use the sofa beds.'

Regardless of Catriona's assurances, I was daunted by Shona's pointed comment, and I mentioned this.

'Don't listen to a word she says. It's just sour grapes, that's all. Shona would like to run the establishment but although she is hardworking, she can also be moody and, well with one thing and another, that is not the image I wish to present at Wolf Lodge to our guests.'

'And are you very busy, with guests?'

A shadow flickered across her face. 'Not as busy as I would like us to be. Oh, have no fear we are not in financial difficulties. You may see the books if you like. But there is always room for improvement I say, and new blood is just what we need.'

Again, I had that sense that I wasn't being told the whole story, but she carried on talking.

'You have met Shona and Moira. Moira is in charge of the chalet changeovers with Shona helping her. Shona also works on reception. We do half board here, having found that most guests are out and about during the day. There are plenty of places to eat in Kinlaggan itself, so that is never a problem for them. Of course, if they request it, then packed lunches can be made up. If we are busy, then we try and hire temporary staff, but it can be a little tricky.'

She stopped here and for a minute looked as though debating how to proceed.

'You met Robbie last night,' she said after quite a pause. There was a shadowed look in her eyes.

'He clearly has problems,' I said respectfully, remembering Sean's comment.

She nodded at me with a grateful smile. 'I am afraid so. It appears to run in the family which is not necessarily relevant at this stage. Suffice it to say that we do have trouble keeping our waiting on and temporary staff. Not to mention the problem of keeping our guests happy.'

We continued discussing some of the day-to-day details and what my duties would be. As a basic outline, I would be responsible for greeting the guests at reception and generally overseeing that their stay ran smoothly. This meant potentially pre-booking activities for them with local outdoor pursuit centres, a few of which we could offer discounts for if they booked through us.

'In essence Daisy, I need you to be the eyes and ears of Wolf Lodge. To be able to read people and react to them before they even know what they are wanting if that makes sense. This used to be my role and I thoroughly enjoyed it. As fit as I am, I do know it is time for me to take things a little easier. I was seventy-five last birthday and although I am not ready to stop completely, I have the sense to know that it is wiser to put things into place before they are absolutely required.'

I was not lying when I told her I had put her at least ten years younger.

She smiled and said with a hint of Lily's merriment, 'I knew we were going to get on. Now as to New Year's Eve which of course is tomorrow.' She heaved a hearty sigh and folded her hands in her lap to look me squarely in the face. 'It's going to be very busy, although not quite as busy as in previous years, but never mind. It is what it is.'

'How full are you?' Hogmanay should have meant they were fully booked.

Another shadow in those eyes. 'About half full in both the Lodge and the Chalets. Regular guests who come year in year out without fail.'

I pondered this and those doubts flared up in my mind, even as my mouth traitorously issued the words. 'Oh well let's make the most of it shall we? You tell me what I can do to help.'

She brightened at this. 'Bless you my dear, I wasn't expecting to put you straight to work.'

'Why not? Tell me, what's the plan?'

Catriona began to outline the evening's events. There was a festive meal for both the hotel guests and those staying in the lodges. After that, there was a dance with a local band taking place in the ballroom. To top the festivities off, there would, of course, be fireworks in the grounds at midnight.

'It's all rather jolly,' she said with a smile that didn't quite reach her eyes and I couldn't help but think of what Lily had said about the curse. Was the grandfather she had referred to who had killed himself, Catriona's husband? If so, was New Year's Eve one of those times when the loss hit hardest?

'How can I best help?'

'Do you think you could keep an eye on Robbie for me?'

I was not expecting that! My immediate silence was obviously enough to make her expand.

'He will be drinking I can tell you that for a fact. Sometimes he doesn't go near the bottle. Sometimes he is the life and soul of the party and sometimes as you have already witnessed Daisy, he can be an absolute swine.'

I was wary in my reply. 'I will try, but I am not entirely sure how I will be able to do that.'

'Divert him, keep him entertained. Steer him away from any potential fireworks and I don't mean the literal kind. Oh, dear me what am I asking you to do. Perhaps I should ask Shona?'

I questioned this with a look.

'The girl has been after him ever since Miranda left him. His wife,' she explained and waved a hand airily. 'It's a long story, too complicated to go into now. The point is, Shona has been like a cat in heat trying to get my son's attention.' She gave a very unladylike snort.

Quite why anyone would want the attention of such an ignorant brute was beyond me. Luna, who had been settled quietly at my feet rose then and placed her head on my lap with an alert expression on her face.

'Leave Robbie to me, I'll take care of him.' No, no, no! That was not what I intended to say.

'Jolly good. Now if you will excuse me, I must get back to the reception desk.'

Going back into the main hallway I saw Lily sitting on the bottom step of the stairs. She looked at me brightly and I wondered if she had been listening at the door. Luna padded quietly over to her side and happily let Lily wrap her arms around her great hairy neck.

'Would you like to see the ballroom now?' Lily said getting to her feet 'You didn't get chance to see it yesterday. Come on, I think you'll love it.'

She led me through a door on the opposite side of the hallway to the dining room. Then along a corridor where she pointed out a room which was the library, and the billiards room, and then pushed open a set of double doors.

'Wow!'

The ballroom had a marble floor and at the far end, a long row of elegant French windows that overlooked the terrace and the formal gardens. I had been a fan of regency romances in my teens and imagined twirling couples decked out in their fineries, dashing young beaus, blushing debutantes, dark and handsome brooding heroes, waiting to swoop on unsuspecting virginal heroines.

'It's awesome isn't it.' Lily looked pleased with my reaction.

'I'll say. This place is just crying out to be turned into a wedding venue.'

'I know. That's what I want to do when I leave school, be a wedding planner here at Wolf Lodge; actually not just weddings, any kind of event. We could make this place really so much more than it is now.' she said, 'but Mum and Dad are being total pains in the arse about it.'

She slumped down to the floor and leant her back against the wall. Sensing she wanted to talk and for some reason considered me an appropriate audience, I followed suit. Luna snuggled between the two of us.

'Dad wants me to go to college when I finish school to do A levels, I mean how bloody boring is that! And Mum is insisting I join her in America.'

'Your Mum is in America?'

'Hm. With Derek the dimwit.' Lily scowled. Then she tossed her head, her dark hair falling around her face. 'To be fair to him, he isn't so bad. I mean he is dim, but he's nice enough. And stinking rich. Derek Marchant the third, owner of a huge bloody vineyard in California. No guessing as to why Mum went for him then?'

A sensitive subject and not one I was going to probe. I just let her talk.

'Mum wanted me to go with them straight away but there was a huge fight between her and Dad. It was Granny who won in the end. She said it should be up to me where I finished my education as it wasn't my choice that my parents were splitting up.'

I could not resist asking then. 'And did the idea of living in California not appeal?' I knew most of the teenagers I had taught would have jumped at the chance, with or without their parents.

Lily looked at me as though I was mad. 'What and leave Kinlaggan? I mean I have been to California for holidays with Mum, but live there, go to college there? No way. Kinlaggan is in my blood. I can't leave here.' A shadow darkened her eyes. 'It would kill Dad if I left him.' Then, she sat up a little straighter. 'So anyway Daisy, you promised Catriona you will help look after Dad tomorrow night. We need a plan.'

Ah so definitely listening at the door then. 'What do you have in mind?'

'I have absolutely no idea.'

'Oh. I suppose I will think of something.'

'Perhaps you can ask Sean?' She suggested with a quirky little tilt to her head. 'He's totally cool. I am sure he can come up with a solution.'

Not surprisingly when I put this to Sean a little later on, he smiled rather smugly, acknowledging the compliment from the fifteen-year-old. I had wanted to go for another walk after lunch, or at least a drive to get my bearings in the local area, but as Catriona had rightly said in the morning, the bright blue skies had changed unbelievably to a swirling mass of white snowflakes.

The library, a fabulously cosy room with comfortable leather sofas and an endless choice of books was a natural choice to spend the afternoon. We had it to ourselves and sat in front of a roaring fire with a pot of tea between us and some Christmas cake that Alex had made. I licked my fingers appreciatively on finishing the last moist and alcohol-laden mouthful and then prompted him.

'Well then my totally cool wise guy, how on Earth do I prevent that drunken brute from making a total shambles of the night and ruining everything?'

He had one arm casually around my shoulders, his face close to mine and a very wicked look in his eyes as he replied, 'The obvious has not occurred to you then Daisy? A full-on seduction routine that would keep him occupied and away from the drink.'

I slapped him on his leg. Hard. 'Good! I am glad that hurt. For one thing, I don't do seduction, I'm not that sort of woman. I'm not!' I protested at the look on his face. 'Sean Murphy, I'll have you know I am a very respectable, probably boring, middle aged woman, not in the habit of seducing random men, especially boorish, drunken, random men, and doubly especially when I am in…' Just in time I stopped myself from say 'in love' and finished with, 'involved with someone else.'

He considered this. 'Respectable, hmm, boring, well maybe that could have applied Daisy, but I think you are leaving that tag behind. Middle aged? What has a number got to do with whether or not a woman is alluring, tempting, and sexy or not?'

He stroked a finger down the side of my face. Then gently ruffled my hair. When I looked into his face, and saw the lines that ran deep, the signs of a life lived hard at times, that contrasted so sharply to the brilliance of the light in his eyes, I forgot all about the age thing. As he said, it was just a number. He still hadn't told me his age. It didn't matter. Not when he could look at me as he was doing right at this moment.

I reached for him, hungry now for more than cake and I kissed him lingeringly on the mouth. It was a delicious festive tasting kiss. It went on and on, softly, lazily, languorously. The fire in front of us crackled and gave out the occasional pop, but other than that there was only the sense of us two in this cosy room, a world of white outside, and a need to snuggle up close inside.

There was something wonderfully playful about kissing like teenagers in the middle of an afternoon, curled up together on a settee. I had wriggled around and instead of sitting next to him, I was now on his lap and his hand was roaming teasingly underneath my thick woollen sweater. He was toying with the clasp on my bra, and I had enough sense to pull back a little, remembering where we were.

I could see the devilment in him though. 'Sure, and who is going to come in? You told me Catriona and Lily have gone to take some food to a poorly neighbour who lives five miles away. And as for the mad old bastard, sure and he is probably drunk in a corner somewhere.'

'Actually, he is standing right behind you,' grated out a voice that in all truth did not sound in the least bit drunk, or at that moment mad.

I scooted around and off Sean's lap, feeling the heat rise in my cheeks as I saw behind the high back of the settee that Robbie Munro was standing in the library. He was near one of the shelves with a book in his hand. He must have come in ever so quietly and I wondered that Luna had not risen in the presence of someone else. Shooting a glance at my wolf I saw that she was sprawled out like a fur rug in front of the fire, emitting contented doggy snores.

'Ah indeed there you are, 'tis yourself,' Sean greeted him with not a hint of shame, standing up and giving his jeans a twitch to accommodate the obvious bulge of his erection.

I shot him a furious glare, quite embarrassed. It would not have been so bad if my host had been as inebriated as he had last night, frankly I think if Sean and I had been full on at it and stark naked, he would not have noticed. Right now, though I was uncomfortably aware of the scrutiny I was under.

'We didn't hear you come in,' I blurted out, feeling now like one of my pupils in trouble.

'Clearly. I mean don't let me stop you. I merely came in to get a book.

This being the library of course. It's where the books are.'

His tone was mocking, the look in his eyes as he took in my rumpled state something else entirely.

I glared back at him, a defiant lift to my chin, very aware that I was acting out of character. I was saved from digging myself into a deeper hole by Sean announcing blithely.

'Voltaire is it then? Candide? That's a classic if ever there was one. Everything is for the best in this the best of all possible worlds. Daisy isn't that what I keep telling you.'

Robbie looked from me to Sean and snapped shut the book, replacing it on the shelf. 'I've changed my mind. I don't feel like reading after all. I will leave you to continue in peace.'

I could have thumped Sean then when he jiggled his groin once more and winked lewdly at Robbie.

'Ah that's most considerate of you, and it's a marvellous sofa so it is, I am sure you must have enjoyed the odd moment of passion yourself on this very spot. Yes, I can see by the look in your eyes, so you have. But to be fair to my lovely Daisy here, I think I would really prefer to spend the rest of the afternoon in that comfy bed we have upstairs. And what better way to spend an afternoon like this than in the loving arms of a beautiful woman. Yes, tis a lucky man I am wouldn't you say?'

With a wicked smile on his face, that half of me wanted to slap off, and half of me wanted to kiss him for, he held out his hand to me.

'Come on Daisy darling, to bed. Three o clock on a snowy afternoon is the perfect time for a loving, so it is.'

Embarrassment fought with a fiery feminine pride as he led me past the towering figure of Robbie Munro. I had never felt the object of such attention before, never with Gary. He would comment in an offhand way if he liked an outfit I was wearing. But it had been years since he had made me feel as though I was a woman that stirred such a passionate interest in a man.

With heat in my cheeks and a growing feeling of the most decadent lust rising in me, I allowed myself to be led from the library and up the many stairs to the room at the top of the tower. Once there our lovemaking was both playful and fuelled by a desire so intense, I felt sixteen again and in the throes of my first ever crush.

I couldn't wait to get my hands on Sean's lean muscles, and yet I had a fit of the giggles as in trying to get him undressed so quickly we both toppled over and landed on the floor in a heap. Luna, who had woken grumpily from her snooze by the fire to follow us up, gave a disgruntled sigh as if to say, oh they're at it again, and then took centre place on the four-poster bed with a look in her eye that told us both she was not for moving.

The floor was good enough. For now. We would move Luna later. All that mattered at the moment was that the tangle of inconvenient boots, jeans, sweaters and underwear could be removed and then skin could be on skin.

'God, I love the feel of you!' I breathed out to Sean as I wriggled full length on top of him, just savouring that moment of first body contact. His body was as beautiful as a carved statue only living, and breathing, warm and strong.

'I love the feel of being inside you more,' his soft Irish tones caressed me as seductively as his hands moved to lift me up and then raise me back down.

If you could growl with pleasure, I did. An earthy, animal sound that rumbled from my throat and evoked a ripple of laughter from Sean.

'Ah 'tis hungry you are now, Daisy darling. My she-wolf. My beautiful she-wolf.'

He managed to sit up with me, his body as loose and lithe of a man so many years younger, so his hands could trace down my spine, explore each muscle on my back, and lovingly stroke the etched lines of my tattoo. As he tenderly touched the image of the wolf, I felt as though he was touching my soul. The teasing laughter, playful giddiness that had brought us here to this point, was now gone. In its place was something else. Deep, mysterious, and beautifully wild.

Cradled so intimately together, he encouraged me to move on top of him, all the while holding me so close, and stroking my back and the tattoo of Luna. I felt him grow so large inside me I could not possibly contain him. But I did. My body melted into his, burned with the heat of a furnace until like molten metal we were fused together as one.

'Oh God Sean, I can't take this!' I cried out, as the building heat began to send me dizzy.

I could hardly breathe my heart was pounding so hard. The pleasure I felt was too much, but there was nothing that could have stopped me from going wild with him as I did.

'You can take it, Daisy, you must my darling, take it now, take it all, go on, Daisy, take it from me!' His words were soft but insistent. A crooning, murmuring in my ears as his mouth kissed the base of my neck, sucked at my breasts, teased the soft skin under my jaw, and all the while his fingers on my back, lovingly stroking and caressing my wolf.

As the wolf on my skin burned, the wolf within me rose to a peak of intensity that had me throwing back my head, exposing my neck to more biting kisses and so help me I screamed in a manner I had never, ever, done with Gary. Some part of my mind registered that I was glad we were right at the top of the tower with thick stone walls.

Sean then flipped me over, eyes glittering like the darkest of sapphires, he gazed down into my sweat covered face, as he began to let loose his own control. How was it possible I wondered to feel so completely lost in passion as I did with him? It awed me and terrified me in equal measures.

Finally, and I mean finally because his stamina was as breathtaking as his beauty, he lay still within my arms. My heart was still pounding, the blood still rushing in my head when he carefully withdrew and gently pulled me to my feet.

How, I wondered, did he recover so quickly? He led me to the bed where with a disgruntled sigh, Luna was moved from prime position. Drawing back the covers he eased me between the sheets. It was dark outside now, and I saw on the bedside clock it was just turning four o'clock. We had spent an hour writhing together on the floor. I was weak with sated lust and sleepy, but thoughts of what had occurred before we had come up to the bedroom were intruding.

'I am not sure how all of this has helped me figure out a way to deal with Robbie Munro tomorrow night?' I said with a huge yawn escaping my mouth.

He slid into the bed beside me with a glint in his eyes. 'I think you will find a way of keeping his interest somehow.'

'Sean Murphy,' I muttered lazily, 'Sometimes I do wonder if you are an angel in disguise, or indeed a devil.'

'A little of both, my darling Daisy, a little of both.'

And then he behaved in the most devilish of ways that took me once more to the gates of heaven and beyond.

Chapter Nineteen

Dinner last night had been a quiet meal in the kitchen as Catriona had decided that I was to be part of the household. Thankfully, there was no sign of Robbie. Lily had continued to entertain us with her lively chatter. I found it impossible not to respond to her warmth, even though she touched a part of me I had thought would remain frozen forever. Occasionally I caught Sean watching us and I wondered what he was thinking. My enigmatic lover was still a stranger in many ways and I was beginning to think he would always remain so.

I had promised I would help with preparation for tonight and so I left the cosiness of my bed and dressed. Sean had woken me with a kiss, already showered and dressed. I put on a pair of jeans that were comfortably worn and an oversized silver-grey sweater that had belonged to Gerald, and I refused to part with. There would be time later for dressing up and make up.

I had some colour in my cheeks these days, with a touch of the roundness I used to have in my face returning along with my appetite. My eyes, that had become empty windows into a lost soul, seemed to sparkle, a shiny silver, no longer dull pewter. All thanks to Sean no doubt. And in the pit of my stomach there fizzed an unrecognisable feeling that I decided must be excitement.

'Come on Luna, let's go and greet the day,' I said to my white haired, silver eyed companion. 'I'll take you for a walk as soon as it gets light.'

I made my way downstairs enjoying the feeling of having something to look forward to. Already the thought of having to sell my share of Gerald's house back to Gary was less painful. I did not know how long I would be at Wolf Lodge, whether this would be a short term or a more permanent situation, but that didn't seem to matter right now. I also knew that as much as part of my heart wanted it, I did not have a long-term future with Sean. For now, I was happy simply to be here.

Luna padded silently ahead of me to the kitchen, and I was not surprised at her pace. I too could smell bacon cooking. It came as a surprise though to find Robbie at the huge aga wielding a very heavy looking pan. He had his back to the door as I entered, but Sean and Lily were sitting at the table, a pot of tea between them and a rack of toast.

'Hiya Daisy.' Lily greeted me. 'Dad's making bacon, eggs and haggis, do you want some?'

'I suppose I do. It must be this wonderful highland air giving me such an appetite.'

'Or all the exercise you are having Daisy darling,' said Sean with a smile and a wink.

I think I heard a snort from Robbie but he kept his back to me so I couldn't be sure, but Sean and Lily chattered on as though there was nothing amiss.

'Where is Alex?' I asked as I took a seat at the table.

'Having the morning off as well as Mary before tonight,' came the reply as in walked Catriona. 'I have prepared the cold buffet for the guests today. I trust everyone slept well?'

I watched as her eyes skimmed over me and Sean and went to her son. He did not turn from his task, and I suppressed a twinge of anger. Really how rude could a person be? I assumed he was sober if capable of cooking a breakfast, so no excuse for bad manners. He didn't even speak when he served up the breakfast. I couldn't fault the cooking of it, but he put the plates on the table with a graceless clatter, scraped back a chair to sit next to Catriona, which meant he was opposite me and began to eat silently.

Sean spun off into a tale about another of his many cousins that had the astonishing effect of making Robbie laugh. I nearly jumped off my chair. It was so unexpected and surprisingly appealing in the richness of the sound.

I was further surprised when the lights suddenly went out.

'Oh no, not now!' Catriona exclaimed with worry in her voice.

Robbie's response was a succinct, 'Fuck!'

'Shall I get the candles?' asked Lily helpfully.

Although it was morning it was still dark outside and not helped with snow heavy skies.

'I knew we should have replaced the generator last year,' fretted Catriona and I could understand her concern. A hotel with no electricity for New Year's Eve was no good at all.

'I'll try and get hold of Gordon,' said Robbie with yet another string of curses as he realised that he had not charged his phone up.

'If it's the generator then that's no bother at all,' said Sean calmly pushing his chair back and standing up. 'Robbie why don't you show me where it is.'

Robbie's roll of expletives came to an abrupt end. 'You're an electrician?'

'I am,' answered Sean, ignoring my look of astonishment and closing my mouth with a kiss when I had opened it to say that he was an architect. 'There now Daisy, why don't you go and take Luna for a run with Lily while Robbie and I sort this out and then we can all get on with some work.'

'That would be wonderful Sean, would you?' Catriona looked at him as though he was heaven sent.

I watched in amazement as the taciturn Robbie walked out of the kitchen, talking earnestly now to Sean as they discussed what type of generator was installed at the Lodge.

'Come on then, Daisy,' Lily stood up from the table and then stopped to ask her grandmother if she needed any help with the pots.

'No, indeed I'll be fine. You go and take that lovely wee beauty for a good run. Yes here you go now, I thought you would like sliced haggis.'

Luna wolfed the treats that Catriona passed to her from the table and then I went with Lily for an early morning walk in the snowy darkness. It seemed a good as time as any to try and talk more about her father. And I needed something to take my mind off Sean's latest surprise.

Really, who was he?

Lily took me to the gardens of the Lodge.

'I think it looks magical like this,' she said, 'It makes me think of Narnia and the statues in the White Queen's house when I see the topiary animals all covered in snow. I used to imagine as a child that they could come alive and dance. Daft I know.'

I made no comment, thinking of Abigail rushing into my house announcing that Sean had made the snow figures dance. Had he? Had he really done that? Homeless tramp, architect, gardener, children's magician, electrician?

Really?

'Tell me about the family curse,' I asked her as we walked, Luna crazily bounding in the snow.

She sighed dramatically. 'It was all Great Grandfather's fault. He fell in love with a gypsy woman who was camping nearby. She didn't love him, so he ordered her and her family off the land. She refused to go so he got his shot gun out to warn her off. She had a white wolf, just like Luna.' She paused in the telling of the tale, but I had a horrible suspicion how it was going to end. I was right. 'He shot her wolf, so she cursed him and his kin.'

'I think I would kill someone if they shot Luna,' I had to admit and said this out loud.

'I agree,' said Lily ruefully. 'And I wouldn't mind if it was just Great Granddad she cursed cos he deserved it. But it doesn't really help me and Dad now. And it wasn't Dad's fault.'

Back to the present. 'Tell me again exactly how does the curse manifest itself?'

'That the men in the family will never live to old age. Specifically, they kill themselves.'

I tried to be practical in the face of this peculiar conversation. 'And what happened then with your great granddad, and your granddad after him?'

'Great Granddad was found with his head blown off a couple of weeks after they left. At a full moon,' she added as if this was significant and who knows maybe in the world of curses it was.

'And your granddad, what happened to him?' This of course was Catriona's husband.

'He drove his car into a tree.'

I paused for a second and considered this. We had come to the end of the formal gardens and had turned back to face the Lodge. Looking at the old building in its wild but peaceful setting, it seemed difficult to think of two violent deaths within the same family.

'But could that have been an accident?'

Lily shrugged. 'Granny insists it was. She doesn't like to talk about it. And it happened before I was born so I got most of the details from

Moira who has always lived round here.'

'What are the details then?' We began to walk slowly back to the Lodge and my mind was swirling. It was like something out of a gothic novel.

'According to Moira, the coroner put it down to accidental death. It was icy on the roads and Granddad had been drinking. There was a lot of gossip at the time that it was suicide though because they had been having financial difficulties and the Lodge might have needed to be sold.'

From a practical level I could see why Catriona would insist on an accidental death verdict. If there had been life insurance involved, then suicide would have deemed this null and void. Possibly with her husband dying this could have solved those difficulties. I would not have blamed her from wanting to shy from the truth if indeed this had been the case. I would have done the same.

'But perhaps that really was just an accident?'

Lily shook her head and looked at me with huge green eyes. 'Nope. Cos he also died at a full moon you see, Daisy. It was the curse. And Dad gets really moody at times, sometimes he doesn't speak to anyone for days. Not even me. And sometimes... sometimes he even has blackouts when he can't remember what he has done.'

This last bit was whispered with such pain and fear a little more of the ice around my heart melted and without thinking I reached for her.

'He'll be fine,' I said to her in that ridiculously stupid way that adults do when in all probability this might not be the case. She wrapped her arms around me and clung on tightly for a moment and I wondered how long she had been nursing this fear within herself.

'He will now,' she said confidently when she pulled away. 'Because you are here with Luna and that is going to break the curse and then that will clear his name. Look they've got the lights back on!'

The distraction of the Lodge being illuminated again prevented me from asking how exactly Luna and I were meant to do this. And what did she mean, clear his name?

'Come on Daisy, there's loads to do. Look there's Sean. Well done, Sean!' Lily went to hug him. 'And thank you. Dad would have been sooooo grumpy having to sort that out by himself.'

'Ah well we can't have a grumpy dad can we now,' he gave me a grin over the top of her head and then after she had scooted on inside, he pulled me close for a quick kiss. 'You are looking fresh and pretty as the flower you are named after.' Then he shot a sideways glance in the direction that Lily had gone. 'And she is certainly as beautiful as her name, both inside and out I would say.'

His words produced a lump in my throat that I forced myself to swallow. 'Yes. She is.'

'Hm. I saw the both of you hugging out there. It was a lovely sight. Didn't you hold her so tight as though she were your own precious daughter, and didn't she just hug you back in need of a mother so she did. Yes, a lovely sight to see.'

I looked at him sharply, but his expression was utterly unreadable.

'Well then,' he said blandly, 'there is, I believe a lot to be done, so no more time for shilly-shallying Daisy darling, let's crack on.'

Crack on we did and soon the Lodge had more people bustling about the place.

Moira and Shona had arrived from Kinlaggan. Moira greeted me as though I was an old friend, but I was right in my initial assessment of Shona. There was a definite chill in her eyes when she said hello. I thought of Catriona's comments about her crush on Robbie. She was welcome to him!

I said as much to Moira later. We were upstairs going through the bedrooms one by one with the special finishing touches that Catriona had organised for the New Year. For tonight there were a couple of miniature bottles of malt and some exquisite hand-made chocolates as well as the toiletries.

'These look absolutely yummy,' I commented as we checked the first room and laid out the gifts.

Moira was in charge of the trolley with fluffy white towels, and she turned to me.

'They are. And that's why Catriona has asked you to help me with this, not Shona. She has been known to help herself on the odd occasion. Especially with the wee drams!' she finished with a laugh.

I was shocked. 'Does Catriona know? Of course she does, you just said so. But why doesn't she do something about it?'

Moira counted the towels in the bathroom and then she answered my question. 'Because getting good staff these days is difficult and for all her quirks, Shona does work hard.' She gave me a questioning look with a smile on her face. 'Will you be challenging her about it when you are in charge then? Cos I warn you, Shona is already gunning for you?'

'Why? I only met her yesterday.'

'Cos of all the chatter young Lily blurts out. She has been going on about her spell, which of course I helped her to do.'

'Of course,' I said wryly unable to stop the slight roll of my eyes.

She laughed and I saw that she had not taken offence. 'Quite. Anyway, in amongst that was the notion that along with breaking the family curse and stopping her dad from killing himself, which I can see from your face you now know about, she also intends to see her dad get married again.'

She laughed even more as she saw that her words had frozen me in place, my hand just about to put one of the boxes of chocolates on the dressing table.

'Oh behave!' I said to her, feeling rather pleased that I could be so at ease in her company.

I had been sorely lacking in female friends of late as all of my acquaintances were connected to Gary. How refreshing to have this light-hearted banter with a member of my sex.

'I am with Sean,' I said firmly. 'Shona has nothing to fear from me in that direction. Besides,' I added this in a whisper just in case anyone might overhear 'who in their right mind would want to marry that grumpy sod?'

charge him?" I went on. Sheila winked, pausing for one.

"She's cool," met her answer.

"As of all the character young Lily Jabrex too. She had been gazed on about her spell, which of course I helped her to do."

"Of course," I said wryly, unable to stop the light roll of my eyes.

She laughed, and I saw that she had not taken offence. "Take Shivani, in a manner that was the notion that along with breaking the family code and stopping her dad from killing himself, which I can see from you, her you now know about, she also intends to see her dad get married again."

She laughed even more as she saw that her words had thrown me in place, my hand just about to put one of the boxes of chocolates on the dressing-table.

"Uh, behaved," I said to her, feeling rather pleased that I could be so at ease in her company.

I had been sorely lacking in female friends of late, as all of my acquaintances were connected to Clay. How refreshing to meet this light-hearted banter with a member of my sex.

"I am with Sean," I said firmly. "Sean has nothing to fear from me in that direction. Besides," I added this in a whisper just in case anyone might overhear "who in their right mind would want to marry that pig-ugly sod."

Chapter Twenty

It was just after three in the afternoon. I had changed out of my jeans and put on a bright red dress Sean had bought me for as a Christmas present, one of the many from his charity shop jaunts. I still wasn't used to seeing myself in such colours, but Catriona approved when she saw me.

'Och you look lovely my dear, so bright and cheerful and you have such lovely shapely legs. I adore those wee ankle boots, very sexy if I may say so.'

'I am not trying to look sexy,' I had spluttered, and she had laughed even more.

Then we had been kept busy at the reception as one party of guests arrived after the other. As she had already explained, the majority were returning holidaymakers who greeted Catriona like an old friend. I was touched as she introduced me as the newest member of the Kinlaggan family.

The time passed quickly and under Catriona's careful guidance I soon got the hang of the checking in process. It helped that Luna was sprawled across the entrance hall in the manner of a real-life rug. There were exclamations all round when the guests saw her. She was a natural ice breaker. A wolf at Wolf Lodge, how apt.

I began to really enjoy myself and after the first few check ins, Catriona stepped back a little to let me take over. Reception work, or anything to do within the hotel trade had never occurred to me previously and I would not have considered it as a new career if it had not been for that letter getting misdirected in the post. I said as much to Catriona when we had a quiet moment.

'I for one am glad it did get misdirected. However efficient the other lady may have proved to be, she wouldn't have brought a wolf with her, would she?'

I laughed at this. Luna had been the star of the afternoon, bedazzling all the guests with her perfect behaviour and luminous eyes.

'I guess not. What a lucky coincidence it was, my name being so similar to the one on the address.'

'Exactly, and I wish you would tell that to my dear granddaughter. She is convinced she conjured you up here through that daft spell of hers that Moira taught her. I love her to bits I really do, and Moira, but I think the pair of them are completely befuddled.'

'Hm. What's in a name hey?' I tapped a pen idly on the desk as a thought had suddenly popped into my mind.

'What?' Catriona asked sharp as a pin.

'My name,' I said thoughtfully. 'Should I change it back to Flowers when my divorce comes through?'

'You must, simply because Daisy Flowers is such a perfect name and it suits you so well. Your mother was right to call you that.'

'Well,' I said with a smile, 'you would think that she would have called me something else when you consider Dad's name, but you see she was called Marigold, and there was a tradition in her family that females were named after flowers or herbs. I could have been Lavender, or Marjoram, or Thyme.'

'Or Parsley,' added Catriona and we laughed at that. She allowed a tactful pause and then in the quiet that had thankfully fallen upon the reception area, said, 'You are definitely getting divorced?'

'Definitely.' I answered. In my bright red dress, standing behind the desk in the huge hallway of this ancient hunting Lodge, with a wolf at my feet, I felt brave, not sad.

'Good. Now, I think that is all the arrivals dealt with. The evening starts at seven, so I suggest you take the chance to go and have a bit of peace and quiet before you get changed. We don't go in for black tie,' she said, 'but it is a nice chance to dress up if you wish.'

Once more Sean had done his magician's trick of finding just the right outfit at our local charity shop. It was a marvel really that in such a short space of time my wardrobe contents had gone from navy blues, blacks and browns, to bold statement colours with the old silvery grey that brought out the light in my eyes.

The dress I was going to wear tonight was a deep green with a scooped neck line and a swirling skirt that fell to mid-calf, perfect for twirling a highland reel. Not that I knew how to do this of course. After taking the chance to have a quick lie down I began to prepare myself, marvelling as I did so that I was going to be celebrating the new year.

Less than a month ago I'd tried to throw myself under a train.

'What is it?' Sean asked me. He was standing behind me to fasten a necklace around my throat.

My eyes met his in the mirror. 'I was just thinking how much has changed. And all because of you.'

His hands caressed the line of my throat and neck, and he dropped a tender kiss on the exposed skin.

'What have I done?' He twirled me round to face him and then kissed me slowly, and lingeringly on the lips. I melted into him, savouring the heat that reached all the way to my toes.

'You have made me happy,' I said to him simply and I realised that this was true. I was happy.

He rebuffed this with a gentle smile. 'Daisy you have made yourself happy and that's the way of it. Now shall we go and dazzle folk with our good looks, style and witty conversations?'

I laughed. 'Yes. Why not?'

He was dressed rather flamboyantly with a fancy white shirt showing beneath an embroidered waistcoat. This was topped with a velvet green jacket. We looked a well-matched pair. Downstairs, the guests had been invited to gather in the main entrance hall for pre-dinner drinks. The fire was roaring in the hearth, candles had been lit on the wide window shelves and the rich scents of cinnamon and pine filled the air. Walking into the colourful mingle of people with Sean on my arm, I could hardly credit where I was and what I was doing.

Smartly dressed local staff had been hired for the night and I was handed a glass of champagne. As I chinked the glass against that of Sean's, my eyes scanned the room, mindful of the promise I had made to both Catriona and Lily.

'So where is our mad host then?' He asked me quietly so no one else could hear.

'I thought you had got on alright with him this morning fixing the generator?'

He smiled that mischievous smile. 'I did. I like the mad bastard, so I do. But mad he certainly is Daisy. There he is now. I am afraid my darling Daisy your plan may be foiled already.'

Naturally, I had told Sean what I had been asked to do. My heart sank when I saw that Robbie, looking I have to say rather resplendent in full highland regalia, had entered the throng with Shona on his arm. Like me, the younger woman was wearing a green dress, although hers was far more daring, being of emerald satin and displaying a cleavage I could only dream of.

'Damn,' I muttered under my breath.

'The night is young,' murmured Sean with that devilish look in his eyes. 'And if he continues to drink in that fashion, it could well be entertaining.'

Whilst everyone was enjoying the champagne, I could see that in Robbie's hand was a glass of what could only be whisky. There was not much I could do for now and I allowed myself to be distracted by chatting to the other guests. I was conscious that although this was a night for enjoyment, it was also a chance for me to plant roots within this community.

Knowing Sean would quite happily mix and mingle by himself, I flitted from person to person, with a smile and a friendly comment, laying the foundations for my future role. When it was time to go in for dinner, I went to rejoin Sean. At that moment, Moira came over to us declaring we both looked the part and with a bold smile on her face she asked Sean if he would dance with her later. He bowed gallantly and assured her he would. Moira was dressed simply but no less stunning for that in black, with her cropped silver- grey hair sleek and shiny.

'Don't worry if you don't know any of the steps,' she said to Sean 'I can show you how it's done.'

Sean smiled at her. 'I am sure I will be in safe hands with you.'

There was a twinkle in his eyes that told me somehow, he already knew how to do the dances. Then Moira called a man over to come and greet us. He was good looking, younger than her I guessed by about ten years, slim build with brown hair and eyes.

'This is Callum,' she said, surprising me by linking her arm through him, 'My husband. He's one of our local vets.' She made the introductions and I found that I was sitting next to Callum as Moira took a place next to

Sean at the long table.

He was an entertaining as well as an attentive dinner companion, walking the line beautifully between flirtation and friendliness and never once over-stepping it. But I was aware as much as I was enjoying myself, and who could fail to in such surroundings, with a feast being served before us, that I was failing in my promise to Catriona and Lily to look after Robbie.

Lily, looking stunning in a cream lace dress with her long dark hair loose around her shoulders was sitting next to her grandmother and across from her father and Shona. There were a few guests between us and them but every now and then I felt her eyes on me. In them was a silent plea. As the meal progressed and wine followed the champagne, or in Robbie's case more whisky, the noise from that end of the table grew noticeably louder than anywhere else.

'It looks like Robbie is on top form tonight,' commented the gentleman diagonally opposite me. Then he turned to his wife sitting next to him. 'You're a little in love with him Mandy aren't you.'

It was obvious that this was no problem to either of them as Mandy shrugged slim shoulders, exposed in an elegant gown of coffee coloured silk.

'Well what woman wouldn't be darling. It's all that wild highland temper just simmering away under the surface. He always makes you feel as though he could just explode, even when he is being charming with you.'

'I suppose that's his artistic temperament,' said her husband. Stuart looked not in the least bit bothered that his wife had such a crush on his host. 'Always the same artists, mad as a box of frogs I think.'

I spluttered then on my wine, eliciting a concerned pat on the back from Callum. 'Are you alright Daisy?'

'Fine, sorry that just went down the wrong way.'

Across from me I caught Sean's look of amusement. Did he always have to find everything so funny? I was tempted to give him a kick under the table but knowing me I would miss and hit Moira instead.

I cleared my throat. 'I had no idea he was a painter?'

'Gosh yes, and quite a famous one,' said Mandy. 'Have you never heard of RJ. Munro?'

I shook my head. 'Sorry. I love art but I have no idea what is currently popular.'

I was then informed by those around me that Robbie Munro was a talented and highly sought-after portrait painter. It seemed that the rich and famous would clammer to engage his services.

'It all worked very well when his wife was managing him,' said Mandy, 'then when she left him it all went to pot. And of course, there were the rumours following the deaths of those poor women. Not that I believed them for a second. Mad he may be but he's no serial killer.'

'I beg your pardon?' My voice came out as an undignified squeak.

Callum tutted. 'It was all nonsense! Bloody media loving to bring down someone rich and successful.'

'Yes, but they still haven't found out who was responsible have they?' Stuart added and then looked across at me. 'You mean you don't know about this? Where have you been for the last couple of years?'

'No, I don't know what you are talking about. I haven't followed much of the news, I have been caring for my in-laws until they both died.'

'Ah, well my dear, in that case I shall enlighten you.' Stuart looked keen to embark on his tale, but Callum cut across him.

'I don't think now is a suitable time, do you?' He might have been younger than the other guests, but the vet had a quiet air about him that held sway.

The conversation rolled onto more general topics, and I continued with my meal whilst trying to imagine Robbie Munro as a successful high society painter whilst at the same time wondering what the heck had been meant by the other comments. In true female gossipy form, I was made aware of the situation later on in the ladies. Mandy, rather drunkenly trying to re-apply her lipstick was happy to fill me in.

'Fancy you not knowing about those women being murdered. Three I think it was, or maybe four. Anyway, the last one actually worked here doing your job. That was last year some time. I believe Catriona has had a devil of a time filling her position. I mean who would want to work where their predecessor was abducted, then found raped and stabbed to death a few weeks later. Especially,' she added leaning in towards me, 'when the prime suspect on that occasion was none other than our famous host?'

'I really need the loo,' I said squeezing past her and locking myself in the cubicle as I digested this horrifying news.

Could there possibly be any truth in it?

Catriona, Lily and everyone else all seemed so warm and welcoming. I was sure they could not possibly be harbouring a serial killer in their midst, even allowing for a curse ridden suicidal mad man. Back in the dining room it certainly looked as though Robbie was in sterling form tonight as the laughter continued to ripple all the way down the long banqueting table. What had I let myself in for I wondered and decided to temporarily blur the answer with champagne?

When the meal was finally over, we were invited to make our way to the ballroom.

I was right that Sean knew how to perfectly perform each dance. In contrast my efforts were enthusiastic but clumsy to say the least. My partners, Callum amongst them were kindness and charm and soon I forgot my inhibitions along with fears over my host and gave in to the whirling and twirling.

'Goodness,' I said after one dance which involved changing partners and coming back together again so many times, I felt dizzy, 'this is one way of burning up the calories. I had no idea this was so much fun!'

I had ended up with Callum as my partner and he grinned in delight. 'We highlanders aim to please. Do you want to dance the next one or take a breather?'

'I think I really need a breather. How does Sean do it? He has danced every dance, and still he looks as fresh as a daisy,' and then I giggled at what I had said. Yes, really the champagne was kicking in.

'But not as fresh as the Daisy in front of me,' said Callum with a warm smile.

'I heard that!' Moira swirled past with her dancing partner and managed to playfully swat her husband on the way.

I knew though that Callum was only being friendly. Sometimes, in the early days with Gary, some of his friends had made me feel uncomfortable with their comments. As I had got older, frumpier, they had stopped. It was nice now to be on the receiving end of masculine attention. We had just found a quiet corner to cool off a little and have another drink when Lily wove her way through the moving mass of people to join us. Or rather to come specifically to me.

'Daisy you have to help.'

Chapter Twenty-One

'Lily what's the matter?' Instantly I felt guilty.

I had promised I would look after her dad but in all truth, he hardly seemed to need this. Robbie had, along with everyone else, thrown himself into the dancing. I had briefly been partnered with him myself as we went from one reel to the next and while he had looked a little flushed in the face and bright eyed, didn't we all?

'It's Dad. You have to get him away from Shona.'

'Why what's the matter?' I asked again, wishing now that I had not had quite so much champagne.

Callum gently prompted her. 'Lily, you know we are all your dad's friends here, you don't have to hide anything from us.'

By now Sean and Moira had joined us and we all waited for her to reply.

'I heard Shona talking to one of her friends in the toilets. She's absolutely smashed off her head. She is planning on asking Dad to marry her, at midnight but she's going to do it publicly thinking that he will say "yes" if he's in front of loads of people.'

'Ouch,' commented Callum.

'Would it be so terrible for him?' I asked, admittedly not liking the idea of a public proposal either.

'He'll go potty!' Lily exclaimed. 'He absolutely hates being put on the spot and I know he has been drinking loads tonight, and I'm pretty sure he's taken some drugs. He's far too happy!'

I could see this wasn't good and then she went on.

'And that's when he crashes the worst! If Shona makes a public show of him, he'll either get really angry and start a fight, or he'll just go off and ...'

And what, I wondered? Either kill himself or someone else?

Callum stepped in. 'Perhaps I should go and have a word.'

'No,' Sean forestalled him. 'You need to stay neutral. He trusts you as his friend, don't overstep the mark now in his eyes. He is going to need you at a later stage.' Then he said, to my surprise, 'Lily is right to ask Daisy, she is the right person for the job.'

We all looked at him. The thought of tackling a drunken, drug fuelled Robbie was not something I thought I was qualified for. Sean however gave Lily an encouraging nod.

'You go and fetch Luna and bring her here. When you have done that, Daisy, you will go and ask Robbie if he will walk with you outside. I'll look after Shona.'

I had no doubt that he was capable of distracting the younger woman, who was now hanging onto Robbie's arm in a possessive manner. What I did question, was how I was going to entice Robbie into the garden for a moonlit stroll, especially when it was approaching midnight? And given what I had been told, did I really want to?

But Sean, as ever, was persuasive and a few minutes later I had Luna by my side. It was not often she was away from me but on this occasion, I thought my wolf would prefer the quiet of my bedroom to the noise and bustle of the ballroom. Lily had been thoughtful enough to bring me a shawl. As hot as the ballroom now was, it would be freezing outside.

'Thank you, Lily,' I said and slung it loosely around my shoulders.

Then I made my way carefully through the dancers to the other side of the ballroom. Luna, it seemed, knew exactly where she was heading and reached Robbie before I did. I watched him put out a hand to softly stroke her head looking completely at ease with her. As I caught up with Luna, the fiddle player announced that the following dance was to be a slow one, bringing them up to the New Year.

'Lads and lassie's make sure you grab the partner that you want to have that new year kiss with,' he said to a rousing cheer.

Shona flashed me a look of annoyance and then pulled on Robbie's arm. 'Come on, Robbie, you heard him. This is our dance.' Her eyes were glittering. 'You are blocking our way to the floor, Daisy.'

'Actually, Robbie I was wondering if you would come outside with me for a minute?'

He looked surprised, if not stunned by my request and who could blame him? Shona on the other hand, leant in close to me and whispered in my ear.

'I don't know what game you are playing at right now, but fuck off and get out of our way!'

Not a good way to speak to me with Luna at my side. She snarled at Shona, and literally butted her out of the way. Then she opened her jaws wide and took hold of Robbie's right wrist.

'For fuck's sake that bloody wolf is biting you, Robbie!' Shona hissed and a few heads turned as the music grew quieter now for the slow dance.

I must admit to feeling a tad alarmed at the sight of his wrist in Luna's jaws, but to my surprise Robbie had a crooked grin on his face.

'She's not fucking biting me you daft woman,' his gravelly voice, laced with whisky and God knows what else he had taken, echoed rather loudly. I watched as Shona's face became inflamed. Robbie seemed impervious to this. He was looking at Luna who was fixing him with her huge silvery dark eyes. 'She's rescuing me, aren't you? Clever girl.' This was followed by a raucous bark of laughter.

With perfect timing, just as Shona was about to explode, Sean appeared at her side. With a dashing bow, he swept her away into the moving swirl of dancers before she had time to protest. Robbie then offered a rather wobbly bow in my direction and held his free arm out to me.

'Your wolf has requested I join you, and who am I to refuse?'

I then walked with him holding my arm on the one side and Luna, keeping a grip on his other hand. It raised more than a few eyebrows and Robbie played to the crowd.

'What's a man to do when a wolf and her mistress command?'

There was high spirited laughter as we left the ballroom but in the corner of my eyes, I saw the look on Shona's face as Sean gracefully spun her around. It was twisted with hatred. I couldn't think about the implications of this right now though, I had a mad man to entertain in the gardens of Wolf Lodge. But as soon as we ventured outside, I could not stop myself from exclaiming.

'Oh wow, that is stunning! I've never seen such a sky.'

For a moment I forgot everything other than the sheer dark beauty of the sky above me. I released myself from Robbie's hold and walked a little way down between the formal flower beds. There was snow on the ground, but these paths had been salted and remained clear of it. Tilting my head up to scan the heavens, I was awestruck.

'I have never seen a sky like this,' I repeated as much as to myself as to him.

'Aye, it is special,' his voice was close in my ears 'There is nothing else quite like it.' There was a moment of silence, not unpleasant and then he went on. 'It makes you wonder though doesn't it, the sheer scale of it, the enormity of it, it makes us humans look so fucking small and ridiculous.' He gave a harsh laugh. 'Really, why do we even fucking exist? What's going to be left of us after we leave this earth? Fucking nothing. Nor should it either, cos we're fucking inconsequential. We're all just fucking wee dots, grubby little monsters, scratting about trying to prove we're all so fucking brilliant at this that and the fucking other. And none of it makes a fucking difference. None of it.'

The last words held so much pain I whirled my head round to look at him. Was this what Lily had meant when she said his crashes were always worst when he had been drinking and taking drugs? Did he then slump into some kind of depression? I searched for the moon in the sky, relieved to see it was not full. Then I mentally gave myself a kick for even considering such a thing. But there was no denying the despondency that had been in his voice a second ago.

I had to respond to it. 'Yes. but you make a difference to Lily, surely that matters?'

He went very quiet and still, statue like. I thought then, if it began to snow, he would let the flakes fall and cover him until he was no longer visible. The air between us was sharp with the icy coldness of the night. I felt completely out of my depth. Here I was, in this bewitching setting, an inky sky alive with stars as brilliant as diamonds above me, crystalline snow making magical forms of the garden, a wolf at my feet, and a darkly, brooding man towering next to me.

As soon as these thoughts registered in my mind, I had the urge to giggle. I sounded as though I was a heroine in a regency romance, escaping the ballroom for a midnight tryst. I did giggle then and the statue before me moved.

'Och, so you think I am a laughable excuse for a father, do you?'

'No. No, not at all. That was not what I was thinking.' The sudden flash of his temper was alarming. 'I was thinking something completely different.'

'What?'

The word was snapped out less of a question, more an interrogation; as though I was deliberately hiding something from him.

Perhaps a touch of paranoia I wondered, as I said in all honesty, 'Nothing to do with you.'

'Don't lie. You think I can't be a good father to Lily, don't you?'

He took a step towards me, closing the gap until there were inches between us. The next moment his hands grabbed my arms and pulled me even closer. I could see how intently his eyes were staring into mine. Luna sat up a little at his movements but oddly there was no snarling from her. I took this to mean that she saw him as no threat.

Trusting my wolf, far more than I trusted myself, I replied steadily, 'I was not thinking that at all. Why would I? I hardly even know you.'

'What were you thinking then that made you laugh so? You sounded like a young girl.'

Yet another change from him. He flipped from mood to mood it was hard to keep up. Now he was looking at me with a teasing light in his eyes that was making my head spin. I had the ridiculous urge to giggle again. I should not have had so much champagne and then come out into the fresh air. It was sending me giddy.

'You look so pretty when you laugh like that,' he said, his voice now low, quiet and ever so dangerous.

In the background I could hear the revelry from the ballroom ringing in the new year. The noise had caught his attention too.

'Midnight,' he said.

I was trapped in his arms and seemingly turned to stone myself. I shot a glance out of the corner of my eyes to Luna, but my wolf had relaxed on the ground.

'Happy New Year,' I stuttered, my voice sounding most unlike my own.

He titled his head and grinned then, a very wicked, knowing grin. 'Happy New Year, Daisy.'

Then of course he kissed me.

And this of course would have been absolutely fine.

After all, it was New Year's Eve, the clock had just struck midnight. From inside the lamenting strains of *Auld Lang Syne* were clearly audible. Kissing the person you were with, was an acceptable custom. What could in no way be deemed acceptable, was to surrender just like one of those ridiculous heroines I had been thinking about, into a passionate embrace of the sort that quite literally had me damn near swooning.

Daisy really what are you doing? Stop this now woman!

I thought these thoughts but for the life of me I could not action them. A surprised moan escaped my mouth, and an answering throaty growl came from him, as the pressure of the kiss increased. I willingly opened my mouth to let his tongue entwine with mine.

Dear God Daisy, what the hell are you doing?

At the same time another voice in my head demanded more, yes please more. I felt tiny in his arms, weak kneed and weak willed as he kissed me deeper and deeper. The peaty taste of whisky was in his mouth, but I think I was already intoxicated beyond measure for this to have any more of an effect.

I groaned again and this time it was a guilty murmur, 'Sean.'

'Is not here,' was the brusque response. 'You are, I am.' He pulled away from me for a second and in the twinkling night sky I was mesmerised by the look in his eyes. Dark, so very dark, the iris's huge and a reminder that he had probably been taking drugs on top of the alcohol.

All the more reason to pull away now Daisy.

Right now!

Still I didn't.

I must be really drunk, I thought as I watched in slow motion as he bent his head once more. This time I crazily allowed my hands to sneak up around his neck and tangle into his hair, thick and long around his collar.

Yes, definitely drunk.

But even as I tried to use this as an excuse, I knew it was a lie. It was not the alcohol, or the sharp sting of icy cold air that had numbed my brain. It was the physical effect the man was having on me.

Hot, earthy, basic desire; so raw it stunned me.

So much desperation in those kisses and I could not tell if that was from him or me, that there was no way I could just stop. Nor did I want to.

There was a moment when I felt one hand move down to lift the hem of my skirt and the heat increased as firm fingers stroked the length of my thigh and higher still. I had worn lacy pull up stockings for the first time since I could remember and a high-pitched whimper escaped into the night air as those searching fingers found the silk of my knickers and probed beneath.

I felt shame at the knowledge that he must have found me already wet.

Fear at the look in his eyes and the energy coming from him.

Excitement that locked me into place and stilled my voice from demanding he stop.

He somehow pushed me backwards and I was half leaning against the thick wall of a hedge, cold and wet against my back. More urgent movements and suddenly there it was, the feel of him, nudging against my naked skin.

Shocking.

Thrilling.

'I can't, I mustn't,' I gasped in horror both at my actions and the weakness of the words.

'Well, I can, and I must,' he drawled, his Scottish accent thicker and voice rougher with need.

In one urgent movement he was inside me, his hands on my bottom, the bare skin of his thighs under his kilt rubbing against my own. A sharp intake of breath as the air was momentarily halted in my lungs. I couldn't breathe, couldn't move, couldn't do a damn thing, only feel the heat and hardness of him filling me as though I belonged to him.

A moment in my life when everything changed.

Whatever had existed within me before had been banished. There was no doubting the fact that I was opening myself to him, clinging to him, with complete and utter surrender. I thought, half hysterically, of the heroines I had read about in my regency romances. I could not recall one of them being ravished in the moonlight. It always stopped at mere kisses.

And yet here I was, under the glorious light of the moon being well and truly ravished by a mad artist, a possible killer. I must be the one under some kind of curse I thought as I gave in to the overpowering demands of his body and mine.

Until it was impossible to ignore the noises coming from the Lodge. Music had given way to the chorus of people chatting and talking and Catriona announcing something loudly about fireworks.

'Stop!' I panted, terrified that we would be discovered in minutes and equally terrified that this was going to stop before I could explode as brightly as any Catherine Wheel. 'The fireworks!'

'Fuck the fireworks!' He replied and to my horror I saw that he was not going to pull out. 'My fucking land, my fucking lodge, and right now,' he said with a somewhat demonic look, 'I am fucking you.' He increased the power of his movements with each word until all I could do was hang onto him for dear life, biting my lip to stop the screams that I so desperately wanted to let loose into the night.

Moments later he sank his head into the crook of my neck. I thought he was going to bite me like a vampire, which in my semi delirious state would have made a lot of sense and excused my behaviour. But he, like me, seemed to be trying to contain the vocal outpouring that should have accompanied the orgasm that rocked through us both. As quickly as he had entered me, he pulled out, leaving me virtually on my knees at the suddenness of the movement.

'Och sorry, here, let me help you up.'

'I can manage thank you,' I said stiltedly through lips that had now turned wooden even as my limbs had turned to jelly.

'As you please. You're a damn fine fuck Daisy, anyone ever tell you that?'

I raised my hand to slap him at the same time I heard an appalled gasp a few feet away.

'You wasted no time I must say!'

There was more light now being thrown into the gardens as burning torches lit the way for the people to gather on the terrace to watch the fireworks. Thankfully most did not venture down the paths but Shona had done. In the spooky light of stars and torches I could see her face shining with animosity.

'Are the fireworks ready?' Robbie asked her coolly and even I was appalled at his lack of sensitivity.

I saw then that her hand did flare out to strike him, but he was too quick for her.

'Fucking try it,' he warned her as he grabbed her wrist easily in one hand. 'Now, go and do your job and help Catriona set off the fireworks.'

'Bastard,' she hissed under her breath.

'Probably,' he agreed nonchalantly.

To me she added spitefully, 'Don't think I won't tell Sean you've just cheated on him.'

No, no, no, no!

I cried out the words silently in my head, hating myself and Robbie in equal measures. I was not a cheat. Yes. I was. I watched in horror as Shona stomped back up the garden path towards the terrace. Perhaps if I ran, I could get to Sean before she did. But then what? Really what could I say? Shona would still get to him. The heat of desire, as base and unexpected as it had been, was replaced by the stinging chill of utter mortification.

'Is it serious between you two?' Robbie asked me in such casual manner it was impossible to consider how intimate we had just been.

'What?' I spun round to face him and found he was eyeing me thoughtfully. 'Yes. No. I don't know.'

That of course was the truth of it. I really didn't know with Sean. I had never known. I had just welcomed the warmth of human affection and touch after being betrayed by Gary. I winced inside. Now I had betrayed Sean. What did that make me?

'He won't mind you know.'

'What?' I seemed incapable of more logical thought.

'Sean. I don't think he will mind.'

I stared at him as though he was an absolute idiot. 'But we have just...'

'Fucked. Aye, and as I said damn fine it was too, Daisy. He's a lucky man.'

He was making my head spin.

'Well, I would bloody mind!' I exploded and I knew it was true.

If Sean had so casually romped with Shona, then I really would bloody mind. Tearful and confused I swirled away from Robbie, desperately wishing that I had a magic wand and could wave away the last quarter of an hour.

The fireworks were in full display as I made my way back to the terrace. Sean was standing a little apart from everyone, leaning against the stone balustrade that edged the steps down to the gardens. He was watching my progress and I knew then that Shona had indeed spared no time in telling him. With a heavy heart I placed one foot after the other and took each step slowly and reluctantly.

'Sean...' I opened my mouth to speak and I couldn't as my throat was clogged with tears.

Unbelievably he held open his arms and wrapped me up in the sweetest of embraces. I couldn't stand his kindness and I sobbed quietly into the front of his shirt.

'I don't know what came over me, Sean. I really don't.'

I raised my eyes at last, daring to see what was in his own, expecting condemnation but finding instead something entirely different.

'Ah Daisy darling, so you are human after all.'

'Yes but...'

He wiped a finger across my cheeks to clear away the tears. 'But what? You got drunk a little, maybe a lot. You got bewitched by the moonlight and stars.'

'I think you are being too kind Sean. Far too kind. I have just behaved appallingly.'

'You haven't killed anyone. You haven't hurt anyone.'

'Have I not hurt you, Sean?'

He smiled at this, a crooked smile that was both loving and disturbingly mischievous. In the background light of the fireworks, it was difficult to read his face properly.

'You could never hurt me, Daisy. Did you think as you walked out into the garden with him that this would happen?'

'No! No of course I didn't.'

'Well then,' he said as though this was all that mattered. 'Now have you ever seen such a lovely firework display. Oh, and Daisy darling, Happy New Year.'

He kissed me softly, tenderly, on the lips that had just been so devoured by Robbie Munro.

I clung to him with a desperate need of something I could not define and whispered back. 'Happy New Year Sean.'

As I did so I tried to ignore the nagging thought in my mind that if I had not known what would happen when I walked out into the garden with Robbie Munro, had he?

Chapter Twenty-Two

To say I was unsettled by my behaviour was putting it mildly. I spent the next couple of days feeling as though someone else had temporarily inhabited my skin. Whilst this was prickly and uncomfortable, there were the odd flashes when I felt as though I had been allowed a glimpse of another reality.

A world in which a completely different Daisy existed.

A world in which this Daisy was driven by her senses and not practicality.

I was aware that I had already begun to behave a little in this fashion with Sean. More than a little. Inviting him back into my home had been totally out of character. But at least I could hide behind the excuse that I was reeling from the double blows of Gerald's death and Gary's betrayal.

What I had done with Robbie Munro was completely different.

For one thing, I could not use the excuse of vulnerability.

For another, I didn't even like the man, let alone his reputation.

Anyone could fall for Sean. He was charm personified, not to mention the good looks and the lyrical tones of his accent. He was also kind to old ladies, children, and animals alike. As I had said to Moira, who on earth would be interested in the grumpy sod that was Robbie Munro? Apparently, Shona was. Mandy, one of the guests, had also alluded to being attracted to him, despite the suspicion that he had had something to do with the deaths of three women.

They must be crazy.

I told myself this every time I remembered the shocking thrill of how suddenly he had taken me up against the snow-covered hedge. They were crazy. I was crazy. Plain and simple. Never mind worrying that Robbie himself was mad; clearly, we all were. Thankfully for the rest of our stay at Wolf Lodge, I did not see much at all of Robbie. But what I did see of him only added to the notion of him being a few cards short of the deck.

How else could you explain his behaviour?

He didn't speak to me at all, in fact he didn't speak to anyone apart from Sean. I could quite happily have banged their heads together at one point. How was it possible for the two of them to chat so easily after what had happened? I really didn't get it. I observed that with everyone else he was abrupt to the point of rudeness or would go suddenly silent and stare blankly into space as though somewhere else entirely. Then it was time to leave and return home. I had to face clearing out my belongings so that Gary and Corinne could move in, before coming back to take up the position as manager and live there.

'You are coming back, Daisy, aren't you?' Lily was hanging around the entrance hall with Catriona.

Truthfully, I was regretting my decision already. This was all a horribly bad idea. I would go back home, swallow my pride and sign on with a teaching agency. That would be by far the best thing for me to do.

'Yes I am. I just have things I need to sort out at home first.' Daisy will you get control of your mouth!

I shot a look over to Sean. I had told him in bed that morning that I was going to change my mind and once I had returned home, I would pen a polite but firm letter to Catriona. He grinned broadly.

'It's going to make such a difference having you here properly,' said Catriona. 'You took to it like a duck to water, it's like you have always been part of the family.'

I couldn't respond as she then enveloped me in a hug and invited Sean back anytime.

'I promise I will pop back to see how you are all doing. But as I am sure Daisy has explained, I will be occupied for a while helping someone else out.'

I shot him a sideways glance which as usual he managed to ignore. Was this his way of reminding me that our time with was coming to an end. Was this why he had pushed me to go for that moonlit walk with Robbie? Had he tired perhaps of his dalliance with me and didn't know how to tell me kindly?

It was a long drive back home and for the first time since I had got to know Sean, I was uncomfortable with him. He picked up on this, of course he did. We had only been driving for about twenty minutes and he reached over a hand to clasp one of mine and raise it to his lips.

'Daisy darling why so serious? You aren't still fretting over what happened on New Year's Eve are you? If you are, well then that's daft. You were drunk, he was drunk. It was a moment Daisy, a moment. And he is a handsome brute, so I can understand it, I really can. I would fancy him myself if I were that way inclined.'

'He's also a possible serial killer!' I exploded.

'I must admit, I did not see that one coming,' said Sean lightly. 'It certainly makes things interesting.'

'Interesting!' I couldn't help another sharp retort.

In a quiet moment I had managed to Google the details of the story.

It wasn't pretty.

Over a five-year period, three women had gone missing in the local area, only to turn up later raped and stabbed. The first had been a hiker who had been staying at Wolf Lodge. The second had been a married woman who lived ten miles away. Heartbreakingly in her case, she was the mother of a toddler. The most recent, just over a year ago, had been the woman who Catriona had employed to take over her role as manageress.

Two out of three with direct links to Wolf Lodge.

Bad enough.

More damning was the discovery that Robbie Munro had been linked to all of them, including the married woman. He had been conducting an affair with her whilst her husband was away on the oil rigs. Worse, the fact that under interrogation from the police, Robbie himself had declared wildly that he could not remember what he had been doing on two of the three nights in question. He had even gone so far as to beg to be locked up in case it happened again.

Only an extremely expensive lawyer and a complete lack of forensic evidence had prevented him from being charged. A scarf from the hiker had been found in his room, but as his lawyer had pointed out, Robbie had not denied having a relationship with her, if only whilst she was on holiday.

A grim picture.

A womanising man who suffered blackouts and had begged to be locked up.

Forget the notion of a curse, that was clearly his family's way of hiding from the ghastly truth themselves. I thought of all the cases where people related to killers had denied all knowledge of their behaviour. I would always scoff at this. How could they possibly not know?

'Yes, very interesting.' He said again with a nod of his head.

I let out a sigh that was more of an explosion of confusion and mixed emotions. 'Sean you are just so different to anyone I have ever met, sometimes I wonder…'

'What?' He took his eyes off the road for a second to look at me. Dazzling blue eyes so intense in a face creased and lined with a life well and truly lived.

And was that it? Was he so different because of how he lived his life? Homeless and on the streets a few months ago, and yet an accomplished architect, talented in so many other areas that it was hard to keep up with him. Did he simply live his life according to his own random code, in which case me having sex with another man did not disturb him? Me accepting a job with a possible killer did not worry him?

Then he delved into his story telling soul to have me laughing my way out of my discomfort, weaving his Irish magic so that by the time we had crossed over the border back into England I had all but forgotten about my fears.

That night as we lay entangled together once more, I slept easily telling myself that what had happened with Robbie was an out of character oversight brought on by too much champagne and nothing more than that. I even managed to convince myself that the torrid rumours were just that and that there would be a perfectly practical answer to everything.

Violet popped in for coffee the following morning to see how I had got on in Scotland, and I think, because she was feeling a little guilty over Sean moving on to help out her nephew.

'Was it what you expected then?' She asked.

I poured us a cup of tea and served her a slice of fruit cake that Mary had insisted I brought back with us. It was heavily laced with whisky and met with my elderly neighbour's approval instantly. Her enjoyment of the cake gave me a moment for my blushes to subside. A vivid image of Robbie had been in my mind, and I had to shove it back to where it belonged, right out of my head.

'It was interesting,' I said cautiously. I showed her the photos I had taken on my phone, not just of the Lodge and the chalets but of the people there too. Except of course Robbie, he did not feature in any of them.

Violet finished her cake and looked at them carefully. 'It's magical,' she said scrolling through them one by one. 'I am definitely going to book a room. Once I have got my own move sorted out of course. I had an estate agent round whilst you were away.'

'Crikey that was quick.'

'I don't believe in shilly-shallying once a decision has been made. A for sale sign will be going up tomorrow. And at least for you dear, with Gary doing what he is doing, you can, in all essence, just walk away and start your new life.' She eyed me sharply. 'Provided of course that you get a fair price for your half,' she stressed 'including the plot he is selling to the builders. Now, who is this lovely young lady in this photograph running in the snow with Luna? She looks delightful.'

'That's Catriona's granddaughter.'

'And what is her name dear?'

'Lily.'

She had not missed the pause. She said ever so gently, 'Wasn't that the name of your daughter?'

'Would you like a second cup of tea?' My voice was absurdly bright as my hand rattled the tea pot.

Her hand stilled mine. 'It stays with you always doesn't it? I often wonder what my Carrie would have been doing now, had she lived. As I am sure you must do. I picture the life she could have had. I rather fancy she could have been a dancer you know, a ballerina. I had promised her dancing lessons for her fifth birthday.' A sigh as fragile as a snowflake falling to the ground. 'Meningitis.'

I had never allowed myself to even think how my daughter might have grown up. We had had a few precious hours together, long enough for me to decide on her name. Then she was whisked away to intensive care, and I was suddenly rushed into surgery myself. When I had come round from the anaesthetic and the operation that meant there would be no more children for me, she was gone.

Lily.

A daughter named for a graceful, elegant, beautiful flower.

Mine briefly.

'Oh, Daisy forgive me, I have made you cry, how stupid of me.' Violet squeezed the hand she had grasped and through my tears I could see the shine in her own.

I couldn't speak. Literally could not say a word. I had shut my eyes but that did not stop the silent rivers falling down my cheeks. I heard Violet moving about the kitchen, a cupboard door, a bottle opening, a glug and splash of liquid. Then gentle arms around my shoulders.

'You can't hold it in forever, Daisy, Lord knows my dear, I tried that myself. It will send you mad in the end. You have to find some way of peace with it. Maybe, just maybe, the fact that this young girl is called Lily is a sign for you.'

I snuffled, sobbed, shook into her arms, all the while knowing that she understood my pain, my grief because she too had lost a daughter. We had only ever spoken of it the once, years ago not long after I had first moved in with Gerald and Irene. My mother-in-law had told Violet about the loss of our baby girl and Violet had found the way one day to let me know ever so gently that if I ever needed to talk, she would understand.

For ten years I had lived next door to her. Now we were parting ways; me up to the wilds of Scotland, and Violet nearer to her nephew in Manchester. Yet now was the time that finally I was talking to her. I don't know how long I rambled on, but she sat with me, and listened. She encouraged me to drink my tea, now super charged with whisky and finally when the words and tears had dried up, she cut a second slice of cake for me and slid it towards me.

'Sugar my dear, it is so very bad for us, but at times it is exactly what we need. Along with another cup of tea.'

I let her brew up another pot and made no protest at the generous amount of whisky that was poured into this cup as well. It was only eleven o clock in the morning but what the hell.

'So,' she said as she sat down back opposite me again, 'tell me about this Lily. She has obviously made an impression on you and not just for the name.'

Astonishingly I found I could talk about Lily Munro and Violet was right; she had made an impression on me. She was just the sort of young girl I would have imagined my own Lily to grow up to be. Violet was intrigued by the notion of a spell and a curse.

'Sounds fascinating! I really must come up there and meet them all.'

I laughed. 'Well, I am not at all sure about the spell and family curse to be honest. But I can see how seriously Lily takes it. She certainly has reason to be concerned about her father.' This ended with a snort which of course meant I had to expand further. I did so, retaining the more lurid details.

'I would trust Sean in this matter Daisy. If he has no concerns, then neither should you.'

We got to talking about practical matters and she helped me make a list of jobs to do before I could move back up there. It was good to get my head thinking on a less emotional level and Violet could see I had recovered from my outburst.

'Well Daisy, I think I had better be getting along. I have much to do myself. I have arranged for a house clearing company to come this afternoon, which I must confess I am not looking forward to at all. So many memories, it is going to be hard to let go, but I must.'

I promised her I would go round later and give her a hand. 'And then why don't we go out for tea?'

'Ooh the Roebuck?'

'Sticky toffee pudding?' We said at the same time.

'With caramel sauce and vanilla ice cream.' Violet finished with a smile. 'Absolutely.'

We rose from the table and together cleared away the pot of tea, the cups, cake and whisky bottle.

Violet touched me gently on the arm. 'I shall see you later,' and let herself out the back door.

Sean had taken the train to Manchester to meet up with her nephew, so I had the house to myself. Feeling the need to shake off the wooziness, the emotion and the whisky, I grabbed my cheerful red coat, then with Luna at my side, I ventured out to the park. I told myself I was burning off the cake and alcohol before I took Violet out for tea. In reality, I was burning off pain and grief that went so much deeper than anything I had felt for Gerald and Irene, or even for the loss of my marriage.

Back home, I grabbed a quick cheese sandwich, half of which went down Luna's neck, and then made my way upstairs to my bedroom. With a rapidly beating heart, I opened my wardrobe doors. Before I could change my mind, I swiped at the clothes on the rail to root at the back for the box.

Shame was my first emotion as I realised how dusty it was. Shame and guilt that I had let the most important time in my life be shoved away and forgotten about. Well not forgotten, never that. Impossible to forget. Too painful to brave looking at.

Coward.

I had been a coward in not talking about Lily. I had been a coward in not thinking about the suggestion Marigold had made. I remembered how my heart had turned against my mother for her suggestion. How dare she even think that adopting could possibly mend what had been broken?

I remembered now with a clarity that stunned me, how Gary had taken her side, and how my fury had turned against him. I felt the room tilting for a moment. I was no longer there but watching myself witnessing the scenes over again. The difference was I could see the pain in both my mother's eyes and my husband's. I watched as though a film were replaying before my me. How I had shut down. Pushed away offers of help. Withdrawn.

This shocking insight left me winded.

If I followed this train of thought, if I dared to find the courage, I knew what I would have to face. It was not an excuse. What Gary had done was still wrong. He had lied to me. Been unfaithful to me. Tried to cheat me financially.

But I had pushed him away.

This had all taken place in those very early years, but the rot had set in and like a cancer I had fed it. I remembered one of many stories Sean had told me.

'Did I ever tell you the about the white wolf and the grey one that lives within us?'

It had been one morning when I had received another email from Gary about the divorce. I had been muttering and grumbling and he had begun to tell me this old native American tale. Quite where he had got it from who knew?

It went like this.

A child had asked an elder in their tribe why men fight all the time. The answer had been that men have two wolves within them. A white one and a grey one. The white one represents all that is good; honesty, courage, hope, love. The grey one represents all that is bad; deceit, fear, doubt, hate. The child had then asked which one won the fight.

I had asked Sean the same question as he had paused in the telling of the tale.

'Which do you think, Daisy?'

I had shrugged and replied that I had no idea.

He had given me then one of his knowing looks. 'The one you feed the most wins.'

I thought about this now as I held the box of memories.

I had fed the grey one a diet of hurt and resentment and in doing so I had closed the door myself on my marriage. By the time we had moved in with Gary's parents to help ease the burden of Irene's dementia, the habit had been well and truly formed.

It had been easy to throw myself into the caring role, finding an outlet for all that pent-up emotion, when I should have been looking in the other direction. I should have been looking at Gary, at what we had had when we first started out. I should have been trying to find a way to get past our hurt together, instead of somehow assuming the mantle of martyrdom all by myself.

It was like looking in one of those mirrors at a fairground where the image was distorted and hideous. Only the twisted reflection looking back at me, was the very unpalatable truth. I felt quite sick. Luna came to my rescue. My white wolf with the magic in her eyes. She licked my hand and then gently nudged at the box. I pulled on the faded pink ribbon tied in a bow and took off the lid.

The photograph. The tiny snip of downy hair. The delicate crocheted shawl that Marigold had made. My mother had done that? I was lost in a bewildering time warp and only aware that I had not moved a muscle and was now chilly when I heard the footsteps on the stairs. I was not expecting to see Marigold, colourfully dressed in tangerine and black.

Instantly on guard, my body stiffened further. 'What's the matter?' Clumsily I tried to hide what I was holding.

'You are Daisy,' she said, 'you're the matter.'

I tried to read her expression and couldn't, until her eyes took in what I had in my hands and then it was easy to see the pain. I let her carefully take from me the contents of the box and remained silent whilst she handled them one by one. There was no disguising the tenderness in her touch and a part of me began to silently cry inside, that she had never held me so tenderly. Or if she had, I could not remember.

'What are you doing here Marigold?'

'I had a dream last night,' she said slowly.

I experienced a little shiver. Rarely did we acknowledge the Romany blood in the family. It was there, diluted perhaps but there all the same. Rose had always dabbled with tarot cards and palm reading. I shied well away from such nonsense, but I knew well enough to listen on the rare occasions that Marigold chose to disclose something.

'Lots of wolves,' she continued and thoughtfully stroked Luna's head. 'Grey ones, snapping at me. Devouring me. Then this one appeared. And I saw her. Lily. Your Lily. And Mine.'

'What do you mean. Your Lily.'

She twisted her hands together, fidgeting with her amber ring. I had never seen her discomforted before, always so brazen it was strange to witness her looking almost frightened.

'It's my sin you are paying for.'

'What?' Of all the things she could have said I was not expecting this.

'Lily. It's always been about Lily.'

'You aren't making any sense. And what sin are you talking about?'

'I had an abortion.' She virtually spat out the word as though it was a poison pellet in her mouth.

I was astounded and yet still it was not clear why she was disclosing this to me. And why now? And again, what did it have to do with my Lily? She answered the questions in my eyes with a rapid speech as though once she had ripped off the gagging tape there was no holding back.

'It was before I married your dad. My life was very different. I lied to you and Rose when you were growing up. I lived on the streets for a while. I was only young, very young. I had to survive so I did what I needed to. Not proud of it but it had been happening to me anyway so I thought I may as well get paid for it. Got pregnant, got rid of it.'

It was like machine gun fire, each sentence a bullet shattering the ideas I had had of my mother growing up in a close family, not that she ever talked much about them. What did she mean, it had been happening to her anyway? Now was perhaps not the time to ask as she had more to off load.

'I had always told myself if I had a daughter, then my first born would have been called Lily. Well, I did. Only I never allowed her to live. I couldn't see a way out you see. I knew it was wrong. I hated myself afterwards. Took an overdose. That's when I met your dad.'

I knew I was gawping at her in astonishment. This was so not the story

Rose and I had grown up with. Staggered I could only let her continue.

'He was working in the hospital when they brought me round from having my stomach pumped. He was so handsome and kind. First man to treat me with respect he was.' This last bit was said with so much sadness I felt my world rocking once more on its axis. 'He didn't care you see. What I had been before. What had happened. I did though. Deep down that is. Never thought I was worthy of him.' She gave a peculiar snort and I realised then that she was holding back the tears. 'How could I be? Raped by my father and then selling myself to anyone for a tenner, a fiver, when other girls my age were doing their exams and going to college.'

A stranger was sitting on my bed next to me.

A woman in her sixties was telling me she had been raped by her father.

A woman who had been on the streets, fallen pregnant, had an abortion.

The images she had put in my mind collided brutally with my own memories. A mother who didn't seem to care. A mother who constantly argued and fought with my dad. A mother who seemed intent only on having a good time. It was sending me dizzy. Yet I had to get over my feelings and respond to the woman next to me.

I reached for her hand to offer comfort. 'I'm so sorry, Mum.' The word slipped out and for once she did not correct me and insist I call her Marigold.

Beneath the careful makeup, I saw the signs of age on her face, highlighted now as the mask of her pretence was stripped away.

'What have you got to be sorry for? It's my sin. That's why you lost your Lily. I tried asking you, remember, not to call her that if you were to have a girl. But you wouldn't listen. Had your heart set on that name you did, just like I had. Only I got rid of my first daughter and that's why you lost Lily.'

In the face of her punishing guilt, I could only shake my head and protest. 'No. No that's just not true. It wasn't your fault.'

Dozens of memories were flooding through my mind, gushing like a river breaking its banks. I had thought Marigold callous and uncaring in so many of her words and actions, both when I was a child but if I thought about it, more so after the birth and death of my own.

Guilt.

A poisonous serpent.

It had slithered into Marigold's mind so long ago, its vicious forked tongue whispering deadly words in her ears, making her doubt herself, her value, her worthiness. I could see it all so clearly it was as though someone had just floodlit everything and the shocking brilliance of it was blinding. I bit my lip so hard I could taste the blood.

Dark grey wolves, snapping at us both.

I gave an involuntary jerk and looked at Luna who was resting her head between us now.

'Not your fault Mum,' there I said it again. 'Not your fault at all.'

The hand I was holding squeezed back. 'I blamed myself.'

'I see that now.'

'I pushed your dad away, and you two girls. I couldn't bear you calling me Mum. I didn't think I deserved the name. Not after what I had done.'

She knocked the wind right out of me then with this last remark and the next thing I knew I was hugging her tightly and we were both crying.

'Why now?' I asked her a little while later. 'Why come and tell me now?'

She shrugged. 'I told you, Daisy, the dream. The wolves. It was as though Luna here was guiding me. I couldn't stop myself.' She wiped her tears and looking a bit more composed, regarded Luna solemnly. 'You do know she is magic, Daisy don't you. There is enough Romany soul inside of me to tell me that.'

I smiled and it turned into a grin that we both shared. 'Yes, I do know that.' I thought of the tattoo on my back, and how Sean had taken me to have that done.

Sean.

I heard his voice calling from downstairs.

'Hello up there. I got finished earlier in Manchester than I thought. Violet texted me, something about tea at the Roebuck and sticky toffee pudding? I'll book us a table for four then, shall I?' He was in the doorway of the room, silver blond hair windswept around his craggily lined face, eyes a brighter blue than any artist could produce. 'Good to see you Marigold.'

He had always been a little off hand with her, rebuffing her attempts to flirt with him. Now though he entered the room with a gentle smile on his face, the warmth of which was like having the sun shine upon you after a very dark day.

'You've been having some mother and daughter time then I see? Good. All good. Now, let's go and eat, shall we?'

I am sure, but I could not swear to it, that as he bent his head to make a fuss of Luna, he said in her furry ear, 'Good girl Luna, well done.'

Chapter Twenty-Three

In the end, leaving Park Road had been easier than I had thought. All down to Sean of course. He had transformed me from an empty shell of a woman, to a Daisy that I rather liked. I had watched his influence on those around me. Sean had the ability to bring people together and break down invisible barriers. It was as though having exposed my family and the various rifts between us at Christmas, he then went about weaving threads that skilfully bound us back together.

Only as an improved version.

If you asked me exactly how he did this, I could not say. There were no specific actions he took, or at least none that I was aware of. Yet from him coming on the scene, I'd had a visit from my dad, openly expressing his regret in how distant he had been. Followed of course by that shattering disclosure from Marigold.

She had shaken the foundations of everything I had grown up to believe. I talked at length to Sean. He shone his spotlight on the pertinent points and brushed aside what he lightly scoffed as being irrelevant. She had suffered. She had projected that pain onto Rose and me and especially our dad as she had barricaded herself so effectively behind that pain.

When I commented on the peculiar co-incidence of Marigold naming her daughter Lily, his reply was, 'It is a rare bond that binds you together.'

'He should be a priest,' Marigold said to me a couple of days later. Unusually, she had offered to come and help me pack up my belongings. Unusually, I had let her. 'He took my hands just now as I walked through the door and told me to stop blaming myself. I know you told him. I'm okay with that. Other people have tried saying that to me. Including your dad.' She had shaken her head at this point, 'But him saying it, wow. I feel I have been absolved. Are you sure he hasn't been a priest?'

I remembered how I had asked myself the same question. 'No,' I responded. 'But he would have been a very good one.' Then I also remembered how he made me feel when we were in bed together and I blushed. At which point Marigold caught my eye and we shared a moment of laughter.

Even with Gary, there was a lessening of the bitterness that had seeped into my veins. The clarity that had hit me about my own behaviour after losing Lily had stung as brutally as salt into an open wound. I could not however, shy from it. Once it had been exposed, it had to be dealt with. There was a painful conversation just him and me at the kitchen table. Between us the unresolved grief for the loss of our child.

I saw the astonishment in his eyes when I haltingly broached the subject. He had not been expecting it at all. When I had made the phone call to ask him to come without Corinne, I think he had been geared up for a battle. What I gave him instead was an apology. I was not unaware as I did so of the irony of my situation and Marigold's. We had both succeeded in pushing away a very good man because of the pain we had been unable to deal with inside.

I still wished he had been more honest with me. Made a clean break before starting his affair. I still felt used in that he had waited until his parents were both dead and no longer needed care before telling me. But now I could say this to him calmly and in turn, he responded with the apology I needed to take away some of that hurt.

Then we had looked at each other with a desperate sadness reflected in our eyes that told the story we both wished things had turned out differently. Too late now though to start again. His future lay with Corinne and their baby. It was a bitter-sweet parting when it came to it and there were tears on both sides. He said in a rather choked voice that he would see I got my fair share of the garden plot he was selling. I wondered what Corinne would say to that but wisely kept quiet.

A few days later I retraced my journey up to the highlands, only this time without Sean at my side, just Luna. Sean made love to me that last night with a tenderness and ferocity that left me weeping and breathless. Every touch, ever kiss seemed to burn its way into my soul as though I was being branded. He laughed wickedly and then went on to brand me some more. As the soft dawn light broke through the winter darkness I had lain quietly in his arms, knowing with a certainty that did not need putting into words, that this would be the last time I would share a bed with him.

To question it would have been to tarnish it.

You do not put a price on a gift.

You do not ask where it has come from.

You do not ask how long you may keep it.

These were the thoughts that had pierced my mind in those last precious moments when I was wrapped in his arms, when he was warm and strong inside of me, when I felt myself glowing from something so much more than sex.

We dressed quietly, ate breakfast together, and then with a last lingering kiss he put on Gerald's overcoat, tied a bright yellow scarf around his neck which clashed wonderfully with his red polo neck, and got ready to walk out of the door. I offered to drive him, but he had said no. Didn't I have a long enough journey ahead of me? He was happy getting the bus, then the train to Manchester.

'I will come and see how you are doing,' he said with a smile that threatened to break my newly mended heart. 'But you'll be just grand Daisy, I know you will. And you have Luna to look after you.' I watched him walk down the path like a male version of Mary Poppins who had come whirling into my life, magically rearranged it, and now was off with a changing wind. I half expected Luna to disappear with him. But she stayed and I hoped, like the tattoo on my back, she would never leave me.

So, it began. A new life into which I quickly settled, despite my earlier reservations.

§

I would get up very early as my first job of the day would be to check in with Mary and Alex in the kitchen to see that everything was running smoothly for breakfast. Then I would greet the guests as they came down the stairs. Sometimes I would arrange local activities for them, often they just wanted a little chat and a few suggestions as to where to walk or explore. In the evenings I would read up and learn all there was to know about the area.

The weather when I arrived at the beginning of February was rather brutal. I realised that what I had considered suitable winter attire was not going to cut it in the highlands. Moira caught up with me one morning after I had come back from walking Luna. It was a particularly cold day with a wind so icy it threatened to freeze the breath in your lungs.

'I'm nipping into town in a wee while,' she said cheerfully, smiling at the noises I was making as I shed my red duffle coat. 'Why don't you come with me. We can get you a warmer coat, or perhaps some better layers for underneath as that does look cosy. It's all about the layers up here, Daisy.'

'If I put on anymore, I shall look like an Eskimo,' I said pulling at the various tops I was wearing.

Catriona walked through the lobby and overheard. 'Aye but none of those are the right kind. You go along with Moira and get kitted out properly. Wednesdays are always quiet. Why don't you have a wee bite to eat whilst you're at it? You've not stopped since you got here.'

I looked at Moira who nodded eagerly. 'What about Luna? Shall I leave her here?' So far, she had not left my side, a constant, watchful companion.

'I am quite happy to keep Luna company,' offered Catriona. 'I have some letters to catch up on. I am sure she will be perfectly alright with me in front of the fire in the library.'

I was not surprised to see Luna walk over to brush against Catriona's legs and then lope off with her. I was sure she was telepathic. I was also sure that when Catriona was having her tea and biscuit break there would be extra helpings from the kitchen.

Moira's rather battered but reliable old land rover provided the transport into Kinlaggan. In parts it was a bit of a bumpy ride, something I was still very mindful of when I dared to take my car out. Moira though manhandled the vehicle and the icy conditions, not to mention rather a few potholes with the aplomb of a rally driver. And the speed.

She laughed at my expression a few minutes into the drive. 'Don't worry, I know this road like the back of my hand. The only problem is if we run into a logging lorry, then we're fucked!'

I looked at her in horror and she laughed some more. 'Have you lived here all your life?' I asked her as she deftly swerved to avoid a black Porsche that was speeding in the opposite direction.

'You mad bastard,' she yelled out of the window, half-open despite the cold, 'you might have a fucking death wish but I don't!'

'Isn't that...?'

'Aye, Robbie, mad fucking bastard he is in that car. I swear one of these days he is going to wrap it around a tree like his father did. I only hope if he does, he doesn't take some other poor soul out with him! Stupid fucking idiot.'

I really didn't know how to respond to this tirade against the person who was in fact her boss and landlord, as he owned the entire estate. My expression brought more laughter.

'Och don't worry. I love the daft bastard to bits. I've known Robbie all my life and my family has always been close to his. We were in the same class at primary school and high school.' She became then suddenly serious. 'I really don't want him to kill himself, accidentally or otherwise. I wish he would sell that stupid bloody car, it's not right for round here at all.' She gave an odd half grunt then. 'Ah well that would be it wouldn't it.'

'What?'

She navigated the turning that would take us off the treacherous minor road to the main one.

'It has just occurred to me that he only drives that damn beast when he is in one of his moods. Have you not noticed that? No of course not, you have only just got here. It was his wife's car you see, Miranda's. He has never been bothered by fancy cars, not his thing at all. But when she left to go to America of course he kept the car. It's like a black monster he brings out of the garage when the darkness comes over him. Course, you're going to fix all that, so it'll be fine.'

'I'm really not too sure about this whole curse thing to be honest, Moira?' I said tentatively, not wishing to offend her.

'Aye well, regardless of that I still think you being here will make a difference.' She slanted me a sly look that hinted she possibly knew what had happened on New Year's Eve. I was determined though to keep absolutely silent on that matter.

She dropped the subject of Robbie realising I was not going to be forthcoming and soon it was time to park up the car and hit the town. In essence, this was one main street with wide pavements, and brightly fronted shops and cafés either side, snug in its setting with the river not too far away and the snow-capped mountain peaks in the distance.

It had a quaint old fashioned train station at one end with a platform either side of the tracks, and that was that. Kinlaggan to me was like a toy town. Yet it was bustling with friendly people. I loved it. Really loved it. When Moira told me that she had lived here all her life, I could understand why.

Everyone knew Moira and she introduced me. Used to the faceless anonymity back home, I found this all rather refreshing. I also enjoyed shopping with Moira, who like Sean was keen that I opted for bright cheerful colours. Unlike Sean, she was not exactly on the thrifty side.

'Och but it's good quality gear,' she said as I looked at the prices in one of the shops. 'Stuff like this lasts for years as well.' She plucked at the blueberry-coloured fleece she was wearing which flattered her cropped silver hair and blue eyes. 'I've had this ages. Tell her Tania, she'll save money in the long run if she buys the right clothes now.'

Tania, a young, and athletic blond agreed, 'Aye you need to be dressed right for our weather.'

As Gary was going to pay me for his share of the house, plus some extra for the plot of land he was selling, I could afford to splash out a little. I got out my card and put it to good use. We went back to the car to leave the bags in the boot and then Moira led the way to what she declared, was the best place in Kinlaggan for a spot of lunch. For a small town there were a lot of cafés and shops selling pies and cakes, as well as a rather posh looking hotel which I commented on.

'That looks cosy.'

'Aye it's a grand hotel. But we don't go in there.'

'We don't?' Was this I wondered some sort of hotel rivalry thing?

It appeared not.

For once the light hearted side of Moira vanished and she seemed at first reluctant to speak. I was skilled though in holding the gaze of someone, training from my years as a teacher and finally she gave way.

'I may as well tell you. Kenneth Grant who owns that hotel is the father of one of the women who went missing and was murdered.'

I tried recall the details from the internet. 'And why exactly does that affect us?'

'Cos she was the married woman who Robbie was having an affair with. When that came out in the investigation there was all manner of hell let loose. Her husband came back off the rigs and he and Robbie had a real set too just here. Damn near trashed the entire bar they did, what with Robbie being accused of killing her an' all.'

'Right,' I said slowly.

'Course he doesn't help himself at all the daft sod. He gets fearful drunk and tempersome at times,' she said as we pushed open the door to the café on the opposite side of the street. 'Actually, he doesn't need to be drunk. He can be fearful tempersome anytime.'

'So, what happens then?' I asked as I followed her to find a table. 'I mean, does he not get arrested?'

Moira rolled her eyes. 'Ach, this is Kinlaggan. Why bother? Folk tend to like a bit of a scrap around here. It livens things up. Besides, Dougal is his cousin.'

'Dougal?'

'Aye, the local police. And everyone knows that it's likely just the curse anyway on account of his dad and granddad being mad. Mind you, the police that came from Inverness took all that to point to him being a psycho but that's city folk for you. They don't understand these things.'

'No of course they don't' I commented as neutrally as I could and tried to concentrate on the menu.

I ordered something described as a huntsman pie with chips. There was no doubt the highland air had jump-started my appetite that had all but walked out the door last year.

'I'm thinking I will need to buy larger clothes soon if I am not careful,' I said as I began to eat.

'Nah, you'll work it off. Or shiver it off,' she grinned. Then returning to the topic of our mutual employer, her childhood friend and my one-night stand, she added, 'I think it also muddied the waters cos he is a bit of a celebrity.'

I coughed on a chip. 'He is?'

'Aye, he was on that show on telly, you know the one, it's on every night at tea time.'

I looked at her blankly.

'Ah well it was a while ago. It was Miranda you see. She managed him, as well as being his wife. That's how they met, through his art.'

Despite myself I was fascinated, and throughout our lunch I prompted Moira to fill me in on more of his background.

'He used to just do landscapes you see or animals, never having much time for folk. He's a genius at painting animals. You should look at his work sometime. Anyway, Miranda turns up at the hotel, years ago now with her fiancée. You can guess what happened.'

'He didn't?'

She finished a hefty mouthful of her lunch and nodded. 'He did. To be fair I think it was a bet from one of his drinking pals. Miranda was a right cold fish you see and snotty with it. Someone bet him he wouldn't be able to swipe her out from under the nose of her fiancée.'

'Really admirable behaviour,' I said dryly.

'Ah well, he was not having the best of times,' she said, 'his dad had just gone and smashed his car into the tree and Robbie was a wee bit mad as you can imagine.'

I knew grief made people do crazy things, even so I found it hard to like what I was being told about the man. What self-respecting woman would admire someone who casually set out to seduce another for a bet? What self-respecting woman would have sex up against a snowcovered hedge on New Year's Eve with the same man? Enough said. I let Moira continue.

'Anyway, it was at this time that Miranda saw what a talented painter he is, and I think she was interested in him for more than just the sex, which I am told he is very good at?'

Thank goodness for years of staring down teenagers. I held her gaze steadily.

Emitting a disappointed sigh as though she knew I was holding out on her, she went on. 'Anyway, Robbie was not looking for a relationship at all, and so Miranda disappeared back south of the border with her fiancé who she duly married. Robbie isn't that much of a bastard that he had to let the fellow know he had been cheated on.'

'Good to know,' I said solemnly.

'But there was a real hullabaloo a couple of years later when she came back with Lily. Turned out that Robbie had got her pregnant. Well Miranda obviously didn't know who the father was initially.'

This was intriguing. 'What happened? How did she end up marrying Robbie?'

'Turns out her husband needed to have some medical tests done for some weird condition and they wanted to test the wee bairn to see if she had inherited it. Only, as you can imagine, the tests showed that she couldn't possibly as he was not her father. Ergo rapid divorce and virtually zip settlement for Miranda as rich toff husband was furious for being duped.'

'And Robbie then wanted to marry her?'

Moira scoffed. 'Don't be daft! But there was Lily. Aye that was love at first sight I can tell you. None of us could believe how the cantankerous sod softened when he looked at her. So, as soon as Miranda was free, they got married. Only she was a real persistent bugger. She had the knack of getting under a person's skin. You see she pushed Robbie to move down to London and work the art scene, knowing that she could get him huge commissions for portrait work.'

'You surprise me. I wouldn't have thought he would agree to that at all.'

'Hm, well he wouldn't apart from at that time the estate was having financial difficulty on account of his dad being a bit of a fool when it came to gambling. He left a load of debts when he killed himself. The only other love in Robbie's life, apart from Lily, is of course Kinlaggan.'

I mulled over this as our plates were cleared and we ordered a chocolate pudding with a whisky sauce. After a few mouthfuls I asked what had happened to end the marriage and bring Robbie home.

'She thought she could tame him. Have him as her talented pet who just happened to bring in the money and a touch of fame.' Moira paused to enjoy a mouthful of calorific heaven and rolled her eyes. 'As if anyone could tame Robbie Munro, and especially in that environment. He was like a caged beast. I went down once with Catriona to visit him. Why anyone would want to live in London I do not know. You can't breathe! He couldn't handle it, so his drinking got worse and so did his behaviour.'

She shrugged. 'He's a handsome sod though, and with that gloss of fame he had women throwing themselves at him. Which of course, he never said no to. Miranda finally got fed up, but the last straw was when he told this really rich bloke she had got a commission for that he was a gormless wanker and he lost the sale.'

'Oh dear,' I found I was smiling. Which of course I should not have been.

'Aye well, the gormless wanker ended up being husband number three so that was the end of that. And as you know Lily, wise girl chose to stay with her dad. Growing up she had spent most of her holidays at Kinlaggan and for her it was like coming home.'

I had been told a little of this by Lily herself but a much more restrained version. Either way, Moira's gossip session told me three things. Firstly, that I could enjoy female friendship that had nothing to do with Gary, that was a positive. Secondly, the more I heard about Robbie Munro, the less I liked of him. Thirdly, I must be somewhat insane myself to have agreed to work for him.

What other explanation could there be?

Chapter Twenty-Four

Now I was working at the hotel I had a room on the side opposite to the guests' wing. It overlooked the formal gardens and was a lovely room. The only niggle was the fact that as I opened my curtains each morning, it was impossible not to allow my eyes to fall onto the spot where I had drunkenly, stupidly, let Robbie Munro have his drunken stupid way with me.

As soon as my eyes hit this spot, I would experience a sudden bolt of thoughts and emotions. Guilt, shame and an uncomfortable dose of lust. This was then stirred up with a sliver of anger at Robbie and peppered with just a dash of confusion at Sean. What had he been up to when he had pushed me into 'rescuing' Robbie from Shona's proposal? In my weaker moments I blamed him for my behaviour.

Sean.

I should be missing him, and in many ways I was. His humour, his compassion, his wit, his gentle and not so gentle at times lovemaking. He had been like a drug, altering my thoughts, emotions and behaviour. Surely at the sudden withdrawal I should have been suffering in some way.

I wasn't.

I was feeling wonderfully, gloriously alive.

I absolutely refused to contemplate not even for an instant, that this had anything to do with Robbie. It was rare that our paths crossed, as Catriona pointed out, he was far happier either secluded in his studio or out on the estate grounds, which suited me perfectly. I quickly learnt what time he ate his breakfast so I could avoid him. The thought of facing him first thing in the morning was just too much.

On the times we did come across each other, I told myself that my reaction to him was purely menopausal. The increase in heartbeat, the flush of temperature, the heat that ignited in my depths and had me clenching my thighs together - all of this was the blasted menopause.

Nothing to do with the towering presence he exuded, the sheer brawny size of him, the forest green eyes with intriguing flecks of hazel fringed with long dark lashes. Nothing to do with that at all. Or come to mention, the way his mouth, often in a grim surly line could suddenly twitch into a wicked, smile with a hint of the sensuality he had shown on New Year's Eve. Nothing to do with that at all. It certainly was not because of how he spoke in a low toned, gravelly voice. When my spine tingled if he did address me by name, it was yet another cursed symptom of the menopause.

So that was alright then.

I had that all nicely under control.

No need for random thoughts, emotions, feelings to go wildly off piste.

I had enjoyed my fling with Sean and now I could move forwards with my life.

I was not however, impervious to the entirely different effect that Lily had on me. Robbie's daughter was a delight to be around. The first couple of weeks I was at Kinlaggan, I didn't see much of her as she was at school. Robbie would take her the five miles down the winding roads to Kinlaggan, where she would then catch the bus that went on to the larger town of Inverlaggan. As she dashed past me in a flash of navy uniform, she would give me a big smile.

'Cheery bye Daisy, see you tonight.' And always the same question. 'Can I take Luna out when I get back from prison?'

Which put a smile on my face as I replied of course she could.

'Fridaaaay, Daisy!' Lily perched her bottom on the well-polished bannister and slid the last few feet landing gracefully by the reception desk. 'Freeeedom!'

I had to laugh and from behind her I heard a similar sound from Robbie. The noise, so rare from him demanded that my eyes, so determined not to look at him, would do so. He met them with a blankness that was a complete contrast to the fire I had seen that night in the garden. But then he had been fuelled with alcohol and drugs. Catriona had commented only yesterday that he was not drinking as much which she was pleased about.

He certainly did seem quieter.

I was not so sure this was a good thing. I was surprised to find myself thinking that he only seemed capable of switching on any form of light when it came to Lily. He looked right through me as though I was not even there. How was that possible? How could this be the same person who had…? I stopped there because I didn't want to think about what had happened in the gardens.

Instead, I smiled at Lily and teased her. 'I am surprised you are talking to me Lily if you hate school so passionately. After all I am a teacher. One of the enemy!'

'Ex Daisy. Ex teacher. Besides, I bet you were brilliant. I don't hate all the teachers. Just most of them. And the uniform. And the lessons. And the homework. And the revision. And the…'

'Come on lass.' A quiet but firm hand on her shoulder, huge, but gentle.

'Alright Dad.' Then the usual, 'Cheery bye Daisy, can I take Luna out when I get back? And as it's my first night of freedom after six weeks of incarceration,' she dragged this out with style as she started to follow Robbie across the entrance hall, 'will you come with me? And you too, Dad? I've been training her, and I want to show you what we can do.'

She exchanged a cheeky little look between us. 'Please?'

Then I watched her shamelessly use her girlish wiles on the grumpy sod who was her dad and who seemed to be putty in her hands. It was quite amusing to watch but I was mindful I kept my face impassive. The last thing I wanted was for him to think I was encouraging him in any way. Once Robbie had agreed that he would go for a walk with Luna after school she then turned her sparkling green eyes on me.

'You're usually free then aren't you Daisy? You can come with us.'

I dared to shoot a glance at Robbie to see if there was any of the sardonic amusement I sometimes caught in his eyes when he looked at me. But no. Still that empty deadness and in Lily's, a silent pleading that I couldn't ignore.

I nodded. 'Now off you go before you really are late.

I then resumed my task of contacting previous holiday makers who had not been for a while to entice them back for another stay. The longer I was there, the more I began to realise the impact that the ongoing murder stories were having on Wolf Lodge. I had read every article I could find and from the way it was portrayed in the media, it really did not look good. At best, the hotel and lodges were only ever half full.

It didn't help matters that a lot of the locals seemed to positively relish the idea that the Mad Laird up at the Lodge could be a serial killer. Moira explained that the long dark winters led to over-ripe imaginations.

'Och nothing ever happens round here you see. They all love a bit of drama and the grimmer the better at times.'

Moira was happy to chat as she worked, and I think she liked that I took an interest in what she was doing. She bustled about, her trim figure lithe and active with the energy of a much younger woman as she cleaned, polished and prepared the chalets until they met with her satisfaction.

'Is your Sean coming up for the week?' She asked, duster in hand and polish being sprayed generously over a coffee table. Woe betide if a coffee mug should mark it!

'No. I'm not expecting to see him until Easter. He did say he would come up then. He's going to be busy with this project he's working on in Manchester and it's a heck of a trek for just a weekend.'

'Aye I guess so.' Coffee table duly shining, she turned her attention to the glass in the French windows that opened onto the balcony. 'Are you missing him then?' This was said with her back to me as she vigorously rubbed at children's finger marks.

When I replied that I wasn't, she swivelled her head round quickly, blue eyes bright with interest.

'You gone off him then?'

'No. No of course not.' I shrugged. How could I explain what I didn't understand myself? 'I guess it's just that I have been so busy settling in.'

It was a lame excuse and from the smug little smile that appeared on Moira's face, was exactly what she had been hoping for. Shona on the other hand, who unbeknown to me had been upstairs stripping and changing the beds, came into the lounge area with a very sour look on her face.

'If you're done here, Moira I'll start on Red Squirrel.'

As much as I didn't like the younger woman, I was trying to be impartial and I greeted her with what I thought was a pleasant smile.

'Morning Shona. Are you well?'

'Hmm.' She tossed her nose in the air at me and stomped out of the chalet, arms laden with bedding.

I heard a snort from behind and turned to see Moira laughing. 'Aye she's well out of sorts that one. Has been since New Year. I don't know what you did but you fairly scuttled her designs on our Robbie.'

I gave her my best blank look.

Undeterred, Moira went on. 'Och she'd be even worse for him than bloody Miranda and she was a pain in the arse, but at least she gave us all Lily.' Then another one of her killer looks. 'She seems fair taken with you does the lass. I think you're good for her.'

Fragile ground and as much as I liked Moira, I wasn't ready to start chatting about Lily with her. The rest of the day passed easily enough. I was enjoying having my mind occupied again and I knew I had an eye for detail and a good memory which meant that absorbing the routines was easy for me. Compared to teaching teenagers, I found any awkward guests an absolute breeze to deal with.

I had my break time mid-afternoon and went to enjoy the peace and quiet of my room. It was large and square in shape with two deep windows that let in a lot of natural light. The soft furnishings were in various tones of lavender and heather in a muted tartan that was homely but not overwhelming.

I liked to sit on the chair by the window with a tray from the kitchen which I would bring up. Alex, shy with me because of his autism, had fallen under Luna's spell. As a result, when I bobbed in the kitchen at three o'clock to make myself a drink, there would be a tray with a pot of tea, milk jug and sugar bowl, and a slice of cake, as well as some scraps for Luna.

Having enjoyed today's afternoon break, and with Luna gnawing noisily on a venison bone, I turned my attention to my phone. Since that shattering confession, Marigold and I had been in touch more frequently. Neither of us wanted to delve back into the past. It was and always would be too emotionally painful. But what was starting to develop was a flow of communication where we at least showed an interest in the other.

And now I saw a message from her which took me by surprise.

'Well fancy that,' I said to Luna once I had read it. 'Marigold has taken herself off to do a floristry course. Well I never.' Then I acted on impulse and rang her.

She told me she always wanted to have her own florist shop, which would have been ideal given her name. Bizarrely, she had kept Flowers as a surname even after she had divorced Dad, which I knew irritated

Samantha no end. I had always assumed that this was the reason Marigold had done it, but now listening to her it was more than that.

'I suppose you think I am daft doing this at my age,' she said with that old hint of a barrier between us, which I now recognised as insecurity.

'Not at all! I think it's great. You're no older than Catriona and she is still really involved here.' I hoped I was being encouraging.

'It's you who got me thinking,' she said surprising me further. 'I thought to myself, if our Daisy can hoike herself up to the wilds of nowhere and run a hotel, then surely to goodness I can go to our local garden centre and sign up for a floristry course.'

'Absolutely. And you never know, you might meet another nice gentleman there?' I was being brave here as my previous opinions of Marigold's rather colourful love life had not been all that kind.

'I doubt it. But I am not doing this to meet another man. I am doing this for me!'

'Even better.' When I put the phone down, I was smiling.

I had even more reason to smile when I read an email from Violet. She had sold her house to a cash buyer which meant that she could move into the retirement flat that her nephew Timothy had found for her near to where he lived. As her buyer wanted to move in quickly, she would have a period of a couple of weeks where she would technically be homeless.

Violet saw this as an opportunity to come and stay at the hotel. I replied immediately saying I would reserve her a room. Checking the time, I saw that Lily would soon be home, and I had not forgotten my promise to her. A quick change into jeans, sweater and boots and I was ready.

By the time I had finished booking a room for Violet, there was the sound of Lily's voice chattering happily to her father. Within seconds, she appeared through the front entrance, flinging her school bag carelessly across the stone flagged floor of the reception area.

'Lily!' Catriona's voice, crisp yet affectionate, called through from somewhere.

'How does she do it?' Lily rolled her eyes and looked at me. 'I thought I was the one who wanted to be a witch, but Granny seems to do it quite naturally.'

'I heard that young lady,' said her grandmother as she appeared out of the library, reading glasses on the tip of her nose and a book in her hand. 'What have I said about you hurtling that rucksack of yours across the floor like that? One of these days you will hit a guest.'

'How do you know that's not what I am practising for?' Lily gave a cheeky retort but went to snatch up the discarded bag nevertheless and hauling it over her shoulders she began to rush up the stairs. 'Won't be long, Daisy.'

'She wants to show us what she has done with Luna,' I explained to Catriona.

'Does she indeed,' said her grandmother with a small smile as she looked from me to her son. 'Clever girl.' Then she retraced her steps leaving me alone with Robbie.

He just stood there in the hall, hands deeply in his pockets, eyes fixed on some point away from me, his face in profile. I shuffled things around on the desk in the pretence that I had something to do, in order that I did not feel obliged to break the oppressive silence. Under my lashes I did sneak the odd glance in his direction, but he remained unmoving.

I noticed that his hair needed a good wash and he had let a few days stubble grow unchecked. Even the clothes he was wearing seemed to be his oldest and shabbiest, faded jeans, almost frayed at the hems, and a wax jacket that looked so grimy it reminded me of how Sean had used to dress. It was difficult, if not impossible, to think that this man and the dashing, vibrant, whirlwind who had so swiftly seduced me in the gardens was one and the same. He had about as much appeal right now as a dirty dish cloth.

I thought with a shudder that he really did fit the profile of an oddball killer.

I realised I had begun to stare and moved to go and fetch my coat. Walking past him I thought at least he would move slightly to acknowledge me, but he didn't. He just stood there, lumpen, leaden, unseeing. Even more disconcerting. I was in half a mind to not go out but that would have meant disappointing Lily.

'Told you I wouldn't be long. Come on then. Dad, come on. Dad.' I watched as she tugged at his sleeve. A third time, quietly, now, 'Dad, please come with us into the garden.'

The anger of a minute ago changed into something else. Pity? Concern? I wasn't sure. But I got a flash of why Lily was so worried about him. Even for her, he had difficulty in responding as though he was having to drag himself back a very long way from somewhere very unpleasant.

I remembered that he supposedly had black outs when he could not remember what he had done.

Frightening.

'Let's go and see what you and Luna have been getting up to together,' I said brightly.

Lily led the way round to the back of the hotel, through the formal gardens and down the path to the Lodges. There was a scenic play area for children, all very natural in style with wooden built obstacles and a climbing frame. She insisted Robbie and I sit next to each other on one of the raised logs that could be used for balancing, but which also worked as a seat.

It was a joy to see Lily and the wolf playing together. And it seemed to break through whatever dark mood Robbie was in. Not that he became chatty, far from it. He remained silent, but out of one of his coat pockets, he took a sketchpad and a pencil. I was desperate to lean in to him to see what the rapid moves of pencil on paper were turning into, but I shied from that proximity.

'Let me see, Dad.' Lily had no such reservations and she wriggled between us on the bench. 'Are you going to do a painting, Dad?'

'Maybe,' was all he said.

Lily turned to look at me and the light shining in her eyes was touching. 'You should see Dad's paintings, Daisy, he's a genius.' Then, and I should have been prepared for this, 'Dad why don't you show Daisy your paintings?'

I could see the shutter's coming down in his eyes and although I didn't understand his silent response to his daughter's plea, I knew that now was not the right time.

'Lily I would love that, but some other time perhaps. I promised Sean I would give him a ring this evening, in about, ooh, yes ten minutes or so.' The lie tripped easily off my tongue.

I could see her disappointment and I felt a stab of guilt.

'Come on,' I said to her, 'It's getting pretty cold now and the light is fading. But thank you for showing us what you have been doing with Luna.' Then, in the way I would do with anyone else, in other words, anyone apart from a strangely surly, darkly attractive man I had stupidly had sex with, I turned to Robbie and at last addressed him. 'She's done really well, hasn't she? Maybe there are some local dog shows Lily could take Luna to?'

'What?' He stared at me as though I was talking gibberish. Then a brusque, 'Aye. Suppose so.'

We began to walk back towards the Lodge.

'Ooh look a guest arriving,' said Lily as we watched a man neatly park his car and get out.

Robbie merely grunted and strode on into the hotel.

In contrast to her father's behaviour and with a lightning flash of a smile, Lily called over to the approaching guest.

'Good evening, and welcome to Wolf Lodge Hotel, I'm Lily.'

'Ah, and good evening to you to. I remember you from my previous visits, young lady, but I don't believe we have met?' He was tall and slim with dark hair and pale blue eyes behind metal framed glasses, cleanly shaven with a sharp hair-cut. 'Colin McCready. Very pleased to meet you.'

I shook the hand he held out, liking the cool firm touch. 'Daisy Flowers,' I said, having decided upon my move that I would start using my maiden name even before my divorce came through.

'Daisy Flowers, what a pretty name.' His gaze lingered long enough to tell me he found me attractive and then he turned to Lily. 'Lily, this must be your mother then?'

I suppose it was a natural mistake. 'Oh no,' I said quickly. 'Lily lives here, she's a Munro. I'm just the manageress, although I am aware, I don't look like it just now,' I added with a laugh looking at my jeans and boots. 'We've just been walking with Luna.'

'What a fabulous wolf!'

Luna though showed no desire to introduce herself. Maybe she was impatient for the kitchen treats I knew she usually got from Lily after her walks. Catriona came out of the library to check in our new guest. I assured him he was in capable hands, and I turned to make my way back to my room, mindful that I had said to Lily I had a phone call to make.

As I did so, she said to me quietly. 'I wouldn't mind you know.'

'Sorry, what?'

'If you were my mother,' she said, one hand on Luna's neck. 'I wouldn't mind.'

Thankfully, she didn't allow me chance to think of any reply as she disappeared with Luna and left me to climb the stairs, my mind in a spin.

Chapter Twenty-Five

Despite the dark shadow of rumours that hung over Wolf Lodge, there were some regular guests who were happy to return. Colin McCready a bird watching enthusiast was one of them. There was also a family who came to enjoy the many outdoor pursuits which the area had to offer. More than once they went out for the day and asked if Lily could go with them.

'Aye it does her good to spend time with a normal family,' said Moira one afternoon. We had nipped into Kinlaggan for a coffee and cake. 'She misses having a mother around.'

I made a non-committal noise as I stirred my coffee. Lily's comment to me a few days earlier had blasted into my mind like dynamite. I couldn't get her words out of my head.

'Will she go over to America for Easter to join her mum and Derek?'

'Aye that's usually the case. The half-term week just isn't long enough for the travel, and of course the lass wants to be here at Christmas and Hogmanay, so Easter is usually the time she flies over there. She splits the long holidays between them.'

'It's a pity in a way that she won't be here for Easter. My sister Abigail is coming for the two weeks. I know she's a lot younger than Lily, but it would have been nice if they could have met.'

Moira looked understandably puzzled and so I had to give her a brief sketch of my family dynamics.

'Wow,' she said with a wry smile. 'That must be odd having a stepmum younger than you and a sister young enough to be your daughter.' Then with the directness I had come to associate with Moira, she asked the question that others often shied from.

'So how come you and your hubby never had children? Were you just waiting for the right time, and it never happened? I must admit I had given up on having children still being single at the ripe old age of thirty-eight. Then of course Callum came along, and before I was forty so did the twins. They were a surprise to both of us I can tell you.'

I smiled at her. Three-year-old Kyle and Keira were her favourite subject and she would usually have a new photo on her phone to show me. Moira's mother lived in Kinlaggan and shared looking after the twins with them going to nursery so that Moira could continue her job.

'Oh shit,' she said quietly as I still had not responded. 'I've gone and put my foot in it haven't I? Callum's always telling me I am as subtle as bull at times. Let's change the subject, what do you think about our dishy guest of the week.'

The other thing she liked to do was give the male guests marks out of ten in a completely sexist and politically incorrect way.

I found myself saying, 'We did have a daughter, but she only lived a few hours. Her name was Lily.'

She said softly, 'That must have been so painful. Must be still. How old would she have been?' Gone was the flippant gossip. In her place was someone that I was beginning to trust enough to call friend.

'Fifteen, nearly sixteen. She was born on the seventeenth of June. She died on twenty-first of June.'

Moira's eyes grew huge. Her mouth dropped open.

'What?' I had to prompt her again when she didn't immediately answer.

She looked as though she didn't want to say anything, her face wrinkled into a frown.

'You are going to find out anyway, probably best that you know beforehand.'

'Know what?'

'The twenty-first of June is our Lily's birthday. And she will be sixteen this year.'

We looked at each other across the small table in the crowded café. Around us buzzed lively conversations and children's voices from a couple of the tables. But between Moira and I there hung a weighty silence.

Lily Munro had been born on the day that my daughter had died.

It was at the very least an incredible co-incidence. I felt the hairs on my neck stiffen and looking at Moira I had the sense that she was feeling something similar. I thought of her and her spells with Lily to bring me here. I thought of meeting Sean, and Luna and all that had happened since then. I really was not so sure that I believed in co-incidences anymore.

We both started talking at once.

'Yes, he is rather nice.'

'Gorgeous blue eyes and smile.'

We laughed, perhaps a little loudly as we agreed that Colin McCready was pleasing to the eye. We kept the conversation on easy ground, but when we got back to where we had parked our cars, as Moira was now going to pick the twins up from her mums, she hugged me for the first time.

'You mind how you go now, Daisy. I'll see you tomorrow. And if you see that lovely Colin, give him a special smile from me. Only don't tell Callum I said that.'

'I will, and I won't,' I agreed with a laugh if only to put her mind at rest that I was ok.

I drove the five miles back to Kinlaggan, my mind buzzing with what I had just learnt. It had been a big enough shock to hear that Marigold had aborted a daughter who she would have called Lily. And now this.

What if, I thought suddenly, what if somehow the soul of my daughter had not gone to heaven? What if somehow that tiny soul, deprived a life so cruelly had found its way into another body that was coming into the world just as my Lily was leaving it.

Another Lily being born, at the exact same time?

It was a knock-out thought.

It knocked the concentration I usually had for driving. If I had been back home on familiar roads it probably would have been alright. But driving from Kinlaggan to Wolf Lodge in February meant negotiating a winding and narrow road that even allowing for the super efficiency of highland gritters, was still icy in places.

Even then, despite the blurring of tears that had formed in my eyes, and the trembling of my hands, I possibly would still have been alright. Had it not been for that black Porsche driven by a wild maniac. He came hurtling round the bend at God only knows what speed and in my panic and momentary disorientation I did exactly the wrong thing. I slammed on the brakes.

Straight into a super skid.

Straight off the road.

Straight into a tree.

A terrible crunching, metallic grinding accompanied the loud scream from myself and the splintering crack of the tree as we collided. Then a punch in the stomach and face as the air-bag saved my life.

I couldn't move.

I could breathe and I was certainly alive as my heart was hammering away in my chest, but I couldn't move. Fear spread through me verging on blind terror. Then I forced myself to take long slow breaths and exhale steadily. I was shocked. That was all. I began a systematic check of my body, restricted though I still was with the air bag and my seat belt. Then the door was wrenched open, and a thundering voice yelled in my ear.

'Jesus fucking Christ woman. What were you trying to do, fucking kill yourself?'

The rage was icy cold and blazing hot at the same time. An arctic volcano erupting beside me in the form of Robbie Munro. I was still too stunned to speak but I was about to turn my head and glare at him when suddenly strong hands held my neck in a vice like grip.

'No! Dinna move. You may have broken something, you stupid woman!'

Through gritted teeth I assured him I was fine, but this did not stop him feeling his way over my body from the neck down, as far as he was able with the air bag inflated. He did this in a firm and detached manner. Only when he unclipped my seat belt did I notice that his hands were shaking. Daring now to turn my head and look at him, it seemed as though his whole body was shaking.

Now that he knew I was unharmed, or at least safe from serious injury, Robbie wasted no time in dragging me from the wreck of my car. He held me at arms' length from him, dark green eyes, rather wild it had to be said, scanned my face and then looked me up and down.

'You're alright?'

'Yes!' I snapped at him.

Then he shook me. I mean literally shook me. Rattled me like a rag doll. 'You stupid woman, do you not realise you could have killed yourself! Look at your car! Look at the fucking tree!'

Still holding me in his vice like grip, no doubt I would be bruised on my arms, he twirled me around so I could see the damage. It made me feel slightly faint. I could hear the roaring in my ears that told me this was imminent.

Until a hand slapped me across my face. 'Don't you be fainting on me now woman.'

Shocked out of my faintness I spat at him, 'What fucking school of first aid did you go to? And for the record, it was your bloody fault I crashed, you were driving like a fucking maniac – you always do in that bloody car!'

Fear at what had so nearly happened screeched through me and turned me into a banshee. I let rip further.

'Moira said you were going to kill yourself in it one day; well that's fine matey you go ahead and kill yourself but leave me out of it! I want to live!' A sudden blast of memory, sharp, cruel, necessary at this point.

Me and a train platform.

I began to cry as my body turned to jelly. 'I want to live,' I sobbed uncontrollably.

The hands that were holding me had let go suddenly and my knees gave way and sank to the cold, snowy floor. I hugged my arms around myself shaking suddenly. Robbie had backed away a few paces, his hands clutching at his head for a moment, making his dark unruly hair even more tangled and untidy. He stumbled over to the tree and leant his forehead on the trunk. His hands splayed either side and I could see the white of his knuckles.

For a moment I thought he was going to head butt the damaged trunk, his body was as rigid as the tree itself. Then slowly, as if his whole being was in pain he staggered back from the tree, his face grim as he surveyed the mangled car and the shattered trunk. I was still on my knees as he started to walk back towards me.

'I could have killed you.' The rage in his voice was replaced by desolate pain.

I preferred the rage.

'I could have killed you,' he repeated and taking hold of my arms, gently this time, he drew me to my feet. I had got a grip of my tears, but the shakes were still coursing through me. 'Jesus Christ Daisy, I could have killed you.' Then I was wrapped up in his arms, my head cradled into his massive chest. I felt his hands gently stroking my hair.

'I didn't mean for you to get hurt, Daisy. I never meant for anyone to get hurt. I never meant it then and I never meant it now. I just wanted to... I just. You mustn't tell Lily. Promise me you won't tell Lily.'

I was already in a confused state, and he was making me even more muddled with what he was saying. Not to mention scared. He never meant to hurt anyone?

'Tell Lily what? I think I'll have a bit of a problem hiding that I have smashed my car up!'

'Don't tell her that I was going to...' He stopped abruptly.

'Going to what, Robbie?' I asked as I steadied myself and managed to look him square in the eyes.

He was saved from answering directly as at that moment another vehicle appeared on the scene. It was Callum's jeep which was quickly parked a few yards away in one of the passing places. Moira's husband jumped out. He was wearing mud splattered overalls and carried with him a distinctly pungent aroma, but I really didn't care.

'Are you both alright? Aye, I can see that. What happened?' His vet's eyes had quickly given me the once over and then he had turned his gaze to Robbie. I noticed the sharp edge to his voice.

'It was an accident.' Robbie's voice was in turn brusque to the point of rudeness. I was surprised. I knew they were friends for all the age gap of ten years, Callum being the junior.

Callum was used to handling farm animals in pain, and even those at the nearby wildlife park. 'Aye, I can see that. Bloody tree is always causing trouble.'

Robbie shot him a hard glance then as if there was something under the surface of Callum's gentle tone that I had missed. Callum though had turned his attention to me, and I got a hint of why Moira loved him so much. As well as being ruggedly good looking, his smile was one of the nicest I had come across.

'Och, Daisy, we'd best get you checked out. You look like a ghost you do.'

'I'm fine,' I insisted although my body was shaking, and my teeth were still chattering.

'Of course you are, Daisy, but I think you will be finer still if I run you straight into Kinlaggan and let Doctor Dunwoodie take a wee look at you.'

The thought of being scrutinised and asked how the accident had happened was not encouraging. I didn't trust myself not to blurt out the fact that the accident, in my view, was squarely Robbie's fault. I told myself

I was thinking of Lily. I wasn't going to knowingly get her father into any more trouble.

'Really I just want to be taken home. And I am not going in that wretched thing!' I pointed at Robbie's car, slewn haphazardly on the opposite grass verge.

'Right then,' said Callum turning his attention back to Robbie who had now gone very quiet and was just staring at the tree and the front end of my car which was indented in it. 'I can run you up to the Lodge, but we need to shift your car. It's going to need Big Mac out Robbie.'

I stifled a slightly hysterical giggle and Callum explained. 'Ross Mackenzie, he's the local mechanic. Big fella, verra big and not because he is partial to a certain type of burger.' Then he addressed Robbie with more of a snap in his voice. 'Robbie, do you hear me man?'

Clearly Robbie had not. He had something of a zombie expression on his face as he finally took his eyes off the trees and looked at Callum.

'What?'

Callum swore very quietly under his breath. 'Robbie man, will you get in the land rover with Daisy, I think I need to drop you at the doctors first and then take Daisy back. I will ring Big Mac.' He took out his phone and luckily was answered straight away. There was a quick conversation during which time Robbie began walking slowly towards his car.

'Fuck!' Callum shoved his phone in his pocket and moved towards him.

The urgency in Callum's voice broke through the fog of my shock but I was still confused as to why Callum was reacting like he was.

'Robbie, man, you're no' fit to drive.'

I watched as he placed a hand on Robbie's arm to prevent him from opening his door. Leaning in towards him he spoke urgently but I could not hear what he was saying. It was obvious though that Robbie did not like it as he threw off Callum's arm and shook his head.

'I'm fine! There's nothing wrong with me. It was just an accident. She took the fucking bend too fast that's all. Fucking English, they never know how to drive on these roads.'

Charming! I was about to explode at this but a quick look from Callum stopped me. Then he took a little step back from Robbie, holding his hands out in a conciliatory gesture.

'Okay, okay, you know best.'

Robbie merely grunted and reached out once more to open the door. At which point Callum's right arm drew back and suddenly shot forward in an astonishingly quick punch which caught Robbie by surprise, landing him out cold on the floor.

'Callum!'

He grinned at me. 'Och, dinna fret yourself Daisy, I haven't hurt my hand. I'm a member of the Kinlaggan Boxing club.'

'That wasn't exactly what I meant, Callum.'

'Oh.' He regarded the motionless body of his friend on the floor. 'Dinna fret, Daisy,' he said again, 'it's the highland way.'

Apparently, it was also the highland way to get out of his vet's case a large and scary looking needle and pump something into the back of the hand of the self-same prone man.

'Is that legal?'

Callum flashed me that lovely smile and repeated, 'it's the highland way.'

'But does he need it?'

The smiled disappeared. 'What do you think, Daisy? Och I know you haven't been here long. But you know the stories. You know what his father did. You've seen how he behaves at times.'

'But it was an accident, surely?'

'What, him racing in that stupid car at high speed towards the very same tree that did for his father?'

An even greater chill crept into my bones on top of the shock. 'Oh.'

'Exactly,' replied Callum and we both looked at the tree with matching grim expressions. 'But not a word to Big Mac when he gets here, mind. I know the gossip'll fly soon enough, but there's no need for us to fuel it, aye?'

'Aye!' I snapped back at him, angry that he thought I would do so. And then I gave a reluctant laugh as I realised what I must have sounded like.

He was grinning once more. 'You see, a couple of weeks here, Daisy and you are beginning to talk like one of us. Now remember, it was an accident and Robbie has just passed out.'

He said this as a bright red and orange recovery truck came chugging along the road. There had been no exaggeration at the description of Big Mac. He was huge and if Robbie had been standing up, he would have made even him look a bit on the small side.

'Will you give me a hand getting Robbie into my car?' Callum greeted him. 'He tripped in his rush to help Daisy and hit his head on the ground.'

'Wouldn't've thought his skull was soft enough to get knocked out,' Big Mac commented, readily accepting the lie.

There was humour in his voice, but he had such a thick reddish-brown beard it was hard to see if he was smiling. He nodded shyly at me and then helped Callum lift Robbie to his feet. He was waking up which I was relieved to see. Whatever Callum had given him must have been a tiny dose, but it was enough to make him drowsy and disorientated.

'Christ, what happened? Callum did you hit me?' His voice was slurred.

'You see,' said Callum confidently, 'concussion. I need to get him to Doctor Dunwoodie.'

'Aye, reckon you do. Let's get you in the Land Rover then.'

In other circumstances I would have been amused to see the loud mouthed, boorish Laird of Wolf Lodge being manhandled by a red bearded giant as easily as if he was a child. As it was, I was in no mood for smiling. Neither was Callum once Robbie had finally been secured in the passenger seat.

'Big Mac'll take you back, Daisy. You sure you don't need the doctor too?'

'I just want to be back in my cosy room, with a cup of strong tea and probably a very large whisky.'

He nodded. 'Aye, you are turning into a Highlander.'

Bic Mac soon had my mangled car on the back of his truck. 'I'll be back for that beastie once I've dropped you off,' he said after he had also moved Robbie's car into a safer place.

Big Mac was not a man of many words and he drove me back up to Wolf Lodge without talking. He had the radio on in the truck playing music which he whistled tunelessly along to. He parked up in front of the Lodge and helped me carefully out of the truck, my hand absolutely tiny in his.

'There you go lass. You mind you get a wee dram inside you now,' was all that he said.

'I certainly will. And thank you. How much do I owe you?'

'Och, nae bother lass, nae bother at all. Yon car is a write off mind. You'll need to speak to your insurers.'

I nodded, too relieved to have got out of it in one piece to really be thinking about that right now. I was just glad to be alive.

'I'll take it to my garage, and we can sort it out from there when you feel up to it.'

'Daisy, Daisy, are you alright?' Feet scrunching rapidly on the gravel, dark hair flying, face white with fear and Luna by her side, Lily shot towards me.

'I'm fine, honestly,' I reassured her as she nearly bowled me over with the enthusiasm of her hug.

'I saw your car on the truck, but I couldn't see you,' her voice wobbled tearfully. 'I could only see Big Mac.'

I hugged her back, touched by her concern and assured her again that I was fine.

'But what happened?'

Unfortunately, as gentle as Big Mac was in some areas, he was not so subtle in others. 'Och your dad and that black beastie and Daisy here had a wee argument over who owned the road.'

Lily went pale. 'Where is Dad? Is he ok?'

'He's fine,' I got in quickly before Big Mac could make things worse. 'Callum just took him to see Doctor Dunwoodie for a check-up.'

She then asked the pertinent question. 'Where exactly was the accident?'

'The same damn tree that your grandfather had an argument with. Funny that.' Big Mac scratched his beard at this point, clearly considering the coincidence.

Lily's green eyes looked huge in her now very white face.

Fortunately, at that moment her grandmother came flying out of the Lodge.

'Callum has just phoned me.' Catriona thanked Big Mac effusively and once he had climbed back into his truck, she put one arm around me and the other around Lily.

'Tea, scones and whisky.'

'Granny, it's the curse,' Lily began to say as we walked together back into the hotel.

Colin McCready was walking across the foyer as we entered. My head was too full to return the concerned smile he sent in my direction.

'Goodness, Daisy whatever happened?'

Catriona's voice brooked no argument. 'An accident that's all. Just an accident. Nothing that can't be put right with tea, scones and whisky.'

'Exactly,' I said as much for my own benefit as for Lily's. I did not want to believe in the curse as she did. 'An accident. All I need is tea, scones and whisky.'

To which Lily then, in a very teenager like fashion, declared that she had better be having some of the whisky as well in that case.

Chapter Twenty-Six

We sat in the cosy parlour with a fire lit and the thick velvet curtains drawn against the darkening sky. Mary appeared with the requisite tea tray, loaded up with scones, butter and jam. Catriona provided the whisky, choosing a single malt which I protested was far too grand to be used for treating shock.

'Nonsense!'

The amount she poured into my glass proved how ridiculous she considered this.

'It was the curse, wasn't it? Dad was trying to kill himself. I know cos it's going to be a full moon tonight, and that's how it was when Great Grandad and Grandad killed themselves. Great Grandad shot himself but he didn't have a fast car like Grandad did, otherwise he probably would have driven into the same tree and...'

'Lily, have some whisky.' Catriona gently placed a hand on her shoulder in order to stop her pacing around the small room. She guided her to a chair and made her sit.

'Oh.' Lily took the glass which had a far smaller amount and to which Catriona had added water. Then in a much brighter tone she said as if this had just occurred to her. 'But you saved him, Daisy. You see I was right. You are going to break the curse.'

I had happily glugged a few large mouthfuls already. 'What?'

Catriona however was still as sharp as a pin. 'Lily there is no curse. Daisy has not been brought here by any spell of yours. She came because my letter got sent to the wrong address as the ink had run.'

Lily's mouth took a mulish turn as she stubbornly insisted, 'Daisy did save his life. If she hadn't crashed into the tree, then he would have done.'

The awful thing was, I knew she was right. If my car had not been on the road, he would have ploughed straight into it. Deliberately. That was what Callum had realised and that was why he had taken the measures he had to get Robbie to the doctor. But I could hardly tell Lily that. Nor did I want to add fuel to the fire of the curse theory.

Lamely I said, 'Well I am glad that in having my accident, no one else was hurt. It was my fault, Lily, I'm not used to these roads yet, particularly when they are icy.'

I could see the confusion flicker across her face, but Catriona was eager to jump at my explanation.

'You see, Lily, it was just an accident. And the main thing is, that no one was hurt.'

'But why has Callum taken Dad to the doctors?'

I used the same excuse that the vet had given to Big Mac. 'He was in such a rush to help me he tripped and banged his head.'

The reception desk bell rang. I got up to go but Catriona immediately shushed me to sit back down.

'Heaven's Daisy you're in no fit state.' She rose gracefully and went to answer the bell.

Catriona was smiling as she came back into the room. 'Mrs Bramley wants to know if you would like to join them tonight? They are taking Alyssa and William to the cinema at Inverness.'

This was the family that Moira had told me about. Their daughter was the same age as Lily. I hadn't been at Kinlaggan long, but I knew that a trip to Inverness, which was a good twenty miles away, was a highlight for any of the teenagers here.

'Well go and have a wash and a change, they are setting off in half an hour. When you come back down, I will give you some money then if you go out for tea you can pay for yours.'

'I will, thanks, Granny.' Lily dashed back the rest of her whisky with a certain Munro flair and made for the door. Just before going through, she stopped to look at me. 'Daisy, thank you.' She was quiet, but it was her way of telling me that she had not been completely swayed by my story and the excuse it was just an accident.

Catriona watched her go across the hallway and once she seemed satisfied that she was well out of earshot, she came back into the room and closed the door. Pouring me a second large glass and now one for herself, she sat in the chair opposite and regarded me calmly with her dark brown eyes.

'Was he trying to kill himself?'

'I think so. I can't say for definite Catriona, only he can. It really was not my fault.'

I hesitated a fraction here, after all I had been distracted at the stunning revelation that Lily Munro had been born on the day that my daughter had died. A fact that in the turmoil that followed I had almost forgotten. I took a deep intake of breath.

'What?'

I shook my head. 'No, it's nothing. Well, nothing to do with Robbie anyway.' I couldn't lie to her. 'I was a little distracted driving back Catriona, but you know I never speed, and I was aware of the ice. As I approached the bend there was suddenly Robbie's car hurtling towards me at such speed, and the road there is so narrow. I panicked and hit the brakes which of course I know was totally the wrong thing to do. Like I said, I was distracted, so yes in that respect the accident was my fault.'

She had leant forward to the edge of the seat. 'Was he hurtling towards you or the tree?'

Impossible to say for sure and my expression told her that. 'What I can say, is that anyone driving a car that fast, down that road, at that bend and on such an icy day must have some sort of death wish. Even if it is subconscious.'

Her hands gripped the whisky glass, and I could see the effort it took for her not to cry.

'Sometimes,' I said very gently and thinking of that terrible day at the train station, 'sometimes we don't even think it. We just are so lost. It sort of just happens.'

'You've had some experience of this?'

'For a minute, yes. I lost myself.' I told her how Sean had pulled me back and saved me.

I watched as Catriona's careful guard began to slip. Her hands trembled as she sipped her whisky and she let a solitary tear escape down her cheek. She wiped it away and then was brisk once more.

'Well, I don't believe in curses or witchcraft, Daisy, but I do believe in good fortune being sent in some ways. I will forever be grateful that you were there at that moment, even if it did mean you had to hit that wretched tree!'

'Me too,' I said, relieved to see a small smile return to her face. 'But if you don't mind, I really do feel rather sore all over. I think I need to go and soak in a very hot bath, otherwise I won't be able to move at all tomorrow.'

'Of course you must. Here, take the bottle with you.'

'I don't need the whole bottle!'

'You will probably have a hell of a headache later, or in the middle of the night. If you have it in your room, you don't have to come down for some. Oh, for heaven's sake Daisy it's only a bottle of whisky.'

Unspoken I think were the words that it could have been worse. So much worse. If Robbie had hit the tree at high speed, if he had hit my car for that matter at high speed. When I thought about how close one or both of us had come to dying, I reached out and took the bottle.

'Wise girl,' she nodded. 'Now a long soak in the bath and I will get Mary to bring a tray of food up tonight for you. Shush,' she warned me with a flash of her eyes as I opened my mouth to protest. 'You look dreadful and trust me, gossip flies round here quicker than you can sneeze, you do not want to deal with questions, however well-meaning, tonight.'

She had a point there and I submitted to the temporary state of invalid, thanking her once more.

'Dearie me, Daisy, it's I who am thanking you! Now away you go, off up those stairs, bath, early supper, then bed.'

She sounded like a mother. Like the mother I wished Marigold could have been, maybe would have been without her own trauma to shadow her life. Impulsively I leant forward and kissed her on her cheek as I passed her.

'I shall say an early 'good night' then Catriona.'

I was going up the stairs clutching my bottle of 12-year-old Kinlaggan as Colin McCready was coming down for a pre-dinner drink himself.

'Oh hello, I was just going to ask if you would like to join me for a drink in the bar before I have my dinner? But I see you have already started.' He eyed the bottle in my hand with amusement.

I returned his smile ruefully. 'Would I sound like an alcoholic in denial if I said I don't usually drink this early?'

'Of course you wouldn't. I saw you coming in before. You must have had a terrible shock.'

I nodded. 'Hence the early drink and much needed hot bath.'

'Of course,' he said again. 'Maybe another night, before I go home?'

I stood there halfway up the stairs, swaying slightly, it had to be said, as I let this sink in.

'I'm sorry. Stupid timing. Clumsy of me.'

There was a kindness in his eyes and a self-depreciating smile that coupled with his good looks was rather appealing. I told myself that Sean would not mind. I could picture him grinning at me even as I thought this. I told myself that Sean was hundreds of miles away and I was not going to see him for weeks. I told myself that Sean had let me know that what we had shared was magical but in no way permanent. Besides what was I saying yes to, a drink in the bar, that was all.

'I would like that, Colin. Perhaps tomorrow, or Friday. You'll be leaving on Saturday, won't you?'

He nodded. 'Aye, that's right. I own a wee bookshop in Glasgow. A friend runs it for me whilst I am away.'

'Oh, I love books. I used to teach English literature.'

His face was even more attractive as he smiled now. 'Oh well, that's grand. But look, you're dead on your feet and I'm keeping you from your hot bath. Tomorrow then, or Friday?'

I nodded and continued up the stairs. I was relieved to get to the peace and quiet of my room. I drew the curtains, and it was impossible not to see the brilliantly shining full moon, already luminous in the sky. Both that and the stars were so much clearer here, but it was not their brightness that struck me tonight, it was Lily and her insistence on a family curse.

Lily.

Back to what Moira had told me.

It was too much to take in and so I reached for the Kinlaggan. Stuff it, I thought and poured a third, large glass. I really was developing quite a taste for all things Scottish. I went to my bathroom and turned on the taps. Soon there was fragrant steam billowing round the room, and I shed my clothes.

There were bruises on my arms where Robbie had grabbed me hard. Looking at them, I remembered the way he had changed so suddenly. One minute he had been blazing with icy anger towards me, and the next moment, shut down with absolute horror that he had nearly been responsible for my death.

The thought of how close that had been, had me sipping once more at my whisky. My body was beginning to shiver. I tested the hot water with my foot then sank into the bubbly depths. For a few moments I wallowed there enjoying the heat, the scent of the oils I had added and the inner glow that the malt was producing.

But I kept replaying what had happened in my mind, getting stuck on one particular point. Something Robbie had said? It was niggling at me but as is always the case when you are trying so hard to think of something, it proves elusive. No doubt it would pop back into my head some other time. For now, I wanted to forget the whole dreadful experience.

I wanted to shut down any fantastical notion that Lily Munro could possibly be the re-incarnated soul of my daughter, because that was just too, well it was just too much on so many levels that my brain wanted to explode when I thought about it. Colin McCready, the handsome book shop owner from Glasgow was the perfect distraction to think about.

I allowed myself to indulge in a harmless fantasy where someone like Colin, good looking and charming could become a permanent fixture in my life. I loved being here at Kinlaggan and I was enjoying my new job, but after all, it was exactly that – a job.

When the water finally got too chilly, I hauled myself out, nearly slipping as the whisky had gone to my head. I was slathering body lotion onto my skin when I heard the knock at my door. I remembered that Catriona had said she would have a tray sent up from the kitchen so I could eat in my room.

'Just a minute,' I called as I reached for my bath robe and quickly tugged it on.

I was expecting Catriona, or Mary.

I was not expecting Robbie.

'Oh.'

He brushed past me carrying a covered tray which he set down on my dressing table. 'Mary was just bringing this up,' he said bluntly.

'That's kind of you to save her the trouble.' I eyed him warily, wondering what on earth had happened at the doctors but not feeling I could ask him. He seemed subdued, leaden almost and I wondered if he was still feeling the effects of whatever Callum had shot into him. Or perhaps the doctor had prescribed something? However, he was feeling, I was in no mood for a discussion.

'I'll have it when I have got dressed.' I held the door open for him, making it clear that I wished to be alone.

I should have known better. Subtlety did not work with Robbie. He looked at me as though realising for the first time that I was in my bathrobe, something which made me feel ever so slightly vulnerable.

'I need to talk to you.'

'I'm not really…'

I didn't bother finishing my sentence as he was obviously not going to leave. Not judging by the way he went to the whisky bottle and poured himself a large glass.

'Should you be having that?'

His expression was almost comical. He looked at the glass as though I had suggested he was drinking poison and took a large swallow. Resigned to his presence in my room for now, I was about to pour myself another glass and stopped. Look what had happened with this man last time I had too much to drink. Just thinking about it made me feel peculiar and so I was snappy with him.

'I'm not too sure I want to talk to you.'

'Tough.'

Then he started pacing round like a bear in a cage. The dull body language of a few minutes ago was no longer there. It was unsettling to watch. Maybe I would have that drink after all.

'Well talk then if you insist on doing so,' I said pouring a glass of whisky with a touch of defiance. He was making me feel edgy just looking at him.

'You musna tell Lily.'

'What?'

'You musna tell Lily.'

'I musna, you mean I mustn't tell Lily what?' I thought I had already agreed to saying nothing.

He growled then, bear like, fierce. Slamming the glass down on the table he glared at me. 'Do I have to spell it out for you?'

I blamed it on the whisky. I blamed it on the shock of nearly being crumpled in my car. I could have, should have handled myself and his agitated state better. But I didn't. There was something about him that lit a fire in my belly, and it had been stoked by forty per cent proof alcohol and shock.

'Yes. You do.' I returned his glare with a steely look of my own.

'Fucking hell woman, have you no sense?'

It appeared not where he was concerned because I shrugged at him in a completely careless manner. As I did so my bathrobe slipped a little and my hands went immediately to tighten the belt. Behind the dark anger in his eyes came the glint that had got me into trouble before.

Bears can move extremely fast for all their size. This two-legged version was no different. In an instant the floor space between us was gone and he was holding my arms as he had done after the crash.

'Ouch!'

'What?'

'You've bruised me you bloody thug!'

He looked horrified. 'Shit. Show me.'

I couldn't without taking my robe off as the bruises were on my upper arms. So, I just nodded at where he was holding me. He let go instantly. I was not prepared for what happened next. Instead of continuing to harangue me, he sat on the edge of my bed, body language once more undergoing a dramatic change. A wounded bear now sat before me. One holding his head in his hands.

'I'm a fucking monster, a fucking monster, I shouldn't be like this, nobody should be like this, Lily deserves better, oh Christ Lily, Lily, I am so fucking sorry Lily.' He raised tear filled eyes to me. 'Promise me you won't tell her, aye you ken, I see it in your eyes, you know what I was going to do, and I fucking was! That fucking tree! It was calling me, just like it did Dad. You see, I am fucking cursed and I deserve to be! I fucking deserve to be...' he ended on a sob and his hands were tearing at his head.

I was horrified.

I was drawn by an emotion I couldn't name to the depths of pain he was suffering.

'I won't tell Lily,' I got onto the bed beside him, not sure whether to touch him or not. He didn't seem to hear me so in the end I gently placed a hand on his shoulder. 'I promise I won't tell Lily.'

'You promise?' He turned his head to me, hands dropping now to his lap. I could see they were trembling.

I couldn't help myself. I took hold of one of them. My hand seemed so small in comparison but that didn't matter. I think the touch was important. It was like trying to calm a wild animal and touch was a language that broke all barriers.

'I promise I won't tell Lily,' I repeated looking him squarely in the eyes.

Which was a big mistake.

Turbulent, stormy, deep, deep pools of emotion. Sucking me in, pulling me under. Drowning.

I took a sharp gasp of breath, rocked by how connected I felt to him at that moment. It was the emotion. All that powerful emotion he had just displayed. Anyone would have been affected. But not everyone would perhaps have been so stupid to do what I did next.

Another big mistake.

What was I thinking when I slid my arms around his shoulder and attempted to give him a hug? Really Daisy, you think you can safely hug a demented bear? Even one who has just shown you its most vulnerable side? Callum would probably have told me that an animal is at its most dangerous when wounded, and Robbie Munro was as wounded as they came.

Stupid, stupid, stupid, Daisy.

He shuddered beneath my touch, and I held him then, even closer. I don't know how long we sat like that, me trying to absorb some of his torment, feeling his tremors rippling through me like an earthquake beneath me. He held on to me, not bruising now, but clinging in need.

Need comes in different forms though and there was a fraction of a moment when that need changed. He had calmed. His head had somehow found a resting place in the crook of my neck against my chest. I had wriggled a little to accommodate his position and now the folds of my bath robe were slipping, exposing more leg and hint of breast than was safe.

Safe?

Yes, because now I recognised the danger I was in.

My heart seemed to be beating louder and I wondered if he could hear the change in rhythm. Had he picked up on the subtle rise and fall of my breasts, all too aware now of the man who was cradled against them?

He had. I noticed at first the intense stillness that came over him.

That was my moment to move. To pull away with grace and gentleness. But I didn't. Caught in a trap of my own making, I couldn't. I wanted him to do what he did next. I wanted the arms that were holding me to shift and move, so that one of his hands could brush ever so lightly, questioningly against the underside of my left breast over the towelling material of my robe.

He caught my moment of stillness then. The unspoken permission. The hand moved ever so slowly now as he lifted his head. With his face just an inch from mine, he paused to look, to check.

Yes. My eyes silently told him.

Yes. I pleaded silently at him as my lips parted and waited for his touch.

'Yes,' I said ever so softly as that hand slid inside my robe, sought and found my naked breast.

Chapter Twenty-Seven

Within minutes the rest of my body was naked.

Urgent hands, I am not sure whether they were his or mine, untied the belt and slid the towelling fabric from my shoulders. He had clung to me before in pain and despair and now he was reaching for me with a different need entirely. Or maybe it was the same need, just disguised as something else. Either way, it didn't really matter. What mattered was the fever in him that I responded to. Common sense and logic had flown right out of the window and across the mountains.

As hungry as he had been to touch my naked flesh, I was just as greedy.

Between hot, ravenous kisses, I pulled at his clothes, fighting with buttons and zips in a wriggle and a fumble. Then there was nothing between us and we were free to tangle together on the bed. There had hardly been any skin contact at all on New Year's Eve, just the rough sensation of him entering my body. Now every inch of me came alive.

It wasn't seductive.

It wasn't sensuous.

It was wildly – utterly mad.

Almost as soon as we were naked then he was inside me. No preamble. No foreplay. There didn't need to be. I was ready for him as soon as he touched me. He didn't need any encouragement to let loose his desire, but I gave it anyway, wrapping my legs around his waist and clawing at the heavy muscles on his back.

There was a flash of comparison.

Gary.

Sean.

They disappeared in the gasp of a breath.

My thoughts, emotions, morals, all followed my common sense out of the window. I was only capable of feeling and I felt I was on fire. I was a volcano that had been dormant, had begun to rumble with Sean and was now completely erupting.

I was wild.

He was wild.

I kissed him with a craving, with a desire, with a fire that matched his own. I tangled my fingers into his hair and held him close, closer still as he moved faster within me. I let my breath escape in a low drawn out moan as his hands came under my bottom to lift me up further. My eyes snapped open wide at the force now coming from him and my body wilted in complete surrender.

At this point I had become a passive partner.

I could do nothing else.

The energy coming from him was more than I could handle.

It was bruising, raging, out of control.

My body was being pummelled with his in a way that shocked me and aroused me further.

I had a fleeting moment of fear just as the screams were beginning to build in my throat and dizzying pleasure swamped my mind.

Was he a killer?

This was not rape.

But it was wild.

Out of control and wild.

His eyes were shut and as firebolts were exploding from my core, a cold sense of what I was doing washed over me. It didn't prevent my body from responding though as I shook beneath him. My body and my mind were two separate beings at this point. As though I was watching from afar, I saw the intensity of his feelings cloud over his face, but I had no idea what those feelings were.

This was a stranger I was allowing to use my body. To pleasure my body. At this final moment of shared physical ecstasy, there was no shared emotion. He had cut himself right off from me. There were three, maybe four long hard thrusts from him and then a sigh that he seemed to hold back as though this too he dared not let escape.

Then he did open his eyes.

I don't know what he saw reflected in mine, but he looked at me for a second and then closed his eyes once more, rolling off me and flopping onto his back, one arm drawn across his face. I had grown used to Sean's lovemaking that was as tender and caring as it was passionate and steamy. Faced with this cold reaction I was dazed.

And angry.

I was about to tell him to shove off and leave me alone, my earlier compassion and pity no longer in my mind. The snoring put paid to that idea. Cursing under my breath, mainly at what a bloody idiot I had been, again, and secondly at what a bloody ignorant lump of a man he was, I rooted for my bathrobe and covered myself up once more. Then I tried to wake him.

I prodded him. Poked him. Spoke very loudly in his ear. I even slapped him on the face. He did groggily open his eyes at this insult but only for a second and then he turned onto his side and continued to snore. I stared at him, not quite believing my eyes, not quite believing what had just happened. But it had, and there now, curled up on my bed and lost in an untouchable sleep was Robbie Bloody Munro.

'Can't you do something, Luna? Can't you make him shift?'

I looked at my wolf who, used to Sean and me in bed together, had given her usual huff of disgust and removed herself as far away as possible. She now lazily got to her feet, looked at me and then jumped onto the bed settling herself down on the pillow next to him.

'What? You are joking right? You can't possibly want to sleep next to that ignorant monster!' I hissed at her. To my horror, she extended her snout and gave him a lick on his bare shoulder. 'Traitor.' I glared at her, bemused that she so obviously liked the man.

Really, it was most annoying. The least she could have done was to bite him on the arse! Thoroughly grumpy now and aching in even more places than I was before, I stomped around the room looking for something cosy and comfortable to wear. I was going to be sleeping in the armchair unless he woke up. I pulled on my pyjamas and then an old jogging suit on top with a pair of thick woolly socks.

Thankfully, this being a highland hotel there was a good supply of spare woollen blankets on the top shelf of the wardrobe. I pulled out a couple, inched the chair nearer the radiator, wishing that there was an open fire in the room, and reached for the discarded tea tray and whisky bottle.

There was a hearty game broth which had of course gone cold, but I ate it now, taking pleasure in dunking great chunks of the crusty bread into it. This was followed by a doorstop of a sandwich cheese with a savoury relish, also delicious and finally a large slice of apple and cinnamon pie with a small jug of fresh cream. Starving, I ate the lot. Chomping away gave me something to do other than think what an utter bloody numpty I had been.

Again!

At least there was no one this time to witness what had happened and I hoped that no one would find out either. The rich and satisfying food did take some of the edge off my anger and self-disgust. It was hard to be so disgruntled with such a full stomach. Not to mention the rest of the bottle of Kinlaggan, although eyeing the bottle ruefully I did partially blame this for my recklessness.

It seemed that alcohol was not a good idea with Robbie Munro anywhere in the vicinity. It wasn't as if I even liked the man. So why, oh why had I just done what I had done? And aside from blaming the whisky, I couldn't blame it all on him this time because I had gone to comfort him.

You knew then Daisy.

I tried to ignore the voice from somewhere in my head.

You knew then what would happen.

I argued with this voice for quite a while until I eventually fell asleep.

A crash accompanied by swearing woke me. Disorientated and deeply uncomfortable from being curled up in the chair, it took me a few moments to realise what had woken me.

'What the fuck?'

The bedside light came on. Robbie was standing there by the bed, looking as disorientated as I felt. Then he looked at Luna, curled up on the pillow and the rumpled state of the duvet which showed where he had been sleeping. Finally, he cast his eyes downwards and took in his naked state. Which I have to admit, even allowing for my annoyance and bias that he was the most horrible man I had ever come across, was pretty magnificent. And this, of course, only made me more annoyed.

'At last, I can now get some decent sleep!' I checked my watch and saw it was three in the morning.

Like a bear coming out of hibernation he shambled around the room, picking up the discarded items of clothing which he seemed to have difficulty in putting back on. If I wasn't so damn furious, I would have found it highly amusing to see the big hulk of the man dressing as clumsily as a toddler. Twice he nearly fell over trying to put one leg through his jeans and then he pulled his sweater on over his head back to front. As for lacing up his boots, well in the end I gave up and shoved him abruptly onto the edge of the bed, trying to ignore what had happened a few hours previously and tied them up for him.

'Thank you,' he said quietly.

Brokenly.

As though the very act of having to dress had all simply been too much for him.

I was kneeling on the floor, and I raised my head to look at him. Once more I felt flooded with a nameless emotion that washed away the anger and fear he stirred in me. The coldness I had felt beneath the fire of his passion, was for now in a state of thaw.

Exposing a shocking vulnerability as it did so that made me ask, 'Will you be ok?'

Our eyes met and held for a long silent moment. In that unguarded space, a bridge seemed to span the distance between us. Then again, as though he had had much practice at doing this, he withdrew and I saw the light change in his eyes once more.

'Aye. You will not tell Lily.'

'No. I will not tell Lily.'

I made myself hold his gaze. I would not tell his daughter that I knew he had tried to kill himself that afternoon and I certainly would not tell her that we had ended up rolling round the bed together like a sex starved pair of animals. No indeed.

'Good. That's good then.'

I couldn't just let that knowledge hang in mid-air though. 'What did the doctor say?' I rose to my feet giving myself the advantage of height as he was still sitting on the edge of the bed.

He raised his eyebrows and I explained that Callum had told me where he had been taking him.

Robbie snorted. 'Fucking Callum.'

'He is worried about you. And so is Lily.' I gave him one of my hardest stares.

He pulled a face and shook his head. 'Fucking doctors. Fucking pills.

As if that will make a difference.'

'It might do.' It was like trying to help one of my most dysfunctional pupils. 'What has he prescribed?'

He shrugged and then rooted in his jeans pocket for a prescription. He held it out to me.

'Did Callum not think to get this for you at the pharmacy?'

Another shrug, this one accompanied by the merest hint of a smile. 'Saved by a heilan coo in distress.'

'A what?'

'Heilan coo. Or as you would say a Highland cow. I promised him I would get the pills.'

Did I look that gullible? I held onto the prescription. 'I'll get it for you tomorrow.'

'Ah woman didna fash. As if taking some wee little pills is going to make any difference.'

I could be equally stubborn. 'They might. I will get the prescription for you tomorrow. And you will at least try the pills.'

The smile grew into a mocking grin. 'Aye, and how exactly are you going to make me take them?'

'You either take them, or I tell Lily you gave up on her and tried to smash yourself into that bloody tree.'

That made him stand up sharpish. I stood my ground, even though I was so much smaller than him.

'You would, wouldn't you?' He considered this and then his eyes strayed to the crumpled bed.

'I said it before Daisy, you're a bloody good fuck. Maybe that's all I need hey? Maybe I just need a woman like you in my bed to sort me out. Shame you can't get that on prescription hey?'

It was a gauntlet thrown down because I had just got one over him. It worked because I could feel the heat rise in my face, not to mention other parts of my anatomy. Mustering up as much dignity as I could, I went to the door and opened it. Carefully I poked my head down the hallway, checking there was no one wandering around.

'I think you should go.'

When I finally had my room to myself once more, I turned accusing eyes at Luna. 'Well you weren't exactly much help there were you? I mean, could you not somehow have stopped me? And as for cuddling up to him on the bed afterwards, anyone would think he was a really nice person. But he isn't Luna. He's as mad as a hatter for one thing, and when he isn't crazy, he is rude, obnoxious, arrogant and a complete and utter prick, not to mention a possible psychopath,' I finished on a whisper.

Luna regarded me solemnly with her beautiful luminous eyes. We snuggled up together to get back to sleep. As I pulled the duvet around me, I got a faint hint of Robbie's masculine smell. It was hard to say if this was a comfort or an annoyance.

The following day it was business as usual.

Up early, down to greet the guests for breakfast, friendly smile in place, and reassurances all round. Yes, I was completely fine after my accident and no it wasn't anyone's fault other than my own. I wasn't too sure about saying this with regard to my insurance, especially if my car was going to be a total write off. Big Mac cheerfully confirmed this when he rang just after lunchtime. I was at the reception desk and was putting the phone down with a long drawn-out groan when Colin McCready came out of the dining room.

He was whistling but stopped when he saw me. 'That sounded heartfelt.'

'My car is a write off. I have spent ages this morning on the phone to the insurance company who are generally are being unhelpful, telling me that I should have called the police.' I shrugged and held out my hands. 'I didn't know what to do. I've never crashed my car before and given where it was and how dangerous the road is, it seemed the sensible thing to just move it out of the way.' I didn't add that there had also been concerns over the suicidal behaviour of one of the participants.

'Sounds like you could do with a bit of cheering up?' He looked at me hopefully. 'I was going to drive over to Boat of Garten to look out for ospreys. I don't suppose you would enjoy a spot of fresh air if you are free?'

At that moment, Shona also came through from the dining room. I could feel her scowling at me as she listened to Colin's tentative invitation. She had never forgiven me for New Year's Eve. God only knew what she would think if she knew about last night. No doubt I was irritating her now with the attention I was getting from Colin. I was tired, I had a cracking headache, and I was going to have a real knotty problem with my car insurance, not to mention the inconvenience of having no transport.

'Colin that would be lovely,' I said making a snap decision. 'Shona, did I hear you correctly this morning asking Catriona if there were more hours going? Yes, well there are. I usually finish at three but as you are here now, that would work very well. It's all yours Shona.'

'Oh, that's grand,' said Colin with a touching enthusiasm.

I could see Shona was tossing up in her head was it worth refusing just to spite me, or did she really want the extra money? She was trying to save up for a new car herself, so that won out.

'Just give me ten minutes to change,' I said to Colin. A short while later I was ready in one of my new pairs of walking trousers, a petrol blue colour teamed with a deep plum fleece which really suited my grey eyes. The new coat I had bought with Moira was a cheerful red.

'You look nice,' said Colin. 'Bright. I'm not sure you won't frighten the birds away but never mind.'

I heard a snort from Shona.

'Shall I put something else on?'

Moira had encouraged me to go for bright colours as it was easier for the mountain rescue to spot me, should ever the need arise. I had not given birdwatching much thought.

'Don't worry. I am pretty sure they are used by now to folk in bright gear.'

Feeling a little mollified at this, I declared myself ready to go. Then there was another awkward moment as he realised belatedly that wherever I went, so did Luna. Ah, take a wolf birdwatching, probably not Daisy.

'It's okay,' I said quickly. 'I can leave her in my room. Come on Luna.' I went to the stairs for her to follow me back up. At which point she went on strike and refused to budge. 'Luna come on!'

It was the first time ever she had disobeyed me, and I knew damn well she was doing it on purpose. I thought of how telepathically clever she could be and looking into her eyes now I swore she was laughing at me. It was as though she was saying it was okay for me to leave her behind if I needed to go into town, but under no circumstances was it acceptable to go for a walk without her.

'We don't have to go to look at the ospreys,' said Colin good naturedly.

'Oh yes we do,' I replied over my shoulder whilst glaring at Luna and making my mind up. 'Right madam, if you want to stay there you can do.'

I straightened up and nodded at Colin. 'Right let's go.'

'What? You can't leave her there.' Shona was not a huge fan of Luna nor she of her. She eyed the wolf that was now sprawled lazily across the foot of the stairs.

'Do you want to try and move her?'

'No.'

'Well then.'

'But you can't leave a wolf unattended. Health and safety.' In battle mode, Shona folded her arms at me and smiled with satisfaction.

I was just considering this when Robbie strode into the hotel from outside. He stopped dead seeing Colin and me together and Shona behind the desk.

'You going out?'

'Yes.'

'You going out with him?' Hair unkempt, unshaven, eyes rather on the wild side I don't know how he could consider giving Colin such a look from head to toe, but he did. 'Och well.' He started to grin but I shot him a look of warning that halted him in his tracks.

'Colin is taking me to look at the ospreys, which is really nice of him. Especially as I don't have a car to drive at the moment,' I said pointedly.

'Aye, about that.'

'Look we have to get going if we stand any chance of seeing them this afternoon.' Colin butted in with a quiet determination that I rather admired in the face of Robbie's uncouth brusqueness.

'Erm, the wolf.' Shona had her say once more.

'She won't go to her room,' I explained to Robbie and realised I sounded as though I was talking about a child, not an animal.

'Can't say I blame her,' he said. Then surprised me by adding. 'She can come with me.' He walked over to the stairs. Luna immediately rose and to my utter astonishment, she moved to follow him.

'What are you doing?' I called after him.

'Work,' came back the reply over his shoulder.

'Work?'

'Yes woman, work!'

He didn't bother to turn around, but treacherous Luna did and gave me the most, well, wolfish of grins. Huffing back my indignation, I turned to Colin with the brightest smile on my face I could produce.

'Come on Colin, let's go birdwatching.'

Chapter Twenty-Eight

On the drive from Wolf Lodge to Loch Garten, he asked me all the usual questions you would expect from someone just getting to know you. We obviously had a love of literature in common and that made for a very easy starting point.

Then understandably he asked, 'So how did you come to be working at Wolf Lodge?'

I gave him a brief version of getting divorced from Gary and needing a new start. It didn't seem relevant or appropriate somehow to mention Sean at this stage. Although of course he couldn't help commenting on Luna.

'It's quite ironic that you have a wolf yourself.'

He didn't know the half of it I thought as I considered both the tattoo on my back, her mysterious appearance and the fact that the painting in Michaela's studio was from a setting round here.

'How often do you come up here?' I asked him and at quick turn of his head to look at me I berated myself. I sounded like I was keen to see more of him already.

'A few times a year if I get the chance. I like the solitude and birdwatching.'

Looking at his shy smile as he parked the car, and then as he handed me a pair of spare binoculars it occurred to me that perhaps geeks were underrated. He pointed the way through the wooded edge of the loch, and we began to walk until we got to the spot that Colin had in mind to settle down and watch for the birds.

I could not have asked for a more pleasant way to spend a winter's afternoon. Especially after the previous crazy twenty-four hours. It was easy to sit in silence next to him. The only words shared were when he asked if I wanted a hot chocolate from the flask that Mary had provided. Wrapping my hands around the mug I enjoyed the warmth of the drink and a couple of short bread biscuits, also courtesy of Mary.

Our silence and patience were rewarded as I got to see one of the majestic birds swooping down to the loch to deftly catch their prey. I could appreciate some of Colin's enthusiasm. The bird was so close we didn't need the binoculars, so I had chance to get out my phone and take a few shots. I would send them to Abigail who was a keen animal lover. My little sister was impatient to come and visit at Easter and I had already decided to bring her here. I mentioned this to Colin later as we eased the stiffness from our bodies and made our way back to the car as the light began to fade.

'Oh, that would be nice. I am hoping to return at Easter myself. How lovely if I could meet her.'

Then cautiously as though aware he may be crossing a line, he asked, 'Do you have children yourself?'

I shook my head. 'You?'

A look of pain shot across his face. 'My wife was pregnant when she was killed falling down stairs.'

'Colin I am so sorry. That's awful.'

I felt an instant bond with him over the loss of a child, but I could not imagine how I would have felt if I had lost Gary at that time as well.

'What about you? You mentioned you were getting divorced – have you come here to start a new life?'

'Yes, exactly'

'You'll definitely be staying then?' Colin asked me as we got back to the car.

'Definitely.' It was easy to answer positively. 'I mean I hope it continues to work out at Wolf Lodge but even if it doesn't Colin, I think I could make my home here permanently.'

He gave me a shy glance as he opened my door for me. 'No chance of you being enticed away?'

It had been a lovely couple of hours. A beautiful setting. Quiet company. Easy silence and gentle conversation. The uplifting sight of the ospreys. I was glowing inside and out from the warmth of my emotions and the chill of the air. Tingling and alive with joy and enthusiasm.

I answered him with an encouraging smile. 'Maybe Colin. Maybe.'

He seemed happy with this as we drove back to Kinlaggan. 'Could I perhaps entice you to tea at The Ptarmigan's Nest. I'm fancying a venison burger myself?'

The Ptarmigan's Nest was a lively bar in Kinlaggan that served simple but hugely satisfying meals and quite often had live music in the evenings. I had said yes yesterday to a drink at the hotel bar. Going for a meal even a casual one like this was one step further. But after such a lovely afternoon it seemed the natural thing to do.

'I would love to,' I said. Then I remembered I still had an errand to run. 'Will the pharmacy at the health centre still be open do you think?'

It turned out it was and satisfying my sense of responsibility, not that it was my obligation to do this, I nipped in and got Robbie's prescription. I shoved the tablets into one of the large pockets of my coat making a mental note to give them to him later. Then again, maybe it would be safer if I got Catriona to give them to him. I wasn't sure that I trusted myself around Robbie, especially if I had been drinking with Colin.

The atmosphere in The Ptarmigan's Nest was lively with a number of people on holiday. It was still early though, and we didn't have too long to wait for our food. Colin stayed away from alcohol as he was driving but I allowed myself to be temped into trying some of the local stout that was on offer that week.

Then we carried on chatting as we ate and, as before, I found Colin an easy person to be with. He reminded me a little of Sean. He was kind and attentive and had an easy depreciating manner. He didn't have the same sparkling energy about him that my lodger, friend and lover had. But then few people I had met in my life were quite like Sean. If anyone for that matter.

Regardless of comparisons spending the afternoon with Colin was just the tonic I needed. By the time we were heading back to the hotel, my spirits had been lifted and my headache was gone. It was completely dark as we drove back, there were no street lights at all on the road to Wolf Lodge. I cautioned Colin, perhaps unnecessarily as he was a careful driver anyway, to be mindful of the bends in the roads.

'I take it that's the tree then?' As he sensibly braked to take the corner where I had spun off, the headlights caught the spot where I had crashed.

Where Robbie had driven me off the road.

Where that mad lunatic had tried to kill himself.

'Yes,' I said, a trifle breathlessly as the enormity of it hit me once more.

'Sorry. Stupid of me,' said Colin reading that change of mood in an instant.

'It's ok. Really no harm done. Just a ruined car. I just hope the insurance get it sorted quickly although from what they said this morning I think I may have a battle on my hands with them.'

We were both quiet for the rest of the drive home, but it was not an uncomfortable silence. I broke it as Colin was parking at the front of the hotel with an enormous yawn.

'Oh no. I hope I haven't bored you to death?' He said, switching off the ignition.

'Gosh, not at all.' I yawned again. 'Sorry. It's all that lovely fresh air, good food and ale. And company.' I said with a smile. 'I am really relaxed.'

I didn't like to think that I was probably also very tired because I had not slept a wink last night thanks to Robbie. Walking back into the hotel with him, I had that moment of wondering how to say goodnight? Was this a date we had been on? Did I give him a friendly kiss? I burned a little inside at my insane response to Robbie.

I think he was feeling something similar as we did that awkward shuffling thing people do when they are not quite sure of their actions, or how they will be interpreted. We both spoke at once, thanking each other for the lovely afternoon. Then laughed, recognising the awkwardness for what it was.

'Perhaps we could do it again, or something similar if I get chance to come back at Easter?'

'I would like that,' I replied at once.

'Well then, I'll say goodnight.'

Perhaps it was a little cowardly of me, but I was glad that we were now in the entrance hallway, the phone ringing gave me the excuse I needed to dodge the matter of a kiss.

'I'd best get this' I said brightly to him before Shona could appear to answer it.

When I had finished with the enquiry, I made my way upstairs wondering if Luna was still with Robbie. I was surprised that she had not bounded straight into the hallway to greet me as she usually did.

When Robbie had said he was working, had he meant that he was up in his studio at the top of the West Tower? From what I had been told, he had not done any painting for a long time. I had also been told that under no circumstances did he like to be disturbed if he was.

I loitered in the corridor along which was my bedroom and the door to the tower. I dithered, thinking that I had a right to go and get my wolf back. Then I heard the pounding which I recognised as Luna's powerful tread on the stairs behind the door and stepped back.

I was just in time as the door opened and Luna joyfully leapt up at me. I had got used to this habit of hers by now and had learnt to brace myself for the assault. I had not learnt to brace myself for the effect that seeing Robbie appeared to have on me.

He stood there, framed by the doorway of the tower, as unruly looking and as unkempt as earlier. Only now there was an energy about him that was positively crackling. Used to the surly dark side of him, I was completely wrong footed when he looked at me and then without a word took my hand. I no choice other than to be led by him into the tower and up the stairs. I realised that with him it was useless asking what we were doing. As long as it didn't involve us getting naked, I told myself fiercely.

At the top of the tower there were two rooms. One I presumed was his bedroom. Thankfully he did not open the door to this one. The room he took me into was his studio. Like the man, it was chaotic and messy with large canvasses, easels and art materials stacked hither and thither. But the main focus of the room was the easel upon which he had clearly been working.

He was still holding my hand, but I needed no encouragement to be led to the easel. My heart was beginning to pound, and I didn't know why. Perhaps there was a sense of being shown something no one else had been allowed to see yet. Perhaps I was merely reacting to the vibes he was giving off. Luna too for that matter. My wolf seemed positively brimming with energy; more than usual that is.

Whatever the reasons, the beating of my heart went into turbo mode when I saw what was on the canvas. Time stood still and for a moment I was back in my home town, back to that day when I had met Sean, back to meeting Michaela in her tattoo studio.

Two artists.

One used ink and skin as her medium.

One paint and canvas.
Two studios, hundreds of miles apart.
One picture.
Luna by the waterfall with the mountains behind.

It was not finished, I could see that, but it was there all the same. The wolf on my back burned and tingled, that reminder that Luna was imprinted onto my skin with far more than just ink. If I had ever had any doubts before that there had been magic involved, they completely left me now.

I couldn't speak. The painting drew me in, just as Michaela's had done in her studio. Luna stared at me from the canvas, and I was there with her, the waterfall close by, the scent of pine clean in my lungs, the icy cold of the snow topped mountains stinging on my face.

Like Michaela, Robbie's response to my silence was the same. 'You don't like it.' Unlike Michaela's voice there was a scary deadness to the tone as the words seemed to be ripped from him.

I whirled round to face him. 'I love it!'

His whole body seemed to be containing a wildness that could explode at any point. 'You're sure?'

Once more he moved me with his vulnerability. 'Yes,' I said, again feeling as though I was calming a wild animal. 'It is beautiful.'

It was far more than that. But now was not the time to share with him that I had seen that same image before on the wall of a tattoo artist's studio. I didn't think that mentioning the possibility of magic was a good idea to someone in his state of mind.

'I got these for you.' Gingerly I handed him the packet of pills that were still in my coat pocket.

He scowled darkly. 'Ach I told you I have no need for such things.' He nodded his head to the canvas. 'This is my drug of choice.'

I could understand that.

What person would not get a high from being able to produce such a masterpiece? I certainly would. I guessed though that therein lay the danger. What happened when the creativity ran out? Was this his real problem? All these mad ups and downs and suicidal tendencies. Was it nothing to do with a family curse? Was he just a temperamental artist after all? Either way, I had more faith in modern medicine than he seemed to. I held out the pills and held his gaze at the same time.

'You promised me. For Lily.'

His scowl contorted into an evil grimace. 'Och, you are a wicked woman, Daisy. Wicked indeed.'

I couldn't help but feel a shiver of pleasure at his words as he took the packet from me. He was still scowling as he read the directions. Then a smile brightened his face. With devilment.

'I have to take them last thing at night. So does that mean, Nurse Daisy, that you will come to my bedroom each night to make sure I take them?'

'No. It does not!' I snapped, aware that this path would lead to my own insanity. 'I will just have to trust that you are taking them, won't I?'

'Aye.' He tilted his head and gave me a very disturbing look. 'Do you trust me, Daisy?'

It was not something I could answer. Then it struck me as I looked at Luna that I could give him some sort of response.

'She clearly does.'

Determined to remain in control this time, I clicked my fingers towards my wolf, hoping that she would not play any more games as she had done earlier. Luna was quite happy to leave the studio with me, that grinning expression on her face that seemed to say, it's okay, I have got what I came for.

'What's going on, Luna?' I asked her once I had reached the sanctuary of my room. 'What's the bigger picture?'

Obviously, there was one and I mulled on my choice of words to her as once more my mind was filled with the image I had just seen reproduced in Robbie's studio. I picked up my phone and called Sean. It was lovely hearing his warm Irish tones full of laughter as always. And as always, he lightly rebuffed any notion at all that he could possibly, remotely, be responsible for this latest bizarre co-incidence.

'Have you not heard of artist's telepathy?'

'No. I have not, Sean.' I was quite sure that he had just made this up. Used to his ways, I let him ramble on in that charming fashion of his. 'Happens all the time,' he finished blithely. 'So, you're getting on well with him then?'

'What? No. Not at all. I mean...'

'It's alright you know, Daisy, I told you this before.'

'Honestly Sean what happened at new year was just...' It was impossible to lie to him so instead I changed the subject, knowing that I had just given myself away. At least I wouldn't be able to see the wise knowing look in those stunning blue eyes. 'How is the project with Violet's nephew going?'

'Grand, just grand. I am going to come and visit you at Easter when we take a break from it.'

'That would be lovely,' I said to him softly and meant it with all my heart. 'I miss you.'

'I miss you too, Daisy. But you are happy there, I can tell by your voice and that is all that matters.'

We said goodnight and he added with his voice a gentle caress, 'Sweet dreams, Daisy darling.'

As I put my head on to my pillow a little later on, sleep took me to the river, to the waterfall with Luna at my side. And Robbie Munro. Deeply powerful, vividly real, wildly erotic - it was the second night in a row that left me feeling groggy and confused when I woke. For once, I wished I could have a lie in, but it was my job to be up and at reception early.

Colin was one of the guests leaving today. 'Is it possible for you to reserve a room for me for Easter. I have decided I will come back then.'

'Absolutely,' I assured him.

Never mind Sean's odd feyness, and Robbie's dark glamour. Normal, gentlemanly behaviour in the shape of Colin was what I needed in my life. A little voice in the back of my head reminded me that he had also lost a child, something we shared that few would understand. As he was leaving, Robbie came into the entrance hall. Spurred by a little imp inside me I dashed after Colin.

'Drive safely,' I said and aware that Robbie was watching me, I impulsively kissed Colin on the cheek.

'Aye, I will. Cheerybye, Daisy.' Colin walked to his car with a smile on his face and a spring in his step.

As he drove away, I saw that there was a car parked at the front of the hotel I hadn't noticed before. I wondered if I had missed a new guest arriving. Aware that Robbie had now followed me outside, I casually asked him if he knew whose it was. He gave an odd little snort.

'You like him?'

'He's a very nice, charming man.'

He smirked as though this was an insult.

Ruffled, I returned my focus to the car. It was a shiny, gunmetal grey jeep, a popular vehicle on the roads round here.

'Well, whose is it then?'

Robbie shoved his hand into his jeans pocket and rooted out a set of keys. He tossed them to me. 'It's yours.'

I managed to catch them, just about. 'Mine. What do you mean it's mine?'

'Your car is wrecked.' He gave a shrug. 'Insurance companies being what they are, I doubt they'll pay up. I swapped my Porsche. It's yours.'

I gawped at him open mouthed. He had nothing more to say and he just turned his back on me and walked into the hotel leaving me once more feeling utterly confused.

Chapter Twenty-Nine

March was a pleasantly quiet month both weather wise and with the guests. Catriona told me it was wise to make the most of this and I took her at her word. I had a taste for exploring more of the scenery and for watching the wildlife. I also wanted to get to know further afield.

About an hour's drive away there was a beach that was famed for being able to spot seals and dolphins. I mentioned I was thinking of going there one Sunday when the sun had come out after a particularly dreary run of days. Lily had immediately asked if she could come with me.

'You'd better ask your dad if that's okay.' I was sitting in the snug with Catriona, cradling a hot coffee in my hands.

'Maybe Dad can come with us?'

It was not really what I had in mind. I had succeeded very well in avoiding Robbie since that night at half-term. He had been remarkably quiet since then and Catriona had more than once commented that his pills seemed to be working. I was not so sure. There was a detached air about him now; that in some ways was worse.

'Go and ask him then,' I said to her, hoping that she would come downstairs alone.

'I believe your old neighbour is coming up to stay with us tomorrow?' Catriona said.

'She is. She has a gap of a week before she can move into her new flat so she thought she may as well visit in that time. She is coming with Marigold.'

'That will be nice for you. I shall look forward to meeting her if she is anything like you,' said Catriona.

I pulled a face. 'Well not exactly. It was a huge surprise when she rang me last night. She had heard from Gary that Violet was coming up and then asked her if she minded if she came along too.'

Lily then returned with a rather pale looking Robbie. He had grown even more unkempt these last few weeks, hair well over his collar now, and a thick growth of beard hiding his jawline. I realised with a shock that it was probably a good fortnight since I had seen him. He had not been down to breakfast at all, nor had I seen him in the evenings.

During the day he was closeted in his studio, and I knew that Mary prepared trays of food for him. Looking at him now, I wondered if he was eating any of the meals. Catriona though did not appear to notice that her son was looking pasty, washed out, and frankly rather rough.

She beamed at him delightedly. 'Robbie, are you going to Spey Bay with Daisy and Lily, that is good.'

'Are we going in your car, Daisy?' Lily asked as we went through into the entrance hallway to collect our coats and boots.

Robbie had of course sold his Porsche, but he still had his own four-wheel drive.

'Yes. I'm driving,' I said quickly thinking that Robbie looked in no fit state to be behind a wheel.

'Oh good,' said Lily. 'I like being in your new car, it's cool.'

I rather thought so too. There was no doubt my confidence driving round the local roads had improved considerably with the jeep, although I had made Moira laugh uncontrollably the first time I tried to park it at the small supermarket in Kinlaggan. The fact that Robbie had sold his Porsche in order to replace my wrecked car, had also caused quite a few comments.

Catriona had been audibly relieved. 'Thank goodness he has got rid of that terrible machine,' sharing the common view that one day he was bound to end up killing himself in it, as had been the intention that day, which of course no one talked about.

Shona had taken one look at it and muttered something very inaudible but rude sounding under her breath. If she had been frosty with me since new year, the atmosphere between us was now arctic. Moira had greeted the news with a chirpy grin and a nod of her head as if to say, I told you he was interested in you. I had then gone to great lengths to talk about my afternoon birdwatching with Colin.

Now it was dolphin spotting with Robbie.

No. It wasn't. Luna and I were going for a day out and Lily and her father were coming with me. Big difference. Very big difference indeed in the company of the two men. Robbie, quite naturally had got into the passenger seat, although I would have preferred to have Lily sitting there. He brought with him a physical presence that was positively gloomy. It was like having a huge dark cloud next to you – ominous and oppressive. Then I told myself he was on anti-depressants so perhaps I was being unkind.

Lily was her usual cheerful self, chattering away ten to the dozen which made up for the heavy silence of her dad. I wondered if this was her defence mechanism. If she could be upbeat and sunny natured all the time maybe it would cancel out the darkness. She certainly was a lot more effervescent than the girls her age that I had taught back home. Was this because she had a dad that she worried over so much? Or was it just the effects of growing up in such a wildly different environment, with all the rugged scenery of huge mountains, vast open spaces and enchanting forests?

Not to mention the coastline.

Wild, windy, and freezing cold in the sunshine, the tang of salt air was a complete change to the pine forests around Kinlaggan. Lily had been here before and I was happy to let her lead the way, binoculars bouncing around her neck as we set off in search of dolphins. They proved elusive, but that didn't dim the enjoyment of walking along the pebbly shoreline and listening to the waves. There was plenty of bird life to look at although neither Lily nor I had a clue what any of them were.

'Colin would know,' I said as she pointed out one to me.

'Do you like him?' Green eyes, curious as a cat's peeked at me from beneath her dark fringe. She had the furry hood of her coat pulled right up and her dainty face almost disappeared with it.

'Colin? Yes of course. He's very nice.'

'Do you like him better than Dad?'

The silent figure of Robbie was a few yards away from us, hands in pockets, seeming not to feel the cold. He had no hat on and the wind was making his hair wilder than ever. He was looking out to sea as though searching for something other than dolphins.

How could I answer Lily's question?

'He bought you the jeep,' she said as if this should count.

I didn't like to comment that it had been her father's fault in the first place that mine was wrecked. I had gone along with the story that the accident had all been down to my inexperience on the icy Scottish roads, not that Robbie Munro had tried to kill himself.

'Yes. He did,' I said aware that some response was required.

'I think he likes you.'

Cowardly I replied, 'Do you fancy a hot chocolate and some cake at the café?'

'Do I? Dad we're going for hot chocolate!'

Abandoning the wildlife, we went in search of warmth and sugary carbohydrates. There was a small visitor centre attached and I went for a quick look round. It would not be long before Abigail would be visiting at Easter, and this was just the sort of place she would enjoy. Maybe Colin would like to come here as well? I felt an odd twinge of disloyalty to Lily. Watching her looking through the dolphin souvenirs I worried that she was pinning too many of her hopes on the idea of me and her dad getting together.

Hungry sex was one thing.

Being in a relationship with a man like him – completely out of the question.

I shouldn't have thought about the sex because then I was thinking about Colin.

And hungry sex was not the first thing that came to mind.

I was glad when Lily broke into that chain of thought. 'Daisy can I borrow some money? Dad doesn't have any with him. I'm visiting Mum at Easter and I want to take her a present.'

'Of course.'

Having paid, Lily linked her arm through mine, and we went to find a table in the café. Robbie had disappeared into the toilets, and he had been there for some time. I was on the point of wondering whether to ask another gentleman to go and see if he was alright when he came into the café. Lily spotted him first and waved at him.

'Dad, we're here. We've got you a coffee and some carrot cake.' She had told me this was his favourite.

Robbie toyed with it for a few mouthfuls and then pushed the plate away.

'Och, I'm not so hungry this morning. You have it.'

'Okay.' Lily took the plate.

I opened my mouth to say that she had said she didn't like carrot cake whilst we were in the queue. Then watching her eyeing her dad anxiously, I kept quiet. I was thankful then for all the times I had sat with Irene when she had been so ill. I had become adept at keeping up a flowing monologue to fill that gaping chasm of silence. When Lily had finished both her cake and her father's, she excused herself to go to the loo. Robbie waited until she was out of sight and then took a hip flask from his pocket and drank heavily from it.

'What are you doing?' I hissed at him, but he looked at me uncaring.

I noticed then how much his hand was trembling. I also heard a tutting from the table behind us. I suppose it was understandable. He looked a wreck, and it clearly was not coffee he had in the flask. I was reminded of how Sean had looked when I had first known him. Angrily I swivelled round to face the woman.

'And your point is?'

It was a good job that we had left Luna in the Jeep otherwise I think the woman would have got more than she bargained for. As it was, I glared at her with a ferocity that surprised me. The initial anger I had felt towards Robbie when I saw the flask, turned to concern.

'Are you alright?' I asked him quietly, moving my chair slightly so that I was nearer to him and further away from the woman behind me.

Green eyes, not sea clear like Lily's but flecked with hazel tones of a forest, regarded me cynically.

'Define alright?'

Somewhat distracted, thinking that it really wasn't fair that a man should have such long dark lashes, I had to give myself a little shake.

'I mean,' I said with a pointed look at the flask, 'are you supposed to be drinking whisky at eleven in the morning, especially when you are on anti-depressants?'

'I flushed them down the toilet, useless fucking things.'

I withheld my screech, just. 'What? When?'

'Ooh, erm a few days ago, I canna remember.'

I stared at him whilst I tried to recall a conversation I'd had with Callum. I was pretty sure he had said when Robbie started taking the medication, that it would take a few weeks to really begin to work and he was not to come off them without going back to the doctor. I snapped at Robbie and reminded him of this. In return I got the darkest of scowls. The look in his eyes was quite really quite hostile. More than that. A madness lurked there. I felt a shiver of fear as I thought about the gossip.

'They don't work.'

'You haven't given them time.' I pushed back my fear and told myself this was Lily's dad. He could not be a killer. He just couldn't be.

'I'm telling you they don't fucking work! What's the point in taking something that doesn't fucking work?' He shouted and banged the table with his fist making the plates rattle and me, jump.

At the disgusted mutters from the other customers, the manageress came straight over.

'What are you fucking looking at?'

He whirled round in his seat to glare at her. The unmistakeable fury in him was enough to make her take a step backwards. Quickly I got out of my seat and slid between her and Robbie.

'I'm sorry, he's not very well,' I said to her and risked placing a hand on Robbie's shoulder. 'Lily's coming,' I said hurriedly, and I was not lying either. His daughter was on her way back from the toilets. 'I'm sorry,' I added to the manageress with a pleading look towards Lily.

Thankfully she caught my drift. 'Alright. But leave as quickly as you can please.'

A shudder ran through Robbie's body as though he was containing an explosion from within. With an indecipherable grunt he pushed back the chair, thrust his hands deep into his pockets and gave me a nod of acknowledgement, as if to say he got my point. He would behave for Lily's sake.

It was not the relaxing day off it should have been and on the way home I couldn't help but compare the time spent with him to the afternoon I'd had with Colin. As we got back to Kinlaggan, Lily got out of the car and gave me one of those hugs that tore into me.

'That was lovely Daisy, thank you.'

'My pleasure, Lily,' and for her, I meant it.

Wanting to speak to Robbie alone, I asked her if she would take Luna and go and dry her off from her walk and feed her. Once they had disappeared up the steps into the hotel, I turned to him, but he spoke before I could.

'Where have we just been?'

'I beg your pardon?'

'Where… have… we… just… been?' He spat the words out, a wild look in his eyes.

My mouth went dry. 'Spey Bay. With Lily. To look at the dolphins. We went in the café.'

He looked terrified then. 'How long were we there?'

'You don't remember?'

The blank look in his eyes was answer enough. 'Don't tell anyone.' In an echo of the car crash he insisted again, 'You mustn't tell Lily, promise me?'

'But you're having blackouts! You should be in hospital! That's not a secret I can keep.'

I got out of the jeep, needing to be away from him. In a flash he was out and standing next to me, hands grabbing me roughly by the shoulders.

'I mean it, you cannot tell anyone.' There was a threat in his eyes whether for himself or me I couldn't tell.

My breathing grew shallow, but I dared to say quietly, 'Maybe if you hadn't stopped taking the pills?'

He looked deeply angry then and his grip on my shoulders tightened as though he wanted to shake me and was holding himself back.

Just.

Then his hands went to his head, and he smacked at himself so hard his ears must have rung with pain.

'I can't fucking paint.' He stated baldly.

'I'm sorry?'

'The pills. You were going to nag me about those fucking wee pills. I know you were. You had that look in your eye. That bossy teacher look. Has anyone ever told you it's a very sexy look by the way?'

I gawped at him wondering how the hell he could spin things around so quickly. The fury he had shown had vanished and now there was an energy to him coupled with a reckless glint in his eyes.

Trying to regain control, I said calmly. 'Could you please explain that. I mean the not painting. Not the other bit.'

He grinned at me. In contrast to before it was like seeing a rainbow after a storm. 'I mean, Daisy, I can't paint if I take those pills. And if I can't paint, then you may as well shoot me and be done with it. Do you see what I mean?'

I leant back against my jeep. It was not an argument I could counter. I said rather feebly, 'Yes but you shouldn't have come off them straight away.'

Another of those damn grins, taunting, mocking, and annoyingly sexy. 'And you always do what you should Daisy?'

Memories of him inside me flooded into my head and flicked that switch in my body.

Folding my arms against him, against myself, I replied tartly. 'We aren't discussing me. I suppose that's why you are drinking in the morning? You've got some kind of withdrawal going on. You should go and see the doctor.'

'What the fuck do they know Daisy?' Again, his mood changed right before my eyes. The fire and life extinguished in an instant and replaced with a cold deadness. 'There's no cure for a fucking curse, Daisy, I know that, and I know another thing. If I can't paint, I will end up killing myself. So, if drinking whisky in the morning is what I have to do on some days, then drink fucking whisky I will.'

I wondered there and then if it was a good idea to suggest maybe he was an alcoholic. He read my mind and shook his head.

'Ah you're not the first to say it Daisy and I have no doubt you'll not be the last. Maybe I am. Maybe I'm not. I drink to dumb down the monster Daisy, usually that's when I drink.'

'The monster?'

He tapped his head. 'Aye the monster that lives in here. It's a fucking evil one. A big fucking scary black wolf! He comes in and snaps and snaps and fucking snaps at me. And one of these days he will snap so hard they'll be no running from him. No fucking wee pill will hold him off forever. The only time I am at peace is when I am painting. And I can't paint with hands like this can I?'

I was shaken at his description of the black wolf, mindful of Sean's tale of the grey and white ones. He had not mentioned a black one, but I supposed that would be far worse. I looked at his hands and saw how they were shaking.

It was pitiful.

'Oh Daisy, don't try to fix me, lass. I can see you have a mind to. You canna fix what is cursed. But I thank you for caring, Daisy, I do thank you for caring.'

I saw Lily coming out of the hotel and was about to call to her, but before I could do so, Robbie moved in towards me and cupping my face in my hands, kissed me deeply.

'I'll only fuck you up, you know that don't you? I'll fuck your body, and then I will fuck up your mind. It's what I do.'

His voice was low, hoarse, sexy, and frightening. What else was he capable of doing? I forgot about Lily for that second, drawn to him like a magnet and equally repelled by him. I wanted him to rip my clothes off and take me there and then. I wanted to run like hell away from him.

'Oh sorry, did I interrupt Dad?'

He shot back from me as though electrocuted, and I caught my breath in a gasp.

'Lily, Daisy and I were just...'

'Yes. I can see that Dad,' she grinned mischievously at us.

Caught in a trap I scrambled for a way out. It came in the form of my phone ringing. I don't think I have ever been so glad to see Marigold's name flashing up at me. I sought the sanctuary of my room talking to Marigold in a breathless manner as I sped inside and up the stairs. When I had finished speaking to her, I flopped back on my bed, patting the cover beside me for Luna to jump up and join me.

I fell into a heavy slumber and a disturbing dream.

I could see Robbie being hounded, chased by a pack of wolves, grey like those Sean had talked about. But leading them was a huge, black monster of a wolf, full of menace. Within the dream I felt Robbie's fear. I felt his despair. I felt it driving him to the edge of oblivion and I woke with a start and a pounding headache.

Luna, silver eyed, white wolf of mine, stared deep into my soul.

before I could do so, Robbie moved towards me and cupping my face in his hands, kissed me deeply.

"Uh uuh, fuck you up, you know that don't cha? I'll fuck over bird, and then I will fuck up your mind. It's what I do."

His voice was low, hoarse, sexy and frightening. What else was he capable of doing, I wondered. Abusful, for that second, drawn to him like an insane and equally repelled by him, I wanted him to rip my clothes off and take me there and then. I wanted to run like hell away from him.

"Oh sorry, did I interrupt Dill?"

He shot back from me as though electrocuted, and I caught my breath in a gasp.

"It's Daisy, and I were not..."

"Yes I can see that," she grinned into the room at us.

Caught in a trap, I scrambled for a way out. It came in the form of my photo-snapping 'other', think I have yet been so glad to see Shangoonk, rising dashing up at me. I sought the company of my room talking to Marigold in breathless manner as I sped inside and up the stairs. When I had finished peaking to her, I flopped back on my bed, pulling the cover beside me for mum to jump up and join me.

I fell into a heavy slumber, and a disturbing dream.

I could see Robbie being bounded, chased by a pack of wolves, except the those I'd seen had called about, but leading them was a huge, Black monster of a wolf, full of menace. Within the dream I felt Robbie's fear, I felt his desperate relief showing him to the edge of oblivion, and I woke with a start, and a pounding headache.

Lana, sheer-eyed, white wolf of mine, stared deep into my soul.

Chapter Thirty

Marigold made her appearance in Kinlaggan with her usual flamboyant style. Raven black hair curled around her expertly made-up face. She wore a bold, orange woollen dress with a bright red fringed poncho and high heeled black patent leather boots. She looked like an exotic bird arriving from a foreign climate.

Besides her, Violet looked far more in keeping with the landscape, wearing soft grey trousers, a heather coloured sweater and an olive-green coat, feet encased in flat sturdy black shoes. They were smiling and chatting together when I caught sight of them.

'It's like going back in time,' said Violet as she stepped from the train to the single platform. 'What a charming spot.'

Marigold had travelled the World and I was expecting more cynicism from her.

She surprised me when she said, 'Well that has to go down as one of the best views I have seen from a railway platform.'

I gave them both a moment to absorb the scene. Looking down the track was a landscape of peaks and valleys, mostly still covered with snow at their highest points. Then over towards the east in the direction of Wolf Lodge, the full extent of the mountain range was visible, the dark green vastness of the forests sprawling out from the lower levels. The weather gods were on our side today and I was so glad that their first view was in the spring sunshine, the sky an endless blue.

'Welcome to Kinlaggan.'

Violet hugged me tightly. 'It suits you Daisy, doesn't it Marigold?'

'You do look well Daisy. You are positively glowing.' A compliment from my mother – this was new.

'It must be this highland air,' said Violet.

'Or is it a man maybe?' This was true to form from Marigold, but it was said lightly.

'Fresh air, and good food,' I said firmly refusing to think about Robbie Munro. Or that I had been on an afternoon date with Colin. 'Come on, let's get you to Wolf Lodge.'

I helped them with their bags and led the way to my jeep. This provoked a conversation as to why I was not in my old car. I skimmed over the details as best I could but there was no escaping the fact that I had to drive past the tree into which I had crashed.

'Oh, my dear that looks like you had a very close shave,' Violet said with a little shudder.

Not wishing to dwell on this, I pointed out some of the other places of interest as we were passing. There was an outdoor centre that offered clay pigeon shooting and quad biking, not really their cup of tea, but across the road from this there was also a craft centre which I thought might be of interest.

Violet could not contain her enthusiasm when we arrived at Wolf Lodge. Marigold was quiet as she got out of the car, but not in a moody kind of way. She seemed to be absorbing her own feelings about the surroundings, so I let her follow Violet and myself into the entrance foyer without rushing her.

Catriona had wanted to come and greet these particular guests and had asked Mary to put on an afternoon tea for us. Having shown them where their rooms were, we then spent a very pleasant hour in the snug, chatting together and enjoying the splendid food.

It was a revelation to see Marigold conversing with Catriona and Violet as though they had been friends for life. Violet talked about her excitement of moving to a new place and Catriona was interested to learn that Marigold had begun a floristry course. I had never heard my mother talk about a subject with so much passion. Just as my life had gone down a new and very different route this year, so, it would appear, had Marigold's.

I wondered how much of this was down to her confiding in me about her past. Having found the courage to tell me about what had happened to her, was she now able to show a softer, more approachable side? If this was the case, then I was looking forward to spending time with her, as much as I was Violet. As I knew I wanted to take time off at Easter when Abigail was coming to stay with me, I had insisted to Catriona that I kept to my usual hours as much as possible during their visit, and both Violet and Marigold fully understood this.

Violet said the following morning after breakfast, 'I am going to indulge myself in reading a good book by one of these cosy fires. I shall take a few walks around these splendid gardens. If you do have spare time to run me into Kinlaggan or to that craft centre, that will be very welcome. But please don't go out of your way to entertain me. I do understand that you are working.'

Marigold was also keen to explore the gardens and grounds prompted by her new interest in floristry, so on a few occasions I would look out of the windows and see the pair of them leisurely exploring. With regard to driving them around, Catriona was more than happy to act as chauffeur.

'It will be my absolute pleasure,' she insisted one afternoon. 'If you like, I can take you on a tour around one of the local whisky distilleries.'

This suggestion was met with great enthusiasm and the following day they did this, arriving back rather late in the afternoon more than a little tipsy. The next day, Violet chose to join Catriona on a walk alongside the river and through the forest.

'After all,' she said as she wrapped a mustard colour scarf around her neck, 'I am not going to get this opportunity in Manchester, am I?'

'You must come and stay with us again, if you are enjoying yourself so much,' said Catriona. The two of them set off armed with walking sticks, warm waterproof coats and, knowing Catriona, a generously filled hip flask. Which left me with Marigold to entertain.

'Don't worry about me,' she said once Violet and Catriona had gone. 'I have some sketching I want to do.'

'Sketching?' I was checking a booking at the reception desk and paused in my surprise.

She looked a little defensive, wrapping her arms close around her body. Today she was wearing a peacock blue outfit, wide legged trousers and a flowing tunic top and silk scarf. I have to say although I had never had my mother down for an artist of any kind, she certainly looked the part.

'My floristry tutor suggested I have a go at it. She says that it can help you understand how to form displays if you have a better grasp of the structure of the flowers and drawing them can help.'

I could see the sense of this even though I had never tried either activity. 'Go ahead.' There was a stunning winter display of evergreen leaves, holly and heather with a few brave little snowdrops on a table in the entrance hall just by the bottom of the stairs. A trifle mischievously, given that she would be on full view of anyone passing through, I suggested she have a go at sketching that.

Marigold was not deterred at all at the notion she might be any kind of spectacle. 'May I use one of the dining room chairs?'

'I'll get you one and you go and get your sketch book.'

A short while later, she was comfortably settled, and I was free to carry on with my morning's work. In between checking the emails and making replies, I kept glancing over to where my mother was sitting, back very erect and looking thoroughly absorbed in her task. There was a stillness about her that I had never seen before. On impulse, I reached for my phone and surreptitiously took a photograph of her in profile. She had an elegant way of holding her head I had never noticed and her jawline for a woman her age was still clearly defined. Her hair was piled loosely on the top of her head, held in place with an ornate pin.

'You had better not be thinking of posting that on social media,' she said without moving a muscle. 'I can't have my friends back home thinking I have totally lost the plot. Margie from the poker group already thinks I have gone soft.'

I put the phone away. 'I don't think you've gone soft,' I said quietly. 'I think you are just giving yourself chance to do things you never thought you could, because of what you were keeping inside.'

She paused, putting her pencil down. 'Is that Sean turning you into the philosopher then? He's quite a character that one. He certainly turned you around, didn't he?'

We looked at each other across the hallway with its highland themes of hunting watercolours, tartan stair carpet, a pair of claymores crossed over the doorway, and suddenly I had the urge to giggle.

'What's so funny?'

I was quick to cast aside the idea that I might be laughing at her. 'Well really, if anyone had said to us a year ago that I would be getting divorced from Gary and would move to Scotland to run a hotel, or that you would be sitting here sketching a floral display, would you have believed it?'

She smiled at that, a knowing but not unkind smile. 'As a matter of fact, yes I would.'

'Don't tell me you saw all of this in your cards?'

Along with poker, one of her other favourite activities was to hold tarot card readings for her friends. To be fair, whatever she said always proved to be accurate. Rose also dabbled from time to time, but it was Marigold who really had the gift. It had passed me by completely.

'Would you believe me if I said I had?' There was a challenging look in her eye and a hint of the old barriers between us.

Anxious not to lose the ground we had been making up, I answered carefully. 'Yes. I would.'

She gave a satisfied smile and turned back to her sketching.

I thought of my tattoo, Luna, this setting and how I came to be here. 'What did you see then?'

The curve of her smile grew but just then a couple of the guests came down from their room, dressed to go out walking. They stopped to see what Marigold was doing before coming to enquire was it too late to arrange a guided walk on the neighbouring estate. By the time I had sent them happily on their way, guided walk duly booked, and lunch arranged for them as well, I was on edge to see another figure coming downstairs.

Robbie had been keeping himself to himself, these last couple of days. It was only the reassurance from Alex that he was eating the food sent up to the room, that prevented me from phoning Callum to drag him off to the doctors again. I was sure that coming off the pills in the way he had done was a bad idea. But Lily had told me happily that he was busy painting again. Then she had asked if her dad and I were going to go on a proper date?

When Marigold and Violet had met Lily, they had both given me a very probing look. I hadn't dared tell either of them what I had found out about her birthdate. Besides, they had their curiosity piqued in another direction when she had casually announced that her dad and me had a 'thing' going on. After shooing Lily away, I had been quick to throw a bucket of cold water on this idea. Judging from the exchange of looks between my neighbour and my mother, I was not sure it was successful. I was just praying that Robbie would stay locked in his tower room, being the mad, creative artist for the duration of their stay.

So far so good.

But now the mad artist was coming down the stairs two at a time in a burst of energy.

'It's finished! I told you those fucking pills were no good Daisy. It's one of my best, ah I can't tell you how good it is to paint something other than a fucking portrait of some dozy fucking socialite.'

He looked wilder than ever, hair all over the place, paint splattered clothes looking as though he had slept in them and more of a beard than I had seen him with so far. I don't think he had gone near a shower for a good couple of days judging by his appearance. Marigold, not surprisingly had put down her pencil once more to stare.

She gave me a very knowing look. 'Well Daisy, you have gone from one extremely interesting man to another it would seem.'

I glared at her, which of course went completely unnoticed. She was giving her full attention to Robbie who had stopped in his tracks at the foot of the stairs, taking in what she was doing.

'Hello,' she said in her usual flirtatious manner, 'I am Marigold.'

Robbie though was more interested in what was on the paper in front of her. 'Not bad,' he said. 'Not bad at all. But your pencils are crap. You can't do a decent sketch with shite like this.' He took the pencil from her and literally flung it across the hallway. 'I have some you can use.'

Then in a whirlwind of movement he spun away from her to come towards the reception desk. I slunk back behind its protective depths as far as I could. Robbie in this mood, whatever mood he was in, was not to be stopped by a desk, however substantial. Not even Luna could stop him, but then I already knew she adored him in the most maddening of ways. So, my wolf did not snarl, growl, or try to bite him when he swept me up into his arms, whirled me around once or twice, then kissed me on the lips.

It was a quick, hard kiss. Then he seemed to think about this and, ignoring the fact that Marigold was just a few feet away, he clasped my face in his hands and kissed me long, and very thoroughly. It was all I could do to make sure my arms dangled uselessly by my sides. I refused to let them wrap around his neck or show that I was in anyway at all losing myself in his passionate embrace.

'You need a shower!' I managed to snap out when he released me.

'Aye, you're not wrong Daisy. Perhaps you can join me later and give me a good scrubbing? First though you have to come with me. Oh yes, you too whoever you are, you come as well and get some decent pencils. Who are you by the way?'

Not many people had the ability to render Marigold speechless, but Robbie had just done that. Speechless though did not mean devoid of smirking. Trailing after Robbie who was refusing to let go of my hand, I mouthed at her behind his back.

'He's completely mad,' I said silently. 'No really, he is.'

Mad as a hatter.

Barking at the moon.

Suicidal at times.

Homicidal?

That fearful doubt.

Exquisitely talented?

Without a shadow of a doubt.

In the chaos of his top floor studio, Marigold and I stood in complete silence. I of course, had seen the outline of the painting a while ago. The finished article was something else. You could almost feel the biting cold of the icy mountains, smell the hint of pine in the air, reach out and stroke the living fur of the wolf who stared back at you with luminous, magical eyes.

It was alive.

As alive as the tattoo on my back.

Once more the synchronicity of it dazed me.

'Do you think Lily will like it?'

'Like it? Who wouldn't?' Marigold's appreciation was clear in her voice. 'It's spectacular.'

'I'm going to give it to her on her birthday, after the party on Midsummer's Eve. She'll be sixteen. Do you think it's a suitable present for a sixteen-year-old girl? Or should I get her some jewellery perhaps?'

Behind the crazy excitement, there lurked a well of uncertainty, dangerously deep.

'Of course she'll love it,' I said quickly.

Marigold said just as quickly. 'Lily's birthday is at Midsummer?'

'Aye. June 21st.'

'And she is sixteen?'

Robbie gave another nod, followed with, 'Best bloody thing I ever did in my life, even though technically it was a bit of a bastard thing to do cos

I seduced another man's fiancé for a bet, but apart from that, aye, Lily is the best part of me.'

I think, in different circumstances, Robbie's casual approach to fathering his daughter would have amused Marigold. As it was, she had not failed to make the connection that I had. I could see this from the look she gave me.

She waited until Robbie had given her some different pencils then said, 'Thank you so much, and thank you for showing us the painting. It truly is stunning. But if you will excuse us, I have just remembered something I need to discuss with Daisy.'

'Aye no bother. Let me know if there is anything else you wish to borrow whilst you are here.'

'Thank you. You are very kind.'

He cocked his head, hands in pockets and with a twisted smile on his face gave a little grunt. 'I am not so sure your daughter agrees with you.'

Flirtatiously my mother then responded with a touch of her old self, 'Yes, well Daisy has never known what's best for her when it comes to men.'

'I thought you liked Gary,' I said rather huffily to her as we trekked back down the winding staircase of the tower.

'I did. But anyone could see he was going to be unfaithful. Rose could see that from day one. It was just you who was so blind.'

Remembering what my sister had told me my huffiness grew. 'Nice to know who you can trust.'

Marigold stopped so suddenly on the narrow stairs I bumped right into her. 'Damn. Sorry. I promised myself I would stop this nasty behaviour. I gave Rose a real telling off before I came here. I told her she should never have told you about her and Gary.'

'Really?'

'Really.' We were now back down on the first-floor landing and could walk side by side. She continued. 'I want us to have a fresh start, Daisy. I have felt that way ever since I told you about…'

'Lily. Your Lily.'

'Exactly. Telling you was like opening Pandora's box for me. I took the lid off my emotions, and I can't seem to put the bloody thing back down again. Oh damn,' she paused on a sniff and wiped her eye. 'Sean said this would happen.'

'Sean?'

'Oh yes,' she said blithely. 'He told me to ring him if ever I wanted to talk, I mean really talk. I always thought the notion of therapy was utter rubbish, a load of old codswallop. But there is something about Sean isn't there?'

Something about Sean?

Indeed there was and suddenly I was longing to see him, to have him here and to listen to what he would say in response to the myriad of thoughts and emotions that being around Robbie and Lily stirred in me. If he had managed to help Marigold decades after her trauma, surely he could unravel this tangle in my head.

'He is one of a kind,' I said ruefully.

'So it would seem is your Robbie?'

We were now back in the entrance foyer. I looked around to see if anyone could overhear.

'He isn't my Robbie,' I insisted with a stupid flush on my cheeks making my mother's eyebrows lift in response.

'Hmm.' She settled herself back in front of her sketching, hand poised with one of his pencils.

'He's not!' I insisted. 'He's completely not the sort of man I would ever be interested in, especially after Sean, who is so kind, and warm and caring. Robbie is rude, bad tempered and foul mouthed. He drinks far too much, does drugs from time to time, and to cap it all he is a mad as a box of frogs and convinced he is under the influence of some ancient gypsy curse not to mention...'

Her head spun round at this. 'What on Earth do you mean?'

'I really can't talk about it. Especially not here.'

'Hmm,' she said again thoughtfully. 'At three o'clock then. When you finish. You and I need to have a real talk.' With that she turned her attention back to her sketch and left me wondering what she had to say to me.

Catriona and Violet returned from their walk and the suggestion was made that we meet up for a coffee and some cake in the parlour. Wary of getting into any deep discussions with my mother I nodded eagerly but Marigold quietly and firmly stepped in.

'That would be lovely, perhaps later. Right now, I need to return these pencils back to your charming son, and then Daisy and I need to have a little chat about a family matter.'

'Of course,' said Catriona with a beaming smile, probably pleased that someone would describe her son in such a way. She admired the sketches that Marigold had done. 'You must come back some time. I am sure Robbie would be delighted to give you some tutoring.'

I really doubted this, but who was I to comment on what a mad artist may or may not be delighted about? I wasn't too sure what my feelings were at the thought of Marigold and Robbie spending any time close together.

Was that the green-eyed monster of jealousy sneaking in?

Did I think Marigold would be interested in Robbie in that way?

Did I think he would be interested in her, despite the age gap?

Knowing what I did of them, there was a possible affirmative answer to both of these.

Did I care?

I really hated that yes was also the answer to this.

It meant that by the time I had got to my room and changed out of my work clothes into my more comfortable attire of jeans and a cosy sweater with thick socks on my feet, I was in a defensive state of mind, not really in the mood for a long chat with my mother. However, when she arrived with a bottle of whisky and two glasses, I decided to reconsider. I perched on the stool by the dressing table and let my mother take the chair by the window. She set the bottle on the table between us and poured two generous measures.

'I will be working again later,' I reminded her.

'I know. But I think this calls for a stiff drink. It can't be coincidence, can it? Lily, I mean.'

We stared at each other. Her dark brown eyes, with a hint of Romany knowledge in them, met mine, perhaps reading thoughts which I could not hide. I was used to building barriers around my emotions. I had readily erected a wall of protection against the notion that the young girl here was in anyway connected to the Lily that I had brought into the world and so quickly lost. Whatever insane reaction I felt towards Robbie, I was hiding from it, behind a shield of pretence. I was not used to being subject to such scrutiny from Marigold and it was rather unnerving.

'Tell me about the curse then?'

I was even more unnerved by this.

I blinked at her, and she gave a tut of impatience. 'Robbie. He is under some kind of malevolent influence. I felt it quite clearly when I touched his hands earlier.'

'Have you been talking to Lily?'

'Why would I?'

Okay then. Marigold had picked this up for herself. I had no reason to think she was spinning me along, so I told her all that I knew, which was not a great deal to be fair.

She waved her hand at me impatiently. 'Yes, but what about the break clause. You cannot cast a curse without including a break clause, it is not allowed, the curse won't work otherwise.'

Of course it wouldn't; silly me for not realising this. I tried to remember what Lily had said and then Luna got up, stretched out sinuously and howled, long and mournfully.

'Oh hell, of course.'

'What?'

I really did not want to tell my mother this. She would read far too much into it and I already had Lily doing her best to match make with her lunatic father.

Reluctantly I told her. 'It would seem that the curse would only be lifted when a white wolf brought love back to Wolf Lodge.'

'Ha! Excellent!' Marigold clapped her hands and smiled broadly, looking from Luna to me with a glint of what could only be described as delight in her dark flashing eyes. 'That's why you are here. It all makes sense. Curses tend to have a shelf life of three generations anyway. If they are not broken within that time they can last forever. You and Luna are going to set the poor man free from his madness and save him.'

I shook my head at her. 'No. No that is not how it is going to be. Not at all.' But even as I protested and Marigold shared a look with Luna, I thought of all the odd coincidences that had brought me here from having that tattoo.

'Oh bloody hell,' I said with a sigh, realising that there was far more to this than I had thought. 'Pour me another drink would you. I'd better tell you the rest.' I told her the details as I knew them about the three murdered women who all had all been romantically linked with Robbie. 'Is he a killer?'

I was alarmed when she poured herself another glass of whisky and would not at first answer.

'Well?'

Her words sent a cold arrow of fear into my heart. 'There is death within him Daisy.'

'Could that be his suicidal thoughts?'

'It may be.'

'Or,' I said slowly thinking of the black outs he experienced, 'It may be that he has killed them and doesn't even remember?'

I hated myself for saying this.

I hated even more the way that Marigold replied. 'A curse can turn a person into someone they are not.'

Chapter Thirty-One

It was time for Violet and Marigold to return home. Violet was excited about starting her new life in Manchester. She promised me she would come back and visit again and said that she hoped it would not be too long before Sean would also be free to join me once more.

'He said he might bob up at Easter,' I told her as I drove them back to the station. 'Although I did warn him, we may be fully booked, but you know Sean, he has a way with him.'

In the rear view mirror, I saw Violet and Marigold exchanging a glance.

'Is it still on between you two then?' my mother asked with a frown on her face. 'Only I thought that you and Robbie...?' After our chat she was sure we would be an item.

I fixed my eyes on the road, glad to have the excuse not to look at either of them. 'There is nothing going on between Robbie and I, nor do I wish there to be. As for Sean, I love him dearly, but we both agreed that there is nothing permanent for us.'

'That is a pity,' said Violet. 'I did hope that when he finished helping Timothy, that you and he would rekindle your relationship. You are far too young my dear to be single for the rest of your life. And you will soon be divorced will you not?'

Marigold agreed with my neighbour. 'Absolutely Daisy. I am sure you won't be single for long.'

I knew without looking at her she was thinking of Robbie.

Just to be a little mischievous, I said in a falsely casual tone, 'Well of course there is Colin.'

For the rest of the trip to Kinlaggan, I sowed the seeds that there could be a potential romance between myself and the quiet book shop owner from Glasgow.

'I am so glad you have another gentleman to court you my dear. I did feel terribly guilty that you may have lost Sean because of him wanting to help my nephew. Do keep in touch and let me know how things develop. Especially if I may need to buy a hat.' Violet smiled at me warmly.

I hugged her tightly and promised I would. Then I turned to Marigold. Things were shifting between us like the sands moving when the tide washes in and goes back out again, leaving behind a slightly different landscape to before.

'Good luck with the rest of your floristry course,' I said brightly to her, thinking this a safe and neutral topic. 'And keep drawing. You have got a real talent for that.'

She almost knocked me off balance, emotionally and physically, by sweeping her arms around me. I was enveloped into a hug of soft cashmere wool and Dior Poison. I found myself responding. As the train drew away from the platform leaving me alone once more, I let out a sigh, not realising that I had perhaps been feeling a trifle tense.

Yesterday's chat with Marigold had unsettled me. Regardless of her agreeing with the idea of a curse attached to him, this still left a man who was at best, rude, badly behaved and obnoxious, and at the worst, barking mad and potentially a suicidal killer. What woman in their right mind would wish to embark on any sort of relationship with someone like that?

Even if they had had mind blowing sex with them.

Twice.

Even if they did have a daughter with the same name, who was born on the same day your own daughter died.

Exactly.

This was the way to insanity.

Having survived the trauma of losing Gerald and Irene and then my marriage exploding in my face, I was hardly going to open another pandora's box of pandemonium. I had been lucky enough to have a brief and very lovely fling with Sean. I was now ready to create my own life here in Kinlaggan, and possibly encourage a romance with a kind, friendly, sensible gentleman who enjoyed bird watching.

'Are you sure about this, Daisy?'

I could hear the laughter in Sean's voice as I talked to him later. It was just after three and I was having a break. There was just enough daylight left to walk Luna out of the Lodge grounds and along the riverside. A pleasant time then to walk and talk with someone I now considered a very dear friend. It was Sean himself who brought up the topic with that canny ability of his. My mother would say he had a psychic talent to pick up on exactly what I had been thinking about.

'So how is life going with all those brawny highland men Daisy, darling? Have any of them managed to replace me in your affections?'

Even down the phone his voice was melodic and lilting. 'No-one could replace you in my affections, you know that. You have a special place in my heart. And always will.'

He knew, of course he did. Even so he got me to talking about Colin and the afternoon we had enjoyed together. From there I ended up telling Sean what I knew of him.

'I think it would be nice to get to know him better.' I concluded which was when Sean asked me if I was sure about this.

'Yes. I am sure,' I said positively, trying to tune out the laughter I was hearing from him.

'Only I can't help wondering you know, with what happened at new year whether someone else might have had more of an effect on you?'

Now he was teasing me.

I replied ever so haughtily. 'How very ungentlemanly of you to comment.'

'I know, I know. Rotten of me,' he replied in a way that told me he wasn't sorry at all. Then I could hear another voice in the background calling to him. 'Look Daisy I have to go now, I am on site at the moment, you carry on and get to know this Colin chap if that's the right thing for you.'

I was convinced it was.

Over the next few days, it was easy to start feeling bright and full of energy. The intensely cold spell that seemed to have gone on forever, suddenly gave up its grip. The air was softer on the face, the wind less wild in the hair, the afternoon sunlight stretching out that bit further. With the approach of spring, I began to wake up before the alarm clock, not needing to push to get out of bed those first dark and clumsy minutes.

My previous life seemed so far removed I could not believe at times the contrast. Grief still shadowed me from losing Irene and Gerald so close together. These feelings were usually accompanied by pangs of regret for the loss of my marriage. On days like these I would take myself off with Luna in my free time, exploring the forests and mountains, and finding comfort in the solitude and the scale of the wilderness.

I had developed a good friendship with Moira, frequently having coffee and cake with her, although I steered clear of invites to attend her 'witchy' meetings. I had enough of the weird in my life with Sean and Luna and I was never quite sure if she wanted me to attend so she could do as Lily had suggested and cast a love spell upon me.

Lily herself continued to be both a delight and a source of pain. The more I got to know the young girl, the more I found myself desperately wishing that she could have been my daughter. She made it embarrassingly obvious that she wanted me to get together with her dad, especially after she had caught us kissing. I could see that my gentle rebuffs at these attempts were confusing her.

Equally, this was not something I wished to discuss with either Moira or Catriona. Moira because she too thought it would be a grand idea if Robbie and I got together, although I think this primarily was to do with how much it would annoy Shona. Moira, I had learnt was something of a benign mischief maker and liked nothing better than to meddle. Catriona, as his mother, was far too closely involved and for the moment, she seemed to be happy with how he was behaving anyway.

Which to be fair, on the surface appeared to be okay. Nobody saw much of him, but that was because he was cloistered away in his tower on a painting binge. There was, however, a bit of a commotion one day when a white faced guest hurried into the entrance foyer in rather a state. Fortunately, it was on a morning when Lily was at school and Catriona had asked for Moira, Shona and me to have a quick meeting as the Easter holidays were starting at the weekend.

We did not get very far.

We had left the door to the snug open so the bell on reception could be easily heard. The ringing was accompanied by a voice calling.

'Catriona, Daisy, are you there? You need to come before someone gets hurt!'

The four of us looked at each other and shot up. In unison we hurried to the entrance foyer. Alec McGregor, a retired army gentleman who stayed regularly to enjoy the fishing and walking, not to mention the whisky, was standing by the desk.

'Damnedest thing,' he said with a shaky laugh, 'I survived more tours of duty that I can count, and I nearly came a cropper with a painting!'

'What on earth do you mean?' Catriona was the first to speak.

'I nearly had my brains dashed out by your Robbie. He's chucking his paintings out of the tower window. It's a hell of a drop and they are landing with a hefty crash, there's glass everywhere.'

It was far quicker to run out of the Lodge and round to the back of the building than to get upstairs to the top floor. Alec McGregor had not been exaggerating. There must have been about half a dozen broken and smashed paintings, all in heavy glass frames, shards of which were now lying on the ground.

'What is he doing?' Catriona wailed in distress and who could blame her?

Moira shouted up to him, 'Robbie, you daft bastard what are you doing?'

I winced, hoping that most of the Lodge guests would be out for the day.

There was movement at the window as the Georgian sash opened to its full extent. Half of a frame appeared and behind it, the figure of Robbie.

'You're in my way,' he called down, oblivious to the wreckage he had caused and the potential danger.

'Robert James Angus Munro stop this at once!' Catriona spoke as only a mother could.

I exchanged a glance and a smile with Moira who was right beside me.

In a quiet undertone she said, 'I wonder if she will tan his arse?' Then a sly look at me, 'Or maybe get you to do that. He would probably enjoy that from you.'

I poked her to silence the laughter that threatened in her eyes. This was not funny, although Robbie's childhood friend seemed to think it was.

'You're in the fucking way!'

Catriona sucked in her breath. Alec McGregor had come out with us, and I think she was more annoyed at being spoken to like that in front of him than by anything else.

The retired captain stepped forward. 'Are you alright there Robbie? Do you need a hand mate?'

He shouted up in a loud voice but with a casual manner as though this was a run of the mill occurrence. Robbie poked more of his body through the window so he could lean out, rather precariously it had to be said, which made Catriona gasp and clutch at my arm.

'I just need you all to fucking move, I have to get rid of these.'

'Aye well, I can see that, Robbie.' Alex said, 'How about I come up and help you carry them down? That way at least they don't get broken, or anyone gets hurt.'

'No just all of you fuck off and let me carry on!' He leant further forward. I thought he was going to topple out of the window and gasped.

'Jesus!' Shona exclaimed. 'He's off his rocker this time, he really is.'

As much as I disliked her, she had a point.

Alec remained calm. 'Right then Robbie, how many more are there?'

'What? Just two. This one and another. They're not my paintings. I've no idea who painted them but I fucking didn't!'

I shot a look at Catriona and the shock on her face told me what I needed to know. Moira looked equally alarmed. They were his paintings.

Alec of course would not know this.' He turned to face us and suddenly there was the army captain talking to us. 'Everyone just move right back. Daisy, you go over there and stop anyone coming round the corner from that direction, Moira, you go the other way and do the same. Catriona and Shona, over there, on the path. Now.'

It was an order and as such we silently obeyed.

Alec raised his head to Robbie and gave him the thumbs up. 'Right Robbie, it's all clear, you are good to go.'

'Finally,' Robbie shouted back. 'Someone with some fucking sense!'

From where Alec had positioned me, I could not see but I could hear the great crash that followed. And then shortly after another one.

'All done, Robbie?' Alec shouted cheerfully.

'Aye, all done. Cheers mate. I owe you a drink.'

In a quieter voice, Alec called us all back. 'That's got that sorted, now we need to cordon this area off, so no one hurts themselves before it is cleared up.'

Catriona was visibly shaken up. I asked Moira if she would take her inside and look after her. Then I told Shona that she would need to cover for me whilst I cleared up the mess.

'I am so grateful for your help,' I said to Alec later as I opened a bottle of Kinlaggan Malt in the bar, poured him a glass and handed him the rest of the bottle. 'Here, that's for you. And we will be making a reduction on your bill for today.'

Moira's husband then turned up. I had not seen anything of Callum recently, other than in passing on the road to wave to, or perhaps say a quick hello in the shops. After this latest outburst I had texted the vet to tell him that Robbie had stopped taking the pills.

'Are you okay, Daisy?'

I reassured him I was.

'Well, it makes a change from wanting to crash a car.'

He realised that he had made a mistake as Alec looked sharply at him.

'Not that he makes a habit of this,' Callum had said. He gave me a quick look and then disappeared saying he was going to just have a wee chat with his friend.

Then I insisted that Alec had that drink.

'Are you not joining me?' He asked.

I had thought him at first to be rather stiff and reserved and put this down to his military background. Having been so glad of what I now saw to be quiet, efficient calm, I returned his smile.

'Why not. Just a small one though.'

In the space of one week, and again, over a glass of whisky, I had a second person telling me something I really did not want to think about Robbie Munro. The first had been my mother, agreeing with the myth that he was cursed. Now it seemed that Alec had something to add.

'Is he getting any help?'

The fire was crackling in the background, there was no one else in the bar, and it was cosy, quiet and intimate. I quashed my immediate instinct to deny that help was required, especially when pinned down by a pair of sharp grey eyes that had probably seen more than I could ever dream of.

I sighed. 'He was on anti-depressants that the doctor gave him, but he flushed them down the loo. He said they were stopping him painting.'

Alec swirled his whisky round his glass and considered this. 'It's not a doctor he needs to see.'

I half laughed then. 'Don't tell me you have heard the story of the family curse and you believe it?'

'Ach no! Although yes, I have heard of it. I have been coming up here long enough, but not long enough to know his father. I was still in the army then. What I meant was, a doctor is no use for someone like Robbie.'

'What do you mean someone like Robbie?' I cast a quick look over my shoulder to check that no one else had come in to the bar, but we were still alone.

'I'm no doctor myself, obviously, but I have seen a lot of things. And I have known someone else very like Robbie. I have wondered from time to time if he was the same. From what I saw today, I would hazard a guess that I may be right.'

Curiosity had me gripped now. I leant forward, eager to hear more. 'What?'

'Coming out of the army you get to see a lot of folk with PTSD. That kind of disturbed mental state. It's more than just depression, or artistic temperament. Aye, my cousin Stu was like him.' Another long drink and a shiver went down my spine.

'Stu?'

'Aye. A grand lad. Life and soul of the party at times, so much energy being around him was like being around a volcano, you had to be careful you didn't get caught in the lava flow and get burnt. Then there were the dark clouds of ash that could fall, suffocating and deadly.'

For an army man he was being rather poetic but the picture he painted was nevertheless alarming as it did ring bells with how Robbie behaved.

'What happened to Stu?'

'He killed himself.'

Not what I wanted to hear. Clearly not another case of someone being cursed but I had to press on.

'What happened?'

Alec finished his drink and reached for the bottle to pour himself another glass. I declined with a shake of my head.

'Poor bastard never got a proper diagnosis. It was only after he had hung himself that everyone started to put two and two together. Too fucking late then. It didn't matter what label they could have put on it, PTSD, bipolar, any other bloody mental illness – it doesn't really matter. Point being, he was ill. Really bloody ill and we never saw it.'

'You think Robbie is suffering from something more serious than depression?'

He looked at me calmly. 'Don't you?'

He was suffering from something that was no longer to be denied.

Mental illness or a curse? I think I may have muttered this out loud.

He gave a quiet sigh. 'Some would say they are one and the same.'

Then to make matters worse he quietly added. 'And sometimes they don't even know when they are being violent.' Clear grey eyes held mine. 'I am no policeman, Daisy, but what I have seen today would have me agreeing with the detectives from Inverness. He's the right profile for that killer. Och not when he's sane. But the other times?' He swirled his whisky around thoughtfully. 'You get him that help Daisy, before it's too late.'

them to make funny noises," he quietly added. "And sometimes they don't even know when they are being wicked. Last time we had mine." "I am no policeman, Daisy, but what I have seen today would have me agreeing with the detectives from Inverness. He's the right profile for that killer. Och nor when he's sane, but the other times." He swirled his whisky around thoughtfully. "You get him that help, Daisy, before it's too late."

Chapter Thirty-Two

Abigail was coming to stay. I had not seen my little sister since Christmas, and I was looking forward to her visit. Catriona had insisted that I take some time off even though we would be busy. She was happy to do extra, and Shona was saving up for her new car, so she was keen to have more hours. I had a variety of activities planned, from simple walks in the forest with Luna, to taking her to visit the reindeer. There was also a small ice rink in Kinlaggan and this was something I wanted to try.

Colin had booked a room for a week and told me that he was looking forward to meeting my sister. I was warmed to hear him say how he hoped we would be able to go out together. Knowing how he had lost a child himself, I found myself drawn to him even more.

Lily was going over to visit her mother in America and whilst I was sorry that she would not get to meet Abigail, part of me was relieved that she would be absent. She was far too eagle eyed and I wanted to be free to spend a little more time with Colin, without her speculating on a possible relationship with her father and making me feel guilty about this.

I googled PTSD as well as bipolar disorder and a range of other mental illnesses. It was all rather confusing and none of it was encouraging. The way to a diagnosis was not at all straightforward. Worryingly there were plenty of boxes that I could tick with what little I knew of Robbie. Equally, as I had only been on the scene a few months, I didn't feel able to take it much further.

I did try to talk to Catriona after the incident with the paintings. Her attitude surprised me. As pragmatic as she was, it seemed that when it came to her son, she had something of a blind spot. Whilst she was keen to discourage her granddaughter's notion of a curse, she seemed as reluctant to take on board that her son might be mentally ill.

When I broached the sensitive subject of her husband's death and the possibility that a predisposition towards mental illness ran in families, she stuck to the line that Angus's death had been a pure accident and that her son was only being so dramatic as he was such a talented artist.

I talked to Callum about it. He put forward the theory that Robbie might blame himself for his father's death although he would not go any further with this. But at least there was someone who did consider a practical explanation for Robbie's extremes of behaviour, rather than a curse. Neither of us mentioned the other dreadful possibility.

And as Callum put it, you could drag a horse to water but no amount of forcing it could make it drink. Remembering how he had had to knock his friend out in the first place to get him to the doctor, and how he had reacted to the pills, neither of us could see Robbie meekly surrendering to the idea of visiting a psychiatrist. Especially not when he was currently painting so well.

There was a bit of a stalemate and frankly, I didn't think it should be down to me to sort out. I allotted this to the place in my mind, neatly labelled 'to be dealt with later' and prepared to spend some quality time with my sister. Abigail coming to visit also meant that I got to see Dad. As I got out of my car at the station and went to meet them, I thought how reluctant I would be now to go back to my previous way of life. Standing on the platform it was impossible to think of that day back in December, only a few months ago when life had been so utterly bleak and unforgiving.

There were quite a few passengers disembarking, after all this was a popular stop on the mainline, but Abigail was so easy to spot. A whirlwind of movement, brightly dressed in a blue coat, long red hair in plaits framing her pretty freckled face. I braced myself for the impact of her hug.

'Wow you've grown!'

'Why do grown-ups always say that?'

'Mostly because it's true,' I said with a breathless laugh as she squeezed the air out of me.

Behind her was Dad, tall and distinguished as ever. He looked exactly what he was, a successful professional man. He still walked with that spring in his step and every time I saw him with Abigail it was obvious to see how she would keep anyone young at heart. He echoed what Violet and Marigold had said when they had arrived.

'You look well, Daisy, really well.'

His comments about how well I was looking made me realise how dreadful my appearance must have been. I knew from my reflection in the mirror that I had put on weight. My jawline had lost that chiselled look, my eyes were no longer shadowed, and my cheeks were rosy even without blusher. Still, it was nice to hear it coming from Dad.

We had never really been that close, and I had hugged my father-in-law more readily than him, but here, on what I considered to be my new territory, it was suddenly easy to envelop him in my arms.

Dad could only stay one night at Wolf Lodge, as he had to travel back the following day in order to then fly out on his safari. But the three of us ate dinner together and I could see as his eyes took in his surroundings that he was impressed. He promised he would return for a proper stay with us some time, although he was not too sure that Samantha would really enjoy it.

'She does like to be active you see,' he explained somewhat apologetically over a whisky in the bar when Abigail had gone to bed.

'You can be as active as you like here,' I replied and listed the assortment of outdoor pursuits that were on offer, not to mention simply walking through the forests and hiking up the mountains.

'She likes things to be a bit more exotic,' he confessed with a rueful smile. 'This safari really was her idea. I went along with it because I didn't want her to think I was turning into an old fuddy duddy.'

The Kinlaggan Malt had mellowed him as he talked. I could see for the first time perhaps the strain that being married to someone so much younger could be having. Not that the age thing was the real barrier. I think more likely that there were personality differences neither of them had realised. But he was quick to praise her in other ways.

'She really is remarkable you know at work. Since she became a partner in the practice we have gone from strength to strength. We are very lucky to have her.'

I mumbled that she was very lucky to have him. I had always thought that Samantha had set her eyes on Dad because he was the senior partner although I had never suggested this at all. And I certainly wasn't going to spoil the mood now.

'You're different here, Daisy,' he said as we finished our drinks, each of us beginning to yawn. 'Less brittle, softer.'

Brittle? I looked at him in surprise.

'I don't mean that badly,' he said hastily. 'It's just that sometimes you could be, I don't know, a bit sharp maybe. It must have taken it out of you looking after Irene as you did for so long, and then of course Gerald. I see it in my patients at times. The carers, they lose themselves so deeply in others, they become a harder shadow of who they really should be. I suppose it's a coping mechanism for dealing with all of the pain.'

It had never crossed my mind that I had become like this. I had prided myself on being such an efficient carer whilst maintaining my part time job at the school. I never stopped to think what it was taking from me. When I discovered Gary's betrayal, I felt I had nothing left at all.

Dad brought this up now. 'You are okay, Daisy aren't you. With the divorce and everything?'

I waved my arms around me, 'Do I look like I am struggling?'

'No. In fact, it suits you to a tee, Daisy. But what about anyone else in your life? I mean I know there was that fellow, Sean but that didn't seem a permanent thing.'

Amazed as I was that I could be having such a conversation with him I shook my head. 'No. There isn't anyone, Dad. Although having said that I have met a nice gentleman from Glasgow who is coming back to stay here for Easter, so you never know.'

'I'm glad, Daisy. You are far too young to be alone. So, tell me about this gentleman?'

I didn't get the chance because just then the door of the bar was flung open and in strode Robbie. His appearance caused the other residents who were enjoying their quiet after dinner drinks to look up. He barged in as though the place was on fire, there was such a sense of urgency about him. He was in his painting clothes, scruffy jeans, tattered old sweater, sleeves pushed up to the elbows, hair, desperately in need of someone taking a pair of shears to it and stubble that was more of a beard.

Which was okay to a point. What was not okay however, was what came out of this mouth.

'Ah there you are, Daisy,' his gaze landed on me like an eagle fixing its sight upon its prey. 'I need you upstairs now. I need you naked.'

Every conversation came to an abrupt full stop. And who could blame them if their eyes all turned to me? It was not the fire in the room or the whisky in my stomach that made my cheeks burn. I didn't dare look at Dad.

'Well? What are you waiting for, woman?' Robbie stared at me impatiently as though he had just asked me to make a cup of tea or something.

'I'm sorry,' I stuttered 'What? I mean?'

'Do you know this man, Daisy?' Dad sounded a little anxious.

'Never mind who I am,' Robbie glared at Dad, 'I need Daisy and I need her now.'

From the corner of the bar, I heard a woman's voice murmur something accompanied by a giggle.

Trying to reclaim some control, I said firmly, 'Dad this is Robbie Munro. He owns Wolf Lodge.'

Which Dad totally mistook. 'Well, that's no reason to expect you to do what he wants like that!'

'What?' This was from Robbie now and then he shook his head. 'No. I don't want to go to bed with her you idiot. Well not right now of course, I'm quite happy to do that afterwards.'

Now there were a few giggles.

I stood up and hissed at him. 'What the hell are you playing at?'

'Playing? I'm not playing, woman, I'm working. I thought that was obvious. Now come with me and take your clothes off.' He reached for my hand which I immediately snatched back.

'Jesus woman, I need you for my painting!'

'You want my daughter to model nude for you?' Dad said to him with a slight tinge of understanding in his voice. 'Of course. You're RJ Munro aren't you. Samantha, my wife Googled you.'

'Good for her. Yes, I am, and I need your daughter, and I need her now, so if you will excuse us, I have work to do.'

It would have been even more undignified to struggle with the grip he had reclaimed on my wrist and I could only cast an apologetic look at Dad over my shoulder. I was steaming once we had got out of the bar.

'What the bloody hell do you think you are doing making an exhibition of me like that in there?'

'An exhibition?' He had virtually dragged me to the foot of the stairs, and he stopped so suddenly I collided with him. 'Daisy you are a genius.' He pulled me towards him and kissed me quickly and hard.

'An exhibition, yes why the fuck not? Hurry up woman, can't you walk any quicker?'

He completely ignored any protestations that I muttered, rushing me up the main staircase, down the left-hand side corridor, past my room as well as Lily's and Catriona's, through the door into the tower, and up the winding narrow staircase to his studio. I wasn't surprised to see Luna sprawling on the floor like a rug. I had become accustomed to the bizarre way she took herself off to keep Robbie company from time to time.

I could also see that there was a new canvas on the easel in the centre of the room. The painting was a long way from being finished but the outlines were there. It was a forest scene, a moonlit one, with the river that I recognised. It was done with the dark, inky colours of the night, highlighted by the moon in the top right-hand corner. The bottom left-hand corner was mostly empty although I could see an outline which looked like Luna sprawling as she was now.

'Take your clothes off and curl up with Luna on the floor.'

'I beg your pardon?'

'Daisy do you have to be so awkward!'

Me awkward? I stared at him and folded my arms obstinately across my chest refusing to be intimidated by the intensity of the stare he was giving me.

'Look, I just want to paint you lying next to Luna, curled up to her as though she is part of you. That's how I see her. And you. She is part of you.'

I wasn't expecting that. My tattoo began to tingle reminding me that all was not what it seemed when it came to Luna. I wondered how he had picked up on it. Artist's intuition? Or maybe that was part of his madness. Either way it was a hook that drew me in. He could see the change in my expression and that wicked grin slashed across his face.

'C'mon Daisy, it's not like I've not seen you naked before.'

True, but on that occasion, I had been suffering the effects of the shock from the car crash, as had he. Now I was aware of what I was doing. Or about to do.

'You said exhibition? Does that mean people will see it?'

He looked at me now as if I really were stupid. 'What do you think? What? You're worried about your reputation. Most women would be throwing themselves at me now to take their clothes off and be painted by me.'

'Modest, aren't you!'

There was a light of laughter then in his eyes and it won me over. Damn it, I thought as I began to peel my sweater over my head. I was pretty sure that I would regret this, but for now I seemed unable to stop myself.

'Good girl,' he said, and began to busy himself with his brushes and paints. Oddly that made me more self-conscious. It was clear that right now he was not regarding me sexually at all. And that threw me. He looked up as I paused in my underwear. 'Well?'

Defiantly I unsnapped my bra and slipped off my pants standing before him completely naked. 'Will that do?'

Just a flash, quick but unmistakeable, a glint in his eyes that told me that he was detached with his work head on but there was more going on underneath. I felt stupidly glad and then immediately cross with myself for my reaction.

Remember Colin, I told myself. Sensible, kind, good mannered Colin.

'Right, now just lie down on the rug next to Luna for me.'

I had forgotten my tattoo. Being on my back I rarely caught sight of it.

'Who did this?' Robbie stopped me just as I was about to lie down, with my back to him. His hands traced the work that Michaela had done. The touch of his fingers made it difficult to speak.

'A friend,' I said.

'It's perfect,' he said with the respect in his voice for the talented work of another artist. 'Did they have Luna in the studio with them or did they work from a photograph'?

Neither.

Michaela had drawn Luna first of all on picture on the wall of the studio, and then on my back, and then she had appeared. No one apart from Sean had seen the tattoo. So, no one could possibly guess at the oddity of it all. But now I felt naked in more than just body. Somehow, I found myself telling Robbie what had happened.

He let out a long slow whistle. 'You have come to break the curse then, Daisy. It is magic. It is real. That's why I am mad. But you've come. You and Luna. You will break the curse. You will save me.'

I couldn't respond to any of this. I was having too much trouble controlling the feelings that standing there naked with him tracing my tattoo were creating. Instead, I followed his directions and settled myself onto the rug next to Luna.

Which was not unpleasant. The room was cosy, she was furry to snuggle up to, and there was something rather peaceful about it. I found my eyes were beginning to close and I snapped them open with an apology.

'No, no that's good. Asleep. Yes. That's even better. Close your eyes, Daisy.'

I did so, feeling in the first instance absurdly vulnerable. Then the slow steady rhythm of Luna's breathing began to synchronise with mine and I drifted off to sleep.

I awoke to find myself being lifted from the floor and carried in strong arms.

'What are you doing? Put me down. I need to get back to my room.'

'I need you here. With me.' He kicked open the door between his studio and his bedroom.

'No,' I began to wriggle in his arms. 'Robbie this isn't right.'

As deluded as he was, I did not want him thinking that if he slept with me, I would break his curse.

He misunderstood. 'Daisy, you mustn't worry what people think. It doesn't matter that I own Wolf Lodge.'

'That's not what I meant,' I protested as he laid me down on the bed. Then I didn't have chance to speak as he lay next to me, brushed back the hair from my face and began kissing me.

Slowly and thoroughly.

Soberly.

That was a difference.

He had been drinking the last two times we had ended up in bed together. It had been rushed, urgent, rough and ready sex that left no time to think.

After the first couple of kisses, I didn't want to think either, but really, I tried.

I tried to think that this was a messed up dangerous man whose mouth was covering mine insistently.

I tried thinking that this was a suspected killer who was sliding his tongue sensuously against mine.

I tried thinking of the three women who had gone missing as his hands held my face in place so he could kiss me deeper and deeper, and not escape his demands.

I tried thinking of all of this even as white-hot flames of lust were shooting down to my centre and I felt myself pooling with hot wet desire.

All from his kisses. He hadn't even touched me anywhere else yet. There was still time to escape.

Maybe.

'This is not a good idea,' I made a valiant effort to speak as our mouths parted briefly for air.

'It is, it is,' he argued and silenced me with more kisses.

Then I was doomed as he began to explore my body with his hands. As he had traced the delicate lines of my tattoo on my back, he traced every curve and contour of my breasts and belly rendering me more compliant. I moaned my protestations against his mouth between kisses. When his hands slipped lower my moans turned into something else.

Clever artists fingers worked with a subtlety I would not have thought he possessed. Rational thought was lost, and my hips began to move of their own volition. He took his mouth from mine to claim first one breast then another, gentle and caressing. I think I could have coped if he had been drunk and rough as he had previously. I think I could have withstood the demands and walked away.

But this.

This slow, thorough, deeply sensuous touch was melting my thoughts, my muscles, my bones, my soul. Before I knew it, I was arching my back off the bed and thrusting my hips up as his fingers brought me to a sudden climax. He caught the cry from my mouth with a deep hard kiss, and his fingers went deep as I spasmed against him.

The last tremors were still rippling through me when he shifted on the bed and began to tease another shocking orgasm from me with his mouth. This second one was even more intense and without him to kiss me into silence I could not stop myself from crying out. He licked and sucked every last drop of passion from me, coaxing more exquisite tremors from my tender flesh. His greed it seemed had no boundaries.

'Oh God I'm dying,' I moaned as once more I felt his tongue plunge inside me and sent me over the edge again.

Right there, right then, it would have been a very happy death. I was too dizzy with satiated desire to even consider my choice of words or thoughts. The way he was making me feel I no longer cared that he might be a madman. A killer. All I cared about was his touch and what it was doing to me. Limp and drunkenly sated, I shut my eyes and tried to catch my breath, eyes closed, not daring to look at him. There was something far too intimate in this lovemaking that I did not want to acknowledge. Pliant and submissive I let him carefully roll me over.

He had undressed himself now and I could feel the heat of his skin against mine. He moved me so that I was on all fours. Then he traced again the tattoo of Luna with first his fingers, and then his mouth. I can't explain how or why this was so sensitive, but it was. As though the magic that was within the tattoo was responding to his touch.

A response that was as wild and primeval as the wolf on my back.

A need to be taken, overpowered, possessed.

An animal claiming its mate.

Deep.

Deeper still.

Filling me completely.

Then pulling nearly right out only to thrust back in with more power and force each time.

I had to brace myself against the bed head to avoid being slammed into it.

Again, and again until both of us were ragged in breath and covered with a film of sweat.

When I came this time, it was with him so deep inside of me I didn't think I could take any more. He echoed my gasps, only louder, harsher, hands gripping my hips to hold me still as he shuddered and shook against me. Then with a long and heartfelt sigh, he fell sideways onto the bed, still inside of me, spooning into me as I had done with Luna on the floor.

'I have to go,' I muttered sleepily.

'No, you don't. You have to save me,' was his equally sleepily reply.

Chapter Thirty-Three

I woke disorientated, with a heavy arm slung across my naked breasts.

Cursing the fact that I didn't even have the excuse of being drunk this time, I berated myself for being the biggest idiot on the planet, whilst trying to slide out from beneath his grasp without him waking up. For all that on occasions he was known to stay up for nights at a time with insomnia, now he was dead to the world and snoring like a freight train.

'You aren't exactly helping matters, are you?' I whispered to Luna who yawned and stretched lazily. 'I don't know why you are so keen on being best buddies with him, but it is not what I want ok? He's crazy mad and nothing but trouble and I do not want to be involved with him.'

I was speaking to my wolf but really it was myself I was lecturing. Yet as I looked at him sprawled carelessly across the bed, his large muscular frame and harsh features softened in sleep, I felt something tugging within me.

Something that was really, really, stupid.

I immediately stamped down on it and reminded myself that Colin was visiting this week and I had Abigail to look after. I had forgotten that my little sister was in the hotel with Dad. I stifled a groan when I thought of what he must have made of my disappearance with Robbie last night.

With a last look at Robbie, and the painting he had worked feverishly on until the early hours, I let myself out of his room and made my way down the spiral staircase of the tower. With a bit of luck, I would get back to my room before anyone else was about. I don't know who jumped the most when I opened the door at the foot of the tower to come face to face with Lily.

Luck it appeared was not on my side.

'Daisy!'

'Lily!'

'What are you... oh! Oh, that is good. I knew you and Dad were going to be right for each other!'

In the tight confines of the doorway, Lily managed to wrap her arms around me and squeeze me into the tightest of hugs, which of course Luna had to include herself in.

'Lily I must explain.'

'Daisy it's ok, honestly. I am soooo happy. And I can get to tell Mum in person that I am going to have a new stepmum. It serves her right cos she was threatening to insist I move to America with her and Dimwit Derek, and like that is soooo not going to happen. I mean, as if I would want to leave here!'

'Lily, really' I was helpless in the face of her unstoppable enthusiasm. But I tried, really I did. 'I was just modelling for your dad, and I fell asleep, that's all.'

I have never been very good at lying and Lily's arch look, green eyes crystal clear and without the haunted look of her father's had me blushing.

To make matters worse, she then patted my arm and said, 'It's okay Daisy, I do know about sex. And I wouldn't even mind if you had a baby. I quite like the idea of being the totally cool older sister.'

Oh hell. I really had tumbled down a rabbit hole this time.

'I've got to get ready for the breakfast shift. What are you doing up so early anyway?'

'I've got to wake Dad up. He's taking me to the airport remember?'

In my confusion I had forgotten that today Lily was going to visit her mother in America.

'You'd best go and wake him then, he's fast asleep.'

'Did you tire him out, Daisy?' She asked with a grin, deepening my blushes and leaving me defenceless in my speech. Adding to this, she went on, 'oh, so if you and Dad get married, then that will make Abigail my what? Half-sister? No, cos she is your half-sister, so that would be step aunt? Oh that is so funny, wait 'til I tell her.'

I gave up at this point and fled to my room.

Fortunately for me, I did have a tiny bit of luck on my side and Abigail was still fast asleep in Dad's room when Lily had to leave with Robbie for the airport. I just hoped that by the time she had got back I had somehow found a way to resolve this muddle. Meanwhile there was breakfast for the guests to attend to. I had quickly snatched a slice of toast in the kitchen, but I managed to find time to have a cup of coffee with Dad once I had made sure that everyone else's orders were taken care of. Not surprisingly he mentioned Robbie, waiting for a moment when Abigail went to the toilet.

'Has he been cleared of the charges against him then? I don't wish to leave either you or Abigail under the same roof as a suspected serial killer.'

Of course, if Samantha had been following Robbie's artistic career, he would have heard the rest.

With Abigail's safety his concern I could not lie to him. Yet that is precisely what I did do.

'He's not a killer, Dad. A bit crazy perhaps but he's not a killer.'

The tattoo of Luna prickled on my back, and I knew it was her influence forcing the words out, just as I was suddenly holding Dad's gaze with a look that ensured he believed me. And all the time I was screaming silently that I didn't know. I really didn't know. Robbie's dark passionate side terrified me as much as it enthralled me. Dad though seemed content with my answer.

'Is he often like that?'

I sipped my coffee, loaded with two large sugars this morning and mumbled a vague reply.

'I suppose it's the artist's temperament,' he said smearing a thick layer of whisky laden marmalade onto his toast. 'Samantha and I went to one of his exhibitions in London,' he told me to my surprise. Then with a hint of devilment in his eyes he added. 'Samantha will be very jealous you know that he has chosen you to be his muse.' He munched on his toast, his grin widening. 'Not to mention your sister. If Rose finds this out, she'll be on the next train up I can promise you that.'

A sudden stab of fierce emotion followed his words. The notion that Robbie might find my sister more attractive than me, that he might prefer to paint her over me. I did not like to put a name to the emotion these thoughts stirred in my heart.

My heart?

I was in need of a shot of Kinlaggan Malt in my coffee never mind sugar. I gave myself a mental slap across the face, and focused on Abigail, asking what she would like to do for the rest of the day. I had agreed with Catriona that I would continue to cover the early morning shift through this week but then she would take over, or Shona would.

'I want to explore the forest and see the waterfall,' she said excitedly. 'Lily told me all about it last night.' She frowned. 'I wish she didn't have to go to America today, I like her.'

'Mmm,' I said, with another sip of coffee. 'It's quite a walk. Would you not rather go and visit the reindeer?'

She shook her head, red hair free for once from the confines of her plaits. 'No. I want to do that when Sean comes.'

'He might not be able to make it, Abigail. He is very busy at the moment.'

She gave me a look far older than her years. 'He promised me he would come and visit the reindeers with me.'

I decided to leave it there. As much as I was longing to see Sean, I was not sure that I could cope with the speculation in his bedazzling blue eyes. We settled on agreeing to trek through the forest to the waterfall once we had taken Dad back to the station, which we had to do straight after breakfast.

'You be good for Daisy,' he said to my little sister, bending down to kiss her goodbye on the platform.

I thought I saw a flash of regret on his face, and I wondered not for the first time if he was being pushed into doing something he really did not want to do.

'I will Daddy.'

'Mummy and I will bring you back something really special from our holiday.'

'I know,' she said with a wistful note that tugged on my heart strings. 'You always do.'

More hugs and then it was time for him to get on the train.

Then, just as he was closing the door, Abigail called out to him. 'Be careful of the elephants Daddy! Be careful of the elephants!'

He laughed and waved but I felt a little shiver running through me.

I put it down to lack of sleep and decided that a flask of hot chocolate was in order when we went trekking off into the forest. A while later, loaded up with a backpack full of goodies from the kitchen we began our walk. Lily had taken Sean and I on the first part of the route that day back in January when we had stopped at the bridge.

It was one of my favourite walks but a fairly long one and I hoped that Abigail's young legs would be up to the challenge, otherwise I would be burning off my picnic with a lot of piggy backs. I had underestimated her enthusiasm. She tramped happily beside me, out of the Lodge grounds, past the chalets, alongside the river, crossing over at the stepping stones, to begin the walk into the forest.

Luna, my clever wolf, was there to guide her as well as myself, leading the way, always stopping to turn and check that we were following her. I had never seen Abigail in this kind of environment before, wild and free and it was an absolute joy to witness, especially as once we had climbed to a certain point, the track winding upwards now, we could look back at how far we had come.

'It's just like Narnia,' she said happily leaping over a tree stump with the agility of a faun. 'Of course, we really need it to snow.'

I laughed thinking that up here we had only just said goodbye to the white of winter, and now nearly Easter, it was unlikely it would return. Or so I thought.

Abigail declared, 'Sean will bring the snow with him when he comes.'

Her confidence in him was rock solid and I certainly didn't have the heart to dent it. 'Are you hungry yet?' I asked her as we had been walking for nearly two hours.

'No. I want to have my picnic at the waterfall. Lily said it is a magic place.'

Even if you didn't believe in magic, you would be hard pressed to remain unmoved by the waterfall. It left me breathless every time I came here. High on the mountain side, hidden in the thick Caledonian forest, was the raging waterfall, tumbling in three steep tiers down a narrow craggy rock formation. It surged with immense power into a mass of churning white water at the bottom before continuing its rapid way into the river we had just followed.

Lily had told me that this was where her great grandfather had been cursed and therefore was where her father would somehow be saved from it. Abigail regaled this to me confidently as we settled onto a lichen covered boulder at the water's edge to eat our sandwiches.

'She told me that her great grandfather had shot the gypsy's wolf and it fell into the water and died here. That's why it's called Wolf Falls.'

Before I could absorb this she asked, 'How are you going to do it, Daisy? Break the Munro curse?'

I was quite unable to answer. Abigail delighted in opening a bag of crisps that normally her mother would forbid her to have and munched happily as she waited for me to speak. When she realised I was struggling to come up with a reply, she shrugged her shoulders and once again brought Sean into the conversation.

'Don't worry, Daisy. I am sure Sean will be able to fix it, even if you can't.' Then on a total change of subject she said quietly. 'I don't think I am going to see Mummy again.'

'Whatever makes you say that?' I nearly dropped my sandwich.

Another shrug, this one a little wooden. 'I don't think she really likes being a mummy,' she said. 'But Lily said that was ok. Her mummy doesn't really like being a mummy either.'

Once more I was speechless. Searching for a way to distract her from these gloomy thoughts, I tried my best to remember some of what Colin had told me about the birds that could be found in the area. It seemed to work and as sunny natured as she was, we were soon making a game of who could spot the widest variety of birds. We even decided to rename a few of them, the sillier the better.

I was left with much to think about by the time we were making our way back to the Lodge. I really hoped that I would not have Robbie intruding into my time with Abigail, or more pertinently perhaps, into my peace of mind. From the icy stares I received from Shona as we made our way into the entrance foyer, it was clear that Lily had told her that her dad and I had spent the night together.

'Your friend Colin is arriving later tonight,' she said pointedly. 'Does he know what he is getting into with you?'

I ignored her and prayed that Robbie would not appear. Thankfully he didn't, but Catriona did, and she was eager to listen to Abigail's first impressions of the area and how much she had enjoyed the walk. I was glad that I had thought to warn my little sister not to talk too much about the family curse as this would not go down well with Robbie's mother.

Catriona delighted Abigail by taking her to the library and showing her where all the books on the local wildlife were. Abigail was a bookworm by nature, one of the many things I had in common with her, and it was lovely to see her settle into one of the huge leather sofas next to Catriona with a pile of books between them.

'It's alright, Daisy, you can leave Abigail with me. I think Robbie was looking for you earlier, he asked if you would go up to the studio when you got back?'

I plastered a smile on my face whilst once more uttering some kind of inaudible reply. Honestly, these Munro's they were turning me into an incomprehensible fool.

And what a fool, I thought.

I made it to my room undetected by Robbie, and the blissful comfort of my bed was calling to me. But I happened to look out of the window and saw a car that I recognised pull into the forecourt. Colin had arrived. A guilty part of me thought that perhaps I could have a little nap and greet him later. I was pulling back the duvet when out of the corner of my eye I saw more movement outside. There was also a rather merry tooting sound. I went back to the window and saw a multi coloured Volkswagen Camper van looking like it had come straight out of the seventies.

Sean!

Who else?

Any though of a nap was instantly forgotten.

I rushed down the stairs feeling energised all of a sudden. I threw myself into Sean's arms for a hug. He just had that effect. Sunshine on a rainy day, that was Sean. And if the sun was shining as it was today, then he shone even brighter.

'Daisy, darling and it is good to see you too. And sweet little Abigail, here she comes, my hurricane, oh gotcha little one!' He hugged me tightly then swept up my sister who had come running out of the lodge into his arms, lifting her effortlessly high into the air, strong for such a lean man. Then with the easy air he had, he turned to Colin who was unloading his car and held out his hand.

'Hello there, I'm Sean. Would you be wanting a hand with those bags?'

'No. It's okay thanks, I can manage. Daisy, it's good to see you again.'

Not surprising in the face of my enthusiastic greeting of Sean, Colin was a little reserved. Who could blame him? It probably didn't help that Sean was as eccentrically dressed as ever, having decided to go the whole highland style circa nineteen thirties, breeches, waistcoat and all, which to say was something of a contrast to his mode of transport was a bit of an understatement.

But as usual he worked his magic. 'You must be Colin. Daisy has told me all about you. It's grand to meet you so it is. Real grand. I believe you have come to visit Daisy, just as I have come to visit my darling little friend Abigail, so I have. I promised you Abigail a trip to the reindeers at Christmas time did I not and here I am?'

'I like your camper van,' she said, eyeing it eagerly.

Which of course meant that Sean offered to show it to us. 'You see, Daisy, I told you I would have no bother finding anywhere to stay,' he said to me with a wink and that mischievous twinkle. 'Fancy you thinking I wouldn't be able to come because it might so busy with Easter. Would you like a look inside Colin?'

I knew what he was doing. He was making it clear in his own way that he was not a romantic threat. I could see Colin assessing this and with a cheerful nod he accepted the invitation to admire Sean's new mode of transport. It would have been rude to then not go into the Lodge together. Abigail was keen to show Sean where she was sleeping and I offered to go and check Colin in, even though Shona was on duty at reception.

Her eyes had lit up as soon as they settled on Colin, but I caught that flash of intense dislike for me once she realised that he was paying me more attention. She waited until he was picking up his bags and heading to the stairs before unleashing one of her acid comments.

'What's it going to be, Daisy, a game of eeny, meeny, miny, mo? Or are you going to roll a dice to choose? Quite the little tart aren't you under that twee exterior!'

I flushed hotly. She was right in so many ways that I was instantly uncomfortable. I shot a look towards Colin who thankfully had not heard her remark. Sean had though. He sent her a cold look that far out froze any stare she was capable of giving.

'Take no notice,' he whispered into my ears as we followed Abigail upstairs with her chattering merrily away ten to the dozen.

'Maybe she has a point,' I said quietly to him.

'It's bile she has in her veins,' Sean said with a shake of the head. 'Some folk are just like that, Daisy. Sour through and through. You cannot save everyone.'

'Is that what you do, Sean? Save people?'

'Did I not save you that day at the station?' Cobalt blue eyes went straight to the depths of my soul.

I did not answer because there was no need to. He had saved me many times over.

'And is that not someone else that is in need of saving, Daisy?'

I knew before I turned my head that Robbie was coming down the stairs. 'I can't save anyone,' I said quickly and quietly only to have Sean give me one of those deeply penetrating stares.

I certainly couldn't save someone who at best was a crazy artist or cursed, at worst a killer. I watched as Colin and he passed each other, the book shop owner giving that friendly nod and hello, and the artist blanking him in the rudest of ways. The rudeness continued as he walked over to me in that predatory manner he had, briefly nodded to Sean, and then curtly spoke to me.

'Where have you been?' As if I belonged to him.

Furious now at my response to him last night I snapped back at him. 'None of your bloody business!'

'It fucking is my business if I am painting you.

Robbie Munro in a snit was quite something to behold. His whole body seemed to vibrate with ill-contained energy and the look in his dark green eyes was frighteningly intense. Colin had paused at the landing and turned to watch. My eyes were still fixed on Robbie, so I had no idea what Colin was making of all this.

Besides me Sean placed a hand on one of my arms that I had crossed belligerently in front of me. I noticed he also at the same time placed a hand on Robbie's shoulder. I was quite surprised that he dared to do this, but there was nothing tentative about the gesture. He stepped in between us, connecting us both with his touch.

There was instant calm.

I was used to this with Sean, but I could see the shock on Robbie's face. He swayed on his feet.

'Sure, and isn't my cousin twice removed on my father's side, an artist and don't I understand the passion this gives them. You must forgive Daisy, this is all new to her. She didn't mean to be absent when you needed her most. Did you, Daisy?'

Those mischievous blue eyes, dazzlingly hypnotic, wiped away my anger. 'No of course I didn't,' I said quietly with a hesitant smile at Robbie.

I saw in his face at that moment the vulnerability shown when I had caught him sleeping.

Lost.

He really was lost, I thought. As lost as I had been that day at the station.

'I am free now,' I said gently, 'That is of course if Sean can look after Abigail for me?' Which went without saying as Sean nodded beside me, a satisfied smile on his face.

'There you go then. You two go off now and get that painting finished.'

He virtually shooed us towards the stairs as though we were two children he had just told to go off and play nicely together. The smile on his face as I turned back to look at him, his hand on the newel post of the banister rail, told me he was thinking exactly that.

Chapter Thirty-Four

I congratulated myself that I managed to strip off once more for Robbie to put the finishing touches to his painting, and then get dressed before anything else could happen. Major triumph!

'Abigail will be waiting for me to have tea with Sean,' I said firmly.

Robbie gave a careless shrug, as though the thought of having sex with me was the last thing on his mind; most unlike him. It was also very irritating as it had been impossible to lie curled up on the rug next to Luna and not think about what had happened last night.

'Do you want to see it finished?' he asked, and my pique dissolved into scotch mist.

It was quite bizarre to see myself so luminously portrayed in a painting of such magical quality. I looked part of Luna, and she looked part of me, the tattoo on my back as clearly defined as Michaela had done it in ink. I knew that Sean's friend would think it a masterpiece and told him so.

'Aye,' he said confidently. It was hard to consider this was the same man who recently had thrown out so many of his old paintings declaring that he had not even painted them. 'We can start on the next one later.'

I gawped at him. 'I beg your pardon?'

'I told you. I am going to do a series of them, all with different phases of the moon and different settings. You can come up here when Abigail has gone to bed.'

He really was astonishingly bold, as though there was only his way of existence and nothing else mattered. Aware that this obsessive side of him was another unhealthy aspect of his personality, I was cautious about how

I replied.

'Yes. I could,' I said slowly and deliberately, 'but I am not going to. Abigail is my sister, and I am supposed to be looking after her. I can hardly do that very well if I am tired out from spending hours up here with you can I?'

It would not just be the time spent whilst he was painting either although I was reluctant to admit this to myself for now.

'I need to do this, don't you understand?' Obsessive. Compelling. Dark green eyes pulling me in.

I took a step back and kept Abigail in the forefront of my mind.

'I have to go,' I said quietly, anxious not to set him off on one of his rages. Luna trotted beside me but only after going to give his hand a lick.

Dinner that evening was the jolly affair that any meal turned out to be when Sean was around. He had suggested to Colin that we all sit together. I caught a flash of irritation in Colin's eyes that surprised me. But then I told myself to be flattered that he had been hoping to have me to himself or at least to only share me with Abigail.

No one could refuse Sean though and the conversation flowed easily enough. It helped that Sean showed an interest in Colin's passion for birdwatching. Not only an interest I observed with some amusement, a knowledge of the topic which left me wondering once more was there anything he didn't know about?

I enjoyed the relaxed company which was much needed after spending time with Robbie and did my best to stamp out the cruel jibe that Shona had thrown my way earlier. We talked about things to do for Abigail and decided that the first trip on the agenda would be the reindeer trek. Abigail confidently announced that it would snow when we did this as Sean had promised it would.

'Actually, I think the weather forecast for the week is pretty mild,' said Colin. 'I checked it before coming away, although of course I could be wrong. You know what Scotland is like.'

I knew what Sean was like.

Sure enough, the following day the guests were all amazed to wake up to a total white out; apart from Abigail and myself that is. We had a fabulous day trekking over the snow-covered mountain side with our guide to see the herd of reindeer and then feed them.

Sean had clearly decided that he was no longer taking the part of my lover. I felt no sadness at this, only a warm tenderness when I looked at him that made me glow inside. He was happy to spend time with Abigail, giving Colin and me lots of chances to have time to ourselves.

He was very easy company to be with. As we had done that day watching the osprey, he was eager to share his knowledge of the wildlife with me. Equally, he was happy to listen to my tales of the guests which seemed to entertain him and then he would return the favour by anecdotes about his customers.

Without seeming to plan it this way, the next few days settled into a pleasant routine. I would get up early to oversee my breakfast shift and other morning duties. Sean and Abigail ate their breakfast together. Colin was always up and out early, disappearing with a backpack and binoculars and an arrangement with me that we would meet up later in the day.

I was fine with this as my main priority was to see that Abigail was enjoying herself. We made the most of the weather, light snow on the ground and clear blue skies spending as much time outdoors as we could. Often Sean would drive us places in his camper van and we would have lunch cosied round the small picnic table which Abigail loved to do. It was a delight to see how happy she was. On the fifth morning the weather changed, and rain set in. Colin suggested as he ordered his breakfast that perhaps he could take me and Abigail to the ice rink.

'It would be nice to spend the whole day with you, Daisy and I am happy to do so in your sister's company.'

I wondered if perhaps he was still a tad jealous of the time I spent with Sean.

'I think that would be a great idea,' I said to him, sure in the knowledge that Abigail would enjoy it. 'Mind you, I have never skated before so I may be rubbish at it.'

'Don't worry, Daisy, I will take care of you. I promise I won't let you fall over.'

True to his word he didn't.

It seemed natural to take his hand and let him partner me.

Colin treated me in the way that my neighbour Violet would no doubt describe as 'courting'. The touch of his hand on mine was light and not too familiar. The way he placed his arms around my waist to help me skate was gentlemanly and supportive. The words he used to praise my efforts were kind and encouraging. Throughout the time I spent with him, sliding this way and that, laughing and shrieking at my clumsy attempts to appear graceful, there was the extra light of warmth in his eyes that told me he found me attractive.

What woman would not be flattered?

He was good looking with his dark hair and blue eyes that were lively with intelligence behind his glasses, well-groomed with hair cut short and clean-shaven. Just above average height and with a trim body that I guessed was generally kept in shape with all the walking he loved to do on his birdwatching expeditions.

He was kind to Abigail although he did not have Sean's natural manner around children, or even more bizarrely, Robbie's for that matter. I was mindful that he had probably shut off that part of himself when he lost his pregnant wife, and the chance of becoming a father with her. Because of this loss, I found it easy to share with him my grief at my own motherless state. He had clasped my hands within his then and gently said that he thought the spirit of his dead wife had brought us together. I was not sure how to respond to this, having quite enough talk of curses, spells and the like. Pragmatism worked for me. But even so I was touched by his gentle manner.

He was in short, absolutely lovely.

A genuinely nice guy.

With whom it would be very, very, easy to see a happy future.

Blue skies all the way and no dark gloomy clouds on the horizon.

'Ah but, Daisy darling, do you not think that you would find yourself longing for the odd storm now and then? You know, just to liven things up a little?'

I was sitting with Sean in his cheerful camper van watching as he expertly brewed up a pot of tea for us both on the mini stove. I had gone from the ice rink in the morning to a quad bike centre in the afternoon with Colin and Abigail. The week's activities and fresh air had finally caught up with her. After an early tea at the chip shop in Kinlaggan instead of dinner at the Lodge, Abigail had virtually fallen asleep on the drive back.

With Sean promising her a story, she had happily settled for bath time and pyjamas much earlier than she would have done normally. I sat in the bedroom with them, listening to Sean make up a fantastic story about a girl and a magic stone that she had found in a forest.

'You sleep well my sweet child,' he whispered softly to her. I watched as he gently folded something into the palm of her hand. He wouldn't tell me what it was, only ushered me downstairs and out of the lodge into his camper van, telling Colin on the way that he needed to talk to me.

So here we were now, cosied up on the seat with Luna resting between us. With Sean there was never a chance you could avoid his questions. As my mother had pointed out, being with him was a like being with a priest. He rooted down deep to your soul until you had to be honest with him.

'You mean,' I said, knowing that nothing escaped him, 'Would I not prefer the charms, and believe me I use the term loosely, of Robbie to Colin?'

'It's clear that he also has a thing for you. And who could blame him? Do I not know myself how wonderful a person you are to be with?' A gentle, oh so very gentle reminder in the look in his eyes of the times we had spent together, both out of and in bed.

'Oh Sean, stop it. You'll have me thinking I am some kind of femme fatale. And I am not. Really, I am very ordinary. Like my name, remember. I am a simple flower, not a Rose, or a ...'

I stopped there as I was about to say, 'a Lily' and of course he picked up on it.

'She is a rare and beautiful young lady, but you must stop seeing yourself in such a light, Daisy. I had hoped by now that you would have more confidence in yourself. I mean, how many women do you think Robbie Munro asks to model for him?'

I gave him a look out of the corner of my eyes. 'Hhm, maybe only those with a wolf that he has a liking for. I think it was Luna really who seduced him.'

Sean grinned then with that look of pure devilment. 'Oh maybe. Or maybe not. Point being Daisy darling, is that even if you refuse to see it, you have two men who want you. I can see it. That sour puss Shona can see it, and it is stewing in her gut like a rotten bone broth so it is.'

I laughed at his description of Shona. He was right that her attitude towards me had deteriorated even further this week. She no longer made the attempt to hide her dislike of me. If she was not so good at her job, I would even consider asking Catriona to replace her, but I had still not been there long, and she was never rude to me in front of the guests.

Then, because I was not sure when I would next get the chance to speak to him like this, face to face and with no one else around, I dared to ask him about something that had been at the back of my mind for some time now. If anyone could answer this, then it would be Sean.

'Just going back to Lily,' I started off as casually as I could.

'Ah yes, the beautiful girl with the name of your lost daughter.' A totally different timbre in his voice now. 'And from what Marigold told me, that would have been the name she would have given to her first born as well, if circumstances had been other than what they were.'

I forgot at times that my mother had also confided in him, and, that in doing so, had begun on her own path of forgiveness and rediscovery.

'Exactly. Sean what if I tell you that Lily's birthday is the twenty-first of June? That she was born on the exact same day that my Lily died?'

He knew what I was asking.

Could Lily Munro possibly be the re-incarnated soul of my daughter? It was a massive, massive, question for anyone to even consider, never mind put an answer to. Yet I had faith in him that he would do this for me. My heart was pounding in my chest as he got up slowly from his seat. He took my cup from me to rinse it carefully in the tiny sink, before returning to sit next to me and fold my hands within his.

'Daisy, darling, you are going to have to be strong now,' he looked me straight in the eyes and I could barely breathe.

I felt as though my whole life was momentarily suspended.

The moment was shattered by a rapping on the side of the van and Catriona's voice urgently calling.

'Daisy, Daisy you have to come now!'

Sean held my gaze for a moment longer and squeezed my hand. 'Strong now, Daisy, strong.'

He slid back the door of the van. Catriona stood there in the soft evening light looking flustered and grim.

'Daisy you have to come, there is a phone call for you.'

Not a good one either.

I raced inside to the privacy of the office. I don't know what I was expecting to hear when I took hold of the phone. My thoughts had gone immediately to Gary. Eighteen years of being married is harder to wipe out than you realise. Then I wondered if something dreadful had happened to Corinne and the baby which despite the circumstances, I would not wish upon anyone at all.

What I was not expecting was to hear a voice with an accent I could not at first place. I was being asked if I was Daisy Janet Barton? No one ever used my full name, the Janet belonging to Dad's mother who had died just before I was born. The name I still used legally. Serious indeed.

I confirmed who I was and then the voice on the other end told me their name was Rafe Channing. He was one of the guides on the safari that Dad and Samantha were on. I listened intently to his quiet voice but what he was saying was so horrific I had to get him to repeat it twice.

Even then I could not quite believe it.

Sean had followed me into the office, and Catriona was hovering anxiously nearby. I held out the phone to her. In the background I heard her Scottish accent murmuring to Rafe, but at that moment I could do nothing other than to turn to Sean.

Wise blue eyes regarded me with a killing kindness and his arms opened wide to envelop me.

'There's been an accident,' I eventually choked out.

Sean's arms tightened a little more. 'I know, Daisy darling.'

'You know?'

I felt him shrug and pulled away to look him in the face. 'I know these things.'

He would.

But then I wondered, if that were the case, could he not have stopped them from going? A tiny part of my mind recalled a moment at the Christmas lunch table when Samantha was mocking any form of magic or miracles. I remember how he had looked at her and I went a little cold. Had he known then?

'What has to happen, has to happen, Daisy,' he said ever so softly and in an aside to Catriona asked her to go and get some whisky.

The good old standby of Kinlaggan Malt.

I took the proffered glass with a shaking hand and downed the generous measure in one. My head was fighting a battle with my heart. One part telling me this could not be true, the other saying yes it damn well was! I thought of Abigail and how I was going to tell her. Then I had another piercing thought! What had my little sister said to Dad as he had got on the train?

Be careful of the elephants Daddy.

Oh my God how had she known?

It was all too much, and I could not bear even Sean's company at that moment. I needed air. I pushed past him and Catriona, needing to be alone. I heard someone calling my name, but I was deaf to them. Outside the Lodge the sky was a stunning dusky pink. Night was settling in with the promise of a beautiful day in the highlands tomorrow.

I thought of what we had planned for Abigail. A drive out to Spey Bay to dolphin spot. I thought of my little sister and how her world had crumbled and how I was going to have to be the one to tell her. I let out an anguished cry as the weight of this responsibility suddenly dropped onto my shoulders like a mantle of iron chains.

'Daisy, Daisy, what's wrong? You ran out of the Lodge like you had seen a ghost?'

Colin was there beside me, concern written all over his face. I was crying now but I could not speak. He pulled me in towards him. He was a naturally caring man. What man would not seek to comfort a woman in tears, a woman he had expressed an interest in.

I let him hold me, thinking perhaps that if I didn't move, if I just stayed there with him then maybe I would not have to face Abigail in the morning. I settled lightly against his chest, trying to contain my weeping. I felt tender hands touching my hair and when I raised my head, I suppose it was natural that he would try to kiss me.

Human comfort, human touch, a recognition that you are still alive.

Tenderness offered and received with a heart that was aching.

His kiss was soft and gentle.

'Daisy whatever it is, I can help you,' he said huskily as he drew his mouth away from mine.

'I see now. When you said you were too busy to pose for me this week, I thought it was because of your wee sister, I didn't realise you were going to be busy warming someone else's bed! Shona told me you had set your sights on your twitcher friend. Now I know why she just laughed at me!'

Robbie's voice harsh as the gravel we were standing on pounded into my head.

'I'm sorry,' Colin eased away from me, 'I had no idea you two were involved.'

'We're not!' I protested. I could understand his hesitance faced with a glowering Robbie who topped him by a good few inches. I was so angry with him then. What was his ego compared to what I was going to have to tell Abigail? I turned back to Colin. 'I have helped him out with a painting that's all.'

'Ha! And the rest! Aye well Daisy, if that's how you want to play it.'

He was being deliberately cruel I thought, given that there had been no mention between us of any personal involvement. We just happened to have had sex once or twice. Well maybe more than that. And mostly afterwards he totally ignored me, bruising my ego until it was an unhealthy shade of purple.

'Shut up!' I shouted at him and surprised us all by moving away from Colin so I could shove at him.

Hard.

I was hurting and I wanted to hurt someone else.

'All you think about is yourself! No one else matters to you, do they? Well, I am not like you!' I thumped him on his chest. 'I care! I care about people. And tomorrow I have to tell my little sister that her mummy is dead, and her daddy has had his legs crushed and might not walk again!'

I choked back another sob. Leaving the two men calling my name after me, I walked blindly back into the Lodge, a very protective Luna at me side. Through the blur of my tears, I could see Shona lurking behind the reception desk with a smile on her face. I was too distraught to bother thinking about telling her to fuck off. I would leave that for another time.

Sean was in my bedroom waiting for me, whisky bottle and two glasses at the ready. He held me as I cried some more and then the two of us, settled onto the bed, one either side of Abigail, Luna at our feet. We slept with Abigail between us, our hands linked across her, and in the early hours of the morning, as the sun filtered through the gap in the curtains, I watched my little sister stir from her slumber and prepared to shatter her world.

that's all.'

'I do.' And the truth? 'Ace well Daisy, if that's how you want to play it.'

He was being deliberately cruel, I thought, given that there had been no mention or of any personal involvement. We just happened to have had sex once or twice. Well maybe more than that. And mostly afterward, he calmly ignored me, browning my ego until it was an unhealthy shade of purple.

Shut up.' I shouted at him and stamped up all by my visits away from Kevin and could throw at him.

Hard.

I was hurting and I wanted to hurt someone else.

'All you think about is yourself. No one else matters to you, do they?'

'Well, I am not like you,' I thumped down on his chest. 'I etc I care about people. And tomorrow I have to tell my little sister that her mummy is dead, and her daddy has had his legs crushed and might not walk again.'

I choked back another sob. I saying the two men calling my name after me, I walked blindly back into the Lodge, a very protective Luis at my side. Through the blur of my tears, I could see Shona turn at behind the reception desk with a smile on her face. I was too distraught to bother thinking about telling her to fuck off. I would leave that for another time.

Sam was in my bedroom waiting for me a whisky bottle and two glasses at the ready. He held me as I cried some more and then the tea or he pulled onto the bed, one either side of me, a small lamp at our feet. We slept with Abigail between us, our hands linked across her, and in the early hours of the morning, as the sun filtered through the gap in the curtains, I watched my little sister stir from her slumbers and prepared to shatter her world.

Chapter Thirty-Five

How could I have ever resented this little girl coming into my life?

Which, as ugly as it was, I had. It had been hard coming to terms with my father having a relationship with a woman three months younger than myself, stunningly beautiful and clever as well. There had been downright embarrassment wriggling around in my soul like a nasty serpent when the news had come that Samantha was pregnant. Dad, who should have been occupied being a granddad to a child of mine, was instead busy becoming a father again.

Embarrassment and yes, that old monster of jealousy.

Weren't two daughters enough for him?

Did he really need a third when I could not even have the one?

Human nature being what it is, all these thoughts and more unpleasant one besides had rampaged through my mind. Then Abigail had been born and I had been one of the first to hold her in my arms. A bittersweet moment indeed. But who could not fall a little in love with the carrot topped, bundle of joy?

Samantha, not the most maternal of mothers, had been happy to offload her daughter frequently into my care, whether I wished this or not. By this time, I had reduced my teaching hours to give more care to Irene. Samantha assumed that I would naturally step into the role of childminder as she carried on, intent on furthering her own career within Dad's practice.

The chubby baby grew into a lively toddler with a chortling laugh impossible to resist. The lively toddler became a cheeky chatterbox who brought sunshine with her on the gloomiest of days. The eager young school girl entertained a dying lady and gentleman with stories that had all of us laughing. Year by year, she stole a little bit more of my heart, as reluctant as I was to give it, she took it anyway.

And now I was going to break hers.

Her long red hair was strewn over the white linen on the pillow, a soft rosy flush on her cheeks from being so deeply snuggled up in the warmth of the bedding. Softly her eyelashes fluttered and green eyes that usually sparkled with merry curiosity looked slowly around the room, taking in myself cuddled up on the bed next to her, Luna at her feet, and Sean standing with his back to the window.

A frown creased her forehead and there was a shadow in her eyes. She wriggled out from beneath the covers until she was sitting up. One hand was clenched around something. She opened it and held out a shiny silvery white stone.

'Mummy gave me to this last night,' she said in a whispery voice as though she did not dare speak any louder. 'Like that story you told me Sean, about the magic forest, and the star that fell from the sky for the princess to find. She said that I only had to hold it and she would be with me, even if I could not see her, she would always be with me, just like the stars that you can't see sometimes, but they are always there.'

I swallowed a lump and didn't dare look at Sean.

He had known. Of course, he had known.

Had he also somehow sent Samantha to Abigail in her dreams?

It was only seven in the morning but right then I really could have done with a large Kinlaggan Malt.

'Abigail,' I began softly, 'You have to be a very brave little girl now. I have something to tell you and it is going to make you very, very sad.'

Her eyes went huge, and her fist tightened around the stone. 'Is it something to do with Mummy and Daddy?' The softest whisper ever now.

I nodded and struggled to get past the lump in my throat. Scooting up even closer to her so that I could slip one arm around her shoulders and stroke her sweet face with my other hand, I forced myself not to cry for her sake.

'There has been a terrible accident, Abigail. Your mummy got very, very hurt. Abigail, your mummy has gone to heaven to live with the angels.'

'She's going to be a star now? Because she is dead?' Quietly matter of fact, yet not statements, questions. Just making sure.

'Yes, my darling she is dead, and I am sure she is going to be a star, isn't that right Sean?' Tears slid down my face as I turned to him, and he took over.

'One of the brightest Abigail, one of the brightest. I will show you sometime which one she is and then you can see her always.'

'Promise Sean?'

'I promise,' he said to her solemnly and I knew he would do this, and there would be a star that he would be able to pinpoint and make special for Abigail.

'And Daddy? Has Daddy gone to heaven too?'

I sniffed away my tears, feeling utterly useless at this. 'No darling. Daddy is still alive. But he has been very hurt. His legs have been badly broken.'

'Was it the Elephants?'

I held her tightly. 'Yes, Abigail it was the elephants.' God knows how, even Rafe was as a loss to explain what exactly had happened. But somehow on this safari, an elephant had charged. Samantha had been crushed and Dad caught up in the disaster too.

'Will I see Daddy again?'

'Of course, you will darling. But I am not sure when. He won't be able to walk for a long time.' If ever I thought with fear. The logistics of it all suddenly swamped me with a black void of panic. A dead body to get back home, my father stuck in some hospital in the back end of beyond, my seven-year-old sister with no parents to look after her. My head started to swim. I felt Sean's hand pressing onto my shoulder.

'We will sort everything out. Trust me.'

I did and I was so glad to have him there with me.

'Are we going to see the dolphins today?'

Abigail's question took me by surprise. I looked at Sean and he nodded.

'Would you like to go and see the dolphins, Abigail?'

She smoothed the stone she was holding in her hand. 'I think so.' Then without saying another word she got out of bed and went into the bathroom where I could hear the noises of her washing herself and cleaning her teeth.

'Dolphins?' I said quietly to Sean.

He shrugged. 'She's seven. She will deal with this however she needs to.'

I also shrugged my shoulders, my gesture one of helplessness. 'But Sean there is so much to do!' I rattled off the horrific list that was growing by the second in my mind, of arrangements and phone calls that needed to be made. Of the changes that would have to be put into place. Not least, where on earth would Abigail live whilst our father was so brutally incapacitated?

'None of which will suffer for going to see the dolphins.' Sean pulled me towards him and lightly dropped a kiss on my forehead. I softened under his healing touch and melted into his arms, no hint now of the lover, nor did I wish there to be.

He was so much more than that now.

Abigail came out of the bathroom and knelt down to stroke Luna. 'We're going to see the dolphins today, Luna. She can come with us, can't she? I mean she won't chase them in the sea, will she?'

'Luna can come,' I said to her.

I quickly got myself dressed then, jeans and a jumper, no make-up and hair brushed haphazardly. Sean left us, muttering something about a phone call to make and then I sat Abigail down to brush her hair. I had done this many times, yet today this was different. Today this was being done with the knowledge that her mother would never again do this for her. Did she realise this I wondered as her eyes met mine in the mirror?

'Don't be sad, Daisy,' she said. 'Daddy will be alright. He's a doctor. He will be able to tell them how to make his legs better.'

Dear lord, I had a child comforting me! I gave myself the biggest mental boot up the backside possible and asked her how she wanted her hair doing?

'Can I have it in a plait, on the top of my head like the princess in Sean's story? Like a crown?'

Abigail my darling girl I would make you a crown of all the stars in the sky if I could to save you this pain, I thought, as I said yes of course to this and carefully began weaving such a plait.

Catriona had drafted in Moira to help take over my hours for the rest of this week and the next whilst Abigail was with us and I was glad that I did not have to face the guests this morning, or for that matter have to put up with Shona in my place. We went downstairs together hand in hand. I really could not stomach the thought of eating, but Abigail said she would like some porridge with lots of syrup.

Colin stood up as soon as he saw us entering the dining room. I suppose after our kiss last night he was wondering how to greet me, especially in the circumstances. I gave him a watery smile and told him that I was taking Abigail to see the dolphins.

'May I come with you?' His eyes fixed intently on mine.

I felt a moment's irritation, needing to be alone with my sister. Then he added with a boyish smile that he had never actually managed to spot a dolphin in all the times he had visited. It would, I reasoned have been churlish to refuse. He also offered to drive and that clinched it. I had hardly slept a wink last night.

Sean turned up just as we were ready to go. He motioned for me to come to one side so he could talk to me alone. Colin offered to get Abigail sorted out with her coat and boots and said he would wait for me in the car park.

'Sean, what the hell am I going to do?' I said to him as soon as they had gone.

Timelessly wise blue eyes regarded me calmly. 'You my darling Daisy, are going to take that little girl to see the dolphins and give her something to make her smile. And I am going to sort everything else out.'

'How? Sean there is so much to do. I have to speak to so many people.' Not least, I suddenly realised, Samantha's family. What on earth were her parents going through now? I had only met them once at Dad's wedding and, to be honest, had not liked them, but right now that was irrelevant.

And then I had a sudden and intense thought that rocked me. What if they wanted to take Abigail to live with them? It would be natural as they were after all her grandparents. But they lived in the Cotswolds and that was hundreds of miles away!

'Don't panic,' said Sean softly, reading my mind effortlessly. 'First we ascertain how badly injured your father is and how soon he can be transferred to Scotland.'

'Don't you mean England?'

'Slip of the tongue,' he said smoothly. 'Then we discuss with Samantha's parents what to do about bringing her home. I can do that if you give me their number. No don't look at me like that. Your priority is Abigail now. You can speak to them later by all means, but really, do you want that conversation just now?'

I shook my head. No, I really did not. Right now, a trip to see the dolphins was all I could cope with.

'Then off you go now. And enjoy yourself with that lovely man who clearly would like to look after you a little more.'

As always, Sean managed to lighten the darkest of moments and I loved him for it. 'Thank you.' I leant towards him to lightly kiss him on the cheek. 'Let's hope we see some dolphins for Abigail's sake. When I took Lily there with Robbie, we didn't spot a single one.'

But as with the snow on the day we went to see the reindeer, there were dolphins in their dozens this time. The weather was glorious, sunny and clear and not a hint of sea mist or fog. We had a clear view of the beautiful creatures as they frolicked and played in the water, so close to shore that you felt you could swim out and join them.

Colin was as enthusiastic at seeing the dolphins as he was about snatching every opportunity to take hold of my hand and ask me if I was alright. He was asking the impossible. I thought nothing would ever be alright again. Yet as I stood on the pebbly beach with the wind in my hair and the sun warm on my face I wondered if meeting him was like Luna coming into my life.

Another little bit of magic.

I didn't dare think just then what exactly the future held, but Colin's kind attentiveness was just what I needed. I wrapped it around me like a comfort blanket, a shield to protect me from what was to come. At one point another tourist came up to us and offered to take a photo of us together, mistakenly thinking we were all a family. Neither Colin nor I commented, and I saw the beaming smile of pleasure on his face as we huddled together so that we could all get in on the shot.

'That's brilliant,' he said, thanking the person and then showed me the picture. 'I'll send it to your phone, Daisy then you have a copy too.'

In the photograph, Colin had his arm around me, and I was naturally leaning in towards him. Abigail was in the middle, and she looked for all the world like our daughter.

It brought a lump to my throat.

A happy family.

Was it possible?

Somehow, out of this tragedy could there be a whole new life for Abigail and me?

And then I had to stop for a second as these thoughts were in danger of escaping like a runaway train. Hang on a minute Daisy! Your dad, Abigail's dad is still alive! You can't just absorb Abigail so neatly into your life with this man because it presents a perfectly complete family picture.

My head was seriously messed up.

Colin picked up on this, but perhaps not the reason why. A little while later when we had gone into the café and Abigail was giving a huge ice cream sundae her full attention, he spoke quietly to me.

'I know we have only really just met, and I know that the timing is utterly lousy, but I am going back to Glasgow tomorrow morning, and I was wondering if there was any chance that you would like to see me again? I mean, in the sense of more than just a hotel guest, Daisy,' he added quickly.

Sitting there in the cafe with him was how it should be. I could not help compare this visit to when I had come with Robbie. It felt comfortable and right. I would be safe, giving my heart to him. Colin McCready was a gentleman who would cherish and respect me if I gave myself to him.

He was the harbour, and Robbie Munro was the storm.

Right now, the harbour looked like the place I needed to be.

Gary had abandoned our marriage. I had lost Gerald and Irene, and now I was faced with a father in a wheelchair for the rest of his life and a little sister to nurture through the death of her mother. What woman would not at this point in her life want to reach for that harbour? Especially when it came in such an attractive package?

'Yes. I would like to see you again, Colin.'

His smiled broadened. 'I hoped you would say that. I thought we had a connection, Daisy. I was just unsure after last night, with what Robbie said.'

It prickled at me that starting a relationship with someone on a false footing was not a good thing. But with Abigail sitting there I could hardly explain.

He went on. 'He has a terrible reputation you know, Daisy. He just uses women. I have seen it many times in the years I have been visiting Kinlaggan. I would hate to think that you were another one of his... victims.'

It was an odd choice of words and I wondered if he had used it deliberately to remind me of exactly how dreadful Robbie's reputation was. His pale blue eyes were regarding me steadily as though waiting for my answer.

'Can I go into the gift shop please, Daisy. I want to buy a present for...' Abigail's chirpy voice had been a welcome reprieve. But then I saw that she had just realised what she had been about to say. For one brief moment she must have forgotten. Her face crumpled into a mask of sorrow and tears began to overflow into the bottom of the ice cream glass.

'I think we had better get back and have some quiet time now if you don't mind.'

'Not at all.' Colin stood up abruptly and I wondered if he was offended.

He drove us back to Wolf Lodge and there was a slight atmosphere between us that had not been there before. Then again, Abigail had insisted that I sit in the back with her. Once back at the Lodge he came to open my door and help Abigail out, asking when he would be able to see me again.

'I really am not sure, Colin. But thank you for today. I have enjoyed the time I have spent with you this week'

'As much as modelling for Robbie?'

Shona unwittingly came to my rescue. 'Mr McCready, will you be dining in the Lodge tonight? We have another guest just checked in who is an amateur bird watcher. I told him we have something of an expert staying with us. He was keen to talk to you if that was possible.'

For once I was glad of Shona's overtly flirtatious manner and the way she appealed to Colin's ego. It gave me the chance to evade his question, coward that I was. I started towards the stairs with Abigail.

In a needy voice, she asked me if I would carry her as she was tired. This was so unlike her I knew that the shock was kicking in. I hitched her up into my arms as best I could, wondering if Sean was around to maybe help me. I was only small and my sister tall for her age. She clung around me like a monkey, her head nestling into my neck. I could feel the beginning of wetness on my skin and knew that the damn was beginning to break.

My legs started to wobble as I reached the halfway landing where the stairs split into two, the left-hand side being for the guests and the right for family and staff. I could hardly see where I was going and hoped I would not trip and fall. An accident right now was the last thing either of us needed.

'For fuck's sake woman, give her to me before you drop her.' Low toned and gravelly, I heard his voice behind me.

With a gentleness I had not seen in him before Robbie carefully detached the now whimpering child from her limpet grasp and cradled her easily in his arms. Without another word to me he strode quickly up the rest of the stairs, taking them two at a time. I was too tired and emotionally overwrought to argue or complain. After all, he had a point. I could very easily have dropped her.

Once in my room, Robbie settled Abigail onto the bed, carefully slipping her boots off and letting them fall onto the floor. I watched as he pulled back the covers to tuck her in snugly. It didn't matter that she was still fully dressed. It didn't matter that it was the middle of the day. We both could see she had gone as white as a sheet, the only colour in her face the redness that was blotching around her eyes as she cried openly now.

'I want Mummy.'

'Aye I know you do,' Robbie said softly to her, lying next to her on the bed as naturally as if she was his own daughter.

He looked across at me with a questioning glance as if to say why was I not there as well? Stunned, I got onto the bed on the other side of Abigail who was weeping her heart out now. I slid in as close as I could and held her whilst she cried and cried.

It seemed to last forever, this river of grief and yet it could only be the very start. I kept thinking Robbie would go but he stayed there, not moving, just watching us both silently. After a while, as Abigail's cries lessened and became more of a snuffling moan, there was a knock on the door. I frowned and Robbie got up to see who it was.

Shona stood there, a scowl on her face as soon as she spotted Robbie in my room. 'There's a phone call for you downstairs.' She nodded in Abigail's direction. 'Her grandma is insisting on speaking to you. Says she had the Irish man on the phone earlier and she isn'a verra happy with him.'

I could have hit her then for her cold dispassion and insensitivity. I think Robbie felt something similar.

'She'll be down in a minute,' he said and shut the door.

Turning back to me he said that he would stay with Abigail who was on the verge of sleep but not quite. I hesitated and then realised I was being a fool. Whatever thoughts I may have towards him he was responding to Abigail in the way he would to Lily. And Luna made it quite clear she was happy with him on the bed with my little sister.

I nodded and went down to face the wrath of Samantha's mother who for some reason managed to pin the blame of her daughter's death on my father even though the safari had not been his idea at all. Then I got blasted for allowing 'that wretched Irishman' to suggest that her granddaughter would be better off being looked after by her big sister in Scotland, rather than with her grandparents!'

I listened to the hysterical tirade which I suppose was understandable given the circumstances, half shocked at the thought that Sean had suggested this, and half delighted. He had also suggested that my sister should make the decision as to where she stayed whilst her father recovered, and not have it made for her.

'The man's obviously a buffoon!' This was screeched into my ear.

Sean was many things. A buffoon was not one of them. I had had enough. As pleasantly as I could I told her I would call her back tomorrow when we had all had chance to calm down and think a little more. Trudging back upstairs I pondered over what she had said. Was there a possibility that Abigail could stay here in Kinlaggan for the time being? Could I possibly, in some small way, fill the gap that losing her mother would create in her life?

It was all too much to take in. And I still had not even had chance to speak to Dad yet. I pushed open the door to my room quietly, hearing as I did so the soft and melodious sound of singing. Robbie was on one side of Abigail who now looked as though she was sleeping, although little snuffles still escaped from her, and Luna was protectively curled up on the other side.

'Don't stop,' I said to him as he made to move. 'It's beautiful.'

He continued for a line or two and then rose from the bed, taking care not to disturb Abigail. 'My Granny used to sing it to me,' he said quietly. He crooned another line as he edged past me to stand in the doorway.

'It's beautiful,' I said to him. 'Thank you.'

He shrugged. 'Ach it's just a lullaby. No doubt that twitcher of yours could do just as well.'

There was a coldness to his voice now as though he had become another person and the chill of it stunned me. He turned away and walked down the corridor leaving me wondering how someone so horrible could sing so beautifully to a child.

Beauty and the beast.

Tired beyond belief I got into bed with Abigail, fully dressed myself and went to sleep.

Chapter Thirty-Six

Colin went back to Glasgow the next day. He promised to ring me as soon as he was home.

'If there is anything I can do, Daisy, you only have to ask,' he said before getting into his car.

'I know. I appreciate that,' I said, wrapping my woollen cardigan tighter around my body. I just couldn't seem to get warm today and had a thundering headache.

He reached towards me for a kiss. I offered my lips up to his but, it was done absentmindedly and I instantly apologised.

'I'm sorry, Colin. My head is all over the place right now.'

'I will ring you,' he said again and then got into his car and drove away.

Part of me wished I could go with him. Anything but face the mountain ahead of me.

Thank goodness Sean was here.

That thought was to go through my head countless times over the next week. I had not expected him to stay for more than a few days when he had first arrived, but he was unshakeable whenever I mentioned the subject of his returning to Manchester.

'I will stay as long as I am needed,' he kept saying and split his time between helping me directly cut through the red tape that was involved in repatriating a body, and indirectly by looking after Abigail who clung to us both like a little lost sheep.

Catriona and Moira were fantastic, taking over my work as much as possible and even Robbie seemed to be on his best behaviour. Twice, at

Sean's prompting, I went to his studio so that he could finish the painting he had been working on of me and Luna.

'How are you helping anyone by saying no to that?' Sean said to me with a laconic smile. 'You know he needs his painting to keep his mind clear.'

He would then look at me with that devilment in his eyes as though he was saying that Robbie needed me for more than just that, and he was having fun in placing me in the way of temptation. Whatever was in Sean's mind as he tried to throw us together, the man himself was remarkably detached from me. The way his dark green eyes looked over me made me wonder if this was the same man with whom I had shared such passionate sex. The same man who had declared in that unguarded moment, that he needed me. That I had to save him. I decided that Robbie was best placed in a box labelled 'stupid moments' and concentrated on Abigail.

It was going to be weeks before Dad would be able to be safely flown home and transferred to a hospital here. There was one more week of the Easter holidays before Abigail was due to go back to school, but the question was, where would that be? At Sean's suggestion, we went for a quiet walk, away from the Lodge and the chalets, so we could have a little chat with her.

I hated to see the change in my little sister.

It was as though someone had snuffed out the spark in her.

A battered old teddy had appeared as her constant companion. When I asked her where it had come from, because she had certainly not brought it up with her, she had surprised me by saying that Robbie had given it to her. The teddy apparently was called Angus and Abigail had taken to talking to it, in a rather amusing version of a Scottish accent.

Angus was with her now as we sat and had a mini picnic of shortbread and hot chocolate with a chocolate flake to dunk and stir. Mary was doing what she could in the kitchen to spoil Abigail in the only way she knew how. We had found a place by a shallow part of the river with plenty of boulders that provided easy seating for us. Sean sat on one boulder, pouring out the hot chocolate. I sat close to my sister as I asked the pertinent question.

'Abigail, darling. You do know don't you that until Daddy is much, much, better you won't be able to go back to your home.'

She nodded. 'I know. You told me. And Sean explained as well. Daddy's legs are too hurt for him to go on a plane and when he is better, he won't be able to walk properly.'

If at all, I thought, if at all.

'That's right. So, we have to think about where you would like to live whilst his legs get strong again. Your grandparents have suggested that you go and live with them in Winchcombe and go to the village school there. Would you like that Abigail?'

She shook her head. 'Angus doesn't think that's a good idea.'

'Does he not?'

Another shake of the head.

'What does Angus think you should do?' Sean asked her from where he sitting, gnome like, folded up legs crossed on his boulder, Luna right beside him.

Abigail bent her head and whispered into the teddy's ear. 'He says I should stay with Daisy and Robbie and go to school in Kinlaggan.'

Across from me I saw the smirk on Sean's face. Everything was fine about that sentence apart from the mention of one particular name. How on earth did Abigail link me in her mind to him?

'I think that's a grand idea, Abigail, just grand. Here would you pass your sister her hot chocolate, she looks like she could do with something sweet inside of her.'

Abigail hopped down from our boulder to fetch the flask that Sean was holding out to her. I took it from her with a smile and poured us both a mug, breaking the chocolate flake in two so that she could have half and I could have the other piece.

'Angus says can he have some too?' She peered at me with sad green eyes.

'Of course he can, darling. Here.' I gave her mine and pondered on the feasibility of what she had said.

There was a lovely primary school five miles from Wolf Lodge at Kinlaggan. Whenever I drove past it, it always looked a cheerful place. But what if they didn't have space for her? I needn't have worried. This could have been down to Sean and his ability to make things just happen, or it could simply have been the nature of the environment I was living in now. Here in the highlands, miles away from any real large city, people prided themselves on taking care of their neighbours, whatever the distance between them.

When we got back to the Lodge after an enchanting walk with Sean beguiling us both with fairy tales galore, there was a bright red mini parked up and a lady sitting inside. I wondered who it could be as, this being the day after Easter Monday, we were not expecting any new guests now until Saturday.

'I'll see you two later,' said Sean with a hug and a kiss for Abigail before letting himself into his brightly coloured camper van, which was parked now as though it belonged at the front of the Lodge. I doubted that anyone apart from Sean would have got away with leaving such a vehicle in this prominent place, but Catriona had taken one look at it, received one of his dazzling smiles and waved an airy hand saying it could stay there as long as he liked.

'What would you like to do now, Abigail?' I asked my sister feeling a little lost myself at how to fill in the rest of the day.

'Robbie said I can do some painting with him if I like?'

This was news to me. Bloody hell, I thought. First Marigold and now Abigail. 'And would you like to do that?'

'Mm.' She nodded. 'Angus thinks it would be fun.' Then she turned her face to me and with a coy look added, 'But only if you come too.'

I was saved from this as the lady sitting in the red mini got out and approached us both.

'Hello there. I spoke to Catriona earlier and she said you would be back around now. I hope you don't mind me calling on you like this.'

She was attractive in a fit, athletic looking way; trim body in snug fitting jeans, walking boots and a bright red jumper that matched her mini. Her dark hair was cut short. I placed her at about forty looking at the lines around her light brown eyes that were full of warmth. She oozed vitality and in my rather exhausted state I have to say I was slightly dazzled by her.

'I'm Petra Gabrysch,' she said, focusing on Abigail as she crouched down to hold out her hand to shake. 'You must be Abigail, and who might this fellow be?'

She managed to produce the first small smile I had seen from my sister in days and for this I immediately liked her.

'His name is Angus,' said Abigail with a touch more of her usual spirit. 'You have a funny name.'

'Polish father, Scottish mother,' Petra replied cheerfully. 'Now Abigail I have been hearing about your very sad news, and I wanted to come here straight away and tell you how very sorry I am about your mummy.' She kept hold of Abigail's hand as she was talking. 'You see I know what it feels like to lose your mummy when you are still a child. It's rotten, isn't it? And scary. Very scary.'

Abigail nodded, clearly transfixed, but then so was I.

Petra continued. 'It is going to mean a lot of changes for you. Catriona telephoned me this morning and spoke to me about you. Someone called Sean suggested that she did this. Is he the fine-looking gentleman I saw you with just now?'

The miracle of a tiny giggle escaped Abigail.

'I thought so. Anyway, Abigail, I was wondering if you would like to come and have a look around our little school here in Kinlaggan? Would you like that?'

Abigail shot a triumphant look at me.

'Do we need to ask Angus about this?' I asked her rather dryly.

She shook her head. 'He's already told me it's a good idea.'

Petra then stood up and looked at me. 'Sorry, I should have said. I am the head teacher of Kinlaggan primary school. We would love to be able to help you and Abigail at this very difficult time.'

I could have burst into tears then and I think she sensed this because she quickly suggested that she drove us down to the village and would be happy to bring us back. The school was closed for the holidays, but Petra gave us both a full tour and then took us into the office.

'We may as well get the paperwork out of the way,' she said, super-efficient as she went to a filing cabinet and began rooting out a lot of forms. 'You'll have to sign everything for now as Abigail's loco parentis for the time being.'

Then it really hit me.

For the foreseeable future I was going to be standing in as Abigail's parent. My hand was shaking as I began to fill out the forms. Stupidly I kept forgetting details and had to ask Abigail at times. Petra had given her a puzzle to play with whilst I was doing this, and my sister answered quietly as she concentrated on what she was doing.

'It will be alright, Daisy,' Petra said to me when I had finished the last one. 'Abigail will be alright. We will take very good care of her here, I promise you.'

As more tears threatened to fill my eyes, she briskly changed the subject to a totally un head teacher like topic and asked me what I thought of Robbie.

I stared at her blankly.

'We have all been wondering if the rumours would scare you off. And Shona has certainly been hoping they would. She has had her eye on him for some time now, although it has been said that someone else might have put a spanner in the works for her?'

'Are you friends with Moira by any chance?' I asked. When she nodded, I added, 'Hm, I thought so.' More than that I refused to say. I had got used by now to the gossip machine that ran without fail at Kinlaggan. But I think she was merely trying to lighten the mood and I could not fault her for this. She drove us back as promised to Wolf Lodge chatting easily to Abigail as she did so.

At least that was one huge problem solved. Next, I had to phone Abigail's grandparents. When I rang them, they had just been discussing arrangements with their local undertaker about the funeral. Part of me rebelled at this given that Dad was married to her, but realism had to take over. Dad was not going to be in a fit state to do anything for a while and for Abigail's sake it would be important that her mother was laid to rest in as dignified a way, as soon as possible.

There ended up being give and take on both sides. When I told them about Petra and the school at Kinlaggan I got the impression that they were rather relieved. There was no point at this stage fretting over what would happen when Dad was finally well enough to be flown back to this country. Sean had managed to make me see that I could only take one step at a time.

One of these was sorting out Abigail's belongings. Dad had packed her clothes for a two-week holiday and that was it. Petra had assured me that there was no rush to get a new uniform for Abigail, but if she wanted this to start the new term, then she was happy to go into Inverness and buy everything that was needed. Once word got round that the newly motherless child was going to be a member of the school, offers of help came our way. Then there were things to be taken care of at home. For this I needed Marigold or Rose. My mother understandably was muted in her condolences about Samantha.

She surprised me though when she snapped at me, 'Of course I will help out making arrangements for your dad when he is back home. Do you really think I could have been married to him for that long, Daisy and not want to help him now?'

As flighty as Marigold could be, there was also a determined streak to my mother which if put to good use could be helpful. Sean had advised me to delegate, so I gave her the task of trying to get as much information as possible from the doctors in Kenya, as to what kind of care he might need.

Another pleasant surprise came in the form of Rose. I had not heard anything from her since Christmas, which was nothing new. Even when we had lived in the same town we could go for weeks without contact. We really did not have that much in common.

Rose also was usually the last in line when it came to helping anyone else out. Her salon and her relationships were always in pole position. I was not expecting her to phone and tell me that she would be coming up to Kinlaggan, and that she would be bringing up a car load of whatever Abigail wanted from her house.

'Really?'

'For fuck's sake, Daisy, she's my kid sister too you know!'

Point taken. I could not argue with that, and I needed all the help I could get. It transpired that Sean would be going back down to Manchester on the day that my sister was coming up which was the last Saturday of the holidays. I was a little shaken by how quickly I had got used to having Sean around again. We were no longer sleeping together but that didn't seem to matter. With Sean in the vicinity, whatever darkness you faced seemed that little bit less frightening.

'You've been absolutely brilliant this last week,' I told him as Abigail, clutching Angus, stood on the steps of the Lodge preparing to wave him off.

'Aren't I always?' He grinned back at me, that devilish light in his eyes. 'Now you look after yourself and this little lady here.' He squatted down to look Abigail in the eye. 'Have you got that stone?'

She nodded.

'Moira knows someone who can have it made into a pendant for her,' I said.

'That's grand. You can wear it all the time then. Just be mindful to take it off from around your neck when you sleep my darling child, but keep it under your pillow when you do. That way Abigail, I promise you, your dreams will take you to your mother.'

'They do Sean,' she said solemnly, and I looked at her in surprise. She hadn't told me this.

'That's my girl,' Sean said and wrapped her in his arms for a loving hug.

'I love you, Sean.'

'I love you too, Abigail. And yes, I love Angus here as well. But I think he is too manly a teddy for a kiss don't you, so I shall give one to you, and one to your sister.'

'Remember what I said, Daisy darling,' he looked me square in the eyes and there was no laughing now. 'Stay strong. And remember Luna will protect you. Both of you.'

He brushed off any attempt to question what he meant by this with a kiss on my forehead that felt like a blessing and then he jumped up behind the wheel of his crazily colourful camper van. I watched him leave with a tooting of the horn and a waving of the hand. I thought, not for the first time, how like the character of Mary Poppins he was - coming into my life just when I needed him the most. There was a hollow feeling in my stomach as the van disappeared out of sight and then a small hand tugged at mine.

'Cheer up, Daisy, Rose will be here soon.'

A couple of hours later, just after lunchtime, there was a flurry of gravel and a fair amount of wheel spinning as Rose's sporty red Mercedes announced her arrival at Wolf Lodge. The weather had decided to be kind and she had made the most of this with the convertible roof lowered. My glamourous sister looked every inch a stunning rose, with her wild dark hair covered by a silk scarf, huge designer sunglasses, and scarlet lipstick.

I waited for the usual slap of inferiority to sting me in the face as she got out of the car. It didn't come and I realised that here, with Luna at my side, in this wild, glorious setting I was truly at home and therefore had no need to compare myself with her. The shock of this knowledge made it easy then to rush forwards with my arms out wide to greet her.

'Rose! Welcome to Wolf Lodge. It's good to see you!'

Considering the last time we had been together she had told me she had slept with my husband as she had with all of my boyfriends, I think she was just as surprised at the warmth in my voice, as I was.

'Good to see you too.' Like Marigold, Rose was not a hugger, but she accepted my embrace with a sudden squeeze and a brush of her glossy lips against my cheek. 'Where's the little one?'

'I hope you don't mind. She was invited to go into Kinlaggan by the head teacher of her new school to meet some of the children who will be in her class. Apparently on a Saturday they have a shinty practice.'

'What in God's name is that?'

I laughed. 'I know. It's all a bit different here. Shinty is the local sport. Sort of a cross between hockey and lacrosse, I think. Sounds a bit wild to be honest from the description Petra gave.'

'Oh well, it will be right up our Abigail's street then. Not surprised she wanted to go. And probably not a bad thing either as it will give us chance to have a proper talk about things.'

I was not used to seeing this more serious side to her, but then a sudden death and especially of someone your own age can have a very sobering effect. I took her inside to meet Catriona and show her around and then Mary presented us with her usual highland welcome for special visitors of a cream tea in the cosy snug.

'Would you like a wee dram as well?' Mary asked my sister.

'A wee what?'

'Whisky my dear? Would you like a wee whisky?'

I had warned her that the locals drank it like water and that now included me if I did not have to drive anywhere! It was only early afternoon, but we decided that given the circumstances it was allowed. My sister was more a gin and tonic and colourful cocktails kind of woman but after the first initial shock at the fiery heat of the malt she seemed to acquire a taste for it.

'Not surprised you are looking so well, if this is the local brew,' she said, surveying me over the brim of her glass.

I was in a pair of my now customary walking trousers, with a plum-coloured top. Casual, but bright and cheerful too. I had not been sleeping too well this last week, not surprisingly but even so, I knew I still looked a heck of sight better than I had last year. I had happily bought a larger size of trousers knowing that the scarecrow thin look was not really a good one. Living here with the fresh air, Mary's cooking, not to mention the malt, it was impossible not to thrive.

'It's a good lifestyle,' I admitted with what must have been rather a smug smile.

'And you think Abigail will be okay here?' For once Rose was not being condemnatory, she was genuinely concerned. 'Cos you know, if it was better for her to stay at her usual school, I suppose I could somehow manage to look after her myself whilst Dad recovers.'

I nearly choked on my Kinlaggan. Coming from Rose, the suggestion that something, or someone, take priority over her salon was like suggesting Father Christmas was thinking of wearing blue.

'It's what she wanted,' I said when I had finished coughing. 'Honestly, I have not put any pressure on her to stay.'

'I wasn't suggesting you had,' she said quickly and then shrugged. 'I don't know, Daisy. I feel kind of guilty somehow.'

I queried this with a look.

'Well, I know I always made out that I really liked Samantha, but to be totally honest that was more to hide what I really felt about her.'

'Which was?'

'Stuck up madam who thought she was better than you and me put together.'

'Really?' I offered her a top up of the whisky, but she shook her head.

'Best not, this stuff is pretty strong, and I don't want to be sloshed when Abigail gets back.'

'Quite.' I nodded and poured us each a cup of tea instead. 'Go on then,' I prompted.

What she had to say surprised me, although I could picture Sean sitting there with us, nodding his head as if to say, see, Daisy, beneath each exterior lies a person you never realised existed.

'She was so bloody clever wasn't she. I mean, a doctor for fuck's sake and with her private education behind her. Not exactly just scraped through the local comp did she? I mean, it was bad enough that she could look down on you with your teaching qualification, but have you any idea what she said to me when we first met?'

I hadn't but I think I was going to find out.

Rose continued, obviously needing to get this off her chest. 'Oh, so you do people's nails do you, what a perfectly frivolous way to earn a living. How lovely to go home at night and all you have to worry about is have you picked the right colour of varnish for someone.'

I snorted with laughter. 'She didn't?'

'She bloody did, cheeky cow. I felt like saying to her, yeah well, at least I had no fucking boss to sleep with to get my own place, I fucking worked for everything I got, and I'm proud of it too. Not everyone can be clever you know and pass exams.'

This was one of those lightbulb moments in my life. How had I not seen that my beautiful, sexy, elder sister had carried around with her a monumental burden of inferiority because she had been in all the lower sets at school. The mocking teasing that I was a dull little bookworm had been her defence and nothing more. Her showy lifestyle once she opened her own salon had been her shining armour against a world that judged on academic achievement. And what had Dad done? Married a beautiful, much younger woman with a professional standing higher than each of us.

'She didn't deserve Abigail you know,' said Rose voicing something I had often thought but not dared to utter for fear of sounding bitter.

'Maybe not,' I said slowly, 'But Abigail has still lost her mother, whatever we may have thought of her, and that has to be our concern now.'

'Abso-bloody-lutely,' agreed Rose. I think this was possibly the first time ever we were in complete agreement. 'I mean, I know Marigold was a bit hit and miss at the mothering side of things, but she was at least there for us until she took off when you were sixteen, and we had each other. It wasn't all bad. Was it?'

It could, I realised now, have been a whole lot worse. When I considered what our mother had told me, yes it could have been a heck of a lot worse.

'No. It wasn't, Rose. It wasn't all bad.'

We discussed the practicalities of getting Dad home and how he would need to be looked after, trying to come up with some sort of plan. I think both of us were getting a bit of a headache with the effort of mentally untangling the knots, when Luna suddenly leapt up from her snoozing position. The door burst open and in came Abigail. Her ponytail was adrift on the top of her head, her cheeks were flushed bright red, her eyes were sparkling, and she was covered in mud.

'I have had the most amazing time! Rose you're here!'

'Maybe Rose won't appreciate a hug right now?' Petra Gabrysch popped her head in the doorway with an apologetic smile. 'Sorry! I did at least manage to get her to take her boots off at the doorway. But as you can see, she is a wee bit muddy.'

Rose, grew in my estimation then, as uncaring of her expensive red dress, she let our little sister bowl into her with one of her scrum like hugs.

'Hello Abigail, looks like you have had fun indeed.'

'Petra says I can probably be on the team once I have learnt all the rules. It's a really cool game!'

'She's a natural,' said Petra and introduced herself to Rose. 'And let me tell you, a good shinty player is always popular at school. I went into Inverness yesterday Daisy. I have her uniform with me in the car. Don't worry about paying me for now, we can sort that out later.'

'I can see that my little sister is in good hands here,' said Rose 'and that is all that matters. Never mind a little bit of mud. How about I run you a bath with lots and lots of my special bubbles?'

'That sounds like a lovely idea,' said Petra. 'Why don't you go with Rose and get cleaned up and I will get your uniform out for Daisy.'

A good plan all round. I got up to follow Petra and she asked me if Robbie was about?

'I've not seen him today. Do you need him for anything in particular?'

Petra flashed a smile. 'No. It's always nice to get a glimpse of the hunk when I can.'

'Robbie? Hunk?' Rose's antennae picked up on this immediately.

Before Petra or I could say anything, Abigail butted in. 'He's the Laird here, that's what his daughter Lily told me. He likes painting Daisy with no clothes on and he's going to marry her.'

This was announced in her robustly loud voice just as we were all crossing the entrance foyer. Rose and Petra stopped in their tracks and exchanged a look of shared amusement at my obvious embarrassment.

A couple of guests, two sisters up for a family Christening also stopped. 'Ooh a wedding, how lovely, Congratulations!' said one of them.

'When is the date?' asked the other.

'I'm afraid my little sister has not quite got the right end of the stick so to speak.' I announced to all who were listening intently, including a stormy faced Shona in reception.

'No, I haven't,' declared Abigail with that obstinate streak of hers. 'You're going to marry Robbie.'

Then she finished with a comment that only I understood the true value. 'Sean told me, so it must be true.'

'Let's go and get that uniform, Petra,' I said loudly, and tried to ignore the fact that Shona was glaring at me as though she would quite frankly like to kill me.

Chapter Thirty-Seven

It was an April morning that was living up to its tradition of sunshine, hail and showers. Very appropriate in some ways as it mirrored my mood and possibly that of Abigail. One minute we were both fine and smiling, excited at the prospect of starting a new school and the next overshadowed with fear, uncertainty, grief. I saw it all reflected on the usually sunny face of my little sister.

It had taken a great deal of encouragement to get her to leave Angus behind on her bed. Petra had said that in the circumstances she would not mind if Abigail took the battered teddy into school. Rose and I both thought that as Abigail was not usually the sort of child to cling to a stuffed toy, it would perhaps set the wrong tone for her on that very first day.

'Kids can be such fucking arseholes,' as Rose had so nicely put it over a malt in the bar the night before. 'One sign of weakness and they are in. Trust me I know all about that. I remember the time when you turned up to school that day with your unicorn slippers in your PE bag cos Marigold was drunk when she was sorting it out. Tracey Gibbons and her crew were going to try and flush them down the toilet until I stopped them by threatening to flush her head down instead. She squealed like a pig when I pulled a handful of hair out just to prove I would.'

I had gawped at her. 'I never knew you did that.'

Rose had then shrugged and raised her glass to me with a slightly mocking smile. 'Lots of things you perhaps didn't see kiddo. You were only two years younger, but Marigold always let me know she thought you were my responsibility not hers.'

With the vulnerability of Abigail now stark in our minds, and the awfulness of Samantha's sudden death, it was time to put aside old grudges and perceptions and start afresh.

In the morning, as I made sure that Abigail's lunch box was all sorted, which of course with Mary in charge it was, I left Rose to discuss the Angus issue. I had also asked her if she wanted to come with us, but Marigold had been in touch first thing leaving a message to discuss something about Dad. My sister thought it better that she stayed to ring her back. Also, as she put it, as I was the one going to be doing this regularly now, it was perhaps better if we both started as we meant to go on.

So here we were, at the small primary school in Kinlaggan with its picturesque setting. It was very different to Abigail's school back home. Lots of differences but lots of similarities. Children were children wherever you went and as we appeared, hand in hand there was a lot of natural curiosity. For all of Abigail's usual enthusiasm, I felt her shrink a little closer to me and my stomach churned on her behalf. Then, with a raucously loud whoop of hello, a boy about her age bounded over to us with the energy of a Border Collie.

'Hi Abby. You're going to be in my class, Miss Gillespie has just told me. You can sit next to me if you like.'

Abigail's grip on my hand loosened. 'It's alright Daisy, I can go and play with Rory now. He's on the shinty team.'

'Aye, I'm the best player, well I will be when I am a bit older. My sister Callie is the captain. That's her over there, the tall girl with the ponytail. Callie, look who's here.'

The tall girl came over with a couple of her friends. 'Oh, hi there, it's wee Abby from Saturday. You played really well for your first time.

I watched as my little sister, was welcomed into a group of other children and felt some of the churning in my stomach melt away. Knowing that Abigail was going to be okay at school was a huge burden lifted from my shoulders. But it would appear that I had unwittingly caused a ripple in the smooth waters of Kinlaggan myself.

I was making my way back to my car, the jeep that Robbie had swapped his Porsche for, to find a woman standing by it. I had the feeling that if I had been a couple of moments later, she may have scratched the side of it. Her fist was closed around her keys and there was a jumpy edge to her. Mind you that could have been because Luna was throwing herself at the window quite ferociously.

It unsettled me enough to snap at the woman. 'Do you want something?'

'Do I want something?' Her body language grew more aggressive in stance. She was younger than me and would have been pretty with sandy blonde hair and brown eyes, if it had not been for the expression on her face. 'It's you who wants something.'

'I'm sorry, I don't even know you so perhaps you have got me mixed up with someone else.'

'Och no! There's only one slut driving round in a jeep like that as far as I know.'

'I beg your pardon?'

'Aye, slut, I did say that. It's you whose spoiled our Shona's plans.'

'What?' I was tired, my head was full of worries over Abigail, and I was slow to fit the pieces together.

She decided it was perfectly fine to prod me in the chest. Luna thudded against the window but could not actually do anything which this peculiar woman had obviously realised. She spoke with venom in her voice and another prod accompanying her words.

'My sister, Shona, was all set to marry Robbie Munro till you came along. And you aren't even satisfied with having him hanging after you. Got your eye on one of the guests as well she tells me. Miss fancy knickers with your hoity toity English accent, and your wee fragile little girl lost looks.'

If I had not been so distraught these last few days over Samantha's death, I might have found this funny. Having been born and bred in Lancashire, I had never considered my accent to be anything other than broad and northern, and wee fragile little girl?

I was a woman with a wolf tattooed on my back and a real one in my car.

Enough!' I slapped away the hand that kept prodding at my chest. 'I do not have Robbie Munro 'hanging after me', and how I choose to live my private life is no concern of yours, or your sister's either. If Shona wants Robbie, she is welcome to him and if she does, she is even crazier than he is. And if you think about poking me again, I will open the boot and let Luna bite your finger off.'

This much was obvious with one glance at my wolf.

She glared at me stubbornly. 'We don't like outsiders here, and especially those that make trouble.'

'And I don't like being threatened either, so if that's what you are doing, you can fuck off!'

I had never told anyone in my life to fuck off before. My, how I was changing. Sean, Luna, what have you done to me? I got into my jeep and with a squeal of the tyres pulled away. Driving back, I couldn't help but consider what she had said.

Why anyone would want to marry Robbie was beyond me, although he did seem to set the local female hearts in a spin, regardless of his reputation. Then the answer hit me right between the eyes as I pulled into the forecourt of Wolf Lodge.

Mad, crazy, potential murder suspect, all of those things.

He was also the owner of Wolf Lodge and the estate, not to mention being a successful artist.

Financially at least he was a good prospect. It did cross my mind to speak to either Catriona or Moira just to get a better handle on how the land lay so to speak with Shona's family, but by the time I had gone inside, there were far more pressing matters to attend to.

Rose greeted me as soon as I set foot back in the entrance hall. Moira was covering my morning hours for the time being, but this was something that could not continue for long as I needed to work to earn my own living. Nevertheless, it was good to see my friend's cheery face behind the desk and to hear her ask how Abigail had got on going to school for the first day.

'Absolutely fine thanks Moira, it seems she is making friends already. There's a boy called Rory and his elder sister Callie? They call her Abby, but she seems to like it.'

'Och Rory and Callie are just smashing. If they've taken a shine to her, she'll do alright.'

'Abby? I like that,' said Rose nodding. 'I always thought Abigail was far too stuffy, but ah well, that's probably catty of me to say that right now. Moira, do you mind if I drag Daisy away, I've just been on the phone to Dad.'

'Dad? Really? Is he okay?'

'As well as he can be with two smashed legs, a broken pelvis and a dead wife,' said Rose in her usual dry tone which did tail off somewhat as she was distracted by Robbie coming down the stairs. She had not met him yet but had heard enough to wonder about him. She stared at him with unguarded appreciation for his masculine appeal.

I stared at him in surprise, thoughts of Dad as shocking as this may seem, thrown from my mind. 'Are you alright?'

He stopped dead in his tracks a couple of feet away from me. 'Aye, why wouldna' be?'

'Hi, I'm Rose, Daisy's sister.' Gorgeous, dark haired, brightly dressed in yellow and burnt orange, Rose waited for the greeting that didn't come.

He was still staring at me.

'You look, er, well different, obviously.'

Different in that the usual scruffy few days of stubble or beard had been clean-shaven away and his hair, the long thick mane had been all but shorn to a dangerous looking crew cut.

'Oh, my hair.' He swiped a hand over his scalp. 'Alex did it for me.'

'Alex,' I said dumbly. 'Alex in the kitchen?'

'Aye. What's the matter? Don't you like it?'

Without the distracting frame of his hair and beard, the intensity of his eyes stood out even more. They were boring into me now, like an eagle about to swoop down on his prey, unblinking. If he had looked wildly masculine before, he now looked as though he was ready to go to war.

'You look very...'

I was saved from finishing my sentence as Catriona appeared a little flustered and checking her watch as she did so.

'Robbie we must get a move on, I hadn't realised the time. Your Aunt Agatha was on the phone to me, and you know how she chatters on so. Come on, otherwise we will miss the flight.'

I had forgotten in my anxiety over Abigail starting school that Lily was due home from America today and would be arriving at Inverness airport.

'Good God son what on earth have you done to your hair?'

It was almost comical apart from the black look that Robbie gave to his mother. With a curt nod to me and not a word to Rose or Moira he stormed out, leaving Catriona to scurry behind him.

'That was Robbie Munro,' said Rose slowly.

Moira, grinning impishly was leaning on the desk with her arms folded. 'Aye, that was our Robbie. Who has a thing for our Daisy here.'

'Oh, don't you start,' I blurted out and found myself telling them

393

about my encounter with Shona's sister after all.

'Ah well it's money problems you see. Their dad is a drinker and he's on the verge of losing the family farm. Which is a shame, but there's only the two girls, and neither of them wanted to get their hands dirty working the land, but equally they want the status of owning it. So, Shona was thinking if she snagged our Robbie than that would solve that.'

Rose looked fascinated and, for the moment, our situation with Dad was all but forgotten. 'And he likes Daisy now does he? Marigold did mention something along those lines. I must say, you certainly have upped the stakes after Gary. I mean first Sean and now Robbie. Well played!'

'I am not playing at anything! And there is nothing going on between us. He isn't interested in any kind of relationship. All he wants to do is paint and…' I was going to say have sex but stopped just in time realising that I could easily be overheard by a guest.

'She's deluded,' Rose addressed Moira. 'Anyone with eyes in their head can see he is mad for her.'

'Totally.'

'I mean, off his head mad for her.'

Moira snorted. 'You don't know how close to the truth you are there.'

'Will you two stop it! Rose hadn't you better tell me what Dad had to say?'

'Oh, yes, Dad. Come on then. Is it too early for the bar to be open?'

'Rose it's only half past nine for heaven's sake!'

'I'll get Mary to bring a hot chocolate through, instead, shall I?' Moira offered and received the thumbs up from my sister.

'So tell me,' I said to her once we were seated in a quiet corner of the lounge bar. 'How was he? Does he know about Samantha?'

Rose nodded and the glibness disappeared. 'Yes. They told him yesterday apparently. He was too sedated before to take anything in. He's shattered obviously, but I think right now his main concern as with all of us, is for Abigail. He was happy though once he knew that she was here with you.'

'That's a relief. I was worried he might have preferred her to go to her grandparents.'

She pulled a face. 'God no. I mean they're nice enough in a very genteel kind of way, but look how they brought Samantha up, would you really want Abigail in that household for long? Anyway, Marigold has been something of a star. It turns out she got hold of Uncle Simon.'

I nodded at her and tucked Abigail into bed fully dressed. It was Saturday tomorrow she could have a shower in the morning I thought. Then I resisted the impulse to crawl in with her. Having my sister sleeping in my bed was not helping my own current insomnia.

'Thanks for keeping her company, Lily.'

'Thank you for before, Daisy. I can't wait till you marry Dad and make everything alright.'

I was glad she was hugging me so she couldn't see the expression on my face. She left me with a now thundering headache. What a day! I was just about to go downstairs to get myself something to eat when my phone rang again.

'You said you would call me later.' It was Colin and although the tone of his voice was light, there was a hint of a reproach in his words.

'It's been a long day,' I said too tired to bother explaining.

'I'm missing you, Daisy,' he said after a pause. A different note crept into his voice now. 'I am counting the days until I can come back and see you again.'

There was no mistaking the inference that he wanted to take things further. My exhaustion was such that I couldn't even think how this made me feel.

'I am looking forward to seeing you too,' I said neutrally. Then I looked out of the window. In an echo of earlier I saw a figure in the grounds with a wolf by their side. It was Robbie's turn to look up at a window and see someone staring down at him.

I talked to Colin absentmindedly, aware my body was reacting to someone else entirely.

read in the library and hardly looked up from her book.

'You know she drinks?'

Again, that shrug and little smile as if to say, well don't we all? 'Besides,' she added. 'Donald is not having the best of times at the moment.'

'Donald?'

'Her father. He does have a wee problem with the drink.'

'He's an alcoholic?'

'Aye that's what I said. I do feel a little bit sorry for her. After all, she did have her heart set on Robbie and I know my son can be a bit of a scallywag at times, but I think she was fair put out when she realised that he has eyes for someone else.'

I clamped my mouth shut. How anyone could describe Robbie as a scallywag was beyond me. I was disappointed that my threat to Shona was not going to be supported. I left Catriona aware as I crossed the hallway that Shona was giving me a triumphant look. I wondered if she had spoken to Catriona before I had had chance to do so.

Deciding it was not worth fretting over, I went off in search of the girls. I was expecting to find them snuggled up together on the bed with Luna between them, eyes glued wide-eyed to whatever series was popular on Netflix. As I knocked on the door though I could not hear any background programme, only Abigail's voice.

'I'm not coming! I don't want to see her in a horrible box! I don't want Mummy to be in the ground all alone in the dark with the worms and the bugs crawling all over her! I want her to be in the stars like Sean said she was... she is, he told me she is, he's shown me which star she is! He's not lying he showed me Mummy's star!'

'Her grandparents,' Lily explained with a nod over to the now hysterical Abigail who was sobbing so hard she could hardly breathe.

'Blast them!' I scooped up my phone that I had lent her and switched it off. I would vent my anger at Abigail's grandparents later. For now, I cradled her shaking body to me.

It took a while before the wrenching sobs subsided and when she had finished crying, she looked as exhausted as I felt. It was only early, and she had not had tea but right now she looked like she needed tucking up into bed. I looked round for Luna, but she had disappeared.

'Dad came down before,' said Lily realising that in my concern for Abigail I had missed this. 'He needed Luna for one of his paintings.'

'It was Kirsty Grant's niece. She kept saying stuff about Dad. It would have been her aunt's fortieth birthday today.'

'Okay?' I said slowly, still not understanding.

The words tore out of Lily as though they had been physically ripped from her throat. 'She was the married woman that Dad was having an affair with. She was the second woman to get murdered.'

I never really swore and certainly not in Lily's presence. I did now though, 'Oh shit. Come here.'

It was the most natural thing in the world to reach across to her and take her in my arms. Another girl weeping her heart out to me. I listened to her muffled words and incoherent sobs that jumbled together.

'What if he did do it Daisy?' The faintest of a whisper and a horrified look in her eyes as she pulled away from me. 'What if he did? I know he has blackouts. Granny won't talk about it, but I know he does. What if this is part of the curse and it's got worse cos he's the third one and what if this is what is going to drive him to kill himself in the end? That's what Morag said. She said he's probably getting ready to kill someone else cos that's what happens with serial killers in all the books and TV programmes. It's been over a year, and he must be getting ready to do it again.'

'Shush, stop now.' I placed my hands gently on her shoulders and gave her the tiniest of shakes to stop the hysterical flow. Yet really what could I say? Everything Morag had said was reasonable. Apart from the curse.

What a bloody awful mess.

'You'll save him, Daisy won't you. Promise me you will. Promise me you'll break this curse and then somehow we can clear his name.'

Stupidly I promised. It was the only way I was going to get her to calm down. Then she asked if I would speak to her year head, and could we not tell Catriona or her dad about this?

What was I getting myself into I wondered as we went into the Lodge?

I asked Lily if she would go and check that Abigail was alright in the hope that this would take her mind off her own problems.

'Here, take my phone. I took some lovely photos of Luna earlier on my walk. I think you'll both like them.'

Then I went in search of Catriona, not to discuss her granddaughter but Shona and her drinking.

'Och I wouldn't worry too much,' she said with a little shrug of her shoulders. 'Shona has never let it affect her work.' She was enjoying a quiet child represented.

'God, I love this place!' I breathed out as I made the most of the time I had before needing to make my way back.

Once more in the gardens I scurried past that place, as I phrased it in my mind and my eyes went to the second floor of the Lodge and to the far corner tower. I stopped dead in my tracks. Filling the window of what I knew to be his studio was the bulky frame of Robbie. With anyone else I would have raised my hand to wave. With him that would have been ridiculous. With anyone else they would have raised their hand to me to wave. Again, with him that would have been ridiculous.

'Ridiculous!' I declared out loud to Luna. 'He is ridiculous. I am ridiculous! And why am I ridiculous Luna, because I can't get the bloody man out of my bloody head. And I can't forget how bloody good it feels when I am in his bed!'

The explosion burst from me. It was a relief to let it out even though as soon as I had, I looked around to see if there was anyone else in the vicinity. Thank goodness there wasn't. Then I had a paranoid thought that maybe he could lip read all the way from there!

'Oh, pull yourself together Daisy Flowers! You just need a good night's sleep that's all. Come on Luna, school run time.'

Abigail came out cheerfully enough. She was always at her brightest either just going into or leaving school. I suppose it was the distraction that helped. I was used though to her gradually grower quieter as we drove back to Wolf Lodge. It was not her home after all.

Lily, however, normally talked non-stop the whole time, but not today. It didn't take a genius to see something was bothering her. Aside from her silence, she was gnawing at the skin around her right thumb until it began to bleed.

'Abby, you go on in now, I just want to ask Lily something,' I said as I turned off the jeep's engine.

My sister dutifully did as she was told without question, another sign of her grief, and then I turned to the older girl.

'Look you don't have to talk to me, but I am a good listener.'

'I got into a bit of a fight at school.' Her green eyes looked defiant and her dainty jaw was set.

'That's alright, Lily. I got sacked from my last job because of a fight.'

A curve of her lips told me I had said the right thing.

I have always been light on my feet and Luna was most definitely silent. There was no intention on my part to catch her out and make her jump, but I did so. There was a guilty look on her face and a sudden quick movement of her hand that made me suspicious.

'Have you got a hip flask there, Shona?'

'I'm Scottish, we always have a hip flask around. You must hae seen Robbie wi' his surely?'

The fact that her accent was more pronounced and the way she was glaring at me confirmed that not only did she have a hip flask behind the desk, but she was drinking from it too. My headache thumped away inside my skull.

'What Robbie does or does not do, is no concern of yours,' I said. I realised as soon as the words were out of my mouth that they were badly chosen.

'Och and I suppose it is of yours hey? You havnae' snared him yet you ken!'

I was not going to be dragged into a ridiculous discussion about Robbie. Instead, I told her that if I found her drinking whilst at work again, I would have no choice but to sack her.

'You can consider this a verbal warning,' I said fervently hoping that I was safe to do this, and that Catriona would not undermine me.

'Really?' She folded her arms across her chest. 'Here's one for you then. You stay away from Robbie. Och I ken that he's daft enough to want to shag any old tart when he's the mood on him. But I've heard Lily talk about you getting hitched? Not a chance. He's mine. And don't you forget it.'

I refused to comment other than to add. 'I'll put it in writing if you like then there is no misunderstanding. Come on Luna.'

As soon as I stepped out into the highland air I felt better. I paused and took a deep breath, sucking in as much of it as I could before setting off at a brisk pace. We didn't linger through the formal gardens, I never did. I always averted my eyes from the place where Robbie had first overruled my senses and carried on until I was on the path that took me down to the river.

Sean had taught me to focus on my surroundings and to revel in the simple joy of nature, whatever clouds there were in my mind. I had taken his advice to heart, and as a result, I was soon far away from the irksome Shona, and the heavy weight of responsibility that caring for a grieving further.

Both Catriona and Marigold advised me to ask Abigail herself what she wanted to do, as did Sean. I expected this of him, but then he was not a mother. I was not a mother. I wanted a mother's view on this and the two that I could ask both concurred that at the age of seven it was potentially too harrowing an ordeal that could leave deep and dark memories. Unless Abigail was adamant that she wanted to be there, they both suggested it was best she stayed away.

When I had this conversation with her grandparents however, it did not go down well at all. I did my best to explain that I had spoken on more than one occasion to Abigail and that each time she had quietly replied that she did not want to go to the funeral.

I had to bite my tongue at the response that I was a gormless half-wit who had no idea how to look after a child, and after all how could I possibly understand the bond between a child and her mother as I had never been one? For the sake of Abigail's future relationship with them, I kept quiet, even though I had a raging headache by the time the conversation came to its abrupt end.

I had about an hour before I needed to go and pick Abigail up from school at the end of her third week and then to wait for Lily to get into Kinlaggan on the bus. We had gone through at least three seasons so far today but for the moment it did look as though Spring was hovering uncertainly, at least for the next half hour or so.

This was my free time and I had already changed into my casual attire of jeans, boots and a chunky sweater. I had kept my hair in the short, feathered style that it had been cut into after meeting Sean, and was glad as it required little maintenance. I had put a little bit of make up on but beneath the blusher and eyeshadow I could see the weariness and pallor of sleepless nights.

'Fresh air Luna,' I said, hating the despondency that threatened. 'Come on, we've time for a walk before the school run.'

A quick blast through the gardens and down to the river would do just the trick. I had got a lot fitter since moving here. I was heavier, having put on at least half a stone, possibly more, but everyone told me it suited me, and I much preferred the Daisy I saw in the mirror these days. Well mostly.

Shona was on reception as we strode through the hall.

He seemed surprised by my offer. He smiled and I felt my stomach jolt. 'Aye that would be grand.'

'Well then, that's that sorted,' said Lily with a note of satisfaction in her voice. 'And it makes so much more sense. Daisy, Granny really needs you here in the mornings, and Dad you really like to paint in the afternoons, so this way everyone gets what they want.'

I couldn't fault her argument. I made sure to avoid eye contact at her final shot.

'That's just how families should be, don't you think sis?'

Abigail who seemed to quite like Lily addressing her like this nodded with a little smile on her face.

At some point I was going to have to sit down and talk with Lily.

Far more important than this though was the grim fact that Samantha's body was due to be flown home the next day. Following lengthy discussions Dad would not be on the same flight. He would be coming directly to Scotland and transported under the care of Uncle Simon to the hospital at Inverness. He had been very pragmatic about this when I had spoken to him.

'Samantha is dead,' his voice had betrayed his feelings despite his words. 'Being on the same plane is not going to matter to her. What matters now is the daughter we brought into this world together. Abigail is alive and you know I have always maintained that our responsibility is to the living, Daisy.'

He would at least be closer for Abigail to visit than if he had been in hospital back home in England, even though it would still mean a good hour's drive each way. Then there was the thorny question of Samantha's funeral and whether or not Abigail should attend. Her grandparents thought she should, and I could understand their point of view.

Equally, she was only seven years old, and she would not have the comfort even of having her daddy with her at the funeral. I was going out of respect for Dad if nothing else, but I was in a quandary as to what to do for the best for Abigail.

When I asked Dad, he seemed undecided as though the whole question was too difficult for him. This could have been the morphine he was on. Uncle Simon explained that in order to cope with being moved, his pain relief had to be increased. Having made the huge decision about flying back to Scotland to be nearer to us, I think Dad was not able to think any shadowy figure was surrounded by a pack of angry vicious wolves, that were not just grey in colour but a menacing black. I remembered Robbie describing the turmoil in his head in a similar fashion. When I had these dreams, it was as though I was given a glimpse into his madness, illness, curse whatever it was.

I didn't like it, or any of the thoughts that followed.

I had enough to worry about with Abigail to spare any mental or emotional energy on Robbie and having bad dreams was not helping at all. By the end of the second week of Abigail living at Wolf Lodge we had managed to find our way into something of a routine.

Lily was fantastic adopting a big sister role with a sensitivity that belied her years. Catriona had stepped in to take over some of my breakfast shifts so that I could get Abigail to school on time. Then it had seemed silly that Robbie was also doing the same for Lily who would then get the bus to the high school in the next town ten miles away.

'This is daft,' said Lily one morning as we prepared to get into our cars. 'Daisy, why don't you let us drop Abby off today and you can do it tomorrow.'

Robbie and I were doing a sterling job of avoiding each other, only coming face to face at times like this. With the barricade of my jeep between us, it felt reasonably safe to look him in the eye. I still hadn't got used to his shorn hair which Catriona scathingly described as making him look like an escaped convict. Without the mass of black hair and dark growth of beard his eyes were more startling than ever, and I found the expression in them more and more unreadable.

'Well, if that's alright with you, and Abby?' Surprising how quickly Abigail had become Abby.

'Nae bother to me.' Robbie shrugged so carelessly I did wonder for a second whether I should entrust the care of my sister to his driving.

'It's up to you Abby?' But already she was opening the door of the Land Rover to climb in beside Lily.

'I'll make sure she is safely in the playground,' Lily assured me.

'That's great, thank you. Both of you.' And then finally some of my brain cells kicked into gear. 'Actually, why don't I do the tea-time run? I can pick Abby up and we can wait for your bus to come in. That way your dad can do his painting in the afternoon without having to stop. If you want to, that is,' I added and braved at look at the man in question.

her small fists into my chest as I tried to contain her grief.

The phone would ring and there would be Sean's voice on the other end. I would hear his soft musical tones gently breaking through Abigail's trauma. She would sniffle away her tears, trudge over to the bed and climb in. Then with the phone cradled to her ear she would listen to Sean until she fell asleep.

'How did she know?' I asked him repeatedly and always the same reply.

'Some of us are born knowing a wee bit more than others.'

Then he would distract me, talking about the project for Violet's nephew but he was typically vague about an end date, or what he may consider doing afterwards. His prospects for the future never seemed to bother him. Whenever I asked, he would skilfully turn the conversation back around to me.

'Which of them is top of the leader board now?' He would ask with that teasing lilt in his voice.

Primly I would remind him that there was not a competition running between Colin and Robbie.

'Ah well, Daisy, you may be wrong there you know. You may not think so, but they might.'

At which point I usually got rather grumpy and ended the conversation, convinced he was laughing at me as he put down the phone. I would retreat into the bliss of a hot bath with a rather large Kinlaggan Malt, hoping to fall into a dreamless sleep. This rarely happened. Abigail would greet me in the morning looking better after a night dreaming of visiting her mother in an enchanted forest, which I was somehow sure was Sean's doing. I on the other hand, would wake feeling exhausted and snappy after dreaming about a horrible pack of snarling wolves.

It was reminiscent of the tale Sean had told me about the wolves inside us all. The grey ones being those which respond to all our dark thoughts, emotions and behaviours and the white one being all that is good within us. I had liked the story when Sean had first told it to me. Especially as it had been after we had been making love and he had been tracing the outline of the tattoo on my back.

'Your white wolf is beginning to thrive,' he had said, dropping soft seductive kisses all the down my spine. 'Never stop listening to her, she is the best part of you.'

Which worried me now as I kept having a dream in which a dark and

Chapter Thirty-Eight

It seemed that I didn't stop running for the next few weeks.

If I thought that my life was busy before getting used to my new job at Wolf Lodge, now it bordered on insanely chaotic. Never had I thought I would want Rose to stay with me but that was the truth of it. She had a much easier way of dealing with Abigail's grief than I did.

But there was her own business to get back to, not to mention Pablo. Her lovely Spanish boyfriend had gone back home at Christmas to see his dying grandma. It turned out that she was close to getting her wish for him to marry a local village girl, as Pablo had been sending Rose texts to suggest that perhaps they should take a break after all. For once, the tables were turned and I got the chance to give my elder sister what was hopefully some good advice.

I pointed out that Pablo was way and above the best man she had been involved with and, given what had happened to Samantha, life was too short to waste a chance of real happiness. Rose had packed her bags to drive back to check on her salon with the intention of then flying over to Spain to track down her man. I felt peculiarly bereft upon her departure.

I longed for Sean to be here with me.

We spoke most days. Often, he would call in the evenings, unerringly picking the times when Abigail was at her most fretful as bedtime approached. From her rambling and sometimes incoherent sobbing that erupted at the end of a day, it appeared that she blamed herself for her mother dying.

'I knew the elephants would hurt them,' she would wail, pummelling

'Yes,' said Robbie. He put a hand up to his head as though about to drag his fingers through his hair and I saw surprise when he must have remembered he had had it chopped off in such a brutal fashion.

I also saw something in his eyes that made me want to run.

Fast.

Like a deer running from a wolf.

'I'll go then,' said Moira ignoring my plea from my eyes for her to stay put.

She had inched away from the desk when the phone rang. She caught my movement to pick it up but was quicker than I, shooing me away with her hand, sensing no doubt that I was going to take cover by answering it. Even so as she began to speak to the person on the other end, it did give me a chance to escape. Robbie could hardly blurt out a proposal whilst she was chatting away. I wriggled past Moira and recalled some of my nimbleness from playing netball as a youngster, side stepping past him to the stairs.

Then I did run.

'Sorry Granny,' said Lily with a smile that told me she was anything but. Typical teenager that she was, she carried on blithely. 'Granny tells me that Abigail is going to live here now, that's totally cool, and she's started at the primary school today? Can I come with you to pick her up? Cos, I mean if you and Dad get married like I said, she will be my sort of sister thing in a weird kind of way.'

This was getting to be a habit and not a good one. First Abigail and now Lily. At least this time there was not the sulking presence of Shona to overhear. Instead, there was Moira next to me who was looking at me wide eyed and nodding her head enthusiastically as though this was a really good idea. Catriona sent her granddaughter another admonishment, only this time there was a hopeful note in her voice.

'Lily really!'

Not to mention him, himself. I mean the man in question. Tall, dark, brooding, now nearly shaven headed and even more dangerous looking than before, fixing me with those incredibly intense eyes.

As though there was a question in them.

Seriously?

I had to quash this fire and fast.

'Lily, getting married is not something anyone thinks about in a hurry. And certainly not at a time like this.'

Dreadful I know, but at that moment I was glad that there was the excuse of Samantha's death to hide behind. Daisy you coward!

'Precisely,' said Catriona, 'As much as it is a lovely idea,' at this point she flashed a look between me and Robbie, 'now is neither the time nor the place to be thinking or discussing such things. Why don't you come with me and you can tell me all about America.'

'Oh alright. But Daisy, can I come with you to pick Abigail up from school?'

'Of course, you can,' I said, relieved that Catriona was diffusing the problem for me. 'She will be thrilled to see you.'

Lily picked up her discarded bag from the floor and went with her grandmother, which left Robbie who was still looking at me intently.

'Would you like me to make myself scarce?' Moira asked chirpily, clearly enjoying herself as Robbie and I stood separated by the desk but pulled together it would seem by some invisible force.

'No,' I said.

'I don't know Moira. There's just so much going on.' I shook my head and gave a half laugh. 'I came here to get over the fact that my husband of eighteen years was going to marry someone ten years my junior and have a baby with her. And yes, I am definitely over that. We're nearly divorced, and the baby is due in a few weeks. But I didn't have any intention of becoming involved with any man. Let alone…'

'Two?'

I shrugged helplessly at her. 'Moira, look at me. I'm hardly a femme fatale, am I? You've seen how gorgeous Rose is and Shona - I'm just, well, ordinary.'

Moira tilted her head back, the computer page momentarily forgotten. 'Why is it, I wonder, that we women, never seem to view ourselves in the same light that others do. I see a lovely woman standing in front of me, with perfect ivory skin, eyes as crystal clear as polished silver, hair a lovely soft warm shade of brown, with a figure most women your age would kill for, a size eight no less.'

'Ten,' I interrupted her. 'Too much shortbread and whisky. I was an eight when I came here.'

She grinned. 'Well, ten then, but a healthy, petite ten. But it's what's on the inside with you, Daisy that you don't truly see. And that my lovely meadow flower is what I think Colin and Robbie see. They aren't blinded by the outer beauty, it's what lies within that counts. Well, alright, I mean our Robbie, let's be honest is a bit of a male slut, but you know what, Daisy Flowers…' She paused and looked at me as though something had just occurred to her. 'I don't think I have ever seen him in love before.'

'He isn't now,' I spluttered, just as the subject of our discussion was coming back into the hotel.

Lily pushed through the door before him. 'Moira, Daisy! Oh it's soooo good to be back! Ooh I have missed you both.' In a manner similar to that which I was used to from Abigail, she flung her bag carelessly on the floor, to rush round behind the reception desk and hug first Moira and then me.

'Daisy I am soooo sorry to hear about Abigail's mum. I mean crushed by an elephant that is wicked!'

'Lily really!' Catriona didn't often reprimanded her granddaughter, but a steely look was sent flashing over. 'And how many times have I told you not to throw your bag like that. One of these days you will hit a guest.'

killer. A mad crazy bastard aye, but not a killer.'

I couldn't tell her that there remained in my head that awful sliver of doubt. I had not grown up with him, so I didn't see him in quite the same light. Then, as if in synch with our conversation, an item came on the lunchtime news. We often had the radio on quietly in the back ground and Moira went to swiftly turn it up.

'Shit! Shit! Fucking shit!'

'Detectives are making a renewed appeal to anyone who may have been on holiday in the area at this time four years ago or on any of the other dates to search their memories once more and come forward with any information, no matter how inconsequential it may appear.'

The voice of the broadcaster then introduced the parents of the young hiker who had been the first victim, desperately pleading with the public for any information at all that might help bring their daughter's killer to justice, on the anniversary of her body being discovered raped and stabbed.

The piece finished with mentioning that although Robbie Munro had been brought in for questioning on all three murders, as he had been romantically linked with all the victims, there was insufficient evidence to press charges.

'Insufficient evidence!' Moira swore again only this time under her breath. 'Just wait for the phones to start ringing now.'

She was right. Two family groups cancelled their lodges, and the bank holiday weekends that had actually been full in the Lodge, were soon half empty. It was a frustrating hour and receiving phone calls from reporters didn't help matters either. We were both getting rather tetchy and on the point of unplugging the phone when it rang once more.

'Hello!' Moira fairly growled into the receiver. 'Och sorry, yes of course I can put you onto Daisy. It's Colin,' she mouthed to me with an exaggerated roll of her eyes.

I took the call, delighted to hear his warm friendly voice after such a tiring morning. He asked how I was coping with everything and then made a reservation for a week in May, which was some consolation for the cancellations we had received. Then he wanted to talk on a more personal level. I promised him I would call him back later as Moira was eagerly listening in. She was also very astute.

'You're not so keen then?'

'Gosh haven't seen him for ages, how is he?'

'He's fine,' said Rose, referring to one of Dad's old medical school friends who had taken a different path to our father, going into private consultancy work in London. But they had always kept in touch and to us he was, Uncle Simon. 'Anyway, he has managed to pull a few strings and talk directly to the head of the hospital where Dad is. He is going to fly over there himself and supervise Dad being brought back to the UK, which means this can all happen a damn sight sooner.'

I felt tears welling up in my eyes. I had hated the thought of him being so far away.

Rose leant forward and squeezed my hand. 'I know. It's a massive help. And you know Uncle Simon, he can sort anyone out. They are planning on getting him on the same flight as Samantha once the authorities give the go ahead to release the body. God that sounds ghastly doesn't it, like something out of a crime drama.'

'Not exactly Cluedo is it though. Samantha Flowers, killed in Kenya on safari, with a charging elephant!'

We both snorted suddenly with laughter, that grim dark humour that can overtake the senses at times like these.

'Shit Daisy, don't,' said Rose, wiping her eyes. 'It's really not funny.'

'I know. It isn't. So, when are they flying Dad back to Manchester?'

'That's just it. That's what he was talking to me about. He doesn't want to go to a hospital in Manchester, he wants to be flown to Inverness. He's going to be there for some time, and he wants to be nearer to Abigail so that she can be taken to visit him.'

It came as a surprise but there was sense to the idea.

The morning soon dwindled away with Rose phoning Samantha's parents and me taking the opportunity to catch up with Moira on the reception desk as to what bookings we had coming up for the next few weeks. I knew by now that ideally the hotel and Lodges should be full from Easter through the summer. Catriona had not liked discussing the matter, so it had been Moira who had told me that the last couple of years had seen a huge drop because of the murders and the association with Robbie.

'It's a bloody good job he has the income from his painting,' she said to me now as we looked at the half empty booking slots. 'And even that won't last forever unless he can get another exhibition to sell. He's not a

'Good, I need you to pose for me again. Will you do that? You don't need to worry. You can keep your clothes on this time.'

He had stopped walking so that he could turn and face me directly. His manner was so confusing. One minute teasing, the next off hand and abrupt. The same went for the expression in his eyes. Sometimes it was frightening to see the bleakness reflected there, and other times the fear came from the burning intensity. Right now, I couldn't figure out at all what I was seeing. All I knew was that those dark green and hazel eyes disturbed me deeply.

As did his next words when I didn't immediately reply.

'I've promised Lily I will behave like a gentleman. No more sex. Not if we're going to get married. She said it will make it all the more special that way. So, what do you say?'

'What?'

'Will you model for me again. I want to do a series of you and Luna together, I told you. Then I can have an exhibition.'

'No, I didn't mean about the painting or modelling. I meant the other bit? Really was he that obtuse?

Judging by the frown that creased his forehead, maybe. 'How do you mean?'

I could feel the thundering beginnings of another headache coming on. With gritted teeth I spoke as slowly and calmly as I could.

'I mean, about us getting married?' It was hard to not weaken under his stare. Especially as we were so close to the hedge where we had had that first explosive encounter.

He infuriated me then with an off-hand shrug. 'Och, well I thought about it the other day. With what Lily said, Abby agrees it makes sense.'

'It makes sense?'

He didn't seem to think this was a problem. 'Aye. You like working here, Lily likes you, you're really good in bed and clearly you are going to break this damn curse, which I have to tell you is an added bonus, so yeah it all makes sense.'

Thundering headache right on cue. 'Let me get this straight. You think we should get married because Lily thinks it's a good idea and because of this curse.'

He nodded and then dug himself deeper into the hole. 'Aye but don't forget Abby thinks it's a good idea too. And Sean.'

148

'I think it would be difficult enough for someone of Lily's age, never mind Abby's.'

'And Lily is very mature.'

'Aye. She takes after her father,' he said with another of those devastating grins. I wished he would stop it. 'And not long now til she's sixteen, can you believe that?'

I was painfully aware of his daughter's birthdate. But what I thought about that was not something I could share with him. Then he spoke again, and I realised that I had not been listening.

'I'm sorry, what was that?' I pushed thoughts of Lily and my deceased daughter out of my head.

'Do you want me to come with you on Monday?'

Samantha's funeral was in two days' time. Catriona had insisted that I took not only the Monday off but also the Tuesday as well. I was travelling down to the Cotswolds tomorrow and had booked into a pub just outside Winchcombe where her parents lived. I would be the only representative of our family. The step-daughter who had been three months older than the deceased.

I was dreading it.

Even so, I did not want Robbie at my side. It would be a difficult enough day without worrying how he was going to behave. I could hardly trust him not to come out with something completely offensive if the mood took him. Then there was the thought of being alone with him in a pub for two nights. Allowing for there being another room available, I did not trust myself in this regard.

'No. Thank you but I will be better by myself.'

'Lily thought I should come with you.'

Now it made sense. In that case I definitely did not want him to come with me.

'Honestly I will be fine.'

We continued walking, Luna trotting happily between us and showing no inclination to want to dash off. I wasn't comfortable with the silence, not in the way that I could be with Sean. Or Colin for that matter. Sitting quietly with him in the bird hide that afternoon for example had been so easy. Just being a couple feet away from Robbie I felt on edge and agitated.

'How is your painting going?' I felt I needed to say something.

laughter. 'It really might be possible after all.'

'What exactly?' I was confused.

Lily, in her typical matter of fact fashion explained. 'The curse obviously. I mean if Abby has seen Nessie, and that only happens to really special people, and Abby is your sister, well then...'

I was still none the wiser.

'See Daisy I told you, you are daft at times,' chirped up Abigail, picking up the thread from Lily. 'The curse needs someone with magic around them to break it. And the wolf of course. And you have Luna, and I have seen Nessie.'

'Don't forget the love bit,' said Lily slyly and Abigail giggled, 'Come on Abby, let's leave them to it.'

Before I could stop her, Robbie's daughter had scuttled off with my sister, leaving me alone with him and Luna.

'Do you want to take a walk round the gardens?'

'Do I want to take a walk round the gardens?'

He grinned then and I was blown away by the jolt I felt in my stomach. Such a light in his eyes. So different from the bleak darkness that often lingered there.

'I promise not to take advantage of you up against the hedge.'

Telling myself not to be disappointed by this and giving myself the excuse that Luna had been in his studio all day whilst I had been in Inverness visiting Dad and then the castle, not to mention Nessie, I conceded that it would be alright to take a walk with him in the gardens.

'Are you warm enough?' He asked me with a courteous look. It was early evening now and although it had been sunny during the day, the clouds had taken the warmth out of the sky.

'I'm fine,' I assured him.

I was used to highland weather now and had a thick fleece over the lighter weight shirt I was wearing with my jeans. It felt a little surreal to be strolling in such a way with the man next to me. In all the time I had spent at Wolf Lodge, I had not actually been in his company that much. And when I had, it had been tempestuous to say the least. It struck me that this was perhaps the first real conversation we had had. He asked about Dad and then about the funeral. He had seen how distressed Abigail had been when her grandparents had spoken to her on the phone and agreed that she should not go.

thing. Especially given the circumstances.'

I paused as we got back to the road side car park and looked down at the castle and the dark fathomless waters surrounding it.

'Abby,' I said quietly as I opened the door for her. 'Probably best not to tell anyone about Nessie. I think she likes to be kept a secret.'

'Duh! Honestly Daisy. Sometimes you are so silly!'

I exchanged a smile with Uncle Simon and thanked him quietly for his idea. I drove him back to his hotel in Inverness and hugged him tightly as I said goodbye. Then I drove back to Kinlaggan, grateful that the little girl who got out of my jeep had a smile on her face.

'Can I tell Lily at least?' She asked me wistfully as she came round to the front of the car. The older girl was coming down the stone steps to greet us, Luna at her side.

Given that Lily had supposedly crafted a spell with Moira to bring me and Luna to Kinlaggan and brewed up goodness knows what else in the way of her hair brained ideas, I thought she was the one person Abigail could be allowed to tell.

'I don't see why not.' I could trust Lily not to scoff at my little sister and judging by her look of delight, she clearly believed that Abigail had seen the monster.

'Och I'm so jealous! Dad, wee Abby has seen her! How cool is that?' Looming large on the steps of the Lodge was her father, as dark and brooding as ever, hands stuffed into the pockets of his paint spattered jeans.

'The wee 'uns seen Nessie?' Robbie looked over Abigail's head to me. He actually seemed to be taking this seriously.

I shrugged. 'Yes,' I said as nonchalantly as I could. 'Abby has seen the Loch Ness Monster. But I have advised her not to tell anyone else.'

He nodded and crouched down to Abigail. 'Absolutely. Abby, you must never tell anyone else you understand. She's got to be kept a secret.'

Abigail nodded. 'I know Robbie. Sean told me that most people don't believe in things like this, but I know they are real.'

'Hm. And you saw her. You really saw her?'

'Oh yes.'

'You know what this means Dad don't you?' Lily twirled Abby round in a delighted fashion.

'Aye. It's possible.' Robbie then astonished me by giving a great roar of

415

'But what about your own practice in London?'

Another pat of the hand. 'Daisy I really only do the odd patient here and there these days. I work because I choose to, not because I have to. I am fortunate that way.'

I let out another huge breath. 'If you could do that, I can concentrate on looking after Abby and giving Dad the motivation he needs to recover.'

'Exactly my dear girl. Ah look, here she comes now. Shall we have our picnic?'

'I saw her.' Abigail raced over to us, red hair flying, cheeks flushed and the lost frightened look she had had on her face in the hospital replaced by an expression of utter delight. 'I saw Nessie.'

'Did you my dear? Do you want cheese and pickle or ham and tomato? Cheese and pickle please Uncle Simon.' She perched herself on the end of the bench next to him.

'So, what did she look like then? Does she have three humps?'

Abigail tore into her sandwich with the appetite of someone who had not eaten in ages which absolutely was not the case.

'No silly. That's only the made-up version. She doesn't look like that really.'

Uncle Simon and I were then told in great detail just exactly what Nessie did look like. From the description Abigail gave us, I had in mind an aquatic version of a diplodocus I remembered seeing in a text book from school, long neck, bulky body, long tail, fins instead of legs.

'Well fancy that,' said Uncle Simon a short while later as we shared a selection of cream cakes he had insisted on buying at the shop. 'It's a good job no one else saw her Abigail, otherwise they might have scared her off with their cameras.'

'Mummy told me she showed up just for me.'

'Your Mummy told you that?' Uncle Simon looked at her and then at me.

'Yes. She talks to me. Sean told me that she would always talk to me when I needed her.'

'Sean?'

'Mm. He's kind of magic. He makes things happen.'

'It's a long story,' I said to Uncle Simon as we began to pack away our picnic.

'Oh well. A little bit of make believe in a child of her age is no bad

144

I watched as she ran off exploring the ancient ruins and knew that if Sean were with us then absolutely Nessie would appear in all her spectacular triple humped glory.

'He is lucky to have survived you know.'

'I know,' I let out a long breath that I had not realised I had been holding in. 'I still can't believe it has happened. Will he ever walk again do you think?'

What I loved about Uncle Simon was that he never shied away from the truth, although he had a kinder way of packaging it than Dad did.

'Given the right motivation and the will to do so, yes I believe he may. But it will be a long road to recovery, Daisy. Very long. Months, maybe years.'

I looked ahead to where Abigail was scampering about. 'Surely she will be enough for him?'

'I hope so. Or he may feel daunted by the task of being her father in a wheelchair and give up.'

I groaned, weighted down by the burden. I could feel those shackles fixing themselves back round my ankles once more. Back into the role of carer. Only now I had the added responsibility of being a mother to a child. Be careful what you wish for, Daisy. You always wanted to be a mother, said the sneaky voice in my head.

But not at this cost.

Never at this cost.

'Have you thought about what you are going to do with the practice?' Uncle Simon asked as he gestured for us to take a seat on a bench.

'Oh hell, Elizabeth, the practice manager keeps emailing me. There are locums in place at the moment, but Samantha's position is now permanently vacant, and I have no idea what Dad wants to do. It is his practice after all, but really can you see him going back to it?'

He shook his head. 'Let me discuss that side of things with your father. I'll take care of that for you.' His hand took hold of mine and gave it a gentle squeeze. 'Did I ever tell you it was because of your father that Marjory and I got married? No? Well, let's just say I owe him the best thing that ever happened in my life, so if I can repay him now then that's good. Besides, Marjory was chomping at the bit to come and visit up here, so now that Daniel is settled in the hospital, I can return with her in a little while.'

'Sean?'

Another nod. 'Aye. I spoke to him about it. He rang the other day to see how things were.'

'Did he indeed. And what exactly did he say on the subject?'

'Just what I said. It was a really good idea and that you should marry me. All part of the grand plan.'

'All part of the grand plan?' I repeated this back to him to make sure I had heard correctly.

Robbie nodded once more and looked at me oddly. 'So, it's agreed then? You'll model for me, and we get married. But no more sex until we do. Lily is adamant about that. And so is Abby.'

I couldn't speak. I mean literally I could not formulate the words to effectively come out of my mouth. I couldn't even say that I was angry. Because to admit to being angry about this was to admit that there was something rational about the whole affair. Whereas it just proved how utterly raving mad the man obviously was. After all, what sane man could possibly consider that to be a marriage proposal? It was laughable. Yes Daisy, far better to find this laughable.

However, I was for the very first time angry with Sean.

How dare he meddle so!

And what grand plan indeed?

I could not articulate a reply to Robbie. Not without creating more of a problem. I feared I might explode if I started to tell him what I thought about his shabby proposal. And right now, I had to keep a sense of calm about me in order to get over the next obstacle of the funeral. Thank goodness I had not said yes to him accompanying me. The thought of a couple of days away from this mad house was starting to look appealing, regardless of the circumstances.

'I can't possibly talk about this right now,' I finally got some words out.

'I understand. The funeral. That's why I offered to come with you. And I meant what I said. I wouldn't jump on you if that was bothering you. Sex at a funeral, well obviously not at it directly, but you know, afterwards. Not respectful. I get that. And I promised Lily. But I can still come with you if you want.'

Unbelievable.

I looked at Luna and swear she was laughing her head off in that wolfish fashion of hers as though she understood every ridiculous word.

Stiffly, I shook my head and began to walk back towards the Lodge. 'No thank you. I will be quite alright by myself.'

'I'll wait till you get back then before I make a start on the next painting. I'm glad that's all sorted.'

Sorted?

Chapter Forty

I had packed the dark grey trouser suit that I had worn to both Irene's and Gerald's funerals when I moved from Park Road up to Wolf Lodge. I'd given a lot of my old clothes away to the local charity shop, encouraged by Sean to refill my wardrobe with new. The suit though he had cautioned against throwing out.

'Always good to have a dark suit to hand,' he had said carefully taking it from the pile I had set aside for charity.

'I hope to goodness I won't have another funeral to go to in the next twelve months,' I had replied. 'Two was two too many.'

He had said nothing to that, and I thought of this now. Standing before the mirror in the small but quaintly decorated bedroom of the country pub I was rather unsettled. I suppose that was natural. Preparing to go to a funeral was never an easy thing and especially when it was someone your own age, regardless of the family connection. But as I zipped up the trousers there was more nagging at the back of my mind.

Like the conversation I had had with Robbie in the gardens for one thing!

What the hell had Sean been playing at talking to him like that? I had tried repeatedly to track down my erstwhile lover and friend and each time had been connected to his cheery answer phone. There had still been no response right through the following day as I had driven to Winchcombe.

Just a few of months in the highlands and I had become used to the relatively traffic free roads. Once back over the border and the further south I had travelled, the more I found myself wishing I had taken the train. I was tired when I arrived at the country pub late on the Sunday afternoon. After the last couple of weeks, it had been a pleasure to have my evening meal alone and then retire to bed at an early hour for a good night's sleep.

My stomach was churning too much to eat my breakfast on the Monday morning, but I managed to get a couple of strong coffees down me. Then it was time to get dressed and once more put on the grey suit. I was never overly comfortable wearing a lot of make-up and somehow it did not seem suitable for a funeral to appear too glamourous. Then again, this was Samantha's family, and I did not want to let Dad down having them think he had a drab daughter who could not be bothered making any effort.

With slightly trembling hands I applied a light foundation, a dusting of bronzing powder, a soft mauve eyeshadow that Lily assured me made my eyes look silver rather than grey, and a touch of a barely there lipstick. I had been to the hairdressers in Kinlaggan and had a quick trim and a touch up of the highlights I now treated myself to.

Dad, I thought would be pleased with my efforts.

Suddenly wishing I had a hip flask of Kinlaggan malt to sneak into my handbag, I made my way down to my car. I could park up at the church and try and calm my nerves there. Dreading the next couple of hours, I failed to notice the car that was parking up in something of a hurry next to my jeep.

'Just in time by the look of things!' Colin, dressed in a black suit and white shirt was suddenly standing next to me. 'You look lovely. I suppose that's the wrong thing to say in the circumstances, but it's true. You do.'

'Colin! What are you doing here?' Stupid question given his attire, but I had not arranged anything with him.

'I know you said you would be fine by yourself, but really I hated the thought of you having to face Samantha's family all alone. From what you've told me they sound pretty tricky at the best of times, and this is hardly that.'

'Quite.'

After my ludicrous conversation with Robbie and my annoyance with what I saw to be Sean's meddling mischief, I wasn't sure how I felt about his sudden appearance. Gary had always made me feel rather incompetent as though I couldn't function without him by my side. A part of me wanted to snap at Colin and say 'really if I say I am fine, then I am fine'.

'Shall I drive in my car. That way you can have a drink?'

The part of me that had longed for the hip flask gave in.

'Colin that would be lovely thank you.' Abandoning feminist pride for the opportunity to have a drink at a funeral was, I considered, a fair pay off. I put my keys back in my bag and got into the passenger side of his car. 'Did you ask your friend to cover the shop for you?'

'Och, I just put a 'closed due to bereavement' sign on the door.'

Smoothly he pulled away from the pub, carefully checking before pulling out onto the country lane. His driving, like everything else, was in marked contrast to Robbie's erratic approach.

'But it's hardly of someone close to you.' I looked sideways at him, thinking how good looking he was, especially suited up. Dark hair freshly cut, clean-shaven, intelligent blue eyes behind his glasses.

'I know. But it's to support someone close to me though.' We were paused at traffic lights, and he turned to look at me, a hopeful boyish expression on his face. 'You do understand that don't you, Daisy? I do want us to be close?'

I didn't answer at first. I was considering the difference between his approach and Robbie's. He must have taken my silence for doubt because he went on rapidly.

'I'm sorry. Stupid of me. Lousy timing. Stupid. Forgive me.'

'Not at all. I am touched you made the effort to come, and I will be very glad of your company.'

I really was.

The whole affair was awful from start to finish.

Samantha's parents were hostile in their grief and their attitude seemed to have passed to their family and friends. It was painfully obvious that everyone considered it a scandal that Abigail was being deprived of the opportunities that her grandparents could afford to give her. It was also commented on that she would now be even further away from them than before. Colin was the perfect gentleman, gallantly brushing aside all criticisms that came my way. He made it clear that Abigail's choice to stay in Scotland was not of my making.

Second to that was the fact that little was asked in the way of Dad's health and that did rather fire me up. Realising that a funeral was not the best time for a provocative argument, I opted to douse my flames with gin. Only as my sister Rose could have told me, this was not a good idea. I had never been a heavy drinker. I still wasn't, although it had to be said I had developed a taste for Kinlaggan malt. They did not have any of that here, hence the gin.

'Good job I came,' said Colin at the end of a wearying day.

He had to help me fasten the seat belt in his car when it was finally a respectable time to leave. All of a sudden, it seemed a difficult thing to do.

'Thank God that's over with!' I rested my head on the back of the car seat and closed my eyes. 'Miserable lot!'

'Hm. They were rather...'

'Exactly. Even someone as nice as you is struggling to find a word to say how bloody awful they were.'

He laughed softly 'They were rather difficult. I thought you handled everything brilliantly, Daisy. Although perhaps you have had a tad too much to drink?'

'You're probably right.' I opened my eyes and looked across at him as he drove us back to the pub. 'Do you mind? If I am a little drunk?'

'Daisy if you can't get a little drunk at a funeral then it's a poor do. And I know you would not have done so if you had been driving, so you can blame it on me.'

'Exactly! All your fault, Colin.' I slapped him playfully on the thigh.

He caught hold of my hand and raised it to his mouth to kiss. His car was an automatic and he kept hold of my hand, effortlessly steering with the other one. I was happy to let him do so. The human contact was comforting. When we arrived back at the pub, he sheepishly told me he had been unable to book a room for himself and would it be okay if he shared with me. At this point I was happy to say yes.

It would be comforting to have the company.

Comforting?

Really Daisy?

In my gin soaked mind that might have been what I was thinking. Sober, I would have realised precisely what Colin was hoping for. But my abilities to react sensibly to the men around me were limited to say the least. Add alcohol to that equation and well, frankly it would appear I turned into something of a slut.

The door had barely been closed when Colin pulled me close into a fervent embrace.

He kissed me deeply, tilting my head back a little to increase the pressure and open my mouth so his tongue could delve into mine. I wobbled on the high heels I was wearing and fell backwards a little. There was more of a stumble and then the bed was behind my legs, and I fell onto it.

There we were, all suited and booted and wriggling around the bed, me in a gin infused state and Colin becoming increasingly aroused. I had not experienced many encounters with boys whilst at high school but suddenly I was back in the bedroom of one boy I had liked and who had liked me in return, before meeting my sister Rose. A vivid memory of us half clothed and frantic with passion as teenage hormones surged wildly. The sounds of his mother returning home had stopped us before we had really begun, and I never did get to lose my virginity with that boy.

I had really, really, liked him too.

My first real crush. The hurt of seeing him with Rose a couple of weeks later was as painful as only teenage heartbreak can be. Ridiculous now in my middle forties to be thinking of him. But I was. Briefly. Enough to respond with a crazy desperation to Colin as he feverishly tried to get me undressed. It didn't seem necessary to have lingering foreplay.

My jacket was shrugged off, the buttons of my shirt undone, and that too quickly was thrown aside. Then my bra followed suit and the next thing I knew Colin was squeezing and biting at my breasts in the manner of one starved of nourishment.

Billy, the boy I had had a crush on, had just about got to that part. I remembered now the fear that he would be disappointed in the size of my breasts. I relied as a teenager on a deep plunging push up bra to give me all the help I could get. Yes of course he had been disappointed, or so Rose had taunted me later. Rose with her ample breasts that needed restraining rather than lifting.

The ghost of that sixteen-year-old squirmed inside me and the forty-six-year-old woman took satisfaction in the delight that Colin was taking in my body now. Between kissing and biting, he was groaning and muttering breathlessly.

'Oh Daisy, I want you so badly, it's been such a long time since I've been with a woman.'

'Well get on with it then,' was my drunken response.

'What? Of yes, yes of course, sorry, hang on.'

My head lolled a little on the pillows as he left the ravenous devouring of my breasts to unzip my trousers and tug them down my hips. I lifted up my bottom to help him and pushed at my briefs to slide them down a fraction but that was all I could seem to do. The room was beginning to spin.

'Oh god, Daisy I really want to fuck you.'

'Fuck away then,' I airily waved a hand.

He proceeded to do so. Still pretty much clothed I was aware that he had shifted his own trousers enough to free himself and then he was inside me.

In and out.

In and out.

In and out.

Huffing and puffing.

Huffing and puffing.

Huffing and puffing.

So, is this what all the fuss was about, I wondered as Billy heaved up and down on me, exerting as much effort as he did sprinting round the school running track.

No, no, no, no, no, Daisy. Not Billy. You are not sixteen. You are forty-six and this is Colin.

Oh Christ Colin!

Yes, that was definitely his face inches away from mine, contorting now, with his eyes squeezed shut behind his glasses. He had kept his glasses on?

'Oh, Daisy, oh Daisy, oh Daisy, I'm coming, I'm coming, I'm coming. Oh my God I'm coming!' He finished with a triumphant shout as though he had just crossed the line at a race and come first.

Again Billy, winning that hundred metre sprint at sports day shot into my mind. Go away Billy! That was years ago. I was having trouble keeping focused on that fact. I was also having trouble breathing now as Colin had collapsed in a heap onto my chest.

'Oh, Daisy that was the best. Oh my God I can't believe how good that felt. Was it okay for you? I mean you did come, didn't you?'

Had I?

I don't think I had. I am pretty sure I would have remembered. Right now though I had a far more pressing concern than reassuring Colin about his prowess in bed. I gulped and franticly gestured for him to move.

'Bathroom,' I managed to get out with my hand across my mouth.

'What? Oh, yes, I see, hang on a minute. We seem to be a bit tangled up.'

In his gentlemanly fashion he withdrew from me and tried to help me off the bed. But he was right. My trousers were still around my ankles as were his and neither of us could move very well. I was also hindered by the odd phenomenon of the room moving on its axis.

I lurched forward as soon as I got halfway to standing up, tripped up over my trousers, banging my head on the door frame into the bathroom, and promptly threw up all over the floor. As I lay there thinking I was dying, I could at least console myself with the knowledge that my sour smelling vomit had landed on tiles and not the lovely carpet.

Considerate even when drunk.

'Oh dear.'

I was vaguely aware of Colin hovering around me and the pair of us trying rather clumsily to clean up the mess with copious amounts of loo roll. Then, when he assured me the bathroom was in a decent state, I crawled back to the bed. Having kicked off my trousers and knickers from around my ankles, I was completely nude, but I didn't care.

'Are you alright, Daisy? Shall I get you something to eat? You didn't have anything at the funeral.' Colin was perched on the end of my bed looking at me in a concerned manner.

I groaned and blinked, opening my eyes. He had a point. Now that I had emptied my stomach of the gin, I realised I was actually more hungry than tired.

'What time is it?'

'Seven o'clock.'

'Now wonder I'm starving and no wonder I got so drunk. All that gin on an empty stomach was a recipe for disaster.'

I threw aside the covers and began, still rather wobbly it had to be said, to look for my clothes. Not my suit, crumpled and abandoned on the floor, but my jeans and a sweater I was far more comfortable in.

'I hope you don't think our lovemaking was a disaster?' Colin said as I managed to get my sweater on the right way after three attempts.

'What?' Would it be rude to confess that I had almost forgotten already that we had made love.

Made love?

Sex?

Definitely sex.

We had definitely done that.

My mind and my body were at war. Not to mention my heart and my morals. Standing there swaying and feeling that if I did not eat something soon, I would pass out, I realised this was not the right time to think much, let alone talk.

'I need a burger.' Dimly I recognised that this was more in line with my sister Rose's behaviour patterns than my own.

'A burger?'

I nodded. 'Hm. A big fat juicy burger with lots of cheese and onion rings, and chips.'

'Are you sure?'

'Hm. They do them in the bar 1 downstairs. Come on.'

'Erm you might want to, you know, just brush your hair maybe first?'

He had a point as I saw when I checked my reflection. My hair was looking wild, my eye make-up was smudged as well as my mouth looking rather smeary with the lipstick all kissed off. I tidied myself up whilst Colin used the bathroom. We then went down to the bar, and I devoured a huge juicy burger after which I felt much better. An enormous sense of relief began to settle on my shoulders. I had got through the funeral.

'That better?' Colin asked as I sat back in my seat and heaved a big sigh.

'Much.' I finished my glass of tonic water and nodded. Then I began to talk to him about Abby and Dad and how things were going but before long he interrupted me.

'I know this isn't probably the right time, but you always seem so preoccupied when I telephone you at the Lodge, and really it isn't the sort of thing to do over the phone anyway.'

I was not expecting him to place a small square box on the table and open it to face towards me revealing a simple but lovely diamond ring.

'Daisy would you do me the honour of marrying me?'

I snapped the box shut. 'Colin I can't! I mean, I know we like each other.'

He looked understandably a little hurt. 'Like? I love you, Daisy. I know it's all a bit sudden. But neither of us are getting any younger and look what happened to Samantha. Life is too short to waste chances.'

I squeezed hold of his hand to soften the blow. 'I know. And I do care for you. It's just well, with Abby and Dad, I really can't think of anything else right now.'

He nodded. 'I understand. Of course I do. We'll keep it our little secret for now. No point upsetting anyone until things are a little easier. In the meantime, shall we go back to bed?'

There was such an expectant look of hope in his eyes I didn't feel I could refuse. It was like saying no to a puppy. Back in bed he made love to me once more. This time, alert and aware of all I was feeling, I was aware that I really was not feeling much at all. I responded, but was I swept away?

'That was so good, Daisy,' he said as he had done the first time, and then added. 'I love you.'

I feigned sleepiness and replied with a drowsy, 'Hhm.'

When he began to snore quietly beside me, I lay with my eyes wide open, desperately trying to block out the voice of Robbie telling what a fine fuck I was. And with it the memory of how he made me feel.

But Robbie Munro did not love me.

I squeezed his little black hand to soften the blow. 'I hope,' I said, 'it's just well with Abby and Dad. It's all cart-shuffle and that right now.'

He nodded. 'I understand. Of course. He— We'll keep it out just once for now. No point upsetting everyone until things are a little better. In the meantime shall we go back to bed?'

There was such an expectant look of hope in his face, I didn't feel I could refuse. It was like saying no to a puppy. Before bed he made love to me once more. This time easy and sweet, or all I was feeling. I was aware that I really was not feeling much at all. I expected, but there was a feeling —

'That was so good, Daisy,' he said as he had done the first time, and then added, 'I love you.'

I feigned sleepiness and replied with a drowsy, 'Hm.'

When he began to snore quietly beside me, I lay with my eyes wide open, desperately trying to block out the voice of Robbie telling what a huge fuck I was. And with it the memory of how he made me feel. But Robbie, I now did not love me...

Chapter Forty-One

My mind was a whirlwind as I made the long drive back up to the highlands the following day. I felt shabby that I couldn't respond more enthusiastically to Colin's lovemaking or his proposal. I was angry at myself for not being able to appreciate this lovely man and what he was trying to offer me, and stupidly angry at him for putting me in this awkward position.

The closer I got to Kinlaggan, having stewed over things for a good number of hours, the angrier I grew at all three men.

Sean.

Robbie.

Colin.

Couldn't they see how overloaded I was?

Had they any idea the scale of my worries over Abigail and Dad?

No. Of course they couldn't, because they were men and, in my experience, men didn't think that way.

Thank goodness I had the wise, if sometimes slightly wacky company of Moira to fall back on. By Friday of that week, having dodged Robbie as much as possible, fended off Colin's phone calls with equal measure, and failed to track down Sean, although Violet emailed me to tell me he was constantly on the phone to her, I was in something of a grumpy mood.

'You look like you could do with some fresh air and a good stretch of the legs.' Moira had called into reception to check on the amount of people staying in one of the chalets this coming weekend.

I looked at the clock. The morning was dragging; it was only eleven. I had a lot of catching up to do from taking Monday and Tuesday off for the funeral. There were emails to reply to and Catriona had been asking me to have a look at our website to see if we could update it. But the thought of escaping for a brisk walk with Moira was too alluring.

'You're right. That's just what I need.'

'Why don't you ask Shona to cover for you from one o'clock? You know she needs the extra money and then you get a wee bit more time.'

As reluctant as I was to ask any favours of Shona, it did make sense, and this is precisely what I did. Ten minutes past one came and I was ready in my walking gear waiting to meet Moira, Luna at my side. Shona and I did not exchange much by way of conversation other than for me to pass on any necessary details she needed to know.

'Where are you going?' She asked Moira with her usual sulky expression on her face.

'The waterfall and back. It's been pretty dry this week so I can show Daisy the cave.'

'The cave?'

'Aye. You can get behind the waterfall when it's not been raining so heavy and there's a cave there. Lily and I both think its magical.'

I rolled my eyes at her. 'Well as long as you don't start casting any spells on me that's fine. I bet Abby would like to see that some time so it will be good if I know where it is.'

Forty minutes later, having kept up with Moira's fast pace and feeling smug that I could now do so, we had trekked deep into the glen that then rose with its steep hills either side of the river, coming to what was one of my favourite spots.

Wolf Falls.

'I love it here,' I said as I paused to catch my breath.

'It is magical,' said Moira with a smile on her face, her cropped silver-grey hair now slightly damp and curling from the spray. 'Come on. I want to show you the cave.' Nimbly she began to climb up the rocks on the left side of the waterfall.

Less nimbly I followed, Luna staying with me all the time. Some of the rocks were slippery and there was a steep drop into the water, but I trusted both Moira and Luna to follow their routes.

'Watch yourself there now, that's it, one last step and brace yourself, here we go!'

She took hold of my hand and pulled me. I could see that at one particular spot it was possible to pass behind the water without getting too wet. Then as she had said, we were in a cave which I agreed could only be described as magical.

'Wow,' I was struggling to find other words.

'I know, it's amazing isn't it.' Our voices echoed in the mountain cave, distorted by the sound of the rushing water. 'This is where Callum proposed to me.'

I don't think she was expecting me to groan at this comment but all I could think of was Colin and Robbie and the dilemma in my head. I told her about Colin's proposal.

'Colin? He's proposed as well? Lily told me Robbie had.'

I snorted at that, and the sound bounced back at me. 'I would hardly call it a proposal.' I told her what Robbie had said to me in the gardens.

'Hhm. Well, that's just his way. He told Callum he is going to marry you. He's planning on announcing it on Midsummer's Eve. Lily's birthday.'

'I know when Lily's birthday is!' I snapped and immediately apologised. 'Sorry. Sore point.'

'Aye you said about Lily. Really strange that,' Moira looked at me thoughtfully in the dim eerie light of the cave. 'So, what are you going to do? For God's sake, Daisy, if your answer is going to be no, then please tell him before then.'

'I have!' I protested. It struck me as highly ironic that I was going to be put in the same position that Lily had asked me to save her dad from on New Year's Eve. Only then, that was to save him from publicly being asked to marry Shona. Somehow it seemed to be okay to have the tables reversed.

'You're sure about that? Cos for Robbie to tell Callum it must be pretty fixed in his mind.'

'Oh hell. I told him I couldn't really think about anything with Dad being so ill and Abby to look after.'

'Am I hearing excuses Daisy? And what about Colin? Have you said the same to him?'

'Pretty much,' I replied and then realised we should be making a start back. We began the descent from the waterfall, taking care not to slip. One trip and a very nasty accident could occur.

'Who is it to be then, Daisy?' Moira asked what I suppose was a reasonable enough question once we had got back to the forest floor. 'And does anyone else know about Colin?'

'No! I haven't told a soul, only you, so please keep it that way for now.' She nodded and I continued. 'I honestly don't know Moira. I am in such a muddle. I came here to be independent. Not to find myself in the middle of a love triangle with two men.'

She laughed at that. 'Ah but which one is the true love?'

'Don't. You sound like Lily. I can tell you for definite, Robbie only wants to marry me because he thinks it will be convenient and he has this stupid notion that it will break this bloody ridiculous curse that everyone goes on about!'

Moira stopped me then and placed a gentle hand on my arm, but the look in her eye was quite steely. 'Not ridiculous. You told me yourself Marigold agrees he is cursed, she felt it. And anyway, how do you know Robbie doesn't love you? Just because he hasn't said so? Really Daisy?'

We walked on for a while in silence, the water, gentler now as it meandered beside us in a wide stretch of river, accompanying the bird song.

'Are you mad with me?'

'Daisy no!' Moira shook her head and smiled, the gentle look back in her blue eyes. 'But I suppose I am troubled. I love Robbie like a brother. And I have seen him so troubled in the past. I know that car accident was no accident. And that side of him is only ever a heartbeat away. But since you came, it does seem to be holding at bay. I mean I know there's been the odd mad moment, but nothing like how he used to be.'

'I can't marry someone Moira just to save them from themselves,' I said ever so quietly and hating myself for it.

'But what if you are saving yourself in the process? Have you thought about that?'

I stopped dead in my tracks. Partly because of her words and partly because my tattoo felt as though it was on fire. It always was at this point, with the forest on one side and the mountains behind us. Just like in Michaela's painting, just like the one that Robbie reproduced without ever even seeing it.

The signs were all there.

I had been brought here for a reason and that reason seemed to be Robbie Munro.

But why?

How?

I knew Sean was somehow involved. He had to be.

But again, why and how?

Until I knew the answer, I was damned if I was going to play along like a puppet on a string. I said nothing of this to Moira knowing it would only add fuel to her fire. I just asked her to once more promise to say absolutely nothing to anyone about Colin's proposal.

'I'd hate to upset Lily for one thing.'

'Absolutely,' Moira promised, and I shoved my head back into my sand bucket of indecision.

I picked Abby up from school and then we went to have a quick hot chocolate in our favourite café whilst we waited for Lily's bus to come in. On a Friday she had an extended games session, so this usually gave me chance to treat Abby.

'How was your day?'

A question I had asked her many times before when I had picked her up back home to help Samantha out. Only now it had far more weight behind it. I couldn't just let her chatter on and not pay attention. Everything she said mattered now. Really mattered. Her class teacher Miss Gillespie had pulled me to one side as they tumbled out into the playground like unruly puppies off the lead.

'I am just a little worried that she may not quite grasp the situation with her father,' the young and very earnest teacher told me. She then went on to describe how in circle time that morning Abby had told them all that her daddy had been badly hurt, but it was okay because he was soon going to be able to walk again. 'She does know doesn't she, that this may not happen?'

I felt a little cross with her and on top of my frustrations with the men in my life I had to rein in my response. Now though, seated in the café, in answer to my question, Abby reached into her bag and drew out an exercise book.

'We had to do a story for literacy. About something magical happening. I could have written a story about Nessie,' she dropped her voice to a whisper at this point, 'But Robbie said that had to be a secret, so I did this instead. Only Miss Gillespie didn't really like it because she said it wasn't proper magic and I told her it was. I think she's a bit silly if she doesn't believe in magic.'

'Let me see.' Curious, I took the exercise book from her.

On one side there was the narrative, about how her daddy had been badly hurt by an elephant, but it was all going to be alright because he was going to walk again. When he got better, he was going to take her horse riding. On the opposite page was a drawing depicting this. That background headache began to pound once more. I was saved from commenting as the bell over the shop door clanged and in walked Lily, school tie loose around her neck, skirt rolled up to mid-thigh and long dark hair carelessly messy.

'Hey you two! Cross country was cancelled thank God! Thought I would find you in here. Am I too late for a chocolate? Hiya little 'un what's that a picture of?'

I went to fetch Lily the same order that we had and listened as my little sister confidently told her that Dad was going to get better because of magic.

'Of course, he will. But you know if you really want that to happen, we could always do a spell and the best place for that is the cave. Have you been to the cave yet Daisy?'

'As a matter of fact, I went there today with Moira. It's amazing and yes Abby, in answer to your next question, I will take you there but promise me girls you don't go there by yourselves. Those rocks are really slippery and if you fell into the water well...'

Abigail's eyes were round with excitement, but Lily nodded solemnly. 'I promise, Daisy. I would never put Abby in danger. Are you going to take that picture to show your dad tomorrow?'

Abigail nodded. 'Yes. It will cheer him up. He promised me that when he came back from the safari, he would take me for a riding lesson for my birthday. That's why I drew it'.

I was cringing inside at this and tried to be very tactful. 'Abby darling, Daddy really might never walk again, however much you wish for it to happen.'

She rolled her eyes. 'Daisy don't be silly. It isn't just me wishing it would happen. Sean said it would.'

'Sean?'

'Yes. He phoned me when you were away, when you were...' she gulped and her voice trembled. 'When you were saying goodbye to Mummy for me. He phoned and asked me what I wanted for my birthday.'

'And you told him'?

'That she wanted to go horse riding with her dad cos he had promised her,' Lily finished for my sister who was looking a bit teary right now. 'I was with her when he rang. She had him on speaker and I heard him say, 'well then Abby, my darling girl, if that is what you wish, then that is what you shall have.'

She mimicked Sean's accent brilliantly, but it was not sufficient to lessen the anger I felt. Did he indeed? No wonder he was not returning my phone calls. I changed the subject as quickly as I could and then we made our way back to the Lodge. It had been a tiring week and I was half longing to see Dad at the hospital tomorrow and half dreading it.

What would his reaction be to Abigail's story and picture? Would it inspire him to not give up, or would it plunge him into a deep depression at the realisation of what the future held for him? The doctors and Uncle Simon had made it clear how remote the chances of him walking again were.

I was filled with trepidation the following lunchtime as Abigail and I set off to the hospital. My state of agitation had not been helped by the fact that just as we were about to leave, Robbie cornered me in the entrance hallway. Lily was by his side, as was Luna; traitorous Luna who positively adored him and was always happy to be left in his care.

'Will you be free this evening then to model for me?' Blunt to the point of rudeness.

'Abby can watch a film with me, can't you Abby?' Lily jumped in and Abby nodded enthusiastically so no escape there.

My little sister made it worse by adding, 'Daddy will think it's a great idea for you to be in another painting. Especially if in this one you are wearing clothes, Daisy!' She ended this on a giggle.

'Aye, it's alright wee' un,' Robbie looked seriously at Abigail. 'I've made a promise to Lily here that I won't take Daisy's clothes off again until we are wed.'

More giggles exploded from Abigail, and I abruptly agreed that I would model for him, anxious to get out before anything more was said. I tried not to think about being alone with him, but it was on my mind all the way to the hospital.

I held on tightly to Abigail's hand as we began the long walk down the maze of corridors, not paying attention to anything other than how was Dad going to react to her picture, and how was I going to get myself out of a marriage proposal. Two even!

'Daisy, are you doing your best to ignore me?'

'Hello Marigold, have you come to see Daddy?'

Abigail tugged at my hand and made me stop. There beside us in the corridor, amongst the bustle of other visitors was my mother.

'Yes, darling I have.'

Wearing a sunflower yellow dress, and with a red and white polka dot scarf holding her mane of cleverly dyed dark hair back from her face, I had to admit my mother was a delightful splash of colour in such drab surroundings. But what on Earth was she doing here?

'I told you,' She said, in reply to my question. 'I am here to see your father. Lead the way Abigail,' she said setting off walking, her red stilettos clicking sharply on the floor.

'I get that,' I continued, as we turned from one corridor into another, 'but this is Inverness, it's not exactly a bus trip away.'

'I know that dear. Which is why I caught the train. Ah, is this the ward? Right, why don't you two go and have some time with your father and I will go and speak to that rather dishy young doctor over there. Off you go.'

I shoved aside the vagaries of Marigold's actions and releasing Abigail's hand I watched as my little sister rushed on ahead to the side room where Dad lay. She seemed better able to cope than I with the sight of him so thin, pale, and trying so desperately to hide the pain he was in. Equally the various tubes, and machines he was attached to did not appear to disturb her either. Ignoring my protests that she shouldn't, she carefully squeezed herself onto the edge of the bed.

'I miss you Daddy.'

'I miss you too angel.' His voice sounded a little stronger than last week and I was grateful for that. 'Hello Daisy,' he turned his head as I hovered in the doorway. 'Come in darling. What a treat to see two of my beautiful daughters. And I believe Rose is in Spain right now?'

I nodded and pulled the chair for visitors close to the bed. 'That's right Dad. She's gone to sort things out with Pablo.'

'I am glad. I think he's the right one for her. Sometimes you don't realise things until it's too late.'

I wasn't quite sure what he was referring to, but it didn't matter as Abigail then gave him her picture.

'I did this at school for you Daddy.'

I hoped she didn't see the flash of pain in his eyes as he read the story and looked at the picture.

'My teacher is silly though, Daddy because she told me that you were not going to walk again, and I told her you were because that's what Sean said, and he always gets things right.'

Dad choked back some tears. 'Do you think I can put the picture here, so I can see it every day until I get better? Would your teacher mind?'

Abigail frowned. 'I'm not supposed to tear out pages of my literacy book. Rory did that and he got into trouble.'

'Oh, give it here,' I took the book and very carefully tore out the picture. 'There you go Dad. It's a lovely picture Abby and I am sure it will cheer Dad up to see it. Don't worry about Miss Gillespie, I'll sort her out.'

'You've changed, Daisy. I like it.' Dad smiled at me and then his eyes widened in surprise. 'Marigold, what the bloody hell are you doing here?'

'I would have thought that was obvious Daniel. Abigail darling, why don't you come with me to get a drink for Daddy and let Daisy have a little chat with him now?'

'How was it then?' he asked as soon as Abigail was out of earshot.

I was still blindsided by the appearance of my mother, and it took a second to realise he was asking about the funeral. I took his hand and gave him a version that I thought would give him some comfort. Then told him about our idea to have a memorial service for Samantha when he was better.

'You think that is going to happen, do you? I will get better?' Ruefully he looked at me.

I looked at Abigail's picture and squeezed his hand. 'One day at a time hey Dad. One day at a time.'

'Exactly!' Marigold came back into the room with Abigail. 'One day at a time, and lots and lots of positive encouragement. Which is precisely where I come in.' She smiled broadly. 'I've finished my floristry course so there is nothing tying me down for now. It's coming up to summer, so I have found a lovely retired couple who want to rent my canal boat until October.'

'I have found a super little maisonette to rent right here in Inverness. It overlooks the river and it's only a hop, skip and a jump from the shops, bus route and train station. I can come and visit you, Daniel, and nip up to

Kinlaggan to see Daisy and Abigail whenever I want. Isn't that marvellous!'

I wasn't sure that Dad agreed with this, but Abigail summed it up succinctly. 'That's super Marigold, because Daddy is going to need all the help he can get to help the magic work.'

'Exactly little one,' said my mother, ignoring my frown and patting my little sister's hand.

'Seriously?' I asked her a short while later. We had both stepped out of the room to give Abigail some time alone with Dad. 'I don't get it. You and Dad fought like cat and dog. You couldn't stand Samantha, not really, I know that. So why go to all this trouble?'

'Oh, Daisy. I thought Sean had done a better job of mending your heart than this. Don't you get it? I know I was a cow to your dad whilst you were growing up, but I explained that was because I felt so damn guilty over what happened to me. I pushed him away because I didn't believe I deserved to be loved by him. But did I ever stop loving him, Daisy?'

She looked at me as though I should not have needed to ask the question.

'You can't wrap love up into neat tidy boxes, Daisy. It's messy and untidy and it doesn't behave how you want it to. Real love, Daisy is like a wildfire, it burns out of control, and it never goes out, even when the flames have died down, the embers still glow.'

Great, I thought as I walked out of the hospital with Abigail holding my hand and skipping along quite happily now. I was caught up between two marriage proposals, my little sister was convinced a miracle was going to happen and my mother appeared to be still in love with my dad after all this time.

Chapter Forty-Two

May brought with it a gorgeous spell of good weather and the realisation that I was utterly useless at facing up to matters relating to the heart. I was practical. Sensible. I had been a teacher for heaven's sake. My father was a doctor. Fair enough, this was offset by Marigold and her Romany blood line, but I told myself that my veins had somehow missed out on that portion. I was not influenced by her tarot cards and crystals in the way that Rose always was. Neither did I consider myself akin to Moira and Lily with their fascination for spells and curses. When my mother asked me what was troubling me, apart from the obvious, and would I like her to use her pendulum to give me an answer, I said no.

Absolutely not.

When Moira suggested lightly that perhaps she could cast a divination spell to help clear my mind over which man to say yes to, I said no.

Absolutely not.

Reluctantly, I had to admit that I did believe in magic. I had to with my tattoo a permanent reminder and Luna as a companion. But, and this was a huge but, I absolutely refused to let it have anything to do with the choice of which man I would say yes to.

Assuming of course that it would be a yes.

I found myself growing ever grumpier as the moods of everyone around lifted in contrast, no doubt as a result of the warmer weather and longer days. Even surly, morose, brooding Robbie was less of a growling bear these days. His hair had started to grow back a little and his beard had come through once more. He was on a mission with his paintings, and they seemed to be going well, so his moods also appeared to be lighter.

I chose to ignore the oft repeated comments from Lily, Catriona and Moira that he was so much better since I had come along. I turned my back on the dagger like stares from Shona that grew sharper every time she overheard. I resolutely refused to acknowledge that time was running out.

'It's not a good look you know,' said Marigold to me one Saturday afternoon at the hospital. I had gone there without Abigail as she was in a whirl of excitement over playing in a school shinty match.

'What isn't a good look?' I replied snappily. Most of my replies were snappy these days.

To my irritation, Marigold and Dad exchanged what could only be described as a smugly parental look.

'Having all that sand in your hair.'

'What sand? I haven't got any sand in my hair.'

A chuckle, would you believe it from Dad. 'I think your mother means from the bucket you are clearly sticking your head into over something.'

I stared at them both. Marigold in her usual flamboyant style was dressed in a purple jump suit which, to her credit, she somehow managed to pull off at her age. Dad looking brighter following a further operation to insert pins into his hips, was wearing new stripy pyjamas that she had bought for him. Really, I thought with some indignation, they had waited until I was in my mid-forties to decide to get their parent act together? Unbelievable. But apparently so.

'Why won't you tell us what's on your mind?' Marigold asked and fingered the crystal she wore around her neck and used as a pendulum.

'There's nothing on my mind! Well apart from Dad obviously, and Abigail.'

'It's nothing to do with that artist fellow you are going to marry then?' Dad explained how Abigail had told him all about it and how Lily and she were in cahoots over what style of dresses they were going to wear as bridesmaids. 'I do hope you will wait until I can come, even if it is in a wheelchair?'

'I haven't said I am going to marry anyone!'

'Ooh is there someone else?'

'No! Yes! Oh, I don't bloody know! For fuck's sake!'

'Menopause,' said Dad knowingly. 'You never used to swear, Daisy.'

'I'll do your cards for you love,' Marigold rooted in her bag.

'I don't know what was worse,' I snapped standing up and preparing to go, 'you two when you were fighting, or now getting on so well. I'll leave you to it.'

Round and round in my head it went, a never-ending circle.

Abigail settled more and more into life at Kinlaggan.

Dad began to look as though he was making progress.

But I was constantly in a spin.

Maybe, I wondered as I drove away from the hospital once more, the reason Robbie was no longer acting quite so crazy was because he had transferred some of his insanity onto me? As I passed the twisted tree where the accident had happened at the beginning of the year, I momentarily considered crashing right into it, if only to stop the crazy train of thoughts in my mind.

Colin was on the phone most evenings.

Robbie had inveigled me into modelling for him.

Colin repeatedly told me he loved me.

Robbie talked about the practicalities of being married to me.

Colin wrote long, poetic letters to me which Luna invariably chewed up.

Robbie stared at me hungrily whilst he painted me, Luna sitting adoringly at his feet.

Colin talked about wanting to make love to me again, leaving me feeling detached and remote.

Robbie crept into my dreams leaving me waking flushed and aroused.

Colin was an absolute gentleman of sound body and mind.

Robbie was a womanising scoundrel of dubious mental state and reputation.

It was enough to drive me to drink, apart from my sense of responsibilities. I was, for the time being, Abigail's surrogate mum. Having missed my own daughter for the last sixteen years, I was not going to ruin that in any way. I had felt guilty at missing her first shinty match, but it had been at her own insistence. She didn't want Dad to not have one of us to see him on a Saturday.

'It's alright, Daisy,' she had said with a glimpse of that cheeky smile that had been missing since her mother died, 'Robbie and Lily are going to come and watch me. If we win, can we all go to tea together?'

Oh Abigail! Do you know I can't refuse you anything at the moment?

When I arrived back at Wolf Lodge to find a triumphant Abigail, freshly scrubbed from the shower as apparently she had been *"as filthy as Sean when we first met him"* – her words and clearly spoken in admiration for this state. I was press ganged into going to tea to celebrate the victory.

It was hard to not feel uplifted by her chirpy mood and considering what she had had to deal with I gave myself a hefty kick up the backside and did my best to make the most of it. Abigail's choice of tea for a treat was pizza and there was a good Italian bistro in the heart of Kinlaggan. As Robbie was driving, I said yes to a large glass of wine. And then another one. It was, I reminded myself a celebration for Abigail after all. When the dessert arrived, along with a sparkler for her, I may well have had a large whisky.

Or two.

I needed something to numb the headache that was a constant friend these days. It would be so easy, I thought, sitting there with the two girls and him, to lose myself and simply say yes. To be Lily's stepmum, wouldn't that really answer my prayers? Looking at this beautiful young girl who could so easily have been my daughter spun my thoughts even faster. How could I even contemplate Robbie's daughter being a substitute for my own?

Wrong. So wrong.

Yet it could be so right.

In the midst of these thoughts my phone sent me a message from Colin, attached with it a photo he had taken of us the day we had been to see the dolphins. With it, a comment that he couldn't wait to tell everyone our good news. I blinked. Had I missed something? Colin's text went on to say how excited he was about us getting married. I hadn't agreed to anything had I?

I ordered another whisky.

'Are you alright? Only you know what happens when you have too much of that stuff?' Robbie said to me as we left the restaurant.

'I am perfectly alright thank you. I just have a headache that's all.'

'Och well I know a good cure for a headache,' he said in a low and disturbingly sexy tone of voice close to my ear.

'Dad, I heard that,' Lily piped up. 'No sex 'till the wedding remember.'

'Is that all grown-ups think about?' Abigail asked pertly, fastening her seat belt.

'No Abby, it is not!' I replied hotly, refusing to look at Robbie who was struggling to control his laughter.

However, later on it was very much on my mind.

Abigail was asleep in the bed she shared with me. The moon was high in the sky and I could not sleep. I had drifted off as soon as my head hit the pillow then woken up with a start. I could see from the flashing light on my phone someone had sent me a message. Surely Colin would not be contacting me now? It was nearly one in the morning. Then I panicked thinking something had happened to Dad. Sitting bolt upright, sleep was instantly gone from my mind.

It was a message from Gary.

Corinne had given birth to a baby girl and they were going to call her Annabelle.

I thought I had completely healed from that angry hurt.

I thought the wound was no longer there. But I was wrong.

I sat on the edge of my bed and my mind went back to that dreadful day when I found out that my daughter had died. Back to another dreadful day when Gary told me he was leaving me, that he was going to be a father. Back to that feeling of emptiness and despair.

Shockingly so.

The moonlight shone through a gap in the curtain landing on Luna's white fur as she lay on the foot of the bed. She raised her head and looked at me. Silently she moved and walked to the door. I had to follow her, knowing without questioning where she was leading me. My footsteps were light on the thick carpet, my hand steady as I turned the handle on the door to the tower.

He was awake as I opened the door.

'You dreaming too?' He didn't seem surprised to see me there. He was standing by the window, looking out into the moonlight wearing only pyjama bottoms. 'Blasted dream I get every time it's nearly a full moon. Pack of angry black wolves snarling at me, coming to get me. Biting at me until I have no choice but to run myself off a cliff or... something.'

A terrible note in his voice that made me shiver.

I was mindful of dreams I had had in a similar vein. Not just the grey wolves that Sean had talked about, these were black and carried desperation of the soul with them.

I shook my head. 'No. I got a phone call that woke me.'

'Ah. Hello beautiful,' he said to Luna as she walked to where he was standing. 'Beautiful white wolf come to chase away the black ones hey?' I watched silently as he stroked her big furry head. Then he raised his eyes to look at me with a question in them. 'I thought we agreed no sex till the wedding.'

'I haven't agreed to anything,' I said, aware of a burning both on my back with my tattoo and deep inside my core. 'Wedding. Sex. Or the lack of it.'

'Yet still, here you are.'

'Still, I am here.'

The air crackled between us. An electrical storm right there in the bedroom. Neither of us moving.

I was the one who gave in.

'Are you going to do anything about it then?' I replied and blaming it on the moonlight, I shrugged off the over long t-shirt I wore for bed and stood there naked.

Did he?

Oh yes.

And then some.

It appeared that abstinence for Robbie was not a natural state of affairs. He swept me up in his arms, crushing me to his chest and sought out my mouth as though I could provide him with cask strength Kinlaggan. His kisses had the same potent effect on me. A couple of minutes was all it took for me to be groaning with need and leaning into him as my knees began to tremble.

Very gothic romantic heroine, all of a flutter and ready to swoon.

Well so would you if you were on the receiving end of such deep and hungry kisses, held within an iron ring of muscled arms and feeling the growing strength of him against your belly. What woman with any shade of red blood in her veins would not react as I did?

With a throaty moan and a whimpering plea.

Please don't make me wait.

Please don't be timid with me.

Please throw me on the bed and fuck me as hard as you can.

I didn't say any of this, I didn't need to. He did just that. Picked me up like a featherweight, pretty much tossed me down on the rumpled covers and with his mouth covering mine he was inside me in an instant.

'Christ, Daisy I've missed this.'

His voice was husky in my ears, lips nibbling and biting at my neck as he clasped my bottom in his hands and pulled me closer and closer still to his quick hard thrusts.

'I've missed it too,' I replied in a few breathy gasps, unable to string the words too close together because of the impact he was having on me.

In me.

Each drive of his hips making me jolt and shudder.

It was a confession I would never admit to in the daylight. But here, now, in this tower room with the light of the nearly full moon streaming in, with the full hard length of him deeply embedded in me, I could not lie.

I had missed this.

I was drugged.

Bewitched.

Spellbound.

Enchanted.

I was all these things, because how else could I behave as I did? How else could I react to him when every brain cell told me he was bad for me; dangerous, mad, cursed? Maybe even criminally insane. I could not possibly react to such a man. I could not possibly want such a man. It could not be me.

It wasn't I told myself.

Another Daisy came to life in his arms.

One that urged him on, swore at him to fuck her harder.

Scratched at the muscles in his back with her nails.

Bit down hard into his neck as her body bucked, shook, and trembled.

Cried out uncontrollably as his last few thrusts verged on the point of brutal.

Another Daisy indeed.

A Daisy who terrified me. Wild. Passionate. Not in control.

Our breathing was hard, ragged, heavy. It took a while for it to settle. I could feel his heart racing against mine as we lay entangled together. He was still inside me making no attempts to move. Thrusting aside the comparison with Colin who withdrew almost immediately, politely enquiring as to whether it had been okay for me, I lay there, weighted down by him.

Claimed by him still.

A part of him.

Where I belonged?

A tiny voice in my mind argued with the feelings of terror that this passion stirred in me.

'By Christ did I need that. I've said it before Daisy, you are one hell of a fine fuck. I've never had better.'

There was the bucket of cold water I needed over my head. I was just providing him with a need. He, at that moment, had just provided me with a need. Which now my heart rate had settled down I felt ashamed of. I had used him in this instance just as much as he had used me. No words of love, just sex, that's all it was. My sense of shame poked at me angrily. Bloody Gary sending me that text in the middle of the night. Couldn't he have waited until morning when I would have been in a less vulnerable state of mind?

I let my anger spill out. 'Well, you're not bad at fucking either,' I said and attempted to shift from beneath him.

I did not mean for him to take it as a compliment. 'Och Daisy, you're definitely the woman for me.' He laughed and before I could protest, he began kissing me once more.

Really not fair, I thought. Really so unfair. I should not now react in such a way. I should feel satisfied and be able to walk away. But that other Daisy was taking over, responding already to his kisses. Shifting my hips, I felt him harden within me once more. Surely it couldn't be as fast and furious this time? He might have the stamina but I'm not sure I did. But no. He teased me back into life, finding a burgeoning rhythm and then surprised me by withdrawing.

Now was the moment to retrieve some dignity and coolly return to my room.

Only I couldn't move as he was still pinning me to the bed, wriggling his body downwards, covering every inch of me that he had painted with kisses. Then he came to the one part he had not painted. With a gentleness that contrasted with before, he parted my legs and then lowered his mouth to begin exploring me with his tongue. Already sensitized from earlier, the feel of his mouth against my flesh sent shockwaves through my body. Instinctively I jolted and tried to move away. This was too much. Too intimate. Too exposing to lose control with him this way.

But he wasn't for having me move, large hands clamping my hips in place and as his tongue circled and probed, I lost the battle in my head. I sank into the sensations, as though I was falling backwards off a cliff, and I really no longer cared about the drop. He could do what he liked. And he did, his hunger for me as arousing as the touch of him itself.

The climax when it came was sharp, so sharp it verged on the painful and I cried out aloud. Then whilst my body was still rippling with the aftershocks he was once more inside me, eyes focused on my face, registering with a glint in them, the effect he was having as I fell apart beneath him.

No control whatsoever Daisy.

Only a couple of weeks ago I was letting Colin make love to me. Lying there with him, letting him think I was going to eventually say yes to his proposals. Staying silent whilst he declared his love for me. And look at you now Daisy! Romping around another bed with a man who fucks you wildly and only wants to marry you for convenience's sake. And I let him! I had somehow, turned into something of a slut and I really wasn't sure I actually could blame it on the moonlight.

Regardless of the reasons for my slutty behaviour – moonlight, magic, malt whisky, any combination of these – I awoke a few hours later in Robbie Munro's bed with the realisation that I could not possibly marry Colin. I was disappointed in myself as I considered what I was giving up, and perhaps even more disappointed in myself as I let Robbie take me once more.

There was a desperate hunger between us that made no sense whatsoever and frankly I was tired of denying it. Rumpled, aching, yet in a state of blissful physical satisfaction, I finally left his room at around five in the morning. I still had some standards I wanted to maintain, and I did not want Abigail waking up without me.

I looked at her still fast asleep and felt my heart bursting with love. Luna gently crept onto the bed beside her. I sat there for a while stroking my wolf and watching my little sister sleeping. In the fresh light of the morning, that damnable moonlight back in hiding, the news that Gary had sent me no longer seemed to matter. Sean's tale of the white and grey wolves popped into my head. I didn't want to feed the grey wolves of bitterness and resentment. The white wolf within demanded that I reach for my phone and send a congratulatory message wishing them both well.

That done, I wondered if it was too early to phone Colin especially on a Sunday. Then I had the sudden urge to go and see him. He was far too nice a man to turn down over the phone. Could I possibly drive down to Glasgow and meet with him face to face? I thought it was the decent thing to do.

Decision made, I went to shower, so aware as I did of Robbie's lingering touch on my body. Never mind my tattoo on my back, I felt like he had tattooed himself all over me. Maybe that was why it had never felt right when Colin had made love to me. Robbie Munro had got there before him and imprinted himself on me. I wiped the soap out of my eyes angry at this thought, not liking how it made me feel. Dressed and refreshed I went once more back to Robbie's room. He was still in bed. A slow lazy grin spread across his face when he saw me.

'Back for more so soon?'

'No!' I snapped at him. 'I need you to look after Abby for me. I have to drive to Glasgow.'

'Glasgow? Isn't that where that bird watching twitcher fellow lives?'

'Yes.'

He smirked. 'You've come to your senses then lassie and realised he can't offer you what I can?'

More like I was completely insane. 'Never mind that. Will you look after Abby for me or not?'

'Aye right enough. Shall I come and sit with her until she wakes?'

'Would you?'

He nodded and went to quickly dress in jeans and a rumpled checked shirt. Then he picked up one of his many sketch pads and some pencils and followed me back to my room.

'Don't fret yourself. I'll look after her until you get back. And Luna of course.'

My wolf was still curled up on the bed next to Abigail and I could see it would make a beautiful sketch. Already he had forgotten I was there, so calm and still with a pencil in his hand. I felt a tiny, tiny, shiver of something that I did not want to put a name to. A feeling that made me feel so scared and vulnerable, and so totally alive at the same time. It could not possibly be called love. Surely?

I slammed the door on that thought and, leaving him to it, went down to my car where I phoned Colin. The whole of the drive I questioned what I was doing. When I met him at the park he suggested, I questioned again what I was doing.

'It's Robbie isn't it?' He said as we sat on a bench together. 'I can tell by your face.'

'I'm so sorry. I had to tell you in person.'

'Does he love you?'

My reply was a blank stare.

'Well do you love him?'

Another blank stare which was not very erudite of me.

'Sex then?'

I blushed and had to look away from his lovely kind blue eyes.

'It could just be an infatuation you know. I understand that. He's a very charismatic man. And I know I am very ordinary.'

'Colin you are far from ordinary! You are one of the nicest men I have known.' I reached for his hand and squeezed it. 'I am so honoured that you would want to marry me.' Tears of genuine regret filled my eyes at this point, and I think it gave him some comfort to see that I was not throwing this away lightly.

'It's just, there is something else between Robbie and me that I can't explain. Not just the sex. Something, just something else,' I finished lamely.

'Something else?' He said with an odd note in his voice. He took his glasses off then to clean them. 'Something else?' He repeated looking at me and I thought I saw a flash of anger in his eyes.

Then he put his glasses back on and I told myself I was mistaken. And if he had been angry, it would have been understandable.

'I really am sorry, Colin. I hope you understand.'

'Oh, I do. I understand perfectly.'

'Will you still come and stay at Wolf lodge? I wouldn't like to think I will never see you again.'

This wasn't perhaps true on my part but I felt I had to throw him a morsel of comfort.

'Don't worry Daisy. I am sure we will see each other again.' He smiled and I felt reassured that we were at least parting on reasonable terms.

I kissed him then, a kiss of farewell and walked away wondering if I had just made the biggest bloody mistake of my life.

Chapter Forty-Three

I had turned down one marriage proposal and in doing so I had boarded a runaway train that I could not get off as it accelerated. I began to see, all of us at Wolf Lodge, began to see a lighter side to Robbie. As though the knowledge that I had ended things with Colin had released something within him.

He would grab at me playfully in passing, robbing me of my breath and my senses as he kissed me so thoroughly it made me dizzy. Then he would laugh. Which in turn made everyone else lighten up their own moods. Catriona was delighted, as was Moira, not to mention the girls. It appeared that I had no escape from the engagement that was coming my way as the weeks ran into one another. With each passing day, it seemed that someone else in Kinlaggan had heard the news.

I was often reminded of the fact that people thought he and Shona were going to marry. I heard far more than I liked about the state of things for her family. It would, I was told repeatedly be a real shame when their family farm was repossessed. This was said as though I had something to do with it.

I did what I was good at and found yet another sand bucket in which to stick my head. Let them all worry and fret about Shona. I certainly wasn't going to. For one thing, I was watching the strain on Abigail's face grow a little deeper each time we visited Dad. His progress was painfully slow. I worried that she put too much store in Sean's magical ability to make things alright.

The other reason I did not pay much attention to Shona and the gossip was because I was losing myself in Robbie. There was a ridiculous charade being played out by all concerned. Robbie and I were pretending that we were absolutely not spending a couple of hours each night in bed together. Lily and Abigail giggled and joked that we were having to behave ourselves until the wedding, although I was convinced Robbie's daughter knew the truth.

Catriona kept giving me wise knowing looks and commenting that she knew her son was never mad. He just needed the love of a good woman. Moira put it more crudely, observing that shagging each other silly was obviously a tonic for someone under the influence of a curse.

Rose, tanned from the time she had spent in Spain, paid us a flying visit with Pablo, sporting a stunning engagement ring on her hand. It seemed that the quiet, thoughtful Spaniard had tamed the rambling rose. The dying grandmother had turned out to be dying after all. Before she had, she had given Pablo her blessing to marry Rose, if he gave up his restaurant in England and returned home to Spain, thinking that Rose would never agree to this. She had not bargained for Rose's thorns. Having decided she was not going to lose her man, she promised there and then that she would sell her salon and move to Spain as soon as possible.

Pablo wanted to visit Dad, to belatedly ask his permission to marry his daughter. Crowded in the small hospital room I couldn't help but wonder at the dramatic changes that had happened within my family in such a short space of time. I had never seen Rose looking so happy. Softer. Gentle. Teasing me with kindness in her eyes, not malice. Gentler too the relationship between Marigold and Dad. The ghost of Samantha was lingering but I suppose the length of time that they had been together before counted for more than I had realised.

'It's all change, kiddo,' said Rose to me in a quiet moment before she set off with Pablo, 'your turn to be happy now. You never were, you know. Not with Gary. He was never right for you. You're a wild flower after all, Daisy. You need a little wildness in your life.'

Me wild?

Well maybe I was.

With Robbie certainly.

Did I set out much hope for our future?

One of those sneaky grey wolves kept darting in and out of my mind. A grey wolf called doubt which reminded me time and time again that

Robbie did not actually love me and that I was a fool for turning down Colin. Surely, I realised that this time of sunshine and laughter with Robbie was a mere interlude and that it would pass as quickly as it had come.

I did my best at these times to push these thoughts away and focus instead on Abigail and Lily. Even then I was besieged by another damnable grey wolf of dissent, another voice taunting me that I was only playing at being a mother. Neither girl was mine to call daughter.

Doubts.

Demons in my head.

My cure for them to seek out Robbie and lose myself in his arms. If this was all a touch of madness and it was not going to last, then I may as well make the most of it whilst I could. I think he felt the same way. There was a desperate greed and urgency to our lovemaking as somehow, we both feared this would not, could not last. Yet still he had not uttered those magic three words I so longed to hear and that Colin had said to me.

'I love you Daisy.'

Three small words that I was desperately hoping to hear before Lily's birthday, before our official engagement. I felt it with his body as he claimed me again and again. I sensed it in his kisses, that left me drunk with desire. I heard it in the cries of release as he poured himself into me. I saw it in the paintings he did of me.

But still, he did not say it.

'I can't live without you now Daisy, you know that don't you.' He said this to me. He said it not only when we were tangled between the sheets, he would say it not caring who heard. 'The madness will go when you marry me. I know it will.'

Catriona beamed when she heard him talk like this. Moira winked and would whisper something quietly about Lily's spell being a success. Shona would look on stony faced and tight lipped. I could say nothing, only respond to the spark in his eyes that lit a fire within me I could not deny. How had I ever thought I was beyond passion? It had hit me in the hardest of ways and it didn't even have to be in the middle of the night for Robbie to suddenly declare he needed me.

Needed.

Not loved.

Needed.

'Shona, take over from Daisy will you,' he said one morning.

I had just got back from doing the morning school run and was ready to do my stint on reception, but Robbie had other ideas.

'I've got to change the bedding in Osprey,' snapped Shona who had her arms full of clean linen.

Robbie displayed that quickfire temper. 'Do it later, I need Daisy now.'

Can I be forgiven for falling prey to the sense of power that gave me? I was a victim of blind infatuation and desire and having already thrown common sense aside in turning down Colin, I may as well be hung for a sheep as for a lamb. So went my train of thought, as ignoring Shona's barely disguised grumblings I let myself be swept away.

We didn't make it to the bedroom.

That, announced Robbie, was too far to go.

He rushed me into the library, slammed the door and locked it behind us. For a second, I remembered that time at when I had first arrived with Sean and Robbie had caught us kissing on the sofa in this room. Then, thoughts of any other man or any other time were robbed from my mind. I was wearing a summer dress and within moments of Robbie closing the door he had me pressed against it, my skirt up and my knickers down.

'Hurry,' I urged him as if he wasn't going fast enough.

Mad like teenagers. I was close to giggling at this thought but saw by the look in his eyes that Robbie was far from giggling. Jeans unzipped and the thick hard length of him exposed he wasted no time in entering me. The shock of it as always made me gasp. That first moment of penetration, the fullness, the heat. It seared into me every time, branding something into my soul.

I was empty without him. Missing a part of me. Only when we were joined as deeply as this did I feel really alive. Completely whole. That was how it had been with him from that very first time in the gardens and that was how it was now. Locked tight together, barely moving, just feeling the heat rise rapidly between us.

Our mouths met and he pressed his lips against mine with the same wild fierceness as he ground his hips against me, hands gripping at my bottom to somehow pull me in deeper and deeper. I moaned against his mouth feeling myself coming even though he had hardly moved within me. He didn't need to. He just had to be inside me. So hard. So full. So close.

His mouth broke free of mine to let out an anguished groan. 'Oh, Christ Daisy, I need you.'

'You have me,' I moaned back. 'You have me.'

'They're close,' he muttered, biting into my neck and thrusting even harder inside of me.

'Who's close?'

I could barely think, reeling as I was from the sudden climax that had turned my legs to jelly and my mind to mush.

'The wolves,' he growled into my neck and then kissed me with the desperation of a dying man. 'The fucking wolves,' he breathed heavily a few minutes later. 'They're coming Daisy, I can feel them. This time they're going to have me, I know it.'

He was pounding me against the door now and anyone walking past must have wondered what in hell was going on. For a second, and then the noises we were making would have made it obvious. I didn't care. All I could care about was the man clinging to me, using me, drowning in him. And he was close to drowning I could see that.

'I won't let them,' I gasped breathlessly between more urgent kisses. 'I won't let them.

'Save me, Daisy. Save me,' tortured words that accompanied the wracking shudders of his body as he came with a force that stunned me.

I held him.

Long silent moments, only our breathing now audible and the rapid beat of our hearts pounding away. He was trembling and not from the aftermath of his orgasm. Fear was rippling through him. Fear had driven him to my arms. Fear was making him weep.

'I'm scared Daisy.'

The wetness of his tears against the skin of my neck rocked me, as did his words. This great hulking brute of a man was crying into my shoulders. It didn't last long. Just a few smothered sobs and then swallowed as hastily as he withdrew from me.

'Robbie?'

I stared at him in confusion, hating seeing the now blank look in his eyes. As though once the heat of passion had gone there was nothing left. Nothing at all. It was frightening to see.

'You must not leave me, Daisy, whatever you do, you must not leave me. I swear I will go over the edge if you do.'

'I'm not going to leave you,' I promised and took him by the hand towards the sofa.

His jeans were still unzipped and that was fine because I had not finished with him, even if he thought he was done. I nudged him backwards until he was sitting down and then before he could say a word I knelt down in between his legs.

'I'm not going to leave you,' I said again and gently took hold of him in my hands. 'Whatever madness is coming I won't leave you.'

Then I could talk no more as I lowered my head and began to softly caress him with my tongue. He was vulnerable now in more ways than one and I used my mouth to show him how much he could trust me.

Cat-like licks along the length of him, recovering quickly from his previous orgasm. I sucked at the taste of us combined, that salty tang of male and female scents. I swirled my lips around the tip of him as he began to pulse and throb once more. Opening my lips as wide as I could I enveloped his hardness into the wet soft cavern of my mouth. It was my turn now to take him as deep as I could in this way. As far as I could go to the back of my throat.

I felt his hands reaching for my head.

Fingers began to tangle in my hair, as his hips rose to meet the rhythm I was playing out with my mouth. I wondered if he would feel the need to press me down harder, but no. It seemed he was content this time to let me fully take control. The touch of his hands on my head remained light, stroking, caressing.

His breathing grew shallower, and I wanted to look in his eyes when he came. As fluidly as I could, I rose up from my knees and shifted to his lap, sliding down upon him and clenching my thighs around him.

'Let me see you,' he said hoarsely and his hands reached for the hem of the dress. Up over my head it went along with my bra tossed to the floor. 'You are beautiful Daisy.' He murmured as he cupped my breasts in his hands, leaning forwards to take one nipple and then the other in his mouth.

I felt beautiful with him.

I felt wild and womanly and beautiful.

Sean had begun to mend my heart.

Robbie had completely captured it.

Gentler now than before and with healing in mind, I rocked with him, rode with him, brought him along with me on wave after wave of sensation as the pleasure built. It was my pace, my tempo and I felt him ease into the comfort I was trying to give him. A comfort that took us to a place where I was cradling his head against my breasts, his hands were holding my waist as the release came in long drawn-out tremors from both of us. Entwined together, slick with sweat, damp with tears, a lovers' embrace.

'When you two have finished there's a phone call for Daisy from the hospital.' A sharp rapping on the door and Shona's cold tones barked through the wood.

'Dad!' I scrambled to get into my clothes. 'I have to take this call.'

'I know.' He went to unlock the door but before opening it, he grabbed me gently by the arms. 'What I said Daisy, I meant it. My head has gone like it has before. I can't stop it. It's a swirling mass of darkness, black wolves tearing me to pieces inside my mind.'

I thought of the dreams he had. The dreams I had. The black outs. The murdered women.

'I don't know what I do at times.'

'I know.'

'It's coming up to a full moon.'

'I know.'

'Are you coming to take this call or not?' Shona again.

I reached up to kiss Robbie swiftly on the lips and whispered into his ears. 'I am not leaving you.' Opening the door, I felt the icy blast of hatred from Shona, and I wondered how long she had been standing there. Had she been listening to our lovemaking? Surely not.

I didn't have time to fret about her feelings now, Dad was more important. Although, when I got to the phone at reception, it turned out it was not that urgent after all. He had been ringing with good news. Having tried my mobile three times and got no answer he had resorted to ringing Wolf Lodge directly.

'The doctors have said it might not be too long before I can start physio,' his voice was the most cheerful I had heard it in weeks.

'Really?' I was staggered at this good news, which was contrary to everything the doctors, including what Uncle Simon had said.

'Hmm I know, it's nothing short of miraculous which is another funny thing I have to tell you. Quite peculiar in fact.'

'Go on.'

'I had a phone call from that Sean fellow last night.'

I pricked up at this. Sean had still been avoiding my calls. 'And?'

'Well do you know, he asked me straight out did I believe in miracles?

Knowing how pragmatic Dad was, I thought I knew the answer to this, but I was wrong.

'I said of course I did.'

'You do?'

He laughed then a sound I had not heard in a long time, and it warmed me down to my toes. 'I'm a doctor and a father of three beautiful daughters. How can I not believe in the miracle that is life!'

'And what did Sean say?'

'That was the odd thing. Now let me get his answer right. Oh yes, he said, "well that's alright then". And blow me this morning, the doctors are telling me they have never seen anyone heal from such injuries quite so quickly.'

I put the phone down both relieved and disturbed by what Dad had told me. Then I was too busy to worry about this as Shona announced that she was going home and I would have to bloody well change the linen in Osprey and cover her evening shift in the dining room as well.

'What do you mean you're going home?'

'Family crisis,' she said with a cold look in her green eyes as though daring me to argue with her. 'Catriona says I can have the rest of the day off. And maybe tomorrow as well.'

Inwardly I was groaning at the thought of the extra work, but I was damned if I was going to let her see that.

'That's fine,' I said with a cheery smile. 'You take all the time off you want.'

'Don't worry. You're not getting rid of me that easily,' she replied with a smile that was most unpleasant. 'You think you've got him all snared don't you, but you don't know everything.'

'I thought you said you had a family crisis to sort?' I really did not have time for her.

This proved to be a mistake on my part. Perhaps if I had taken the time to push her at that moment, I might have been able to prevent what happened next. But I didn't. My head was still scrambled from Robbie's frantic lovemaking and Dad's odd phone call, so I dismissed Shona's comments as sour grapes that would have no effect on me at all.

How wrong I was.

Chapter Forty-Four

It seemed that the dark wolves were not just snapping at Robbie over the next few days.

In the build up to the summer solstice, which coincided with Lily's sixteenth birthday and the next full moon, the weather also took a wild and unpredictable turn. The skies were grey and heavy. The gentle summer breeze became gale force winds that ripped up trees and carelessly tossed broken branches in the way of any unsuspecting driver. The downpours when they came, filled the rivers to the point they became overflowing raging torrents.

Mother Nature was having a rare old fit of temper.

The atmosphere at Wolf Lodge was no better.

No amount of sex pulled Robbie back from his depression, and it was not for lack of effort on my part. We communicated with our bodies but the light-hearted side that had only just begun to appear had vanished as quickly as the summer sunshine. He hardly spoke and was brusque and offhand with everyone apart from Lily and Abigail. His daughter watched him like a hawk and pleaded with me to do something.

'I can't bear it when he's like this Daisy. Can't you just hurry up and marry him so that it makes him better?'

She asked me this one day as we came back into the Lodge after collecting her and Abigail from school. Shona was on reception with a couple of guests checking in. Robbie came down the stairs, Luna at his side. It was his routine to paint in the afternoons and then take a break when his daughter came home from school. It had become our family time together, Abigail blending seamlessly into the mix. Only today it was apparent that not even Lily was on his mind as he came to an abrupt halt in the middle of the entrance foyer.

'Who the fuck are you?'

This was churlishly addressed to the young couple who had booked the best room for their honeymoon.

Shona opened her mouth to speak but he continued with a rapid fire of insults.

'What do you think this is, a fucking hotel?'

The young man, a burly looking fellow in his thirties put a protective arm around his new wife and replied sharply.

'I should fucking hope so the amount of money I am paying. But if you don't want my money, I can take it elsewhere. I'm not having my wife spoken to like that. Not on her honeymoon.'

'Dad!' Lily rushed to his side and tugged at his arm.

Alarmingly he shrugged her off, a blank look coming into his eyes, replacing the fury of moments ago.

'Who are you?'

'Dad!' Lily turned her eyes to me in horror.

'We'll be leaving then,' announced the male guest as his wife understandably declared she didn't want to stay.

Shona it seemed was incapable of halting them and torn between going to Lily's side or preventing the guests from departing, I chose the latter.

'No please wait, let me take you straight to your room and of course dinner tonight will be on the house by way of an apology. Mr. Munro is not very well at the moment.'

Robbie was still staring wildly around him as though he didn't even recognise his surroundings let alone anyone in them.

'I might consider staying if dinner was included every night,' the newly married Mrs Frodsham then announced, receiving an approving nod from her husband.

For a second, I could not reply as Robbie suddenly came to life and marched out of the lodge into a torrential downpour, Luna at his side.

'Dad!' Lily called after him. And then she turned once more to me. 'Daisy, stop him!'

'Well? Can you do that? Dinners included all week?' Mr Frodsham pinned me down, the chance of a bargain break, more appealing than taking the moral high ground.

'Yes of course we can,' I smiled sweetly, biting down the impulse to snap at them. 'Let me show you to your room.'

'Daisy!' Lily called after me but right now I had to try and salvage what reputation we had left.

Having mollified the newlyweds and settled them into their room, I found Lily and Abigail taking refuge in the kitchen where Alex was supplying them with large quantities of hot chocolate and cake.

Five months into me living at Wolf Lodge, Alex now at least would shyly say hello to me but other than that he preferred not to speak and carried on with preparing the meal for later.

'Do you think I can have some of that?' I asked eyeing the huge cake that the girls seemed intent on demolishing between them.

Lily scowled at me but slid the plate across the table.

'You're going to change your mind, aren't you? You're not going to marry him after all.'

I couldn't think of anything to say. I had never seen him so unbalanced. I delayed my response by greedily shoving a huge piece of the cake into my mouth, desperately needed the sugar fix.

'You promised you would save him, Daisy, you promised.'

Had I been so stupid as to make such a promise?

'If you really loved him, you would have gone after him, not looked after those stupid guests!'

Did I really love him? It seemed so bloody complicated. I questioned once more my decision in turning down Colin's proposal. I could have been planning a nice simple wedding to a normal, ordinary man, with no madness to consider, or curses, or murder charges! How easy would that have been?

The doubt must have shown in my eyes as Lily then hotly declared, 'You're going to leave, aren't you?'

The pain in her voice got through to me. I pulled myself together. 'Lily, I had to stop those guests from leaving. You know how difficult things are with the Lodge. The last thing your dad and your grandmother need is for anymore bad reviews. What else could I do? And really, could I have stopped your dad?' I spoked as gently as I could but with a firmness that necessary to penetrate her anguish.

'I suppose so,' she said quietly and pulled the plate back towards her for another slice.

'Don't get upset Lily.' Abigail was sitting with the battered teddy who never left her side apart from when she was at school. 'Angus told me everything will be alright.'

The spikiness that Lily had briefly displayed, so like her father, melted away in the face of Abigail's innocent remark.

'Oh well, if Angus says everything will be okay then I am sure it will be.'

'Not just Angus. Sean said it would be alright too.'

Bloody Sean I thought, grumpy with him suddenly. I knew that my mood was mostly because I considered myself to be at fault. I had let Lily down in going along with the idea that I could change her father, make him better, break this curse, clear his name, whatever!

I could no more do that than Sean could make miracles happen in the way he had promised Abigail that Dad would be well enough to walk and even take her horse riding one day. Regardless of Dad's recent sudden improvement, it was a load of horse shit.

Irish baloney and charm.

Oh really?

The tattoo on my back prickled and burned.

Really Daisy?

All those co-incidences leading you here.

Really?

Another headache began to drum inside my skull.

A two-legged version of one came into the kitchen in the form of Shona. 'I need to speak you.'

'Go on then.'

She shook her head. 'No, I need to speak to you in private.'

Thinking there was going to be some other family drama of which a lot seemed to be occurring lately resulting in her darting off at odd times of the day, I gave her a nod and told her I would be with her in a minute. I needed to at least finish my cake!

'Well then,' I said to her having made her wait a good ten minutes when I went back out to reception.

She had a sly look on her face. 'You should have come quicker. There was a message from the hospital. Your Dad has taken a turn for the worse. You have to go straight away.'

'Bloody hell Shona why didn't you say!'

'I didn't want to upset Abigail.' I doubted this was true although I was glad she had spared my sister this news.

Even so, she could have made me understand it was urgent in some way.

'Why haven't they rung me directly?' I asked checking my phone whilst rushing around to grab my bag and my coat.

'You know what reception is like here when there's a gale,' said Shona and she was right in this.

'Any sign of Robbie at all?' It was till sheeting down outside and even though it was barely five o clock the sky was grimly dark.

'No,' she replied looking at me with an odd expression on her face. 'Well, are you going to stand there dilly dallying wondering about Robbie or are you going to get going and see if your dad is dying? You don't want to be too late, do you?'

I gave in. 'Oh fuck off Shona.'

My satisfaction in expressing my feelings lasted as long as it took me to race to my jeep getting soaked in the process. My fingers were shaking as I fitted the key in the ignition and then switched the wipers on full speed. I hated driving in weather like this, and briefly considered trying to ring the hospital to double check. Then I thought of the time I had already wasted eating cake.

Eating cake Daisy whilst your dad could be dying!

Oh God please don't let him be dying, I prayed as I pulled away from Wolf Lodge into the howling storm. Then an even more desperate plea. If he was dying, please let me get to him in time. A flash of lightening made me jump, quickly followed by a crack of thunder. Somewhere out in this was Robbie Munro wandering like a madman. Another prayer to the almighty.

Please God keep him safe from harm.

A second one. Please God don't let him harm anyone else.

Don't let him be a killer.

Then no more thoughts of prayers other than please let me get to the hospital safely.

The road from Wolf Lodge to Kinlaggan, where I could pick up the main route to Inverness, was bad at the best of times and this was about the worst driving conditions possible. Even allowing for the four-wheel drive Jeep, I still felt nervous as I negotiated each twist and bend of the unlit road, praying that I would not meet any of the logging trucks coming in the opposite direction.

Thankfully, the timing was on my side at least. By now most local work traffic would have gone for the day and no tourist would be stupid enough to venture out in weather like this. I didn't meet a single vehicle until I approached that notorious bend where Robbie's father had killed himself and I had crashed into the same tree.

I always slowed down at this point and I was glad I had done so now. Half across the road with its hazard lights on was what looked to be a camper van. The rain was so heavy it was hard to tell. My heart immediately swelled with relief.

Sean!

Somehow, he was here, and everything would be alright. My earlier temper with him disappeared in a flash. I braked carefully and pulled into the passing place at the side of the road.

'Sean is that you?' I yelled above the racket of the rain.

The bonnet of the vehicle was up, and a figure hunched over. He was wearing a long wax jacket with a wide brimmed hat pulled down low over his face. I smiled to myself thinking how much Sean loved his hats.

'You've grown a beard,' I said to him as I caught the first glimpse of his face.

Then I realised it wasn't Sean.

'Sorry I thought you were someone else?'

'Did I disappoint you with that as well Daisy?'

I knew the voice but not the face.

'Sorry?' The rain was coming so hard now I had to wipe it from my eyes it was dripping from the hood of my coat.

'I said did I disappoint you with that as well Daisy? I just can't compete with Robbie, can I?'

'Colin?'

He looked different. A growth of beard and no glasses. But even allowing for that it was the expression on his face that made him hard to recognise.

'I told you I would see you again,' he said as he released the prop on the bonnet and lowered it shut with a slam.

Then he moved towards me quickly, raised his right arm and my skull exploded with pain.

Chapter Forty-Five

The wind was howling and the rain was lashing against the window. I sensed that I was not in my bedroom. I was dreaming I concluded, succumbing to the heaviness of the pounding in my head. Dreaming a jumbled nightmare of being bundled up into a dark confined space. Of movement that made the pain in my head worse and nausea rise in my throat. Tumbling from where I was lying to fall with a bump on the floor of the ship.

I was in a ship?

It felt like it was rocking so maybe I was.

In the dark hull of a ship?

Rolling around the floor like a loose parcel.

Definitely a parcel.

I had turned into a parcel.

All neatly tied up with a ribbon round my mouth.

Not a ribbon, a gag.

Not a ship at all.

Not a dream but a horrifying nightmare.

I choked back the vomit that threaten to spill out through the material that was tight around my mouth. Awareness filtered through the grogginess of my head. Absolute dark, no light whatsoever. Movement yes there was that, and engine noise. More bumping and bouncing around and I rolled once more, banging painfully into something. I seemed to be wedged in a small space but when I tried to move properly, I realised that the sense of being a parcel was due to the fact I was tied up.

Fear then swamped me and churned my stomach.

I could no longer hold back the nausea and vomit spewed against the cloth, spilling back into my mouth. I coughed, choked and spluttered and levered myself to a semi upright position, retching as I did so. Some light did then wash over my surroundings. A flash of lightning gave brief illumination. It was enough to at least make out that I was in a camper van similar to the one Sean had.

Full recognition then.

Colin.

Colin had been there, looking very different but it had been him. I felt the pounding in my head which increased as the knowledge hit me as hard as whatever he had used to knock me out. Colin had tied me up and was driving off with me.

It was too ludicrous to consider, and a hysterical snort escaped my lips. Yet consider this I must. There was no denying the discomfort I was feeling with my hands and feet tied up tightly. Or the sour smell of vomit that now clung to my nostrils with the sodden gag in my mouth. No denying any of these facts.

Colin had knocked me out, tied me up and abducted me.

Abducted, raped, stabbed.

The fate of three women all with connections to Robbie Munro.

My mind went into blind panic. Heart rate shot up in terror. Sweat broke out on my body.

I willed myself to go back to sleep. This was a nightmare. It was not real. If I went back to sleep, then I could wake up again and I would be back in my room at Wolf Lodge. But every bump of the road, every turn the van took, every jolt that rammed through my body, told me this was no dream, no nightmare. This was real. Eventually we came to a halt and the sliding door on the side opened.

A torch shone into my face, the only light in surrounding darkness.

I screeched something unintelligible at him from behind the gag.

He climbed into the van and sat on what I made out to be the bench that I must have fallen off earlier.

'What was that Daisy? Oh, I do apologise, here let me remove this. You seem to have made a mess of yourself, how unfortunate.' He shone the torch over me, speaking as though addressing a careless child, not a woman he had just abducted.

'What the fuck are you doing Colin?' I ground out once he had removed the gag.

'Hhm. Good choice of words Daisy. What the fuck am I going to do with you once I have fucked you? Because that's what you like isn't it? Only you like it best with Robbie Munro don't you. I wasn't good enough for you, was I? You're such a disappointment Daisy. I thought you were going to be different.'

His calmness was more chilling than anger would have been. Or so I thought. His next words told me just how much danger I was in.

'I was going to marry you, Daisy. I bought you a ring! I didn't do that with the others. You were special. You were going to be the one who stopped it all. But you had to go and spoil it didn't you, you stupid bitch!'

He leant down towards me then, spittle dropping from his mouth onto my face which he gripped painfully in one hand, fingers pressing hard into my jaw.

'Why did you have to be like the others Daisy? Hm. Tell me why?'

I couldn't answer, his grip was vice like.

'You could have been my wife!' he hissed. 'But you threw yourself at him, just like Kayleigh. You betrayed me, just like she did!' He finished this with a blow across my face that split my lip and brought blood into my mouth, a metallic taste on top of the vomit.

'Kayleigh?' I croaked thinking that the more I kept him talking, the more I had a chance to escape.

Wrong thing to say. His face darkened, eyes narrow and cold without the shield of his glasses.

'She betrayed me. It wasn't my baby. It was his! She taunted me with it, said I wasn't man enough to father a child.' He laughed then. 'That was when I pushed her downstairs. I was sorry afterwards of course. It was too quick. She didn't realise what was going to happen. I was so cross with myself. She deserved to be punished and I had robbed myself of that chance.'

'You said she had fallen because of her slippers.' I don't know why I said this, it was irrelevant really.

'I could hardly tell you the truth now Daisy, could I? I thought you were cleverer than that. Then again, you fell for Robbie so that puts you in the same bracket as Kayleigh. Only you were supposed to be different! Don't you realise I fell in love with you!'

He swiped at me again, the other side of my head taking the blow this time.

'I was going to take you anyway, but it could have been different if you had just said yes to my proposal. Why didn't you say yes Daisy? I could have saved you then. You wouldn't have had to die like the others, you stupid bitch. Stupid. All you had to do was to say yes and then I would have taken Shona instead.'

I spat the blood from my mouth. 'Shona?'

Another laugh, a very unpleasant sound. 'Stupid woman. Any fool could see she was trailing after him like all the others. She was going to be my next one. All the women pathetic enough to fall for the charms of Robbie Munro. And the best thing of all, as I realised on my first trip to Kinlaggan, was his own reputation. That ridiculous story of a curse and his own behaviour fell right into my hands. He was the perfect suspect especially as he was the only link between the women.'

'But why?'

'I told you! Because of Kayleigh. That bastard met my wife at one of his exhibitions in Glasgow. He stole her from me, and then she mocked me. Robbie Munro fathered a child with her when I couldn't.'

As sickening as it was, I began to see the whole picture. 'So, you decided then to what, murder every other woman that he got involved with, to punish Kayleigh and him together?'

'Clever don't you think. Especially as the bastard is convinced he is mad anyway.'

'But you mentioned Shona.'

'Of course, but then I saw you with him that day when I arrived at Wolf Lodge. Do you remember, you were walking with him and his daughter?'

I remembered the moment we had met. 'What made you change your mind?'

'I saw the way he was looking at you. I could easily have taken Shona and will do so when I have finished with you, but I could see how he really wanted you. So, you had to be the one.' Then another explosion of mad fury. 'But you made me fall in love with you! And you turned me down!'

'I'm sorry, I'm sorry,' I said cowering from the blows that now rained down on me as much as the rain lashed against the sides of the camper van.

'Oh you're always sorry, aren't you? Always sorry when you realise your mistake. But sorry just isn't good enough.'

He was breathing heavily now and all traces of the mild-mannered Colin I thought I had known had vanished. He gave me another resounding clout around the head that sent me dizzy and then I felt tugging around my ankles, a sudden sharp hot rush of pins and needles as my legs were loosened from the rope. But before I could possibly move, I was weighted down with him kneeling across me.

'No!'

His hands reached for the zip of my jeans. This could not be happening. I thought back to that time after the funeral. I had been drunk and confused him in my mind with sixteen-year-old Billy my first real boyfriend. I wanted to cry. This was not Billy, nor was this the Colin I had been with that time, the man whose lovemaking had left me detached and unmoved by his lack of passion.

I had felt nothing then but this time I was going to feel pain. It was too dark to see his eyes, but I could feel it in the rough way he ripped down my jeans. There was a cold sting of something metal and I winced. He had cut through my knickers with a sharp blade. I swallowed hard at the details I had read about the other women.

Repeatedly stabbed.

'Please don't,' I was not above begging.

'It's too late Daisy. It's your own fault. All… your… own… fault.'

These last words were accompanied by jabbing pains as he began to thrust himself inside me. Instinctively I backed away and he responded by slamming my head brutally on the van floor. I stopped struggling then and lay limply in a heap telling myself it would soon be over.

It was. As suddenly as it had begun, I felt him shrivel within me. He continued thrusting away his breathing becoming as frenzied as his attempts to drive deeper inside me. He was failing.

Laughing was not a good idea. But it slipped out more of a disdainful snort. I was being raped by a man with a doughy soft dick.

Laughing was a really bad idea.

Seconds later I was screaming with pain.

Something hard, solid, rigid was being rammed deep inside me.

'Is that hard enough for you Daisy, is that how you like it?' He pressed me down with his weight, his breath hot on my face as he continued to ram the object in and out in a sick parody of sex.

Red hot pain was making me whimper and I had to then beg in earnest. 'Please, please stop, I'm sorry I laughed. I promise I won't laugh again.'

He was laughing though, a triumphant sound. Whatever it was he had used he pulled it roughly out of me. I felt the wetness that must have been blood trickling between my legs and then once more he took his turn. Only this time he was hard enough and used it to punish and humiliate me, adding pain and injury to what he had already inflicted.

There was no way I could possibly compare him to Billy now.

He left me numb and trembling when he had finally finished.

'Now,' he said softly as he tied up my ankles once more but left my jeans pulled down around my knees. 'Tell me that was better than Robbie.'

I bit my lip to stop myself screaming at him that he could never be the man Robbie was. I played dumb only that didn't work either.

'Tell me that was better than Robbie!' he shouted, and I felt that object jabbing at me again.

'It was better than Robbie,' I screamed at him.

'I think you're lying.'

'No, no I'm not,' I sobbed. 'It was better than Robbie. You are better than Robbie.'

'Hhm. Pity you didn't think that before. Never mind. We can have our fun now can't we.'

He moved around the van and then a small light came on. I saw then the object that he had had in his hands that he had used on me. It was his torch.

He caught me looking at it and smiled. 'I could have used the spanner I hit you with. Which would you prefer next time? I'm not that inconsiderate Daisy, I will let you choose your own sex toy, if you are good.'

I rolled over to my side then and vomited on the floor.

Chapter Forty-Six

It happened multiple times that long dark terrifying night.

As much as it was brutal, agony beyond humiliation, I kept myself going at the thought that whilst he was doing that, I was still alive. I was not being sliced with a knife or stabbed until I bled out like a pig. In between, I had to listen to the rest of the story. Morning was approaching, not that there was any real light coming into the van with its blackout blinds fully down. But the storm had abated, and I could hear birds singing.

I wondered if Robbie had got back to Wolf Lodge last night. I had not stopped wondering about him. At the foulest of moments when Colin was hurting me the most, I forced my mind to take me to the shelter of Robbie's arms. How could I have got it all so horribly wrong? He was my harbour and Colin the terrifying storm that would dash me onto the rocks; not the other way round as I had once thought.

Stupid, stupid Daisy.

What would Robbie be thinking now?

What about Dad?

I groaned out loud as I remembered what had been blocked from my mind with the shock.

'Dad.'

'What? Oh, your dad. He isn't dying don't worry. That was just the ruse I needed to get you to drive out alone.'

My throat was parched, he had barely given me anything to drink, just a few sips of water, my head was spinning from the blows, and I felt sick with the pain that was burning inside me, but I had to ask.

'What do you mean? It was Shona who gave me the message.'

'Ah yes Shona. Have you any idea how much she hates you?'

I wriggled around on the floor to try and ease some of my discomfort whilst he talked down at me from his seat on the bench.

'She's prepared to do anything you know to marry Robbie and have his money. I realised this when I rang and spoke to her to cancel my reservation in May after you rejected my proposal. She asked me if there was any way I could persuade you to change your mind. I asked her how far she was prepared to go. Rather a long way it would seem.'

'I don't understand.'

'We met up. Not at Kinlaggan of course, that would have been stupid. She said she wished that you would end up like the other women who Robbie had been involved with and I told her that could be arranged.'

I stared at him in horror. 'She said that?'

'She really doesn't like you.'

'She knows you killed the other women?'

'I did not directly tell her this, but yes I think she realised. The stupid woman didn't think to consider that I would go back for her once I had dealt with you. I am not going to stop until Robbie Munro gets thrown into prison or kills himself. But she provided me with the perfect way to get to you. We arranged that I would come up and stay in the area and she would monitor both your movements and his and when the time was right, she would let me know.'

It took a while for me to process this, but Colin seemed happy to sit there regarding me smugly whilst I absorbed it.

'But what is everyone going to say when I don't return?'

'Ah well, that's where we are going to have a little fun. You see, Shona told you that the hospital had rung. But no one else knew that did they? She will tell everyone else that you have had cold feet about marrying Robbie and that you have run off with me instead. That should be enough to send Robbie over the edge and in a day or so once I have finished with you, I will go back for Shona. I let the police find the other bodies, but I am afraid my dear Daisy I will have to bury you. I'm going to leave Shona at Wolf Falls of course. That will fit nicely with that story of the curse and put even more suspicion on Robbie.'

I was stunned.

He talked so calmly, as though he had thought through every detail, and it seemed he had. But one point stuck out and I dared to voice it thinking it might buy me some time.

'What if they don't believe Shona. Lily will never believe her even if her father does.'

'I am so glad you mentioned that. Both points in fact. Which is why you are going to make a telephone call to let them know that it is true and that you are coming with me to get married and will not be returning.'

There was a certain logic to this I supposed, and I saw the chance to get help by making that phone call. An idea that was quickly squashed.

'And don't think about trying to tell them the truth. If you do that you will only put Lily in danger.'

'Lily?' I went cold thinking of Colin getting his hands on her.

'Don't be stupid. I don't want her. But neither does Shona,' he smiled nastily. 'She is quite prepared to hurt Lily if she doesn't get what she wants, which is to marry Robbie. Yes, she is that cold. I rather like that about her. It's a shame I am going to have to kill her when this is over. It would be tempting to wait a while and see if she gets rid of the child anyway. After all, if she does end up snaring Robbie, the last thing she will want is for his brat to inherit Wolf Lodge which would be natural, so yes possibly, I might take my time with her and see how that plays out. It will be interesting to see if she does have in it her to kill. Not everyone does you know.'

I was already cold with fear, pain and shock. Now I felt my blood freezing.

'So, you had better sound convincing then when you make your phone call. May as well do it now. It's morning.'

He had already got my phone and asked me what the code was to unlock it. There was no point lying so I told him whilst I tried to think as rapidly as I could.

'Hm, Robbie, here we are, here's the number.'

'I won't be able to convince him!' I said quickly. 'Even if I try, he will know something is wrong. And Lily won't believe me either, no matter what I say but please don't let Shona hurt her. I will speak to my mother and tell her, and she can let everyone know. They'll be more likely to believe her, just please don't let Shona hurt Lily.'

'You could be right. You are sounding a little hysterical right now.'

Really?

'I can't find your mother on the contact list.' He scowled at me.

'Speed dial number three.' I told him and waited breathlessly as he pressed the number.

'No funny business,' he reminded me and put it on speaker.

'Bloody hell Daisy it's a bit early to phone. What's the matter?' Marigold's voice sounded sleepy and not surprising as she was a night owl, not usually rising till at least nine.

'Mum I have some news for you, I couldn't wait to tell you Mum.' I said praying she would not give me away.

More alert now I heard her voice. 'Go on I'm listening.'

'There's been a change of plan. Do you remember you did my tarot cards for me Mum and you said I had to make a choice between two men? Well you were so right Mum, and that's exactly what I have done. I was making a big mistake choosing Robbie, Mum, just like Rose made that terrible mistake over Pablo, do you remember how she got that so wrong. Well, that's just what I have done with Robbie. I am going to marry Colin instead. So can you please tell Robbie for me, because I just can't face him, he scares me Mum, really scares me. So can you do that?'

'Are you with Colin right now?' Marigold's voice asked calmly and clearly.

He said in a barely a whisper, 'Tell her the battery is dying.'

'The battery is dying Mum. I have to go now. I love you so much.'

'That wasn't so difficult was it. I can just picture the scene when your mother telephones Robbie with that news.'

I closed my eyes hiding the hope that Marigold would be able to make sense of my ramblings. Then my thoughts went to Robbie. Had he made it home last night? Given the state he had been in he could be anywhere. What if he had already succumbed to the depression and despair and ended his life? The fear of that thought was almost enough to overshadow the danger I was in.

'Now, how shall we pass the time Daisy?' I hated the way he laughed then. 'Oh, look at yourself. In fact, do you know I think I will take a photo so you can see how degraded you look. There you go, smile now for the camera. I said smile,' this was accompanied by a kick to my stomach.

I sucked in my breath against the pain and twisted my mouth into a grimace of a smile.

'Not so much of the pretty wildflower now are you Daisy?' He showed me the image of a woman I did not recognise.

'You'll be even less pretty by the time I have finished with you,' He put the phone to one side and fingered the knife that was never far away. 'But I don't want to get covered in blood just yet so don't worry, we can just resume our other fun and games. But Daisy you must realise now, any noise from you and I will kill you instantly. It's daylight and although we are well off any track, you know how people ramble up here.'

'Where exactly?'

'In the forest at the top of Wolf Falls. I rather liked the idea that you could be so close to home and suffering so horribly, dying on the doorstep. So near and yet so far Daisy, so near and yet so far.'

Wolf Falls.

I thought of the first time I had seen them.

The painting in Michaela's studio.

I thought of my wolf tattooed on my back.

Luna!

How had I not thought of her before?

Luna who had disappeared into the storm with Robbie. Where was she now?

I called to her silently. I felt my back beginning to burn as Colin released the ties around my ankles which meant he was going to rape me again. He had removed my clothes during one of the other assaults along with my boots and socks. I was naked, battered, bleeding, my hands still tied. I was as vulnerable as it was possible to be.

But I had a wolf tattooed on my back.

A wolf that was part of me.

I screamed out silently to her.

She answered with the heat in my back and a rage within me that was savage and wild.

He knelt down exposing himself as soft and flaccid, torch in hand ready to injure me until my pain made him hard.

It was my turn to inflict pain.

Luna's strength and speed, not mine.

Bare feet that snaked back quickly to then snap forwards and kick him right on that soft handful of flesh. Killer or not, he doubled up in agony. I aimed another blow from the floor at his head and he staggered to one side.

Awkwardly I stumbled to my feet. I had seconds, if that. He grabbed at my left ankle, and I nearly went down. Wildly I stomped on his throat winding him enough to release his grip on me. My hands were still bound, and I fumbled with the catch on the door praying that he had not locked it. He hadn't and I fell backwards out of the van onto the forest floor, pine needles and fallen branches the least of my worries as they prickled my naked skin.

Now I had to run and run I did.

Like my wolf.

Sure footed and fast with breath in my lungs that carried me beyond my own weakened state.

The wolf within me ran for her life.

Chapter Forty- Seven

I ran blindly, yet not blind.
   I knew where I was going.
   She knew where she was going.
   To where this had all begun.
   To a waterfall where a wolf had been killed and a curse had been laid.
   To a waterfall with a cave that I hoped to hide in until it was safe to come out. I knew I could not make the distance all the way back to the Lodge, not even with Luna's magic speeding me on. He must have known where I was going, of course he would. It was the straightest route back to the Lodge.
   Soon I could hear the racket of someone following me in haste. Ahead of me I could hear the falls. Would I get there in time to disappear behind the waterfall without him seeing? Surely, he would not know about the cave. I was doomed if he did.
   Doomed it seemed I was.
   The energy that had got me out of the van and away from him was dwindling. The forest floor seemed determined now to trip me up, the branches clawing at me, slowing me down. Magic could only go so far I thought as I sobbed out Luna's name in desperation. My legs were like jelly and every step I took jarred my whole body with pain.
   But I wouldn't stop running.
   No matter how feeble my progress now was, I would not give up. I would not fall to the floor and wait for him to finish me off. I would not give him that satisfaction. At last, the trees thinned out and the waterfall

came into view. Which meant that I could run a little faster now. It also meant I was clearly visible to Colin if he was not far behind.

I had missed my chance of seeking shelter in the cave.

As I made my way towards the rocks at the edge of the tumbling falls, he came out of the forest and saw me. I froze for a moment, caught in the freezing spray from the waterfall, my trembling limbs shaking in earnest now. My feet slipped a little on the wet rocks and I saw him smiling.

'You aren't going to get away from me Daisy.'

Fight, flight, or freeze.

I had fought.

I had taken flight.

I had now frozen.

My eyes fixed upon his and he calmly walked towards me. I was locked rigid in fear, unable to move a muscle apart from shivering wildly.

'Daisy!'

I couldn't even turn my head to look. That knife was glinting at me, as shiny as the mad look in Colins' eyes.

'You're too late Munro!'

Colin shouted down the steep hillside from the top tier of the waterfall to the bottom where I was guessing Robbie now stood. He leapt to join me on the rock at the edge of the falls and pulled me to him, the knife now at my throat. I felt the prick of it nicking my skin.

'For the love of God let her go!'. Robbie shouted hoarsely, his voice breaking as the wind carried it up to me. Anguish and pain ripping through every syllable.

'You can watch me as I kill her.'

It didn't seem to matter to him now that this would unravel his neatly laid plans. His joy would be in seeing Robbie's face as the knife slid across my throat. He turned me around so that I could see Robbie and he would see the fear on my face. I felt him harden against me, sickened that he was aroused.

Sickened and terrified.

This was going to be my final moment.

'Daisy!' Robbie shouted once more as he raced to climb up to me.

'You won't be quick enough!' Colin laughed.

No. He would not. But a wolf brought to life from a tattoo. A wolf who could only be magic. Yes, she could move quick enough.

Through the misty spray of the waterfall, she launched herself at him, knocking us both to the floor. I rolled as far away as I could without falling over the edge.

He screamed and rolled, the knife still in his hands as her jaws clamped around his throat.

Then they both fell over the edge into the raging torrent.

"Though the misty spray of the waterfall, she launched herself at him, knocking us both to the floor. I rolled as far as I could without falling over the edge."

"He screamed and rolled, the knife still in his hands as his fingers clamped around his throat."

"Then they both fell over the edge into the raging torrent."

Chapter Forty-Eight

Churning, roaring, white water.

The falls were in full spate after the storm.

Luna and Colin were swallowed up disappearing into the foaming white mass.

A white raging beast that torrented down the craggy route of the rocks, in three distinct tiers of which I was at the top and Robbie at the bottom.

'Robbie!' I screamed above the thundering power of the water.

He had seen Luna fall in.

He had shouted her name.

He had not hesitated.

He dived into the water at the lowest level, not quite as tumultuous there but deadly nevertheless. Then bobbing up like two corks out of the froth, the prone bodies of Colin and Luna, no longer tangled together. Each motionless and a horrifying amount of red now swirling in the water and turning it pink.

'Luna!'

I screamed hoarsely and hobbled on shaking legs down the narrow treacherous path that would take me to the bottom level. My hands were still bound, and my balance was unreliable. Twice I stumbled, slipped on the wet rocks covered partly in lichen and moss. My breath was painful in my lungs, chest tight with fear and dread. By the time I made my pitiful progress and reached the lower level where the rocks flattened out and the water was slighter calmer, they had all gone. Robbie, Luna, Colin, swept down river and out of sight.

I sank to my knees and howled in despair.

Get up Daisy, get up!

A voice within me urged me to my feet, bleeding and sore as they were now after my barefoot run through the forest. I carried on, praying over and over that Robbie and Luna would both be safe. Luna loved the water, she loved swimming.

She would be fine.

She had to be.

The blood was Colin's.

Only his.

I told myself this over and over as I weaved my way along the river path, which at least was now on the flat. I knew that in a while the river came to a slow shallow bit where, in dry weather, it was almost possible to wade safely across it and for children to paddle in from the pebbly banks.

Please God, bring them to safety.

I should have been surprised to see Sean standing there, but I wasn't.

Nothing could surprise me anymore.

He was wading in the water towards the floating forms of Robbie and Luna. It looked as though Robbie had my wolf in his grasp as he lay half on his back, half on his side, letting the current take him along. He wasn't moving and his eyes were half closed, blood visible at his temples.

Luna was still.

I collapsed on my knees once more feeling utterly helpless unable to do anything with my hands tied.

'Save them Sean, oh please save them.'

He was in the middle of the river now, standing strong against the flow which because of the storm was still quite powerful. Painfully slowly, or so it seemed, he pulled them both out of the water and onto the bank. His cobalt blue eyes regarded me steadily as he laid Luna's limp body gently next to where I knelt.

'Oh no, no Sean. No. This can't be happening, save her Sean, save her.'

As I wept at the gash in her chest which had robbed her of her life, he silently unbound my hands. The physical pain as blood rushed through to my numb fingers was nothing compared to the pain in my heart right now.

'I cannot Daisy. But he tried to, and that is what counts. He was prepared to die for her.'

'Oh God Robbie, don't let him be dead too, no Sean not him as well.'

Uncaring I was still naked, nothing mattered now, I moved to his side. 'Don't be dead, don't be dead. Please Robbie, you mad bastard I love you, don't be dead.'

He coughed and spluttered, spewing forth a mouthful of river water and groaned. 'I love you too Daisy.' Those three words I had longed to hear. Then he passed out.

'Oh God Robbie, wake up,' I cradled his head in my lap, crying uncontrollably.

'He will,' said Sean softly placing a gentle hand on my shoulder. And then I felt him pass me the shirt he was wearing. 'Here Daisy, darling, let's get you covered before the others arrive.'

'Others?'

'Sure, and have I not already phoned for help. They'll be here soon. Now I had better go and get that wicked bastard out as well I suppose.'

With a grim note in his voice, he went back into the river once more. I took my eyes away from Robbie and Luna and saw that caught in some low hanging branches on the far side of the river was the prone form of Colin.

I felt sick as soon as I saw him, and I hoped he was dead.

I hoped he had drowned.

He hadn't, but he was dead, no doubt about it.

'She took him Daisy, even as he plunged the knife into her, she took him.'

Sean hauled out his body with a super human strength and tossed him disdainfully on the floor away from me, Robbie and Luna. Colin's eyes were staring glassily, and I could see what Sean meant. His throat was torn to ribbons.

But Luna, my beloved white wolf, had died in saving me.

I knelt between her body and Robbie's and wept, clutching at her wet fur in the vain hope that somehow the magic that surrounded her would bring her back to life.

Surely it would.

I looked at Sean. 'Can't you do something? She's magic Sean, you know that. It's your magic as well. Sean please.'

Sean crouched down beside me as Robbie slowly stirred but my wolf remained still. 'Daisy darling, all magic has its purpose and its limits. What is done cannot be undone. She is gone.'

He held out my arms then and enfolded me in his embrace along with Luna as I wept inconsolably.

Robbie began to move. 'Did I save her'? He suddenly sat up ramrod straight 'Daisy did I save her? Oh Jesus no! No, no no!' He reached to take Luna from my arms, tears streaming down his face.

'The bastard got her. I'll kill him, I'll fucking kill him, I'll rip his fucking throat out!' he staggered to his feet and was gently caught by Sean.

'Luna's already done that, Robbie. He's dead.'

'He's dead?'

'Look there he is. He's dead Robbie.'

'He was going to kill you Daisy, I couldn't get to you in time, I couldn't save you. But Luna did, Luna saved you and now she's dead. Oh God Daisy, I am so sorry. I tried to save her, I tried.'

I couldn't bear his pain on top of my own. 'I know you did Robbie. I saw you jump. You risked your life to save her, and I will never forget that, ever.'

He looked broken and defeated, the most vulnerable I had seen him. Then his eyes took on another focus as though seeing me properly. 'Christ Daisy what did that bastard do to you?'

I couldn't speak and it was his turn to hold me, as more of the shock began to course through me.

'Hush now darling, it's alright, I've got you. I swear I will keep you safe from now on. No bastard will ever hurt you again. Oh God Daisy, don't cry like that I can't bear it. It's over Daisy, whatever he did it's over he can't hurt you or anyone else again.'

'But Luna,' I couldn't grasp the idea that my wolf was dead. I was still hoping for that miracle.

'Luna saved you and that was her job and Robbie risked his life to save hers.' Sean spoke with a solemnity in his voice I had never heard before. 'It is over.' He said these last three words with a finality that made Robbie and I both look at him.

He was standing, bare chested as he had given me his shirt, with the sunlight glinting on the silver blond lights in his hair, his blue eyes more dazzling than the sky that was beginning to clear and the smile on his face warmer than any sun.

'It is over.'

His words were a blessing bringing an end to a curse.

Chapter Forty-Nine

Eventually police and medics arrived.

Sean filled them in sharply and concisely, no trace of the glib Irish blarney now. His voice was cold, clipped and dispassionate. The medics took one look at me and wrapped me up in a blanket, treating me with the gentlest of care. I protested that I did not need carrying all the way back to Wolf Lodge on a stretcher, but they smiled and tucked me up, nevertheless.

Marigold was waiting on the steps of Wolf Lodge by the ambulance and police cars. Catriona had made a valiant attempt to keep Lily and Abigail out of the way but there was no stopping the girls from charging out having seen our return. They did falter somewhat at the stretcher with the body bag and on seeing Sean carrying Luna's limp body they both burst into floods of tears. Then Lily was clinging to her father and Abigail was clutching at my hands, her young face white as a sheet as she saw what I looked like.

'I'm alright,' I said through my tears. 'I'm fine honestly, I look worse than it is. Really it's just a few bruises.'

Over my little sister's head my eyes met those of Marigold's. She knew how much I was lying.

'Go on girls, in you go with Catriona now, Daisy and Robbie need to go the hospital. Sean, will you take me with you?' There was no stopping Marigold when she had made her mind up with something.

'Of course, I will. Hush now girls, no Luna did not suffer. It will have been quick. Ah, Alex thank you, will you take her from me now and look after her for me till we get back.'

Out of the corner of my eye I saw that Alex had astonishingly left his safe domain of the kitchen and was carefully taking the dead weight of Luna from Sean. Then Shona was frogmarched out of the Lodge loudly protesting that she knew nothing any about any of it. By now the painkillers that one of the medics had given me was starting to make me drowsy and as the ambulance began to drive off, I closed my eyes and briefly sought solace in sleep.

At the hospital Marigold had barged into the room within minutes of me being admitted.

'You'll be alright Daisy,' she said nodding her head and shooing away the doctor who was about to examine me. 'Whatever he has done, to you, you will be alright.' She stood by the examination table and clasped my hands in hers. 'It is over,' she said in an echo of Sean's words earlier. 'You survived and that's all that matters.'

'I really do need to examine her,' came the quiet but firm voice of the doctor who I knew would have to file every little detail down for the police report.

'Well, I am staying young lady, and if you think you can remove me you have another thing coming. I am her mother. A woman needs her mum at a time like this.'

'I quite agree,' said the young female doctor who had already winced at some of my injuries. 'But a little more room would be helpful?'

Marigold nodded. 'Of course. Daisy I will be just here, the other side of the curtain. I won't leave you.'

She had tears in her eyes as she got up and took a seat at the other side of the room. Then I tried to blank everything out as the doctor gently but thoroughly assessed the injuries that Colin had inflicted. I needed stitches internally and for some of the cuts on my face. But no lasting damage had been done I was told gently. Then the doctor carefully amended what she had said. No lasting physical damage. The look in her eyes told me there would be other scars.

When it was over, Marigold came to my side once more. 'Is that it? Can I take my little girl home now?'

'We should really keep her in for observations,' said the doctor but her voice was half hearted as she spoke. I think she knew full well that Marigold was not going to settle for that.

I had never seen my mother without any make up or jewellery. She had obviously thrown on the first clothes that came to hand and had not even brushed her hair that morning. She looked older than I had ever seen her, but in my eyes, she had never been more beautiful.

'She needs to be with her mum, don't you Daisy.'

I choked back my tears. 'Yes, Yes I do.'

Sean had told Marigold that I had no clothes and she had quickly packed a bag. 'I'll help you dress,' she said once we were alone.

She didn't say anything as I slipped off the hospital gown and reached for my clothes. But I saw her expression as her eyes took in the marks on my body. I watched her mouth tighten as I couldn't help but wince in pain as I carefully pulled my jeans up.

'Come on love, let's get you home. Sean is waiting.'

So was Robbie.

He had been checked over by another doctor and had also refused to be admitted for observations with Sean promising he would be looked after.

'Are you alright? I mean… och Daisy, I don't know what to say to you, lass.' He stood there in the hospital corridor; dark green eyes shadowed with an unreadable expression.

'Telling her you love her might help right now,' suggested Marigold from where she stood next to me, half supporting me as I took each painful step.

Next to Robbie, Sean grinned.

'Aye well of course I do,' spluttered Robbie. 'I'm going to marry her, aren't I?'

Marigold was not for giving up. 'Yes, but have you actually told her you love her, or for that matter asked her to marry you?'

Her voice carried enough for the nurses and staff nearby to pause in their work and look over expectantly.

'Och this is embarrassing,' said Robbie shuffling his feet and going red in the face.

I found myself grinning despite myself. Robbie Munro could be made to blush. Who knew?

Then it was me with the scarlet cheeks as he suddenly squared his shoulders and said, 'Daisy Flowers, I love the very bones of you woman, and not cos you're the best fuck, oh no, I didn't mean to say that. Shit, let me start again. Christ Sean help me out here.'

'I think you are doing just fine,' said Sean shushing the laughter around us with a hand. 'Go on you can do it.'

Robbie huffed out his cheeks and started again. 'Okay, no swearing this time. Daisy Flowers I love the very bones of you, I want to breathe the air you breathe, I want to hold your hand and walk with you under a moonlit sky, I want to see the sun rise with you and watch it set with you, I want to grow old with you. Daisy Flowers will you marry me?' He finished by going down on one knee.

The whole ward was now holding its breath and exploded into cheers when I said yes.

'About bloody time,' said Marigold as Robbie then got up and kissed me thoroughly.

We made our way back to Kinlaggan, Robbie and I sitting in the back of Sean's car. He was no longer driving the camper van for which I was thankful. On the hour long drive I had chance to finally ask some questions of my own.

'Sean how did you know to be there?'

He sent me one of those looks in the rearview mirror. 'You know me and my whims and fancies Daisy. My project with Timothy had just about finished and I had a whim to come and see you, so I did. Do you like my new car?'

Whims and fancies indeed!

Yes, I did like his new car and I knew that I would never be any the wiser as far as Sean was concerned.

Marigold then added her part. 'I knew you were in trouble,' she said turning round to look at me. 'When you rang and called me Mum like that. So many times. Daisy it breaks my heart that that was the way you could let me know something was terribly wrong. I should never have stopped you from calling me Mum.'

'You had your reasons,' I said softly and as our eyes met, I knew now there was even more of a bond. We had both suffered brutality at the hands of a man.

'Maybe Marigold, Daisy could start calling you Mum now,' said Sean in that lilting gentle voice.

'I would like that,' she said her eyes still on mine.

'Me too, Mum,' I replied and wiped the tears away sniffling as Marigold reached into her bag for a tissue. Then I thought to ask about Lily and

Abigail. 'What do the girls know?'

'The basics,' said Marigold. 'As far as we knew them anyway. They were up all night with both of you missing. Moira is covering the Lodge and has roped in Callum to help. Catriona has cancelled the bookings for the next couple of weeks.'

'She has?'

Marigold, nodded. 'She's kept the chalets open, but we agreed that you and Robbie would need the Lodge as quiet as possible. And it will be mayhem for a while you do realise once the story gets out.'

It was.

More police interviews followed with the detectives who had been involved in the previous cases. Shona was charged and although there was some local opinion that she was innocent in all of this, I remembered how Colin had told me the steps she had been prepared to take to, including harming Lily. I went through everything again and again, but they were patient with me, and I always had either Robbie, Sean or Mum by my side.

But no Luna.

She was gone and that was a pain that was unbearable.

That first night, after what seemed like the longest day of my life, I lay naked in Robbie's arms, and I cried a waterfall of tears that landed on his chest and were gently wiped from my eyes. Lily had insisted that she sleep with Abigail as she had done the previous night when both Robbie and I were missing. I was glad that the girls could comfort each other. Glad beyond words that I had Robbie to comfort me.

My wild, crazy, boorish highlander was now the harbour I needed after all I had been through. He held me close, stroking the lines of my tattoo on my back where Luna had first come into my life. His lips gently brushed the top of my head and with a catch in his voice he spoke in tones I had never heard him use before.

'I'll help you mend, Daisy. I promise you that lass. If it takes the rest of my days, I will help you mend. Not just from Luna, but from what he did to you. I swear it lass.'

When the tremors of shock and grief ran through me, he held me close and in his arms I felt safe. Bruised, battered, bereft, with him I was whole. I cried even more as I realised this. The night passed with me sleeping fitfully, waking from dreams that were not dreams but flashbacks to what had happened. He would hold me then, rock me back to sleep until I jolted awake once more.

Eventually the dawn broke through the night. My first thought on waking was Luna. My second thought was that today was Lily's sixteenth birthday. I must have said it out loud because Robbie, who was sitting in the chair by the window, watching me whilst he drank a cup of coffee, smiled and nodded his head.

'Aye I know. Can you believe it. My wee baby is sixteen years old. How did that happen?'

Out of nowhere it came. 'I had a daughter named Lily. She only lived a few hours. She died on this date. Sixteen years ago.'

Robbie went very still. He lowered his cup to the deep ledge of the window sill then looked at me steadily those forest green eyes no longer full of turmoil and pain, shining now with a sense of wonder.

'Och Daisy, that's too uncanny for words.'

I sat up in bed, unable to stop myself from wincing at the pain that my movements wrought.

'Shit Daisy, let me help you,' he was at my side in an instant. In silence he helped me dress and I watched the light in his eyes change once more to anger but this time I knew the anger had a direct cause and was not one of madness.

'I'll be alright,' I reassured him, although the sight of my reflection was something of a shock. Not even the cleverest use of make-up would hide the pallor or the bruising. When I had at least brushed my hair I said quietly, 'I never stopped grieving for her. For Lily I mean.'

Once more those strong arms wrapped themselves around me and I felt his lips brush against my ear. 'Nor should you,' he whispered. 'But Daisy, do you not think there is something more than a little...'

I pulled back slightly so I could look directly into his eyes. 'Oh yes. More than a little. In the same way, Robbie, there was more than a little about my tattoo, about Luna, about your curse, about me coming here. More than a little.'

'Aye you're not wrong there.' He released me and dragged a hand through his hair, which had grown back somewhat from his stark crop a few weeks ago. 'It's gone though, Daisy, the curse, the madness. I know it's gone. Cos of you being here, everything. Luna.'

'Luna.' I shook my head tears once more filling my eyes. 'Luna. Lily. Oh Robbie.'

'Come on lass. Let's not ponder the whys of it all. What's done cannot be undone and what is to be done is ours to do,' he said with an astonishingly philosophical view. 'Today we must bury Luna, and we must also celebrate Lily's birthday.'

I nodded, the look in his eyes giving me courage.

And that is precisely what we did.

After breakfast, we trooped in a quiet little group – me, Robbie, Lily, Abigail, Catriona, Mary, Alex, Moira, Callum and Marigold who had stayed the night, with Sean, as serious as I have ever seen him, carrying Luna's body, which was wrapped in a blanket of the Munro tartan.

He had been up already, and the grave had been dug, in a quiet spot by the river where she used to love playing so much. If it had not been for Robbie holding me so close, I would have wrestled Luna's body from Sean's arms. I think both men knew this. I couldn't speak for crying, as Sean knelt and carefully lay her body in the ground.

We all wept.

Apart from Sean.

He steadily filled the grave and patted the earth down firmly when he had finished.

'Of course, she will have a marker,' Catriona announced gruffly, blowing her nose as she did so.

'And a bench maybe so you can sit here and remember her Daisy,' added Marigold.

'Excellent ideas ladies.' Sean smiled at them both then he leant on the handle of the spade he had been using and his gaze fell upon all of us. 'But now, this is also a day for celebrating. Lily it is your birthday and believe me, Luna would not want you to be sad for the rest of this day. Wipe away the tears and let us go and be thankful for what we have got.'

It was impossible to not respond to his beguiling charm as it always had been. Everyone turned to go, apart from me. My feet would not co-operate.

'It's alright,' Sean said quietly to Robbie who was glued to my side. 'You go on with the others. Daisy and I need to have a little chat.'

He waited until we were alone, with the sound of the water from the river and the rustling of the leaves in the trees, a soft summer's day, gentle after the storm the other night, before taking hold of my hands.

'Daisy darling it is time for me to leave now. No, no more tears.'

'Will I see you again?' The thought that he was going out of my life as well as Luna was too much, and my voice cracked with pain.

'You will.' A brief dazzling glimpse of that smile and the light in his eyes that melted any fears away. 'I cannot say when. But I promise you Daisy darling, one day, you will see me again.'

'And Luna? Will I ever see her again?'

He held my face gently in his hands then. 'She is with you always Daisy, she is as indelibly imprinted on your soul as the tattoo is imprinted on your back. I promise you Daisy, Luna will always be with you. By your side, in the shadows, in the darkness, when you stumble, when you fall, when you fear – Luna will be with you. In the light, in the joy, in the laughter that is to come, Luna will be with you.' He pressed a kiss on my forehead.

'She is the white wolf within you.'

Epilogue

'That all went rather well then in the end?' The dainty dark-haired woman with flashing black eyes smiled at Sean as he made his way up to join her on the rocks at the top of the waterfall.

'Indeed it did Michaela, indeed it did.' He greeted his friend with a kiss and then sat with her, cross legged like an elf, the spray of the water lightly kissing over them.

'We didn't anticipate Colin's part in it, though did we?' Michaela turned her beautiful face to him with a dimple in her cheeks as she grinned. 'That wasn't part of the plan.'

'We did not. Ah well, we cannot pull all the strings, as tempting as it is to do so at times. But I think over all it turned out well.'

'I agree.' Michaela was thoughtful for a moment as she looked at the waterfall where three generations ago, she had cursed a man for shooting her wolf. 'I think we made a pretty good team there Sean. Daisy and Lily are re-united, Robbie is free of his curse, Marigold and Daniel are back together again; all's well that ends well.' Then she started to laugh, and it was a musical sound; too beautiful to be earthly. 'But really Sean, stampeding elephants, whatever made you think of that one? We'll never get back to heaven at this rate.'

His laughter joined in with hers. 'Ah well, she made me angry, so she did, not believing in miracles like that.' He gave a careless shrug. 'You should never mock the idea of miracles, you know that. Tis a dangerous thing to do. Oh yes, a dangerous thing indeed.'

MAY YOU FIND YOUR WHITE WOLF WITHIN.

Ingram Content Group UK Ltd.
Milton Keynes UK
UKHW042045140323
418521UK00001B/40

9 781915 472151